Books by John Calvin Batchelor

The Further Adventures of Halley's Comet (1981)

The Birth of the People's Republic of Antarctica (1983)

American Falls (1985)

Thunder in the Dust: Images of Western Movies, by John R. Hamilton, text by John Calvin Batchelor (1987)

Gordon Liddy Is My Muse, by Tommy "Tip" Paine (1990)

Gordon Liddy

Linden Press

Simon & Schuster

New York London Toronto Sydney Tokyo

Is My Muse

by Tommy "Tip" Paine

A
Novel
by
John
Calvin
Batchelor

Linden Press
Simon & Schuster Building
Rockefeller Center
1230 Avenue of the Americas
New York, New York 10020

LINDEN PRESS/S&S and colophon are registered
trademarks
of Simon & Schuster Inc.

Designed by Chris Welch
Manufactured in the United States of America

1 3 5 7 9 10 8 6 4 2

Library of Congress Cataloging-in-Publication Data

Batchelor, John Calvin.
Gordon Liddy is my muse by Tommy "Tip" Paine.

I. Title.
PS3552.A8268G6 1990 813'.54 89-13439

ISBN 0-671-69078-7

The author gratefully acknowledges permission to
quote from the following works:
*Alexander Pushkin: Collected Narrative and Lyrical
Poetry,* edited and translated by Walter Arndt
(Ardis, 1984). Reprinted by permission of Ardis
Publishers.
Meditations by Marcus Aurelius, translated by Max-
well Staniforth (Penguin Classics, 1964), copyright
© Maxwell Staniforth, 1964.
"The Ballad of Paladin," lyrics and music by Johnny
Western and Richard Boone and Sam Rolfe, ©
1958, 1986 by Irving Music, Inc., (BMI). All rights
reserved; international copyright secured.

Contents

(Moscow, Hollywood, Houston, Bavaria,
Ohio, Miami, Down East, Arizona)

AUTHOR'S NOTE

This is wholly a work of my own imagination. While the genesis of certain characters is based upon my experiences and readings, these characters are dramatic distortions, fantastic constructions. None of the conduct of the characters, none of the descriptions, are true or intended to reflect upon, relate to, or disparage anyone living or not. Also, I put real people into imaginary places and events and made up their dialogue. In sum, it's a novel.

Men read by way of revenge.
—CITIZEN PAINE, *Common Sense*, 1776

1

Mother Treason

Tip Grows Up;

My Red and Black Paladin

Russia in winter is the time of gambling and treason. Moscow, at the pinnacle of eleven centuries of Russian winters, is the best place to find both. Russians love gambling. They hate treason. And because human nature is as upside down as not, they are as good at what they favor as they are at what they despise. This is a yarn of a boy and a girl who were very good gamblers, who betrayed their country, Holy Mother Russia, who let me watch it happen for twenty-five years, and whom I can write about now because they're gone and I miss them. Also Tip wants to make some guesses, because I believe I lost my two friends to sci-fi/spy guys like me, though *they* are not make-believers—agents of our Agency (CIA) and their State Security (KGB). When I get to these rude bunches, they shall be rudely identified as the Keystone Ops and Three Million Stooges.

(Who is Tip? Tip is I, now middle-aged, a traveling salesman of make-believe. Nothing high-hat, I promise; I've sold a deal of gleeful sci-fi/spy books, and I've put my name on a few movies of same. If you've bought them, thanks. I make it all up on small elegant machines, and I travel on big amazing ones. Mostly I travel.)

My first trip out of America was to Moscow, when I was eleven, and I've been going back and back ever since like a fellow who's gotten turned around so that the return fare is ticketed the wrong way. How I got to Moscow the first time was that in 1960 I was a boy scout in a troop on Philadelphia's Main Line that was sponsored by a very, very old Quaker meetinghouse. I am not a Quaker today; my Puritan heart is standoffish. But back then I was a tenderfoot, curious about the meetinghouse, and I would occasionally attend services by myself rather than car-pool with my family to the Presbyterians. I didn't understand about the inner light of the Quakers, which moves men and women to sit quietly for an hour, makes some rise to relate a heartfelt anecdote, holds the few Quakers together like cones around an evergreen. I only understood that quiet is hard to do at eleven and therefore strangely challenging. I sat there on a plain wooden bench in a small white room and listened to the cars outside, the steam radiators inside, the slow breathing of the ancients, who did most of the talking. Also I noticed that the other kids were wimps and girls. I was a manly Boy Scout and therefore special, as I could never have been at my own Sunday school.

One January Sunday after service the ancient Mr. Abernathy pulled me aside. "How are thee, young man?" he began. "I have seen thee here before." Frightened, I explained that I was just a Boy Scout from the neighborhood. We were outside the beautifully built meetinghouse, which sits on a stone-wall-enclosed rise that was topped by those melancholy elms that were still alive back then. Mr. Abernathy assured me I was most welcome at the meetinghouse, then asked my name, school and age (I was overlarge then too). I went away that day feeling that I had done something wrong.

That next week Mr. Abernathy called my mom and proposed a strange adventure. Philadelphia's Quakers were sending a peace mission to Moscow in hopes of arranging a summit between President

Eisenhower and Soviet boss Nikita Khrushchev. Mr. Abernathy's meeting had been awakened in prayer and informed by reflection that they should send as their representative not one of their ancient selves but a youth. It was Mr. Abernathy's further illumination, after he had chatted with my scoutmaster, that I was the correct youth—trustworthy, loyal, helpful, friendly and so forth down to typical.

Mr. Abernathy was so certain of himself that my mother refused for me. Events tumbled. I was suddenly an imprisoned celebrity fighting with warden mom for a furlough. Mom said, "Moscow is not like New York, Tipster, where you *hated* it. Moscow's worse. You don't speak Russian, and you don't know—they spy on everyone there! The Quakers are crazy to go." And then she accidentally provided my deep motive: "Besides, you've got school."

Too true, Mom; I love you. If you recall sixth grade, you know how in not much more time I was on a plane to Moscow via Reykjavik, London, Helsinki. This isn't travelogue, it's time encapsulation, but I'll pause to note that I was bewitched by what I saw en route—a TWA Super Constellation, volcanoes, London rain, Helsinki darkness—and by the evening we reached Moscow, I was a tenderfoot of adventure. The Quaker couple who foster-parented me, the Monroes, were newlyweds, without kids yet; they offered a slack leash. I stayed close through customs and the bus ride to our hotel, the very famous, very elite National, off Red Square. By dawn the first day I was ready for action. I had memorized *Life* magazine since 1956. I knew this was where the reds lived. I knew what the Cold War was; I could feel it out there. With a child's lack of limits, Tip the American cowboy was ready to scout out *red* Indians. Let's go!

Instead the peace mission began—conferences, museums and churches, more conferences. Action absent, they talked in two languages most futilely, since Russia's theme in those days was best defined as *Nothing goes.* I'd traveled half a world to a Russian meetinghouse. I listened to the few cars outside, the steam radiators inside, the grownups breathe. I also watched the amazing snowfall that began late morning every day and never really stopped. That cold was darkness visible. What did I care about the Metro, Ivan's bell tower, the Tretyakov collection, the Bolshoi opera, something

called Soviet friendship? Late February in Moscow is make-believe
itself. Walking sounds like rock 'n' roll Rice Krispies. Breathing is
sucking icicles. Everyone's bundled up, quick and most cheery (I
didn't know what vodka did then). I didn't want man-made wonders
like disarmament. I wanted what I know now to call pastoral Russia
—the winter, the blizzards, the endless forest steppe. Nonetheless at
each day's end I was still an imprisoned celebrity, fighting now with
Quaker wardens. I bartered. I had seen kids my age sledding in the
Lenin Hills when we bused out to Moscow University, so I brought
up how well I could take care of myself if I was dropped off with a
sled. Pick me up on your way back.

The Quakers are kindly people with a ferocious yearning for
achievement that often looks like competitive piety. They do not say
no; they do not say yes; they say, "Way will open." I wish I'd been old
enough then to understand their parleys, especially that big one in
the Kremlin's Old Senate building. (It must have worked some miracle, for the following spring Ike did rendezvous with Khrushchev in
de Gaulle's Paris, the U-2 melodrama notwithstanding.) However,
what lesson Tip got out of the mission was that peace is dull. On the
fourth day I was provided excitement—a Russian foster family and a
playmate.

2

Meet the Pallikins. They were not a typical Moscow family, but what
did I know? What do you know? Momma worked as the night concierge on our floor at the National Hotel. She was sharp-eyed, rosy,
chubby, and she regarded her three children as future Lenin scholars.
She collected me from the Monroes at dawn, and we rode the Metro
and then a bus until we arrived at a drab new housing district far from
Red Square. Poppa met us happily at the door. He was a robust clerk
at a tool-and-die factory outside Moscow. The two grandmas were
cooking breakfast while caretaking the two little girls, whose names I
missed. Then there was Trifon, my guy, whom I liked right away.

He's called Trifya at home. I mangled it okay. He called me Tipya (dear Tip). His first words to me are gone, but close to was careful English: "I love this blouse."

He meant my cowboy shirt. I had been wearing my Boy Scout uniform over long johns since Philadelphia and the day before had surrendered it reluctantly to the hotel laundry. My mother had packed my bag around the concept of death by freezing. Fortunately I had convinced her to stick in one of my choice possessions, a raggedy cowboy shirt, two tones, patched, studs and worn-down fringe.

I patted my shirt and replied to Trifya in English, loudly as if he were deaf, that it was what cowboys wore, you know, good guys, Roy Rogers, Gene Autry, the Lone Ranger. Trifya chomped his potato pancakes, nodding dreamily at my explanation. We eight were crowded into the tiny kitchen of their closely packed three and a half rooms. The grownups listened to me, exchanged suppositions, urged Trifya to interpret. He, a dark, rapturously intense kid, already handsome like what kids call the leader of the pack, had the only English in his family and asked me, "Cowboys. Yes? Bang, bang, yes?"

Tip accepted a lesson of the Cold War. Moscow was so far outside America that its kids were hazy about cowboys. Truth, Trifya was precocious, he'd guessed correctly. I turned instant salesman and asked him for the Russian words for horse, cow, West, cavalry, Indians, wagon train. Trifya provided most of what I asked. Without verbs or modifiers, I briefed them. Poppa roared in approval. He was a war veteran and knew the world via propaganda about the American army. Momma did too, but she didn't step on Poppa's colorful social history lesson.

By the time I arrived at Trifya's school, to spend the day with him, he was galloping for cowboys. The Russians have their own version, called the cossacks, and we got good quickly at bilingual tall-tale-telling. Still I report honestly that nothing travels so well as America's make-believe wild West. Forget agitprop about liberty; just show those movies to kids anywhere and you have made America stupendously free forever in their minds' eyes. I liked the cossack yarns, but Trifya absorbed Roy Rogers, Trigger, Bullet, Dale Evans. Meanwhile we were moving through the school day, and when we arrived at the

time for the English lesson I was Trifya's living show-and-tell, an icon
to fifty Russian gapers. The teacher stood by and let me preach cowboys. School was never such pleasure, never would be again.

After school there was ice hockey practice on a natural rink that
lay between the schoolhouse and a brickworks. Comrade Brickworkers idled at rinkside to cheer the boys. As ice hockey was new to
me then, I discovered that Russians play fast, fair, and to death by
exhaustion. They don't bash like our pros do; they keep their eyes on
the puck and skate hard. Resting at play is forbidden, while I could
see that for the grownups, resting at work is desired. I skate badly;
however, Trifya stayed on my heels and showed me what dancing on
ice feels like. I did not have a playmate back home who came even
close to his agility and felt special, as I would not all those locker
room years ahead of me overhearing the in-crowd jocks brag of con-
quest.

The important turn came after dinner, at the again crowded Pallikin table. Momma announced that it was decided I did not have to
return with her to the National Hotel until the next day. I could
spend the night with Trifya. He did his homework in a wink, leaving
plenty of time for more cowboy stories.

It was then that I had my strange genius. My mom had packed me
a deck of playing cards in case I got bored. When Trifya brought out
his chess set to instruct me in a game yet foreign to me, I produced
the cards. He grinned and whispered that I should hide them, explaining, "Babushka, no, no." He meant his grandmothers, who
regarded cards as gambling and gambling as sin. They were
prerevolutionary women, with falcon eyes for impiety. We let Tip get
massacred at chess until they retired to pray, and then, because we
were granted the kitchen/bedroom to ourselves on account of my
celebrity status, we got out the cards by the gas pilot light.

Trifya did not know war, memory or gin, my best games, but he
learned them instantly and beat me faster. I moved on to the most
grown-up game I knew, five-card draw poker. Again Trifya was
keener and quicker. Poker isn't a Russian card game, he'd never
heard of it, but he understood two pair instantly and mastered the
thrill of the draw as if he'd been born to the game. Losing again, I

chose to compete by relating poker to cowboys. I said it was the cowboys' only game, they never cheated, and they shot the bad guys through the ace they had palmed. Trifya was silent in awe. I was winning the East-West tussle at last, so I got very fancy and told a long story.

The most splendid cowboy story I knew then was the weekly tv series "Have Gun—Will Travel." You trendy folk might not recall, but once upon a time boyhood tv was dominated by cowboy shows, and in 1960 my opinion was that the top gun was Richard Boone playing the San Francisco gambler and gun for hire, Paladin. Every Saturday night at nine-thirty, his calling card announced thirty perfect minutes of wild West justice. Paladin's calling card read: "Have Gun—Will Travel." There was a knight chess piece in profile below and then: "Wire Paladin/San Francisco."

The best part of the show for me was the part that I didn't understand. After the setup of the week's fable, with Paladin beckoned by telegraph wire from his luxurious digs at the Hotel Carlton, there was a cut to Paladin in gunslinger black duds. Black was all wrong for a good guy, but that's why I loved it: it uncommoned sense. You did not see Paladin, you saw a tight close-up of his midsection, of his black holster with the silver chess knight emblem. Then Paladin would quote something so amazingly strange that I knew I had to be a smart cowboy someday so I could talk like that. Paladin might say, "'Nothing in his life became him like the leaving it...'" And then he'd add, "William Shakespeare, Macbeth, Act One, Scene Four," and draw his pistol at the camera. All you could see was the gun and the black, black cowboy duds. Cut to action.

As I finished my telling, Trifya was staring at me. He mispronounced: "Pa-la-din?" I wrote it down and corrected: Paladin, like his name, sort of, Pallikin. (I didn't know what a paladin was to tell him; I thought it was just a name. I even thought Paladin's first name was Wire.)

Starry-eyed Trifya corrected himself: "Paladin."

I mistook his fascination for confusion. I thought by adding more details about the black clothes, the plots about the rescues of innocents, that Paladin never took his hat off, lost at poker or shot a man who didn't need shooting, then I could convince Trifya that it was a really neat show, which he'd enjoy when it got to Russian tv. I then went very far into the future, as it turned out, though at the time I was being boyishly thorough. I sang him the supremely catchy Paladin theme song:

"Have Gun—Will Travel, reads the card of a man/A fast gun for hire in a savage land/His . . . [I mangled the verse] the calling wind/ A soldier of fortune is the man called Paladin/Paladin, Paladin, where do you roam?"

Trifya repeated the verse like a tape recorder. Such ability didn't impress me then. I assumed everyone could memorize foreign languages instantly. We translated like playing charades. The toughest line was "a soldier of fortune," since for literal-minded lads like us it comes out "soldier of wealth."

What was most significant was that all the while we talked that frigid Russian night, snowy outside and our breath making vapors inside, Trifya was riding over the threshold and into make-believe forever. It was spooky to watch. I'd never seen someone leave the earth while sitting on it. I'd also never been treated like Scheherazade, so that no matter what I said, I was believed in absolute wonderment.

Nevertheless my emphasis remained workmanlike—not just on Paladin but on all the cowboy stories I had to tell yet. (I was the overfed American boy, with so much to choose from that when "Bonanza" came on that next fall, I would transfer my top-gun opinion to the Ponderosa.) Eventually I tired of talking and tried to get us back to poker. I dealt another hand and was explaining what a straight flush was, when Trifya showed me his cards without a draw. He had two aces, a spade and a heart. I said that it was good but he should remember that two pair or three or four of any kind could beat it. He drew three cards. What's detail is detail; believe or not later. Trifya came up with the aces of diamonds and clubs. He had four aces—the unbeatable hand, if you're not sure what a royal straight flush is. I shook his luck off by saying I had to shuffle better. I also told him that four aces was the Wire Paladin hand, all right. Trifya returned the truth in Russian, and I figured out the translation: "I am lucky, Tipya. I'm always lucky."

Yes, Trifya, you were lucky; you were the black-hatted ace of spades, a true Paladin. I think now that maybe if I hadn't given you my deck of cards as a farewell present (the Pallikins gave me a small bust of Lenin), or maybe if I hadn't rhymed your name with Paladin's, or maybe if I'd come a winter later and preached Hoss Cartwright, the bloated angel, or maybe so much—then your luck would have been different. Maybe none of this. You're still my friend, and I miss you like my cowboy youth.

3

On to the red ace, the dear heart. It was nine years later, the winter of 1969, when I used my make-believe return ticket to Russia. I was a junior classman at Haverford College, traveling once again with a Quaker peace mission.

I once thought it devious to claim I'm a Yale man, a sci-fi/spy alum like Patrick Hale (1778) and William Buckley (1950). Tip was fooling, carried away by envy. He graduated tiny, suburban, Quaker-founded Haverford College, about five miles from where I was born, in Bryn Mawr Hospital. Back in 1969 Haverford College was not the precious little bundle of brains it is today; it was pink-blush liberal, waiting for Lefty to circle the dorms again, crying, "Stop the war!" It was Peacenik U., so smugly righteous that the SDS was regarded as egalitarian.

However, I was not persuaded by politics then, since I had none, only slogans. On campus I was mashed potatoes, a language-major jock, who was not comfortable with either the many high-minded Marcuse vegetables who called drugs "recreational" or the few low-minded meatheads who were my teammates when they were not salting female pork chops. In four years I joined no cause except football, lacrosse and the Greek Club's production of Aristophanes nonsense.

But then that one winter I did sign up for a dove airlift to Moscow to search for peace in Vietnam.

I was twenty, toweringly gangly, with wire-rim eyeglasses and a cowlick, as overserious as you get before you become legally of age to vote and lose. Our peace mission was organized around the fairy tale that a Quaker named Richard M. Nixon was now in the White House and it was proper for brother and sister Quakers everywhere to associate themselves with Mr. Nixon's secret plan to end the war. None of us college boys believed this. It was just a glib scam to secure alumni underwriting. Our motive was wanderlust, though there was the detail that Bryn Mawr girls were accompanying us. We fourteen boy pilgrims (five Quakers, four Marxists, two Maoists, two space cadets and Tip) arrived in Moscow after changing planes in Helsinki. The Bryn Mawr girls traveling with us arrived approximately the same time, at the front of the plane. What I'm saying is that it was profoundly not a coed enterprise. I was the veteran of our pack. I spoke better Russian than our hip junior faculty leader, Mike Miller; I spoke better French, German, Spanish and American then our sweet Intourist guide, Comrade (Miss) Illina, who was waiting for us on the bus that slowly transferred us to the grandiose and elite Moskva Hotel, off Red Square.

I could detail Moscow for you like my present neighborhood, the Upper West Side. Why? What you need to know is that in February it is cold, snow-packed and drab. When I was eleven it was another Philadelphia to me; when twenty, it was profoundly other to me; today it's all prejudices.

Some facts can be assembled. To be a Great Russian is regarded a privilege. To live in Moscow is regarded God's blessing. To believe in God is regarded superstitious and probably disloyal. Back then, 1969, the Communist Party of the Soviet Union was returned unchallenged to power for its fifty-second year. A moody, backslapping hack named Leonid Brezhnev was the boss of bosses; he believed in nothing but keeping his job, hunting stag in the Urals and drinking. The Communist Party's latest reigning theme was best defined as *Nothing goes, maybe.*

If comparisons help, their army was in Czechoslovakia with tanks and in deep trouble everywhere. Our army was in Vietnam with tanks and in deep trouble, etc. Brezhnev looked like the boss; Nixon did too. Today I know 1969 better than any year since. The only genuine news that year was the moon race and my youth. We won the moon in July; I continued young. Add up the tanks, rockets, spacemen and earthy girls and boys, you get another reel of the long-over-budget Cold War.

If I'd written this then, I would have wasted words on the sensational details of our visit to Moscow. We collegians were a few of the very few Americans in Russia that year either not under orders or AWOL. To idle in the lobby of the Moskva Hotel was to occupy the ground-zero target for Western philosophy. You could hear history quibbling. My compatriots ran off to the American Embassy, the Vietnamese Embassy, the Canadian Embassy (curious, that), and then to museums, the opera, the Kremlin. Hip Haverford prof Mike Miller said, "It's happening, Thomas, it's happening!" Tip (who pretended to be Thomas a few years, to shed high school Tommy) agreed. Frantic Intourist guide Illina said, "You must tell them the curfew is sincere, Comrade Paine, it's sincere!" Tip (who liked whoever this Comrade Paine was) agreed.

They were both right. It was also the Cold War. It remained very cold. I know now that I had as much chance to make sense of it as I did to make sense of Livia Logan, the long-nosed Bryn Mawr blonde who roomed three doors left of mine at the Moskva Hotel. In her way, Livia Logan was armored, fueled, moonstruck, expensive—my philosophical ground zero.

On the third day I tried a cease-fire in all directions and rang up the Pallikins. In nine years I had sent Trifya one Christmas card, featuring a picture of my family, and this had been my mom's idea. Trifya had returned me one note, featuring a photo of his family, I'm sure his mom's idea. I did not feel guilty about this. Adolescents shirk detail.

When a young woman answered my call, I announced myself in crisp Russian. It was Marya, Trifya's baby sister, now a teenager, who began formally and then emoted, "Oh, Tipya, yes, yes, you're in Moscow, here! And Trifya, he's home now, you must come and see him. Trifya's always—he's always! You must come. I'm here with Poppa now, he's sick, and Momma's at work. Yes, the National. Go see her. We're the same, yes, the same."

The Pallikins were not the same. Marya was not falsifying, she was hoping. I walked over to the National Hotel to call on Momma. My collegiate Russian upset the sentries, since I lacked a hotel pass. My intention upset the chief concierge, since order is the aim of hoteliers. But soon enough Momma appeared at the office. Her rosiness was gone, her chubbiness was grown, her questions were sharp. "Comrade Paine, why are you here?... You called Marya?... Yes, Trifya's home, from the army.... Yes, a visit. It can be arranged.... Tomorrow morning, call for me here."

If this sounds suspicious, I missed it. The next morning I rendezvoused with Momma again. She was relaxed, just off the overnight shift, and chatted pleasantly on the long Metro and bus ride home. I caught her up on my last nine years. She shared little beyond current Trifya news. He was home from army service, to begin school again. Momma was proud of Trifya in the abstract; she communicated displeasure in the specific, such as, "He's not kept up with his English.... He played hockey until he broke his foot; too many little bones to mend.... And your momma, she must be very proud of you. A peace mission again. It's good. Soldiering's also good, but now, your President Johnson, well... Your Russian is excellent; how did you learn?"

I corrected her only once. It was President Nixon now. She accepted the detail like a momma. "Politics," Momma said. "It's enough to care for the family, don't you agree?"

Da, Momma, I love you, and when we arrived I greeted the family with my proper Russian gift of bread and salt as soon as I walked in the kitchen. The Pallikins kissed and hugged me wholeheartedly. I appreciated the sweet Marya and the lovely older sister, Katya, but I was keenest about Trifya. He was in uniform and looking like a poster. His boyish good looks had become obviously handsome—a chiseled face, coal-ember eyes, curly black hair. I had outgrown him, but he was so gracefully fit that I felt ever more lumpy. He said, "Tipya, those eyeglasses, the Lenin scholar—see, Momma, here's your professor at last." I heard instead: Tip, what happened?

Poppa stayed in his sickbed, so we five sat down to breakfast, served by Momma's mother, the remaining babushka. Russians eat heavily when they can, for the cold, and any meat or dairy product is a treat. The table that morning was indulgent. I did not mean to offend by refusing; it was just my nervous stomach. Momma asked, "You don't like meat and milk?" Trifya volunteered, "I'll eat his portion, Momma; no one will know." Momma shrugged, a maternal confusion, and spoke proverbially: "The cock crows before he eats too." Again I missed the weight of the remarks.

Trifya overwhelmed me with questions about fashion, starting with my clothes and travels, and moving then onto his favorite subject, movies. "Do you go to the cinema, Tipya, often? Do you see our cinema? No? What do you see?"

I answered quickly. I meant to entertain, not compete. I knew they wouldn't recognize the pretentious fads I listed—Bergman, Truffaut and Fellini; Bogart, McQueen and Sellers—nor would they understand my joke that I'd felt foolish at *Yellow Submarine.*

As I finished, Trifya was staring blankly. His sisters delayed breath. I summarized simply: Just foreigners and tough guys; Peter Sellers was a silly guy.

Momma said, "We have them too."

Trifya chomped another sausage and asked, "Tipya, no cowboys? You don't go to the cowboy movies? I've seen two now. *Red River*—" Momma clanked cutlery. Trifya added, "—about socialist brotherhood prevailing over capitalist exploitation. We went to it in—last spring. And years ago I saw another John Wayne film. *Fort Apache*—" Momma rose huffily. Trifya added, "—about the massacre of the Native Americans by the capitalists."

I ignored his politics (not inaccurate, just unclever) and said that he'd seen two of the best westerns ever made.

Trifya's smile was victorious. After breakfast, when Momma had retired and the girls had gone off to school, we boys took a walk in the cold sun to philosophize about John Wayne. Trifya did not mention capitalism again. He knew John Wayne was a monumental hero. Russian boys understand everything about heroism the moment they read Pushkin and Tolstoy. Soon we were far from his apartment, at his old school, standing with the brickworkers and watching schoolboys play ice hockey on the natural rink.

"Tipya," he exclaimed, "you don't know how I've missed your stories, you don't know!" This was tender, and for the first time I let myself see Trifya for what he was, a boy without much, in a country that permitted less. I said I was sorry we couldn't go to a cowboy movie festival right now. Trifya waved my wish away while introducing his twin surprises.

The first was plenty. She came slipping across the ice from the school side, her fur cap flopping over her dark curls. She leaped into Trifya's bear hug and grinned her signature, a huge mouth under a Roman nose. "Oh, Trifya, you feel so good!" she exhaled in Russian, then spoke to me in British English: "You don't remember me, Comrade Paine, but I do you. I'm Tina. I stood over there the day you helped Trifya score his goals."

"She was a poor hockey fan," said Trifya, "but the school brain." He crooned, "My luckiest draw, Tina."

"Brute!" protested Tina, boxing his ears, the first time I actually saw this done. She corrected him in English to me: "I'm his affianced."

I congratulated them in Russian. This got me a kiss from Tina and her proverb about Trifya: "He's got a boot flap for a tongue."

I laughed with her, though Tina was much too smart to make simple jokes. She meant it menacingly too. Russians think in proverbs. The best speak of truth, most of food and folly, the darkest of suffering. Tina was many facts; I only need to summate. Valentina Meyerkhova was truth for a lifetime, a banquet for any fool, a person who knew suffering intimately. For she was also born a beautiful woman amid Russian misogyny, granted a good brain and an ornithology degree amid Russian cruelty toward the New Man and the old wilderness, burdened with a sense of proportion and loyalty amid big bossness and petty horrors—in all, a dear heart who was so much in love with a lucky fellow that she stood by him past the end.

That's many tomorrows. That day Trifya demonstrated his second and most dangerous secret. "Sing that song, Tipya," he pleaded, "the

Paladin song, for Tina, sing it—I could never remember the words!"

I'd stopped singing at twelve, but I played along, speaking the translation, "Have Gun—Will Travel, reads the card of a man . . ."

Tina applauded. Suddenly Trifya moved away from Tina, whipped his greatcoat back and drew a deck of cards from a black pouch on his hip. He recited his own version of Paladin's ceremonial poetry: "You're the kind that always loses,/Bliss and you are all at odds:/ You're too sweet when chance refuses/And too clever when it nods." He shuffled the cards in the air like the cardsharp he was, and added, "Alexander Pushkin, 1825."

I was dumbfounded, not merely by his prowess but also by the intensity of his make-believe. He was well out of Moscow, off the planet, what the word means: starbound.

Tina pulled him back. "Show-off," she scolded. "What kind of a host are you?" Then to me, "He's been waiting to do that for nine years."

Meanwhile Trifya had fanned the deck inside out and done that neat card trick of picking out whatever you want. He produced four aces. "The Wire Paladin hand," he said. "It never loses, but it's my experience you don't need it. Poker's more blissful than the odds."

"You offend Pushkin," chided Tina. Then to me, "He's got a flap for a tongue, cards for wit."

"You don't need wit either," Trifya defended, "if you're holding the high hand."

The lovers' spat faded in our fun. I had three more days to play and was greedy like a lover, since I was stuck on both of them. There were many things I should have seen about their lives, many questions I might have asked. Young Tip concentrated on enjoying himself and on one more vanity, being a show-off too and displaying my beautiful Russian pair to my peacenik compatriots.

It was not easily done. Trifya was available to me during the days, on compassionate leave from the army because his poppa was dying of heart disease. But Tina's class schedule and institute job at Moscow University blocked out her days. Nighttime was out; there was a perpetual curfew in Moscow then, especially for young soldiers, since a tanker on leave from Czechoslovakia had tried to assassinate Brezhnev in the Kremlin yard the month before. I proposed breakfast at Trifya's home and was rejected because Momma would not approve of strangers. I proposed supper, perhaps in my room, and was rejected because Trifya and Tina could not get into my hotel without a pass. Finally, on my last night in Moscow, Tina constructed a plan. There was a bakery near the university that daring students used as a bistro on the weekends. I asked if this still wouldn't be trouble for Trifya. Tina said, "He's used to it."

My collegians were ripe for the chance to meet Russian youth at last. In a week of peacemaking they had been delimited to foreigners like themselves. Correctly, I didn't trust them; they smoked dope in their rooms and complained about the vodka. I aimed to travel to Moscow University looselipless. I had to tell our hip prof, Mike Miller, who recklessly invited his reckless new paramour, our Intourist guide Illina. Otherwise I kept my guest list tight. I invited two guys I liked, Tex the space cadet and Mark Weinstein the prelaw Maoist, and of course I invited the lovely nymph Livia Logan, who did know my name: she used it twice when she agreed, "Thomas, that'd be cool, Thomas." It turned out to be even more cool, because she could bring along two girl pals.

The proverb says, "It was worse than wrong; it didn't work." This applies to Leninism as well as it does to my expedition. It was stupid to lead hipsters into a Moscow bakery that was so deliciously hot with Russian yearning that the Cold War seemed burned out of the evening. Their side did fine. We capitalists acted out. It was a tiny space opening onto the ovens and the loading docks. The Russian kids used it to make romance. It was one of the very few places where they could go to hang out free of envy's way, for they were the elite, they knew that, they were headed toward privilege. Unfortunately my kindred of capitalism looked upon them as shabby state-tech squares who needed cram courses in brand names.

Soon my compatriots were preaching the triumph of the free world via shopping sprees. Even Tex, who didn't know better, kept emphasizing to Trifya that he didn't like his jeans until they were grungy. Even Mark Weinstein, who did know better, said cigarette burns in a sweater made it better. The Bryn Mawr girls were agitprop in motion.

They gave away all their makeup and started a seminar at the adjoining table on birth control devices versus the pill. When Mike Miller got rolling, he took on two Leninists about the superiority of American paper products.

I felt ashamed. I was learning that when you dump Americans in desperate lands, you get tv goes to Mars. Also I could understand what the Russians were saying about us. Their proverbs broke down before their eyes. "Learn good things," one girl said. "The bad come naturally." Yes, but how come, asked another girl, the bad wore such beautiful shoes? "We're related," said a boy. "The same sun dries our rags." Yes, countered another girl, but why're their rags so pretty? There were also many curses for what we were, what we had, which the Russian kids knew they could never have no matter how hard they worked and yet we American fools treated as disposable fads.

The worst of it, though, and why I recount this episode, was with regard to Trifya and Tina. They glowed in their plainness, they addressed my friends as if they were my family. Trifya took to Tex, as I'd thought, and soon they were using Tina and me as interpreters for their sojourns along the Rio Grande. Tex said to me, "He's a cowhand, all right. Get the right duds on him, and I'd have him ridin' range in a week." I translated. Trifya misunderstood the "duds" reference and looked hurt. He was very proud of his uniform, a junior lieutenant in the signal corps.

Tex tried to mend fences. "It's cool threads, man, boss buttons 'n' all, it's just not you." Trifya brightened eagerly, saying he wouldn't always be in uniform; someday he'd have jeans and cowboy boots like Tex's.

Trifya brought out his cards to demonstrate his true talent. His cardsharp's shuffle got the Bryn Mawr girls' rapt focus. Livia Logan had startled at Trifya's beauty immediately. I wasn't jealous, not truly. But then Trifya turned over his deck with one hand and said in broken English, "Gentlemen, the game is poker."

Golden Livia interrupted him like a vulgar princess. "Poker's a pig's game, man. Let me show you what cards're for."

Trifya surrendered his cards to her amiably, but I knew he was shocked. I didn't have time to explain the "pig" reference; today that would be "macho" with more bite. Livia and her two pals surrounded Trifya to read his cards for him.

I moved over to entertain Tina, who was trying not to scowl at Livia Logan. Russian women bypass jealousy for strangling. Tina patiently pretended to be telling me about the falcon population of greater Moscow, while she recorded every seductive word directed at her Trifya. Mark Weinstein crowded in to flirt with her. Again Tina patiently pretended to listen. But when Livia and cronies sighed once too often, Tina spoke hotly to me.

"If that's what he likes, powder and breasts," said Tina, "I can do that too!" Mark Weinstein drew back from her fury. Tina switched to proverbial Russian to me: "'The church is far, the road is icy. The tavern is farther. I'll walk carefully.' Do you understand, Tipya? I can be church and tavern both. He'll never leave me. Never."

I apologized for my serpent of a date. I explained that card reading was an old college-girl game. Tina said, "The cards are what he loves. I must love them too." She laughed. "I'm his luckiest draw."

Yes, Tina, you were all of that—body, belief and draw of joy, the ace of hearts. You were also very, very smart. I can guess that Trifya would never have got so far on that icy path if you hadn't been with him. Why didn't you stop him? I know the answer. You loved him no matter what he did. But still, why? I guess I'm just looking for a way to help you now.

4

Diamonds are next, along with plunder aplenty. By 1981 I had passed through the politics of war, poverty, marriage and divorce, to arrive at my first sci-fi/spy sales. (What this means, if you're curious, is that I got drafted, clerked for the National Security Agency, got loose, clerked on New York's Grub Street, got married, found a clerk to end it, got smart and started to make it all up clerking for Tip.) I had just enough surplus to exercise my return ticket to Russia again. I needed the trip to clear my head of some strange family trouble in Persia (which I won't include here; perhaps another day). Also there was a loony Texas bankerette to avoid and a screenplay to recover from. My grand solution was a February Finnair junket for twenty-two days in the Soviet Union—Helsinki overland to Moscow, enplane to Armenia, Georgia, the Black Sea and the Ukraine, back to Leningrad and out.

In twelve years I had upped my average and written Trifya twice, once from Scotland, where the NSA's wisdom posted me at our sub base, and once again from New York, where I hit bottom reviewing my kind of trash for an arts rag. Trifya had not replied, but Tina had, enclosing pictures of their baby the first time, then their three babies the second time. Her notes were warm and slightly vague. "We are well, hope you are. I am a researcher at the institute. Trifya's still in the army." Then, "I am a doctoral candidate at the institute. Trifya's in the civil service."

I thought none of this odd. I thought, They're happy, I'm not; get to them and admire.

Admiration is a calming thought, and it put me in contrast to the fretful Canadian ancients on my Finnair tour. We were badly undersubscribed because the Californian contingent had canceled en masse. The Cold War had heaved an iceball into everybody's face when the Soviets brilliantly decided to play ice hockey with Afghani heads (invasion, December 1979), and President-elect Reagan brilliantly speechified with the idea that the Russians were very bad guys (Inauguration Day, January 1981). The early Cold War theme of Nothing goes was in reruns. This made neutrals like Canadians very queasy. I liked them plenty when we boarded the train in Helsinki and they sent a legation of white-haired farm ladies to ask me, "We understand you know about Russia?"

I did and kept the wonderfully witty gang who crowded into my compartment entertained as the Moscow Express rolled into grim Russian winter. There was routine folly at the border when the cranky Border Guards searched us for nuclear weapons. One sheep farmer refused to get up from his bunk so the guard could look under the bed. The sheep farmer protested, "I'll move, mister, when you ask me politely." The Border Guard shouted, "You'll move when I tell you!"

I was called in to arbitrate. I thereby called the goons down on my compartment for a truly vain moment. Border Guards are lowlife who are also members of State Security (KGB), the aforementioned Three Million Stooges. They don't like foreigners and hate those who can speak Russian proverbially. Two of them failed to find a secret compartment in my canvas bag. An officer arrived to pounce upon the several copies I'd brought along of my first novel, *Eat the Songbirds*. He couldn't read English; he might not have known Churchill's postwar jest to Stalin about the future of Eastern Europe: "The eagle should let the songbirds sing." But he knew that the bald eagle on the dust jacket should not be grasping that steppe eagle so rudely, the one colored red and branded with a hammer and sickle. I gave him a copy, said he would enjoy it, the bad guys were war, pestilence, famine and death. He almost took them all. He almost confiscated my life's work. But no; he said, "Novelists are crazy. You're not a poet, are you?" Offended, I bent a proverb for him: "The bells toll often in Moscow but not for dinner *or poets.*" He smirked and approved me as harmless to Mother Russia.

Moscow was tidy drab this time. The Olympics the previous summer had rearranged reality. It's called Potemkin villaging, for the famous fake village a Tsarist minister once built to woo foreigners. Soviet bigness had taken on Moscow, cleaning up depots, hotels, roadways and as many drunks and grumblers as could be spared. Of course it was now six months later, and the facades were crumbling. We waded through the falling plaster to arrive at the hilariously gargantuan and elite Hotel Rossiya, off Red Square, two thousand rooms that mysteriously connect to just four elevator banks.

I helped our Intourist guide shepherd the elders to bed rest, then I raced off to buy an expensive fox fur cap for myself and a bottle of pepper vodka for my visit to Trifya and Tina. My tour had only had three full days in Moscow. I aimed to be quick, before the Canadians found me out a deserter. I called the telephone number Tina had sent me, failed. I tried the Pallikins' apartment, failed. Shucking manners, I taxied to Trifya and Tina's address in a newly built housing district east of the city. No one home. The neighbor in the hall mistook me for a prosperous Muscovite and said that the Pallikins might be at their dacha. I asked again and learned a second address, well south of the city.

This was news. To have a dacha is privilege, though it's usually just what we would call a cottage in a former peasant village. I couldn't phone them, since there isn't directory assistance in Moscow; you know or you don't need to. I rang the two numbers I did have off the hook that night, failed, as I did for two more days. Meanwhile I busied myself happily with the Canadians. They loved everything strange, and Russia is where there is no Western familiar. The Canadians enjoyed the Kremlin churches, museums, opera, the cultural whirlwind; and I enjoyed their superb questions to our guide about primary schools, produce, livestock. (If you want to enjoy Russia, go with farmers.) And then it was the last night, and I was frustrated. I should have written ahead, but then why should they be absent midwinter, a bureaucrat and a doctoral candidate? That was good employment but not time on your hands. And where were the Pallikins? I could have tried the National Hotel. Truth, I didn't want to upset Momma again, not before I found Trifya. Tip hatched a bold plan. Hire a taxi and go south. I'd be back in time for our Aeroflot flight to Armenia.

Dead winter, flaking snow, black and ferociously cold, Tip hip-hopped for adventure. My taxi driver, Feliks Andreyevich, liked my Russian, rubles, scheme; mostly he liked the dollars I promised for a success. "Crazy American cowboys! A blizzard coming! I can drive! Make the getaway!" His cowboy reference was to the three ten-gallon hats I'd brought as presents for Trifya's children and the cowboy boots for him; for Tina I had a Bloomingdale's survival kit. Feliks tanked up at his black market dealership, and we slalomed down the Tula road. Feliks kept himself happy with my vodka while he kept me alert with his driving and questions: "Do Americans like music in the taxi? I can get that—jazz or the rock?" and "They raised my fees, the blackguards; this was going to be a good year." I mentioned that Washington was grumbling about making it a very bad year for everyone.

"No! Afghanistan?" Feliks puzzled. "Who cares about that? Wasn't it enough that I lost so much business last summer?" (You remember, Yankee Doodle didn't ride his pony to the Moscow Olympics.)

It was past ten when Feliks found the village turnoff. We stopped short of a neat forest settlement of dachas. Feliks supposed, "High party, your friends high party, are they?" (He actually used the Russian word for extreme privilege in the Soviet Union, *nomenklatura,* which translates "high party" and is equivalent to our CEO class.) I said they were *not* high party and invited Feliks along for warmth and eats. Feliks pounded down a caretaker's door to get good, exact news: *"Da,* the Pallikins are home, who wants to know?" I played the prosperous Muscovite again, and we hiked across a sublimely moonlit snow field. It was not going to blizzard; that had been part of Feliks's bartering technique.

Tina answered the door and jumped into my arms. Her scent was pinewood and brandy. "Tipya, out of the sky, Tipya, how I needed you here!" We were welcomed into a sumptuous home, Finnish trappings, Russian embellishment, including icons, antique weapons, fur rugs like a zoo. Tina herself was wrapped in a fox-trimmed robe over a French dressing gown. Feliks reacted to the wealth by lowering his head and shuffling like a serf. There were two babushkas, who surrounded us with orders to get comfortable and then brought out supper in fast stages. Feliks vanished into the kitchen with the babushkas.

Meanwhile Tina was boozily garrulous. "If I had known... when did you arrive? Leaving tomorrow! Trifya will be *désolé....* He's away till March.... I like the winters here best.... I should wake the children: what wonderful hats!... And boots, oh, Trifya will love them; he doesn't have anything so grand! Bloomingdale's!"

This is sufficient for you to understand this was not simple beautiful Tina the scholar but rather a woman of worldly means. Her wedding band adjoined a large blue-cast diamond trimmed with sapphires. The French word *désolé* was arch Russian pretension of the Tsarist school. She knew Bloomingdale's so well she already had some of its paraphernalia. The hardest evidence that she had been transformed was the Greenland falcon over the fireplace. A magnificent rare bird, *stuffed*, in the home of a bird-lover. I speculate now that perhaps this sacrilege was her sense of shame.

I held back then. It's not obvious how to say, I don't believe you! But when she brought out the family pictures in splendid painted frames so I could see the children it all got so obvious that I did too. There was Trifya through the years, first in uniforms that grew gold leaf and medals, then out of uniform and in elegantly cut Italian suits, ever more handsome and photogenic. The three details that upset me were: first, the famous blue tab on his dress-uniform tunic coat; second, that the Italian suits were black on black over black; third, that the backdrop was not just Moscow or forest steppe. I recognized Scandinavia, Vienna, mosques, Rome and Havana sunshine.

Tina was very, very smart. She knew what she was doing. If I saw, I saw. I stared at the pictures, and one hurt more than the rest: Trifya in black in the rain outside a casino that could have been Monte Carlo, holding up a poker hand to the camera, four aces and a jack, the Wire Paladin hand.

I saw everything. There was Pallikin the gambler and face for hire in the service of the baddest guys in his country—State Security, the infamous blue tabs, the execrable Organs, the KGB, the Three Million Stooges. Trifya was a secret policeman. In sci-fi/spy talk, he was black ops.

What did I say? Something evasive such as how beautiful the babies were, how beautiful Tina had been, pregnant. Tina grinned. She had already read the flap on the cloth copy of my book I gave her. She'd also read the back cover of the paperback, where my NSA clerkship was brandished like a sword. Tina asked, "Is it so different for you, Tipya, another peace delegation?"

I spoke flatly that it was different for me.

She returned proverbially, "When you lie down with wolves, do you get up?"

I said that you *could* get up, fleabites and all.

Tina went past politics to philosophy. She patted my book jacket and her pictures. Her diamond flashed. Then she said, "In the Motherland, the fleas are very big, like carrion birds, and some look like Momma."

If this were one of my sci-fi/spy yarns, I could preach prejudice to you. How State Security is a caste in a country that profoundly believes in castes, being former serfdom with the lords turned out. How State Security recruits from its families, and that when you are born to the breed it requires self-destructive dissent like turning from preppie banking to get out. How State Security divides into directorates, the first being the most famous for its cloaks and assassins (cf. Le Carré, Buckley, et al.), the second being the snitchiest for its spying on foreigners in Russia, the fifth being the foulest for its spying on Soviet dissent, the eighth being their NSA and the ninth being their bodyguard goons. In sum, how State Security is cruel, clumsy, stupid, obvious, remorseless like street gangs, greedy like Wall Street, vain like Hollywood. I could also tell you all this with specifics: how a handsome boy named Trifya went from ice hockey to high-stakes traveling during the Brezhnev era when *Nothing goes, maybe* prevailed, when the Stalinists stopped mass murder and perfected mass corruption. But I'm not selling that tale. I lack the details. What I did have that night with Tina was the one necessary detail to Trifya's fall into betraying his own country. It sounds as trite as it is. *Momma was KGB.* Likely Second Chief Directorate, the snitches of the KRO—a nighttime concierge at the elite National Hotel, where foreigners were bunked. Momma was a stooge, and she had made her only son one too—ambitious motherhood, achieving childhood. Trifya's matinee idol looks, passionate talent for gambling and make-believe cowpoking, had done the rest.

I still don't know how he worked. He was probably First Chief Directorate, the glamour boys, but he might have been a loaner to any of the other gangs. He traveled widely, and that suggests the Operations Department, equivalent to our Clandestine Services. You call them spies. They call themselves agents or field men or case officers or ops. What did he do? That's simple: what he was told. I'm guessing intelligence gathering, maybe some bagmanship. The gambling is my only insight. I'm guessing that what State Security did with Trifya was put him in their idea of a Gambling Department because he had the luck to pluck three of a kind and the sense not to try to fill an inside straight. Poker's profoundly not a Russian game, it's as foreign as longhorn steers, so it's probable he played all casino games. But poker was his favorite. It's the one game of chance for which there are no house odds. And what use to the Stooges? Besides raising a little cash, Trifya could locate the heavy losers. How easy to turn a gambler into an asset if you know he has debts he can't pay or swag he didn't earn.

I can't guess more. Why should the Three Million Stooges even want a Gambling Department? Does our CIA have one? I don't know. There's this: When in doubt, Russians imitate the West. Could it be as silly as this—that the Stooges believed sci-fi/spy guys like Ian Fleming? That they wanted a bevy of Bonds out there? Perhaps, but what they got from me was my Trifya, a Pushkin cowboy in black, who was also a wealthy man in a country that suffers famine every winter.

I did not solve all this that night. What I've told you is guesswork that I worked up later. I passed another hour with Tina, avoiding secrets and eyes. She faked bliss. I faked admiration. Blame it on the Cold War, Tip. I beckoned Feliks from the kitchen, said that I had a plane to catch and a blizzard to avoid (thanks, Feliks), and we parted in true Russian tears.

Tina wept. "When are you coming back?" I didn't know. "You must write Trifya everything!" Yes. "You must marry again and raise a family too, now that you're rich and famous." Maybe. "Be happy, Tipya. Life is good." I didn't say anything wise.

5

When Tip was coming back was the winter of 1985. I wrote ahead this time because I wanted to see Trifya, and Tina's reply said they would both be in Moscow in March. The careening Cold War had canceled direct flights from New York, so I changed to Aeroflot in Helsinki and arrived in Moscow in an ice storm that only a Russian pilot could enjoy. I was traveling alone this time, three days in Moscow, overland to Leningrad, and out.

Tip's ambition was the usual salesmanship. The Soviet publishing house (there's only one, though it has many names) had upset common sense by dangling a contract for two of my books. Theirs was a selective strike, skipping my anti-Stalinist trash and going for my running-cur-capitalism trash. Who knows what they were thinking? I thought them clever. They could package me as a revolutionary brother by using my name incorrectly: Tom Paine. Russians are balmy for descendants of famous rascals. They have societies of them, and one of the members, a Decembrist degenerate, met me at the airport with my Intourist factotum. (The Decembrists were a fairy-tale gang who one weird day decided to oust the Tsar with glory. It was 1825, and they were executed for premature idiocy.)

A century and a half later, my Decembrist was named Boris Groomin and he was happy ever after for his dead forebear. Boris was also a member of the Writers Union (all the print that's fit to news) and started off oilily to me in English: "A distinguished colleague, a socialist poet, very glad, glad."

I returned to him in Russian that I regarded poets to be paper enthusiasts who clogged our post with junk mail. Boris and Comrade Intourist recognized Yankee humbug and had me at the National Hotel straightaway. I was an American best-seller paying top dollar who had cash business with the Ministry of Culture. Result, anything I wanted, extra if I paid for it.

It was early *glasnost* then. I don't think the word had yet emerged as the latest Russian theme, best defined as *Everything goes, maybe*. Gorbachev, in harness eight days, was busy mugging for tv. The Russians had finally found a thug who was good in the glass and young enough not to have a blood-soaked wardrobe. It made them unhappy. "All our hustle to get here, and now we're supposed to change?" Like the foxes they think they are, the Russians were positioning themselves for ice dens crumbling. The Cold War was due a temperature adjustment. Thaw and mud season coming. If I sound suspicious, perhaps I've read the wrong books.

What you need to know was that my business with the Ministry of Culture was satisfactory. They bartered, I signed, they smiled. Now I had ruble royalties that I could spend only here. Boris and Comrade Intourist wanted to celebrate. Did I want to meet poets? Translators? Yevtushenko? I called Trifya and Tina to make a date that night at a poetry reading Boris recommended, East European twigs championing new leaf Gorbachev.

Boris was not a blind degenerate. As soon as Trifya and Tina arrived at the poetry reading, he spotted them as high party and lowered his head. This actually pleased me. Trifya was magnificent in black. "Tina's read me your books," said Trifya, "so exciting, all your cowboys. . . . When you mention John Wayne, I weep." He was weeping then, Russian joy, and with Tina's tears I shed Yankeehood, hugging and kissing back. My childhood chums were beautiful people. I felt special and admit now that their politics seemed irrelevant. Truth, I was proud of them. They were Russian successes. I knew many American successes who deserved the knife the Three Million Stooges keep at throats. This was self-deceit, of course; only the knife deserves the knife.

The poetry reading was superbly coy, rhymed verse that managed paeans *and* irony. Tina and I laughed, Trifya applauded the handsome Polish female poet. She versified contraception, abortion, stillbirth. I teased Boris that the Writers Union wasn't vetting as well as they used to. Get smart, censors: gynecology is a fearful metaphor.

We lined up for autographs afterward, and Tina dared me to flirt with the poetic Comrade Polish Fem. Boris must have said something snitchy to her, because soon enough she came over. When I mentioned how well she'd do in New York, she, Zofia Brandys, dropped Russian for French and said all she needed was sponsors, did I know one?

Nice move, Tip. Hide for decades from home radicals, and you volunteer to escort a divorced Polish Catholic redstocking to a Moscow café so heaped with high party frolickers that the sable skins in the room looked pleased for their last sacrifice. The vodka I *refused* destroyed me. Tina played matchmaker. "He's very progressive, Zofia; he thinks poetry is perilous."

Zofia played arsonist. "In Warsaw, lackeys are progressive."

Trifya urged me to tell Zofia how many slaves worked in my New York penthouse. (Thanks, Trifya.) Zofia asked me enough literary questions to confirm I was an illiterate nincompoop on five continents, and then she asked me how many abortions I had had. She was serious. I was her hot new simile for America. Only the tortured reason of poets explains why, when we dropped her off at the Ukraina Hotel, Zofia said she'd never had so much fun in Moscow, tomorrow night would be fine, pick her up at eight. (Thanks, Tina.)

The next evening started out a rerun—my limo, Boris quaking, Trifya and Tina loose, Zofia droll. I had spent the afternoon at Trifya's, recounting my adventures. Trifya had kept his own confessions to his travelogue and cowboy-movie-going. I asked him about Havana mostly, where they had vacationed, and he did say that he regretted never having visited Las Vegas so he could see the wild West, especially Monument Valley. (Make a note of this; he said no Vegas.) Of personal interest, Momma was pensioned, living in a dacha near his own. His sisters were well-married mothers. Our cautious chat made avoiding the obvious easier. His three boys wanted to hear about Hollywood, and I made up enough to be believed. Their apartment was a town version of their dacha, though the stuffed falcon was absent and the trappings were French modern. Tina came in from the beauty parlor to supervise supper. They didn't have Park Avenue wealth, more what we call comfortable upper. For Russia, though, they were out of sight.

Boris underlined the distance when he bowed to Trifya at the curb and said, "Good evening, Comrade Colonel." Trifya returned, "Boris Leonovich, we're all friends, let's enjoy ourselves. We're going to— what the cowboys say—*wet our lips.*" We laughed, Boris buttoned his lip, soon Zofia began a lusty soliloquy. What aroused her was competing with male pride of place. She treated Trifya like a prince, Tina like a tower damsel and me like an armrest. And Zofy could drink!

She downed those fancy five-cup glasses and propped her rich body on my shoulder to announce, "Why are American men so tall? I'll tell you. Their lovely hot-air heads..." If you know randy bashers like Zofia, you also know how, when we piled back into the limo for another dash to booze, she climbed on my lap like Marilyn Monroe gone cocky. I appealed to Trifya for relief.

Tina declared, "It's good for you."

Zofia asked Tina, "How can they feel so good and be so empty?"

Trifya spoke up. "Perhaps, Zofia, you would share Tipya with a roomful of emptiness?"

Trifya's playful remark alerted me. He meant to show Zofia that I was not entirely an idiot and neither was he. The limo sped us to a Warsaw Pact soiree on the other side of the river. How sleek Trifya was at the door when a goon asked for our credentials. Trifya's cowhide billfold said *carte blanche,* and then, to account for the goon's backpedaling, Trifya introduced each of us to him like treasures. The soiree was otherwise worthless. Comrade fraternal brothers were weathering the March run-up to thaw-crazy Gorbachev's first spring party plenum by whoring in the front rooms and gambling in the back. The Cold War was slush in your drink, and the roulette table was a currency exchange. There was no poker game, which disappointed me at first, then not. I was not tempted to ask Trifya to demonstrate his sinister passion.

Boris volunteered to vet the prostitutes and left us. We watched the craps table and then took two empty seats at the baccarat game, what the Europeans do because they can't figure blackjack. Trifya played Tina's hand, and I showed Zofia how to wager. When I accidentally won a pile for her with my dollars, Zofia ignited, squeals and wet kisses. Zofia was an extremist by nature; gambling turned her raven head like a denunciation. "You will take me to American casinos," she threatened, "and I shall make love to you like a gangster's moll when I win." I told her that back home not even gangsters could beat the house odds. She was not listening, now threatening orgasm if she won again.

After too much of this, we had to figure how to pry our ladies from the table. Trifya reached over to fold both their hands; then to counter Zofia's protest, he started a bizarre distraction. He pulled me close to Zofia's face and gestured to the lair of Eurotrash. "Now, Zofy, listen to me," began Trifya. "My dear Tipya is a poet of the invisible. He knows about spies, all spies. He can tell you, face by face, who the cowboys are. Look now, for yourself, then ask him. He knows."

Zofia demanded, "What cowboys?"

I mumbled, "Cowboys?" I glanced from mug to Stalinist mug. As far as I knew, there were no real cowboys here. What did he mean? Trifya whispered the answer into my ear. A little KGB joke, and I did laugh. We eased over to the red curtains. I pointed outside. I was showing Zofia a cowboy town in searchlights. Across the street was the new American Embassy chancery under construction.

"Hot-air balloons, not cowboys," said Zofia.

Suddenly Trifya did his dear turn for me. "Sing it, Tipya, sing our song for Zofy, tell her how wild the West is, how beautifully wild." Embarrassed, I obliged his intensity, "Have Gun—Will Travel, reads the card of a man..."

Tina slid against her man and grinned her signature. He brought forth his deck, shuffled in midair. I expected his favorite card trick. He had arranged an innovation.

"Forty-eight cards," he said, displaying the deck in a fan. "Where could the aces be?" Trifya plucked two aces from Tina's blouse, making her coo. He plucked one more from my breast pocket. "That's three," he said. "Tipya sees the invisible fourth."

I did but was afraid of braless Zofia's blouse, so I came close enough to indicate, and she shook loose the card.

Trifya laughed. "My dear brother Tipya, I love you." Then he added his favorite Paladin/Pushkin quote: "You're too sweet when chance refuses/And too clever when it nods."

Still, to this day I do wonder exactly how far Trifya meant his sleight of hand to go. He was a professional. He didn't permit cards to beat him. Why, then, Trifya, why did you say there was a cowboy in the room? Why did you show off our chancery? Why did you want me to fetch the ace of clubs from Zofia's pretty chest? Am I uncommoning my sense? Was it just chance? Did it mean anything when it fell to our lusty feet?

6

That club, it tumbled the rest of the year. I'll add a Russian metaphor: Thaw brings impassable mud. Sci-fi/spy calls 1985 the year of the spooked.

At summer's start, one of our midlife cowards named John A. Walker, Jr., was turned in *by his wife* for selling out the U.S. Navy to their Three Million Stooges. Not for politics, just cash and hormones.

At summer's end, one of their midlife cowards named Vitaly Yurchenko walked into the astonished arms of our Keystone Ops. Importantly, Yurchenko was a very high stooge at the KGB's First Chief Directorate's Operations Department. (One of Trifya's compadres?) Again, Yurchenko sold out not for politics, just cash and hormones. Soon Yurchenko was singing low comedy to our side. It was suggested that the American chancery building I'd shown to Zofia that night in Moscow was more bugged than Moosehead Lake.

Soon after, it was revealed to our Keystoners that one of our junior ops in Clandestine Services, a soulless bumbler named Edward Lee Howard, was selling out our Moscow station. Again, not for politics, just cash (he actually buried it in the Arizona desert) and of course hormones. It was funny enough, but then our Keystoners bungled the pursuit of the coward Mr. Howard so badly that he vanished into the desert, a free-lance clown until he wandered into the Stooges' care in June 1986 at Vienna.

There was worse. Spy dust in Moscow. A British-run Moscow mole in jeopardy. A KGB-run Washington mole at the NSA. But let that pass. I've made my point. Mud season.

Tip knew none of this. Neither did you. Nor am I making this up; I couldn't plot such farce. I did wonder, when Yurchenko's subsequent escape from our ops and repatriation to the Stooges turned up on tv, how it might play in Moscow. It played slapstick here, since Yurchenko strolled out of a Georgetown restaurant like an addict rethinking detox. Tv provided more fun the following year when the

Marine guards at our Moscow embassy were accused of fornicating with Comrade Mata Hari. The embassy was subsequently emptied of its native staff and declared so penetrated that visiting State Secretary Shultz had to debrief in a big van.

Why this all might be important is that I was suddenly back in Moscow in January 1987, for the weirdest confab yet fashioned by the Cold War. The Ministry of Culture had invited every Western media nabob they could persuade to come over and hobnob with Gorbachev. I was a late-invited guest, asked overnight to replace a real writer, perhaps because I was outselling Comrades Sontag, Allende and Mailer *combined* behind the Iron Curtain.

I didn't have time to write ahead. I called Trifya and Tina's apartment as soon as I was bunked at the Rossiya. I thought nothing when there was no answer. They owed me a return Christmas present, but I'd had a VCR tape of their Black Sea vacation the previous summer, so we were almost even. The breathless schedule of the lit-crit claque didn't permit me to call again until the second afternoon. Still nothing, and I was annoyed. I figured the babushkas were refusing to pick up, and answering machines don't yet suit Russia's sense of caution. I assumed Trifya was away and Tina was off being glamorous.

By Friday, after an eerie display of East-West gang snobbery at a reception in the Great Kremlin Palace (think of Livia Logan as a Lenin Prize, Zofia Brandys as a Pulitzer), I was dreading another mass sup with my kindred of capitalism. One anecdote does for all. I was eavesdropping when the sensational sci-fi/spy guy Gore Vidal proposed that America and Russia, both northern homed, convene an alliance to combat the clattering of the third world to the south. The reds loved it. So did I. With one wry proposition (I presume he was kidding), Mr. Vidal had uncovered a certain profound Soviet contempt for law. As for the more sincere flirting around me, I don't despise the two-faced Sontag crowd (two enough?); I just don't understand their apologia for the bad guys, and my ignorance slips toward rude thoughts. You don't pet with the Kremlin! The reds are date rape, and they *never* apologize. Have you ever heard the Communist Party apologize? To just one of the uncountable dead, destroyed and missing in its seven decades of devilment? Show me the letter. Gorbachev in Italian suits and his French-remade wife were the same old secret policemen. I knew a secret policeman; he was a friend of mine. Trifya never apologized, and I was almost proud of him for that, and I was almost adjusted to the fact that we were never going to talk candidly about his treachery.

Then it was the weekend. No answer in Moscow should mean they were at the dacha, so I rang through twice without result. This meant nothing. But then, trapped at the hotel by the brutal cold that year and with incorrigible compatriots whose idea of Saturday night was skulking around with celebrity dissidents, I decided it was okay to be very bold.

I called the Pallikin family apartment. Momma answered. I had not spoken with her in nearly twenty years and was affectionate but formal, saying how much I missed seeing her, that I hoped it was not presumptuous to call. Momma listened without comment. I added that I wanted to leave a message for Trifya and Tina.

Momma said, "Yes, comrade, what message?"

In town. Leaving Monday. "Love to all," I closed.

"I'll tell him," said Momma. "My love to your momma, Tipya."

7

This is the end of a yarn without an end. There will be no rescue of innocents nor of the black hat who could palm all the aces. I wasn't trying to surprise you, and you're not surprised, that Trifya and Tina are disappeared. I told you from the first. There's no trickery. Remember I don't have details. For two years now I have used the only sources I have in the genuine sci-fi/spy game—the library reading room—and I've found no explanation as to why my letters go unappreciated.

I have learned that the returning stooge Yurchenko was not executed, as expected, and is being kept available in a reduced state for

Western eyes to puzzle that *glasnost* might actually mean *Nine grams, maybe.* I have also learned that our Keystone Op the coward Mr. Edward Lee Howard is pacing in a glass cage in Moscow, a pet of the Stooges, rewarded like a rat on a leash for having wiped out our cowpoking in Russia forever, maybe. I'm not joking about this. You're not so trendy that you don't care that one very ordinary American lad sold out men, women and children as if they were cow chips.

For a thrill I'll suppose that Las Vegas and Atlantic City (where Trifya never went, maybe) are as bugged as our Moscow chancery, which we're thinking about demolishing brick by brick, and that those blackjack dealers in bow ties at Trump's casinos are as penetrated by the Stooges as were our embassy's Marine guard, which we're replacing with robots.

(Here's a cheap thrill, too, and perhaps why my Trifya and Tina are disappeared. Trifya came up under a gangster named Yuri Andropov. Remember him? Andropov was Boss Stooge 1967–82, Boss of Bosses 1982–83. This current Boss of Bosses, Gorbachev, came up the same way, one of Andropov's pets. The oldest rule of gangland is that when you take over, ice the old gang.)

Tip's end-guessing this way for now. Momma was a stooge, yes, but she loved her Trifya. I don't believe she lied to me when she said she'd pass on my message—as old as Siberia are the mothers who stand by their condemned children. Trifya was a stooge, yes, but he was not ours too. I don't believe he was ours too. Do you? Not Trifya. A double agent? Did you suspect that about his invisible-cowboy-in-the-room game? About his boastful love of the wild West? You don't really think one of the cowboys Howard sold out was Trifya? No. I won't accept it either—that Trifya hoodwinked everyone at the poker table until he got caught palming the aces.

Here's what I figure. What's going on now in Moscow is the latest Russian theme, *Everything goes, maybe.* That means new hands to do the same old dirty work. You hear peace, disarmament, democratization in the meetinghouse news. I hear silences. Trifya was a traitor to his motherland; every day he served the Stooges, he betrayed Holy Mother Russia. He was at odds for a long time and blissful. Then one day, cowboy boots stuck in mud, he was too sweet when chance refused, too clever when it nodded, and so he became misfortune in a savage land. Wherever he is, Tina's with him. He'll never leave her.

Tip's last best guess. Russia in winter is the time of gambling and treason. When it gets very cold again, *Everything reruns, pardner.*

2

Hollywood Before the Mast

I Meet Ahab;

I Get Harpooned

Tip's d o n e t v enough to know that he's "no good in the glass," which is show business talk for poor on camera. There's also Tip's opinions that he's done the Letterperson show enough forever and that the "Today/Morning" gang is yawning, which leaves him cranky with a conviction never to smell their caffeine breath again. Nevertheless Johnny Carson's "Tonight Show" is moon-walking to sci-fi/spy guys, and I blinked once and said yes twice when the booker called my Hollywood agency and they called me. "Tonight" wanted me right away tomorrow night, to replace a Stalinist poet who was *glasnost* bound in East Europe, maybe some other combination.

I was loafing and ice fishing at the time, up at my camp at Moosehead Lake. It was just after Christmas, when Maine's deep woods are white silence save for the wind and the occasional felonious snowmobiler. My solitary holiday had run its course—I am a humbug about Christmas and happy for it. I was supposed to be starting and finishing a new romance of the Cold War. (I write suddenly so as not to think about it; besides, I've done all the research digestible, and the plots are buddies.) Yet I was feeling too lazy to twist, assassinate, seduce, chase, rescue and ironize and found myself keeping the fire too high and staring for many happy hours into another superb xenophobia game in my playmate the Mac. Also my imaginary best friend, McKerr, had been scheduled to show up so we could try one more time to teach me to ski at Squaw Mountain, but his Irish pirate boss had shanghaied him to go buccaneering again. Bluntly, I was catatonically Tip.

For these slim warrants I chose to exit my cozy burrow among black bears and go where I don't belong to get a hard lesson that love and madness are a tricky old couple who entertain bystanders the way hunting season amuses wildlife. Details follow, beginning with packing nothing since my tropical gear was in New York, ringing up the local motorcycle poacher gang I use as a limo service, and suffering a scary dawn ride over slick ice to Bangor for the hop and a half to L.A. and its choice neighborhood of make-believe, Hollywood.

2

I shall surprise you by declaring right away that I like Hollywood; it's been great to me. There are those other opinions, yes, but it's also true that anything that is said about Hollywood is true. Sleazery, thievery, cokery, slavery, pre-Oedipal, postpubertal, creepy rancid stew et cetera party line. As everyone's dearest press agent, Oscar Wilde, said of everyone's dearest humbug, George Bernard Shaw, you can say of Hollywood, "It has no enemies; all its friends hate it intimately."

But not Tip Paine. And it's not just the demilarge checks Hollywood has issued me nor that I get to stay in my agent's mother's Beverly Hills mansion when I go there nor that I am demisomebody there for the five projects that got made. (There are also several of my brilliant hack jobs stashed away like treasure maps; one of which here guides me to prize folly.) None of this business is why. I like Hollywood because I understand what it is. It's New Bedford, Massachusetts, 1850. It's the square-masted whaling industry on the opposite coast.

Take an illustration. Observe the vast Pacific out there, the naked masts of the whalers tied up in Santa Monica Bay. Look closely at the proud financiers called Mr. Goodfellow/man and Ms. Goodlady/person who wait on the quay to sign on another scabrous crew of dregs, children and whiners, who when sent before the mast a year or two will mostly obey the rules, take every whale they can find, melt the blubber down into oil, then sail back again to disgorge the bounty into the hands of the Goods. The famous ships' names are in the whaling hall of fame. My favorites are the Stalinist or Cold War flicks: *King Kong, Hunchback of Notre Dame,* John Ford's corpus, *Body Snatchers, Ben-Hur, 2001, Jaws, Aliens.* You know them as if you'd sailed on them, and that's part of the humor. The audience gets harpooned and converted while loving its predator forever.

Meanwhile the Goods are keeping their counting houses happy, or not, and are trying to convince the bankers to loan them enough to crew the same old ship with a new name, or not. The Goods are very good; that is a fact. They are trustworthy, thrifty, pious taxpayers who live in great clapboard houses that smell pleasantly of plunder. Sometimes they form cartels like UA or Warner's or Twentieth Century but only for tax purposes, because what they love best is to operate independently. It's called being an "indie." Borrow the money, hire the ship, take the plunge into the deep green sea.

As for the scabrous crew, they come and go, and it's Hollywood's smarts to let them have some of the swag, most of the glory and all of the blame. The first mates you know too. My favorites again are the Stalinists and Cold Warriors—Sturges, Hawks, Ford, Kubrick, Spielberg, from all ports and creeds. The harpoonists are obvious—studs like Brando, Brando, Brando. The twist is that the crew mostly behaves when at sea. And when in port it gains useful publicity for meaningless whale oil by being what it is—dregs, children and whiners. Cocaine is their current rum and folly their bed. When not before the mast they will eat, punch, drink, snort, screw, beg, cheat and apologize to anything. Their fate is the same as flesh—mean, desperate, organic. It's not even their fate to bury, because if it's really silly the Goods will name a ship after them and go fishing.

The two correct questions you should ask now are: Who is Ahab? Where is Moby Dick? I could be smart-alecky and reply that Captain Ahab is in his cabin since he doesn't appear on deck until well at sea, where he once again gets to quote scripture to albatrosses and go stupendously mad. I could also remark that the white whale is wherever you aren't looking, he's a confidant of Poseidon and (Ahab's opinion) a familiar of Hades. Yet I must be accurate. Ahab is a major character in a fine book too many educated people ignore, and Moby Dick is a big nasty white whale who doesn't exist.

You have noticed in my salty illustration of Hollywood that I named no captains. This is deliberate. There are no captains. No one is in command. It's a business, not a quest. The truth is that there are no purposefully mad Ahabs, no worthily pursued white whales.

Fortunately for me and other scriveners, the Goods neither understand nor want to that Messrs. Ahab and Dick are make-believe. What this means is that they are always looking for that famous captain to go a-questing. (Candidates like Steven Spielberg are proposed, tried out, then found out as not quite Ahab.) It also means that the Goods believe they need my kind of cartography to place in Ahab's hands when they find him, as if I possessed a secret chart to Moby Dick's patrol area in Whale Alley. It's the best reason why I like Hollywood. I get treated as if I know something it doesn't.

Yes, the word is that the only folk lower than actors in Hollywood are the screenwriters (who aren't writers, thank goodness), and yes, this is true—until you are one who makes money. I had not lost it three times, had made it modestly once, and was now netting it like a Russian trawler. It was why Mr. Johnny Carson's show had called me. The "indie" Goods who owned my latest picture were flacking me as deserving of an Oscar the Harpoonist nomination for my recent work. In Hollywood that post-Christmas season, in brief, Tip was better than hot, Tip was *prehot*.

I ambled out of the eucalyptus caverns of Los Angeles International Airport (it's called LAX on the baggage tags; guess why) still wearing my Maine woolens and wincing at the January heat like a seasoned fisher of persons.

My Hollywood agent, Yakima Kohn, was thorough enough to send a limo to pick me up. He was further thorough to be inside talking on the phone. Yakkie delayed his administration quickly, put the receiver to his chest, began to me, "Slyboots, don't we look warm? Or are we calling attention to ourselves already?"

I mumbled that I was dressed correctly for where my body still thought it was, Moosehead Lake. I added that I'd not had my tropicals and I figured I could let the local tailors rob me.

Yakkie was keener. "No, we're fabulously dressed for this. Don't touch a scratchy scratch. And the thing on your face, we'll trim it a tad and shove you into the lights. They'll love it. 'Nanook Tonight'! We were so worried that this might catch the bunker on us, if you went out there and started chatty-kathy—you talk so well, but you have way too much to say, and it's always never very not not *mishugoss*—but Moosehead Lake! That's your statement! Moosehead Lake! Just tell them where you are! You didn't bring any antlers?"

I asked Yakkie not to tease anymore. My stage fright was replacing my jet lag. It was noontime, and that meant that no matter how I looked, I was due at "The Tonight Show"'s Burbank studio in six hours.

"Antlers is giggles, *bambino*," countered Yakkie, "and aren't we the serious one? But all right, you're my baby, even if you do think too much. Relax now, it's my town, and I'm doing business. Think putting!"

Yakkie directed the chauffeur to drive safely while he continued his telephone administration to a colleague named Faisal. He also presented me with a good luck gift—a custom-built sand wedge. This is Yakkie's loving sense of humor. He is a first-rate human being who is mostly show business and the rest PGA groupie. His late father was a Goodfellow, his ceaselessly generous mother is a Goodwidow, his sister is at an Israeli kibbutz, being a psalm-singing socialist who's way too utopian for my research, and his best friend is a healthy money winner on the PGA circuit. However, the three details you notice right away about Yakkie are none of the above.

First, he is congenitally disabled. His eyeglasses are very thick because he's legally blind; his telephone right hand is pincerlike, with two digits; he walks with crutches because both his legs, born ill-formed and weak, have been amputated below the knees. Secondly, he is homosexually so far out of the closet that even in gay Hollywood he is known as an unusually clear-cut person. Thirdly, he talks funny. His American is Beverly Hills/Yale Drama/agent/golf, his Yiddish is stagecraft, his salesmanship is statecraft. In sum, I have the best agent on the planet. Yakkie took me on when I was nobody but a baby salesman (he said he liked my "lapidarian prose"), and right away I was demisomebody because Yakkie was speaking for me at quayside.

The first time I met Yakkie was back in 1979. He had stopped in New York en route to his latest nephew's birth in Israel via the British Open. I crept into the ludicrous Russian Tea Room and was escorted to his table. I was dumbstruck. He was on the phone, dressed like Yakkie in tastefully happy cream and pastel layers and wearing a Star of David on a small pearl necklace. I thought I was in trouble and tried to evaporate when he rose gracefully on his crutches and offered his pincerlike hand to shake. Yakkie's opening line was, "What are we today?" I was Tip, dressed in Tip uniform, blazer and khakis, and I took him seriously.

It turned out that he was more anxious at meeting me than I would have been at meeting Gordon Liddy. (Yakkie does not think me crazy about Gordon, by the way; he understands about the muse-parrot-on-the-shoulder stuff.) That first luncheon, Yakkie became my friend and confidant forever, though I didn't know it. I thought him extra-terrestrial. He turned out to be primary Homo sapiens, what is called in Yiddish a *mensch*. If anything, I am the sly visitor from a Puritan galaxy. Further, I was never wrongheaded about homosexuality, just college-boy ignorant. After a few years in New York City, I wised up.

(Take another illustration. Once upon a time I was a boy and they were boys and we didn't think about being more than boys. Soon I discovered I liked girls intimately and have not been comfortable since. They discovered they liked boys intimately and have not been comfortable since, though, from my envious point of view, they seem much happier than Tip and have many more friends. The truth of equality is what Citizen Paine said: equal before the law and a republic without lords or slaves. I translate this to America, in these anxious days, to mean that everyone gets a chance to be good or bad the same way; there's no reason to flack one group as more special than any other: race, creed, gender, bucks. This is Tip theory. Tip practice is that Tip-the-visitor-from-afar gets the best of the gender deal. Women and men regard him, he usually regards them, even the scoundrels. And it is Tip's unearned gift that he's always been regarded generously by the nonstraight men he's met.)

Yakkie I love like the older brother I don't have. Also he's a wise gentleman. He's heard my palaver about Hollywood before the mast and has often opined generously, "Whatever you say, slyboots, it's a business, show business." He also says he knows Ahab and Moby Dick are make-believe on paper. He's seen John Huston's smart version of *Moby Dick* five or ten times, looking in on other peglegged heroes like himself, and he has opined, "That fabulous fat white boy steals every scene and he's only on camera the last reel, the naughtiest scene stealer since Fay Wray thought *she* was the star."

We rode the L.A. traffic jam without end into Beverly Hills. I don't know L.A. enough to describe driving around. There are many low points, a few hills, hilarious freeways. North is San Francisco, east is America, south is Mexico, western is a kind of movie that used to make money. For those who make believe, the center of the world is Hollywood & Vine, and the bivouac is Beverly Hills. (The trendy Goods have scattered to other havens, and Beverly Hills is now chock-full of mind and tooth doctors and widows, but it's still Hollywood's sentimental digs.)

Eventually we arrived at Yakkie's mother's tastefully creme-and-pastel palace amid other palaces and gorgeous tropical flora and fauna. Soon enough I was in some wing of the palace, shaving my beard off in the shower (nixing "Nanook Tonight" before Yakkie got tricky), when the phone rang. It's over the pastel toilet, of course, and within easy reach of the pastel Jacuzzi.

"What are we today?" started Yakkie. I grunted. "Still serious? Less Lava soap and more banana shampoo, Tipster. Are you there?" I grunted again; only my mother and Yakkie call me Tipster. "I have good-bad and bad-good for you," he said, "just off the wire. Good-bad is that the 'Tonight' showmen *do* want you; bad-good is that they've delayed your tee-off until Monday*ana.*"

I translated. With four hours to go, "The Tonight Show" had delayed my premiere. I felt much much better instantly, then realized I was stuck with a weekend of stage fright in L.A.

Yakkie continued to soothe. He said that he liked my luck, because now I could rest and get much less thoughtful. Also, he said, this meant I would be doing "Tonight" not with Mr. Carson, whom Yakkie adored but whom he thought a tad too serious for someone as serious as me. Rather I would be out there with permanent guest host Jay Leno, whom Yakkie adored and who he knew would bring out all the sweet warm colors in my B&W bibliographical brain.

Great, I thought, I don't get to meet my hero Mr. Johnny Carson. I get to chat with a guy my age whose jawline alone makes me feel as if I'm watching the Dudley Do-Right cartoon. Was this good-bad or bad-good? I didn't know. It was what Yakkie hates me to call his hometown—Never Never Land.

Yakkie accelerated to agent speed. "I can hear you thinking, unless that's shampoo in your eyes. Don't I treat you well! A sneak screening of Spielberg tonight, which won't be awful... and loads of outtakes from *Ben-Hur* on Mom's vid... and beautiful Beverly Hills REM sleep... and tomorrow, eighteen holes at the club and then a *most* polite party at the marina."

I said that *Ben-Hur* outtakes were okay, but no parties.

"You'll love the marina!" argued Yakkie. "The ocean moves, and we don't. You'll adore the music. Vivaldi and Telemann. And if you're well behaved, I'll let you go to church on Sunday before more golf. Now wipe out the shampoo and tell me you love it."

I said that I was not here for love or money, just tv.

"My thinks-he's-a-tough-guy," said Yakkie, "tell me you love me."

4

Now comes Ahab, along with love and money, the three things I didn't want in L.A. coming at me like a harpoon. Ahab was not at the hyped-up screening of a new Steven Spielberg movie about (what else) Steven Spielberg making movies. Also Ahab was not at Yakkie's fantasy country club with its overlush but playable fantasy golf course. (Yakkie worships golf—though he cannot play—because he worships his best friend and lover, Billy Ben, who was away on Australian links that January.)

Where Ahab abided was at that promised "most polite party" at the marina, which was not a party but a charity benefit for the current fashion, L.A. street gang rehabilitation. I know I've also declared that Ahab is *not*, that he doesn't exist outside of paper, and neither does that fat white boy whale, M. Dick. I'm not trying to trick you any more than I tricked me. This is a salty Hollywood yarn, and as the spectacular former swabbie President Reagan has said often, it's all smoke and mirrors. Well, Ahab smokes naturally and he lives in my looking glass. Here he comes, after some details, and the first trick is that this time around he's very female.

The marina was at Santa Monica sunset. The crowd on the enclosed deck was as polite as charity can afford, so many Goods that the scabrous crew members looked intimidated away from their usual vandalism. Of note instantly was that it was a very male gathering. You want names? You don't know the Goods to hear them, that's the secret of their authority: power makes privacy. The public studs included Michael, Bobbie, Bruce, Tom, Jeff, Tom, Don, Kevin (I'm teasing; my idol Selleck wasn't there—off flacking for the roguish

GOP). You think these studs of Hollywood street gangs don't party together? You're correct. This wasn't a party, it was a benefit, and the boys were present for self-benefit. You call it winter, but in Hollywood it's called Oscar Season. The marina gathering to Vivaldi and Telemann strings might raise money for crack hooligans, but it was definitely a test for screen hooligans to see who was "most polite" enough now to risk nominating (maybe next year) and who this year could be trusted to open the envelopes on camera. The acceptable openers and winners have passed this test and moved on to other polite games, like endorsing presidents. Yakkie hadn't told me (well, the "most polite" had been a soft clue), but this was an all-male prehot closed-set tryout.

The male bonding was why I was unprepared for Kates. That's both names together—Mrs. Kate O'Kates. Her imaginative foes called her "the KO word," and her hired friends said "Yes, ma'am!" instantly. She was no star or director, she was an independent producer, one of the Goods. I was complaining to Yakkie about the fit of my blazer out of the club pro shop and communicating how long I was not staying —fifteen minutes, no more—and he was bartering, "Give me twenty-four, Tipster, even a sitcom gets twenty-four," when Kates stalked upon us and began fishing.

"I'm lucky to find you at last, Mr. Paine," she said, taking my hand strongly to shake it cleanly. Correctly she didn't finish the salutation and name herself. The Goods assume you know them; if not, you're worthless. Also correctly she used the first person plural when she was doing business. "We've called Yakkie about you several times," she said, "and he's told us you hide out in the Arctic. Hudson's Bay? No phone, no tv, no roads, no show."

Flustered, I mumbled, "Call me Tip."

Yakkie propped a crutch against me (whispered her name to me like "Dread O'Dread") and addressed Kates, sounding defense-minded. "I sent in a dog team, Kates. He's here to breakfast with Mom and play golf for me."

"Oh, Yakkie, I like your mysteries." Kates grinned very toothily, like an owner of all secrets. "I won't skip ahead," she said, "but I think we'll keep the tape machines rolling, say late-night network? I've never seen you in the glass, Mr. Paine, and it's good to see you first. The glass is cramped for tall, dark and deep men." She gestured toward the Hollywood studs glowing behind her, all of them low on the horizon like cunning photo reductions of the sunset. "Don't you agree? It's a small mystery why it likes small and cute. You must know."

This was a stealthfully easy question, and this fool went for it, jesting, "Who'd want a big jester?"

As a reward I didn't get a fishhook; I got her cool fingers on my wrist. "You don't wear a timepiece," said Kates, changing bearings, a pro's pro. "Is that because you don't care, like they say? Or do you have chronophobia too, like my son? He was a month late, and I'm still waiting for him to tell me to get off his case, same as his father did—behind schedule." She paused as if she'd just confessed. Her self-deprecation glowed like virtue. "But now you're here, and it's our time to talk—yes?"

Details, all details. Chronophobia. Nice detail, Kates (and a *tough* clue). Kates was a detail person. I argue it was why I liked her so quickly. Sure there was the detail that she was easy-looking, tall, fair and deep—streaked hair, eyes any color contact lens she chooses, original long limbs, hired-on deltoid broad shoulders and coiled legs. She was heavier than fashion or camera permits. Much later she told me that in her college days she'd tried screen acting but that she was "no good in the glass." She said that two children, divorce and too much sport had made her, at forty-one, a pumped-up jockette. What you noticed first and only about that pretty face was the teeth. They were whalebone white and they didn't quit, they just kept coming at you. She talked and fed omnivorously, and she was snacking from a heaped plate of fat California vegetables and tarty dip as she did business.

Meanwhile Yakkie was still fending her off. "We just stopped by on the way from the clubhouse; some free giggles and home for beddie-bye. Get in thirty-six holes tomorrow if I can keep him from church —sensational to see you, Kates, you look sensational, and when Tipster's back in town we'll have lunch on your boat, got one yet?"

Yakkie yanked a brass button on my coat sleeve.

Kates did not wait. "This is now, Yakkie. I want a meeting." She fixed dead ahead on me. The white teeth snapped on a carrot and me together. "We admire your work [crunch] and want to work with [crunch] you, Mr. Paine."

I mumbled, "Please, call me Tip, please."

"We mean *Killed the Beast,*" Kates continued, all sails set. "We've read the treatment [crunch]. Don't ask me how, Yakkie; we've read it."

This was the last jargon I understood between them. The rest was cryptographic show-bizzing and Kates-crunching that translated later to mean that Kates knew there was a script to support my project, wanted to deal, had a major talent agent named Sam who owed her a "package," which means director and actors. She declared she was "suggestible"—that if Yakkie thought I was due "best numbers" after the Oscar nominations, then he should name them now. Finally Kates spread those amazing teeth at me and prophesied, "You want to know my philosophy? It's simple. Like the man said, 'Don't sweat deals, sweat box office.'"

I report *honestly* that she was a vividly human female who for as long as she was dealmaking was larger than life. She ingested those vegetables so fast she seemed to swell healthily. But then Yakkie said the magic words, somewhere in the inflection of the sentence "We'll get back," and Kates reverted to a normal-sized human being. She did not linger; another cool grip on my wrist, a strong whiff of her muscular scent, a fetching "What luck to meet you at last [pause], Tip," and she was gone, only a few yards away to the buffet table, to huddle with other Goods, but as far away as the horizon.

I tried to ask Yakkie, "What?" Yakkie had changed too, from partygoer to evacuee, with me as baggage. We were out of the marina so fast I had to hand my soda glass to the doorman just as Yakkie ordered his chauffeur to whisk us safely to his favorite fantasy restaurant.

"She was coming back," he explained mysteriously en route. "We had to get out before she came back with her boys." I probed and demanded, but he wasn't substantive until we'd settled at his favorite fantasy table and he'd sipped an extravagant glass of wine. For Yakkie, he began bluntly. "Too close, too close, I've got to get new legs, too close."

I protested this talk of dread. I said that I'd seen the subway movie posters in New York. Kate O'Kates—she was an inch-high name on two recent trashy top ten. I argued that she wanted to do our script. (A wacky idea re terrorism but with a happy twist. I had worked it up with Yakkie a year before, after we had simultaneously watched *King Kong* bicoastally while holding open the line so I could once again enjoy Yakkie's adoration of "that fabulous fat black boy.")

"Kates wants to do *our movie,*" I squeaked again, as Yakkie chewed another sip. "*Killed the Beast,* Yakkie!" (If you are so truly trendy you haven't seen *KK* because it's B&W, the last line is the theme: "It was," says the producer, aghast at the gigantic corpse on Thirty-fourth Street, "beauty killed the beast.")

"Forget it, Tipster; not us, not ours, not now, not not not."

"But, but, but," I tried, flailing, "hasn't she got the money, the package, the muscle?"

"She's got it," he said, "she's numbers up the up."

"How much is 'up the up'?" I asked. "Is that like Spielberg was or like Spielberg is?" (Spielberg's my age, so my envious eye makes him my only measurement.)

"She's the KO word," said Yakkie. "What word I hear is her company's going over twenty mil on the two latest."

I asked, "Net?" He didn't react because it was a dumb question. Hollywood publicizes in gross, it speaks in take-home pay. "Net, Yakkie!" I gasped. "Net! Twenty million for trash baskets?" Kate O'Kates was already major Goods, and her best years were ahead of her. She was scrambling the code—hot-prehot-hot. I managed a cynical greedy question: "Not married to Spielberg or such, is she?"

"No," sighed Yakkie. "No. No. She's indie."

Then I achieved my breakthrough genius, the turn being that it was coming this way. (The word "net" had lit my code-happy brain.) Trying to ease Yakkie's mood, I used the famous make-believe name. "Ahab," I said. "Yakkie, *she's my Ahab,* and I'm what she wants as a navigator. We'll go fishing for Moby Dick together! I'll lose my de-mistatus, I'll be net rich! We'll be net rich!"

"Listen, thinks-he-is," returned Yakkie, most unamused. "You don't know what you're saying. Stop thinking. This is business. I'm the agent. You want another, do it. You want me, then—"

"But net, but net," I tried.

Yakkie then used a somber voice I had heard only once before, after a depressed client put Yakkie on hold and botched a suicide. I had been on Yakkie's hold that day, and he'd come back on the line with this bottomlessly rueful tone. What I'm describing is that Yakkie was profoundly serious when he ordered me, "Let . . . it . . . go."

I obeyed. I knew he was leaving the table and my confidence if I said any more. I tooled out my pipe, looked at the menu, fretted that I'd crossed him

Yakkie recovered gently. "We've got Cole Porter kinescope tonight. He's heaven, heaven. You'll flip, and I'll let you think too. Now tell this beautiful boy [the waiter] what we're sampling from his pretty kitchen."

5

The next Ahab sighting of consequence was Monday off the ninth fairway at Yakkie's fantasy country club. It was my second round in three days with three of Yakkie's buddies, and I was Hollywood weary, too much fun and sleep, the sun relentless upon the smoggy January clouds. Yakkie was bundled up tastefully from the midday *sixty* degrees and was riding his telephone-equipped cart alongside me, the prime minister of my every shot in between his chatting with other clients and his mom. Once more I knew that if I could only execute his advice, keep my head down, shoulders level, hands behind the ball, weight back, then I might once see 88 on my scorecard.

Not that day. My stage fright for the "Tonight" taping in six hours had returned to hook every tee shot. I went searching again in the trees for my ball. Yakkie couldn't get his cart through the rough and called from the fairway, "It's there, left, way right," pointing with his field glass. I mucked around many soggy steps and realized there was another golfer, a woman, searching down the slope for her ball off the eighteenth fairway. It wasn't Kate O'Kates; it was one of her foursome. Kates spied me from the fairway, hesitated as if she weren't sure it was me (ha ha), and when I waved in surprise she swelled to larger-than-life size and waved back with there-he-blows energy, hailing through the wind, "Good luck tonight, Tip. I'll be waiting."

I wanted to amble down and flirt but was afraid of Yakkie. I'd already betrayed him in my thoughts and couldn't risk more until hidden opportunity. I did stare long at those long legs. Kates stepped in my direction and I panicked, waving again and jumping back into the brush, to land on my ball. Yakkie, who'd been screened from all this treachery by the terrain, called, "Find it?" I plucked up my ball and walked out to drop for the two-stroke penalty. I got my shot off faster than KK climbs.

The folly of all this is that Yakkie had missed nothing, though he didn't tell me until much later. He knew Kates was stalking me. He knew that she was a member of his fantasy club and that she'd been on the indoor tennis courts on Sunday, where I'd spotted her slaughtering a service. He knew also that she was playing ahead of us on Monday and that she wouldn't be so clumsy as to linger in the clubhouse bar, where I, fool for love, hoped to find her after my round that day. In sum, Yakkie knew that Kates knew that he forbade her.

I knew none of this nor so much more. Those whalebone-white teeth and the elegant six iron I glimpsed through the trees had convinced me, along with Hollywood greed and my own transcontinental libido, that Kates was for me. I mean my make-believe girl, my loveboat captain Ahab. I'm mocking myself because I deserve it; she doesn't.

I was so annoyed with Yakkie by then—he had refused to speak more of Kates since Saturday night—that I dared bring her up in the locker room while he was advising me how to dress out of the pro shop for tv. I aimed to talk subtly, but it probably came out: "What's wrong with Kates? What are you, jealous? I'm not leaving you, Yakkie. She's just a big girl who can take care of herself and maybe me too. Let me try. At least let me try our script with her."

Yakkie's response is stone-written. "I'm sparing you. I'm not bitchy. You want her, go do what you boys *insist* upon doing. I'm going to tell you what you're missing with your trot of the hots. She cheats, Tip-ster." He tapped his field-glass case. "I've seen it."

I asked him what he'd seen.

He gestured toward the golf bags. "Cheats," he said.

I blithered, "Cheats at golf? Are you nuts?" I added conveniently that this isn't golf, that Kates wants to do business, that he'd said so, and that this is Hollywood, where everybody cheats. I felt threatened enough by Yakkie's frown to add the euphemism that always irritates him: I called his hometown Never Never Land.

"Mind me," Yakkie returned. "This *is* business, and no one cheats, not me, not Mr. Moneybags, not you thinking boys. Cheating is what losers did. *Did.* They're history. Snipped, erased, belly-upped. You don't cheat a close-up, and you don't cheat a deal. It's death, boy wonder, cheating is death here. Never never nothing. Business like business. I know it. You mind me. Now and now."

I protested, brilliantly blind insights, such as Yakkie, are you saying that wealthy, successful, dealmaking Kate O'Kates cheats at golf, so therefore she's death? "What about tennis?" I taunted. "Vodka tonics? Taxes? And you say golf?" I gave away my cheating glimpse back at the ninth fairway then by saying that I'd seen her stroke a six iron, she was a terrific jock, why should she cheat at golf? It was too crazy. I laughed. I tried, "Cheats? How cheats? Kicks the ball? Fudges the scorecard? Skips a green?"

"How she cheats is how you're going to find out," Yakkie said. "You're the chatty-kathy amateur. Just remember, you missed it here first, and since I'm the big bad blabber, I'm also saying that cheats at golf is cheats everywhere, thing, time—*mishugoss* forever and ever and ever." He rotated on his crutches and addressed my wardrobe. "Now then. What we are today? The charcoal slacks are tolerable for a college interview. And that hideous white shirt is you, it's *you.*"

6

"The Tonight Show" with guest host Jay Leno sitting in for the ele-mental Mr. Johnny Carson is coming right up, inside a plain soundstage in a plain parking lot in plain Burbank, a neighborhood of greater L.A. But first some remarks about paper-made Captain Ahab of the most unplain whaler *Pequod* out of New Bedford, Massachusetts.

Sci-fi/spy guy Herman Melville, a B&W Puritan like Tip, wrote *Moby Dick* before he went bananas and moved back to New York City. I get a lot out of the book by just hanging around its scenes, replaying its wacky dialogue. *Moby Dick* is best understood as Melville's preliminary madness. He was uncommoning his sense in search of a big air-breathing fish that is anything you want it to be but that I read as Herman Melville himself swimming free from what it is to be a sci-fi/spy guy trapped in 1850 America. Herman was in pursuit of Herman. (I'm trapped likewise a century later, so *Moby Dick* is funny to me, first page to last, and a wordy illustration that though there's no escape, there's make-believe.) The book is heavy on biblical chatter, classical idolatry and whale talk. It's also very, very light on love stuff. It's a first-person fishing yarn that Ishmael, the narrator, makes stunning not because Ishmael's a smart guy but because Captain Ahab is a tough guy. Not thinks he is. Is. We're told Ahab's tall, straight, bronzed, robust, that he looks as if he's been cut away from a stake after a fire has failed to consume him, that he's got a livid white streak branded down his right side. The detail everyone knows best is that white peg leg of whalebone that Ahab plants on the quarterdeck like a pagan pedestal. The impression Ahab gives is raw fury with a mad motive—to kill the wild white animal that took his leg. But there's another detail often overlooked. Ahab was playful, what trendy slang calls a player. He responded to fair weather with a "faint blossom of a look." He did that neat trick with St. Elmo's fire flashing down the harpoon to light him up like neon. Mad as he was, he still plied whaling waters to take a good catch. And even when he lost control and went after Moby Dick like only Ahab could, he played out his role as tough guy with hambone speeches that have a whiff of sci-fi/spy glee, such as, "There's a riddle might baffle all the lawyers backed by the ghosts of the whole line of judges:—like a hawk's beak it pecks my brain. *I'll, I'll* solve it, though!"

My favorite Ahab monologue is during the final battle. It contains choice lines such as, "I grin at thee, thou grinning whale! . . . Oh, oh! oh, oh! thou grinning whale, but there'll be plenty of gulping soon!"

It's Ahab's playful hamboniness and grinning gulping I want you to fix upon. This is another tough clue about Kates, like the one Yakkie gave me about her cheating at golf. A none softer clue is Kates's whalebone-white teeth. Watch them closely, snapping and grinning and confessing in gulps. Try to solve the riddle that might baffle all the lawyers backed up by the ghosts of the whole line of *cruel* judges.

That evening I popped out of Yakkie's limo in the Burbank parking lot fixed only upon surviving "The Tonight Show." Yakkie interrupted his phone call to say he'd pick me up right here when I was released, we'd go to a fantasy restaurant and await the tape-delayed network broadcast. His good luck speech was: "Don't even think putting, make nice and try to smile once for"—he waved the receiver, reminding me I'd called home on the ride to Burbank—"for your mom and mine."

When you do national television, be aware that it's not fun like a circus or glamorous as it looks. It's a business. Nice people guide you to a windowless place that's traditionally called the green room. Modern tv has its own traditions, so "Tonight"'s green room is silver mirrors balanced around the biggest looking glass of all, a discreet tv monitor that demonstrates its obsessive authority by being blank while awaiting the taping of "Tonight." Other nice people provide light snacks and leave you in soundless quiet. There's a clock face, and you watch it. There're other guests too, and amateurs like Tip don't know what's polite to say in a strange room with strangers. The others are here for something, but there aren't name tags, and no one's standing by to do introductions, such as, "Yes, this is [famous head]."

The pros who do tv for a living often arrive with their buddies and chat quietly about unexplained events. If you want to be stonily alone, the niceness of the green room makes it possible to do so in a group, as only a lifeboat might provide. Jay Leno visited us momentarily like a crew coach, but I was too anxious to do more than avoid him, and he let me be. I did stare once at the major guest that night as soon as she came in the room, and it was a mistake. Faye Dunaway

smiled back, said something human like "Hi," and I was terrified by
the time I returned a similar greeting. I failed to find saliva to say
what Yakkie had advised, that she and I had met once before in gym
shorts at my gym in NYC, where I'd helped her with a tricep machine. I wasn't frightened of her, she's nice too, though to have
Bonnie/Milady de Winter seated several feet away being gorgeously
real is not for fickle hearts. I was frightened because this was indeed
the wings of a timeless and boundless stage, and I knew then I was a
watcher, not a watched, a crashed, not a crasher—to be exact, a
nobody, nobody, nobody; smoke is more than I was in those mirrors.

The tv monitor popped bright on cue, and there was the theme
music and Jay Leno doing a nice monologue about doing a nice
monologue. I tried to pretend I was at home. The green room emptied like a lifeboat in reverse: the least shall be last. I kept visiting the
men's room, until another nice person came for me. "Mr. Paine," she
said, "it's time now."

I don't recall any sense but smell—"The Tonight Show" smells like
industrial shampoo—before I was out into those harmful lights and
shaking nice hands. Who knows what was said; I never did watch it.
You're in a time tunnel, and it becomes teleportation and you're
headed into the cosmos as photons forever. By my calculations I'm in
thin space by now, a year short of the nearest next star. I blinked and
blinked to interstellar commuters. The nice audience applauded on
cue. Faye Dunaway had left. Up close, Jay Leno's jaw is calming, as
Dudley Do-Right's must be too.

During the commercial break, Jay Leno, who is also nice, told me
we had only n minutes to go and he'd skip down the scripted Q&A
past my funny name and funnier books to get to my movies. Then we
were back on photons, and Jay Leno said, "Here's a clip from . . ." and
the monitor above the lights was showing thirty seconds of my trashy
hit featuring the Olivier evil scene (picture Prince Hamlet as the
Greatest Pipe Smoker of All Time, Joseph Stalin).

Up to this point I had obeyed Yakkie by making nice and smiling
once for our moms. I was not in control, I was in a script, and I
answered about Moosehead Lake and ice fishing correctly. I must
have said something tv, because the audience laughed. You feel as if

you're being cheered for making a give-me put. Still I was holding on to Yakkie's earlier instructions: "Smart is no-no, it sounds like taunting, and very smart means you're a dog-beater. Don't, Tipster."

Then there was one minute to go, according to the camera guy holding up one finger. You know trouble's coming. Here it is. Jay Leno departed from my script, though he kept to his own. He asked me, "What's next, Tip?" I froze. He tried, "Come on, you can tell us, we can keep a secret, there's only you and me here. [Laughter.] You gonna land a flying saucer in Moscow? [Laughter, and a good idea, Jay.] You gonna try a love story?"

Deicing, I returned that a love story was sci-fi at war with spying, so not for me. [No laughter.] Jay Leno the compleat professional tried his wrap-up query. "Well, we've got spies too, Tip, and we hear you're going to kind of let King Kong win this time, a happy ending, hey, am I right, am I?"

I was freezing up again but not so much I didn't mutter, "Affirmative."

Jay Leno chuckled professionally and said, "Can't wait, we'll get him for a guest appearance if you'll put in a good word for us, but hey, tell him, and please say 'sir,' we pay scale no matter what you weigh."

The audience loved it. And to be fair to Jay Leno, he was not wrong to give away what Hollywood calls "the high concept" to *Killed the Beast*. He was reading from what his research people had given him. Guess who'd given it to them. (Right, not Yakkie.)

"Tonight" was behind me, and I got out of the soundstage and back to Burbank after some nice farewells. I was not clearheaded, too vain to do more than try to remember what I'd just done and left, so I hit the parking lot without noticing it was drizzling. The nearest limo glided toward me, and the chauffeur jumped out. I thought it was a "Tonight" limo, which I'd not needed, so I waved him off and looked for Yakkie's car. The unknown chauffeur continued around to open the passenger door, and there was Kates, snacking on veggies.

"I couldn't wait to see you, Tip. I'm sure you'll be wonderful for thirty million other people," was her entrance line. She looked out from the cozy warmth of her vast German auto and showed those teeth. I backpedaled instinctively. She waved a cauliflower and got cute. "In all the parking lots in all the world, I was just driving by and thought, Why not this one?" And then, me blinking in the rain, she got cuter. "I know you don't know what time it is. [Munch.] Want to go find a clock?"

She was not dressed for scary whaling. She was in burnt earth colors, looking casual and scholarly like a millionaire book-lover. I proudly report that I did not jump headfirst. I mumbled and reached for a miniature tomato on her plate. Then I declared that Yakkie was picking me up and maybe we could meet later, maybe.

"I understand," said Kates most maturely, "I really do. You go home with what got you there, it's what makes you lucky." She laughed, I laughed, we laughed, and there was suddenly a place for us to visit called giddiness. Still I didn't go. I wanted Yakkie. I wanted his de- brief. I wanted his permission.

"Where is he?" Kates asked. (Of course she knew; he was where Yakkie goes when betrayed—away.) "I want to tell him how sorry I am for doing business the other night like that. I was out of line. You're his client, and I respect that." (All this was intimate patter, you understand, because she was no longer using the royal we.) She continued affectionately: "It's this business, Tip. Sometimes when you don't move fast you don't move, do you understand? And forgive me?"

Easy charity is the way to this traitor's fortress heart. But not yet. I was holding to my latest rewrite, where I apologize to Yakkie for Kates, and Yakkie says forget it slyboots, and Kates and Yakkie make up, and we three go off to be friends and make movies, and then . . . Nonetheless my draft needed Yakkie, and he was not showing up on cue to rescue Tip, who didn't want to be rescued. Oh, Yakkie, if you were only less Yakkie and more ordinarily a person who likes to re- peat things until I get it too. But no, Yakkie tells you his theme and then he improvises until you surrender to his genius.

"Do you see him yet?" asked Kates. "Is that his car over there?"

No, no, a few more minutes of eating vegetables with terrific dip and patter about golf, the weather and my camp on Moosehead Lake (anything but the business; Kates was not going to scare me off with that again, though she might have guessed I was way past caring), and then more no Yakkie.

Finally Kates closed the distance. "It's raining, Tip, you can wait in here. I don't—you know—I don't [pause] *like* men like you," and then she hambonily snapped those whalebone teeth on a radish and closed the door on us.

7

We found neither a clock nor Yakkie that night nor for the next weeks that passed out of order. What happened was the love stuff that Herman Melville was very, very light on and I weigh in less at. It's why I'm telling this yarn balanced mostly on the preliminaries leading up to the sail to Katesport, and I'm skipping the shipshape routine once I got there.

I did try to find Yakkie, many times, and the way that's done is you telephone him; he's not a drop-by fellow. I left messages with his associates, his service, and when I finally accepted that he wasn't talking to me, I left a written note with his mom: "Dear Yakkie, Please forgive me or call me and yell. I need you and . . ." It went on in self-pity, always easy when you're feeling righteous because you think you're only half stubborn.

I kept Kates only half informed about my Yakkie search because I was guilty both ways, betraying him and hiding his bizarre opinion of her. Happily she was most busy pursuing her life with me, now a dependent. I was not in love at first, and we didn't bed down at first like celluloid robots. She had a modest leased manse in the hills, and I got my own room right away and kept it. I like talk more than most anything intimate, and Kates played along tenderly. She was smart and understood how confessions work. I provided autobiography in chapter form. She returned her text as if we were reading aloud alternately.

"I'm new at the business," she told me. "I'm not a Hollywood brat, and I didn't pass the bar exam and lever myself in that way: Century City mouthpiece takes over contracts. . . . My marriage ended, and I drifted out here eventually. . . . He got my babies, because he did pass the bar and knows how court muscle works."

Her ex-husband, O'Kates, was not a serious villain to Kates. She'd kept his name (hers was Linnehan), but she didn't care to mention him much. Her father was dead, and her mother and large family were spread out back East in the professions. She'd been born in Baltimore, a Catholic family, and educated by the nuns until she broke away to go to Goucher College, then transferred to Princeton when the Ivy League wised up and went coed. Her law degree at Georgetown had been a slight return to good Catholic girl, but lawyer games and then marriage had undone that too.

"Washington was hot for girl law clerks in the early seventies," she said. "You know, you were there. . . . How it really went was: Get one and forget one. I got married and forgot them." After that there'd been suburban babymaking, a miscarriage and two healthy children in five years. There was also volunteering—hers with a Chesapeake Bay environmental group.

Then came despair. "I was thirty-four and looking at another *fifty* of it, with my mother's long genes. . . . You don't pass the bar and start again with them. You're a gofer, you're somebody's wife, you're a mommy who plays good tennis, you're a four-by-four caretaker. You're nobody, do you understand that, Tip, do you really? *Nobody.*"

I did understand. It's a routine story these anxious days, with too many first-raters out there not in play because they're wives, mothers, simply not gone-gotten salesmen like Tip.

I also understood the trouble that followed the despair. She had an affair with one of the environmental radicals who wanted to depopulate Maryland's shoreline before the residents killed every living thing that wasn't human. "He was a wonderful man and [pause] childish, like you, Tip, really, it's all right. When the no-nuke lobby got rolling after Three Mile Island, he jumped himself up front and traveled everywhere to testify. I loved his commitment; it was like Vietnam again, which I'd missed: big girls were not invited to that either. I started going with him. . . . I hated being away and hated being home. I was still nobody, still his big girl and not me, but for a while I was working for something that . . . Do you know about that too, Tip, what they're trying to do with those nuclear plants, do you?"

I didn't argue back at this or other deep hooks in my brain. She was no-nuke. I'm not. But to qualify my common sense with details about engineering was extraneous then and is now. She could weep about the environment. (Ahab, I note speculatively, was an environmentalist too. He fished like a sport, he didn't exterminate. Today he'd be a radical polarist patrolling Antarctica, that white desert of a Moby Dick.)

Kates's divorce ended her doubts, and the custody case ended her debate. Kates got to be nobody by court decree. By chance she had met a group of filmmakers who were working for public television on environmental disasters. Kates discovered that you could move from gofer to producer in show business without an exam, with smarts and speed.

"Once it starts," she said, "you keep going, project to project, and you meet new people all the time, who hire you on for their work. I got to L.A. by agreeing to work. . . . It's *different* tough than New York. There's work if you're not an artist, but you've got to fight anyway—not to keep working but to get a project better than the last. You know it's *tough* everywhere if you're a woman, a big one, unmarried and hungry. I was *that* and got knocked down. . . . Men, men, they like to knock, and I'm not a *door*. Don't laugh, I'm not a *door!* . . . I got lucky the first time and thought about getting out. But to where? The business doesn't let you; there's always another project. . . . Do you understand, Tip? If I'd set out to be my own company, I'd still be in Silver Spring, playing tennis."

I remarked that she made her success sound like an accidental nonfailure, or perhaps a mystical trick, a door that opens itself.

She returned, "No, it's just a business. But this is the first place I've been where I'm good at what I do. And I like that; I mean, they don't care what I was or what I've done. They don't care! That's everything to me. What I was, a nobody, they don't even ask about it. You don't wear a watch, Tip, and they're like that, like you."

Chronophobic Tip then called Hollywood "Never Never Land."

Kates corrected, "Oh, Tip, it's not that way for me. It's everything!" I remember her flashing those teeth as she emphasized what was stunningly the truth. "I love it! I love them! *They don't care!*"

I could go on, but I've included the important details and enough for me to see again why I did fall in love soon after. I made believe she was a heroine with that magic word "pluck." I go to the movies like you, where pluck shines like the planets. I love pluck and go all the way when it pertains to a handsome, intelligent woman who has tried hard, lost hard, and fought back against many bad breaks and guys. Kates was always fighting hard, a Venus in orbit who was now eager to put her wondrous big shoulders into me too, and I held on. The sex was excellent, I report vainly, and never better than after we'd travel to a Goods confab where she'd done more business. Her production company's headquarters was in Century City, a development where Hollywood now actually abides, in tall glass palaces. Her polished desk was long-stem-rose-adorned and excellent for making love between the thorns. We also made love in the limo, at home with the tv on, and once in a screening room so I could join the Box Office Blues Club. I passed quickly from lustful to adoring to what I mentioned before, dependent. In her business I was a nonplayer, a golf partner, supercargo—in brief, a nobody.

My nobodyhood didn't bother me. I also had a minor status as a scriptwriter, since there was *Killed the Beast* to fuss with. I signed everything, which put me on her payroll. I did flinch when Kates told me that Yakkie's agency had agreed to take points and release me if that was what I wanted. I didn't want that, but I signed away Yakkie too. Kates was what I needed, I prophesied, Kates at sea, Kates at home. I was her mapmaker, she was my Ahab.

Why didn't I tell her she was my Ahab? As Jay Leno says, "Hey, I did, kind of." I told her my Hollywood-before-the-mast illustration and mentioned how Ahab and Moby Dick don't exist but maybe they do, ha ha. She wasn't impressed enough to comment. I let it drift. Maybe I did tell her she was my Ahab. I don't recall exactly. I was in love, that's my dumb explanation, in love, and you don't take notes in love.

I note now that what works in Hollywood love scripts is a cute meeting, then a twist, then the long middle of the movie, where the lovers are angry with each other, then another twist and a happy ending. Add special effects, and it's an adventure love story. It's a simpleminded formula, but don't mess, because like love it works.

For Tip and Kates there was an apparent departure from what works, but not really, if you're writing sad endings. There was the cute meeting (marina/golf/"Tonight"), the first twist (Yakkie), then a month-long development (unwedded bliss) that *seemed* to lack anger. Then on cue arrived the second twist, which was disaster and why the project died in production. Our special effect was madness.

8

The Academy Award nominations were out, and I had one for best screenplay from published material, my screenplay of my book. (I'm not telling you the title, because you might stop renting the VCR tape, disenchanted by my blither.) Kates and I celebrated by trying to eat a whole cheesecake. This is impossible and quickly leads to a food fight and messy sex.

Later I tried and tried to reach Yakkie, since he was the one who'd gotten me the nomination. That failed; Yakkie was ashore, waiting for me to wash up on the beach. When my head settled near earth the next day, I mentioned to Kates that I needed to get out of L.A. for a rest. I asked her if she'd go back to Moosehead Lake with me to get cold, build fires, shun the phone, build more fires. She was eager for it, said she just had to finish some details, that I should get ready for serious downhill at last. "You can't begin by beginning," she instructed me. "The expert trails are where you learn."

I reserved our tickets, and when she couldn't make the date I extravagantly bought open tickets. No again; her projects would not dovetail. It was after Valentine's Day by then, and I had this rash idea that if I could get her alone I might actually decide I didn't want to be alone anymore. I mean second marriage but not L.A. style because that wouldn't work with Kates. "Marriage should be business,"

Kates had said in her autobiographical presentations. "What points do you *get?*" This was a good query, and I thought that if we go to New England I could try some Puritan magic and persuade her wifery was not skulduggery.

The next Friday afternoon Kates hauled anchor suddenly when she arrived back in the limo to surprise me. We were headed to the airport. But not back East. We were Rocky Mountain bound, to a fantasy resort that you achieve by changing planes at Denver and finally sitting in a four-wheel-drive limo with other vacationers wowing at the upsetting moon-bright heights and a beefy cowboy driving one-handed, whose vocabulary is "Hey ya." Along with my fears of speed, drugs, guns and women is high places without wings. Yet another reason I like New England is that the mountains are midgets. Colorado, it's up. I stowed my anxiety. Kates the jockette was ecstatic for the slopes come tomorrow, and after she placed two transcontinental calls she tackled me. "Tip, no more business, I promise, we're free, for three days, free!"

It wasn't the first day; that was me on my ass, whining. Those trails were expert, all right—hooligans, hoods, killers. Kates tired of this by afternoon and we had a good fight. Typical married stuff—you control, you boss—so that later we dined curtly and made up over a chocolate cake in bed.

It was the second day then, Sunday, and it happened strangely. I couldn't face the advanced slope again. At the lift I said that I wanted to practice with the kids on the beginner trail. Kates smiled toothily. "Maybe you're right; you are awfully bruised—such sweet bumps." I added that I'd wait lunch on her and try death again that afternoon. After she'd gone on, I tumbled around sweatily, then sneaked onto the sun deck to smoke my pipe.

Kates was late getting down. I supposed she was soloing one more run. She was an hour late when I spotted one of the he-men from the killer trails and waved defensively. His name was Bo; he'd helped me face death the day before. Bo came over kindly to say, "Hey, yo, your wife okay now?" I was alarmed like a proper husband. Bo explained he'd seen Kates being sick off the trail and had waved down the ski patrol to her. Bo added, "She okay now?"

I raced to the desk phone, got an odd but not perilous report from the ski patrol, raced back to the sun deck, then panicked and tried the room.

Kates answered. "I'm coming right down. I'm sorry, you've caught me making some calls. I know I promised no more business, I'm sorry."

I told her what I'd learned. Kates had been seen vomiting off the trail. When the ski patrol had reached her she had tossed them off and slalomed away.

Kates explained, "That's bullshit. They were trying to hit on me. Big girl out alone. Knock on my door. The creeps."

This was most un-Kates talk. Not the door metaphor but the "bullshit." She was never vulgar, a most polite tongue, and her sudden epithet and angry tone were like punches. It worried me about her, and then it angered me for her. I puffed myself up to call the ski patrol captain to complain about his creeps.

What I learned this time poleaxed me. "No, sir, it's not that way," said the captain. I argued and accused. He was matter-of-fact. "I was there too, sir. We were worried; she was way out of bounds. . . . Sick all over the snow. . . . It's not my business, but my duty is. . . . Your wife's either sick and not telling you, or she's just morning sick, sir. Yes, sir, it was like that."

9

I wish that I'd gone to her and said, Kates, whatever's happening, it's not terrible, I love you, and so forth. Actually I approximated this. It's bad dialogue, it can't work; even make-believe needs a car chase to rescue such bad dialogue.

Mostly I wish that what I'd discovered about Kates was something normally scary like pregnancy.

Instead I botched it worse than I want to recall. I did everything badly, beginning with a barrage: "Are you sick? Are you all right now? What happened up there?" I pestered her at lunch so hard that we didn't go back to skiing. And when she wouldn't answer I pestered her in the lobby, in the elevator and in our room until she fled the room, Colorado and me.

I've been left before, I've done plenty of leaving, but that way that time was wrong. The way she packed was wrong. She didn't flee, she transferred like a seaman to shore, in calm silence. I wanted hysteria, so I tried provocation, bringing up marriage, then asking if she was pregnant? I repeated pregnancy, marriage, pregnancy, wedding, pregnancy, family. She returned nothing, not even disgusted looks. (Truth, there was "a faint blossom" on her cheeks that on another might have broken into a smile.) And then she was gone Sunday by dark. Her last words were business. She showed those teeth and said, "I've had my calls transferred," then snapped shut.

A generous man might have tried a car chase, might have pursued her back to L.A. and negotiated apologies. I did call her but not until I got back to Maine and only because Moosehead Lake was noisy with the self-righteousness in my head. She refused to come to the phone. I abandoned Maine the next day and called her again from New York. More refusal. I tried a telegram, a garrulous letter and, after some rest, a diplomatic letter. Nothing. In due time I got my letters back from her company, along with the junk mail that accumulates when Oscar the Harpoonist is possible.

It was late March soon. By then I had chickened out twice from getting on a plane back to L.A. and her. Why? I report that I was afraid of the pregnancy that I'd vainly assumed was the cause of our breakup. I was also afraid of Kates, who I'd arrogantly assumed was angry with me for forcing myself into her life like a thoughtless sperm whale. More grandly, I was afraid of Hollywood. It wasn't behaving like my neat illustration of whaling after all. It was a business that played fast by rules I didn't understand. I was *afraid*. Yakkie had cut me off. Kates had cut me off. The message I was not hearing was clear: You're outside, thinks-he's-a-tough-guy; stay there. This coward obeyed.

Is that it? If I said yes, you would hoot that you've been cheated. You have been. There's no way you could have solved this riddle with what you've been told unless you've crossed someone like Kates and heard the diagnosis. It's a mind disease. It's not to be solved. When someone goes as far out of bounds as she did and has smarts, speed and wealth, this person is scrupulously in control all the time.

Kates did not make mistakes. The vomiting in snow could have been morning sickness. Or it could have been queasiness from her big breakfast. What found her out in the end was not her conduct but mine. Yakkie said it best in the locker room, that how she cheats is how I was going to find out: "You're the chatty-kathy amateur." I wouldn't let Kates off with silent shrugs. My chatty prying finished us. She went back to her quarterdeck to net mightily and go ever more stupendously mad.

This is how I learned the worst about Mrs. Kate O'Kates. Academy Award night, I was back up at Moosehead Lake, where I'd gone to hide in make-believe Cold War. I watched the ceremonies in dread. I figured that if I won, the Goods who owned my picture would make the speech and I could find the nerve to return to Hollywood to claim my prize and maybe my big girl. If I didn't win, then I'd accept my fate. No suspense, I didn't win, though I heard my name botched as "Thomas Paine." I immediately climbed into another xenophobia game in the Mac. I also wept, which doesn't work when you're extinguishing alien blips. After midnight the phone rang and I answered, assuming it was McKerr.

It was Yakkie, calling from his limo en route to an Oscar fantasy party. "Slyboots," he began, "what are we today?"

I had been prepared for this for three months. I told him I was Genghis f——ing Khan and I ate prisoners.

Yakkie returned, "Oh, my serious baby, we are calling attention to ourselves. We didn't win, did we? I did." (The winner was another one of his clients.) "So, sorepuss, what can I do for you? Want to talk putting? It's time to worry about the Masters again."

I got very serious and let him have it. My condemnation was furious hysteria and redundancy itself, "Tonight" to Katesport to Colorado and his shunning. Yakkie listened with careful sighs. When he was sure I was at a break, he announced that he had arrived at his mom's house and that we needed privacy. He called me back momentarily from his own rooms, asking, "Am I your friend, Tipster?"

When I answered that he was my damned deserting agent, he acquired his rueful tone, his suicide hot line tone, and told me to tuck in my "hurt little paws" while he settled down.

Soon, while he viewed a muted copy of *All About Eve* to back up his sense of humor, he told me the truth about Kates. She suffered from bulimia. It's a mind disease, what is called an eating disorder. It means that after eating you gag yourself until you throw up. Yakkie was terse. He had not known in January. After my betrayal he had made inquiries.

In the business, Yakkie had discovered, Kates was a mansion around a locked room around a hidden file on a wiped disk. Yakkie backtracked to prebusiness. The trail was blank. He reached New York, where many secret files live and where Yakkie has what sci-fi/ spy calls deep-cover sources. Still nothing, too much nothing, too blank a trail.

I interrupted him many times. He chided me with, "Mind me," and "Stop thinking." When I tried to reject his argument—saying that bulimia was impossible, this was ridiculous, how could he be sure?—Yakkie talked tough.

"It's the teeth, Tipster," he said. "You poop up so much, the stomach acid stains the teeth. Kates has a moneybags dentist who does moneybag mouths. Monthly renovation. Dentists like him are in the business. He's also Mom's neighbor. He talks to Mom. Mom talks to me, okay? You can't cheat a close-up, Tipster, I told you."

Her whalebone-white teeth. Her snacking while dealing. Her self-conscious bigness. I had watched and watched and seen nothing.

There was much worse. Yakkie got to it patiently, not skipping a step, because he wanted to help me, not bludgeon me. "I told you she *cheats*, Tipster. *Mishugoss* mouthwash, that's old cheats. This is a new one, and believe me I've seen strange but—not at the treetop. It's *chills*. It's between you and me and the screenplay. Just kidding, checking you're alert."

He didn't wait, no deft suspense required. He had found a guy who had found a guy whom Kates had cheated once very early in her Hollywood career, at the threshold of the door she joked about, where the grappling is meanest. The source went unnamed because he was very sick, said Yakkie, and not going to make it. Yakkie was talking gay Hollywood now, a man who was in deep, deep cover while dying of a cruel disease.

Yakkie said, "He knew her, recognized her, and she canned him because of it. He says she's from Erie, Pennsylvania. A foster family where he stayed a few months, before he ran away. He says she was one of the older foster kids in the family, a little dictator who made all the decisions for the foster parents. Her real name is Monastersky, he says."

I was confused. "Erie, Yakkie? Not Baltimore?" I told Yakkie to make sense.

"Stop thinking!" Yakkie scolded. "My source said Erie. He said she locked him up in the smokehouse or something quaint when he got fresh with her. He was eleven, she was fifteen. But he forgot about this until she canned him on the set. He claims now she denied it and then pretended to can him for theft. She blackballed him, he says. I had my office check. He was canned, who knows why? My office tried city hall in Erie to find the foster family he ran away from. The foster *family*'s name was Monastersky, so our boy'd gotten it wrong. It was a wrong tip, Tipster, but close. Pa Monastersky is dead, Ma Monastersky is lost in a county home. But we got lucky at the nursing home and found a *real* Monastersky daughter, named Babs. She's a mom herself now, a sweetheart. We chatted about movies, she's a great fan, loves Amy Irving, that's the current Mrs. Spielberg to you, Babs wants to know when she's coming back."

I was completely lost. "Foster family? Monastersky? Erie? Not Baltimore?"

"Stop, stop!" shouted Yakkie. "Dear Babs, that's Monastersky to you, does remember a big girl who stayed with her mom and dad after Babs had moved out. A big girl who stayed with the family over a year. Kathy DePaulo. Who went to work for the nuns in the convent."

"Yakkie, you're scaring me!"

"I have more, Tipster. Do you want it now or—" He paused,

reacting to the action in *All About Eve*. When he came back on the line, he finished, "or at lunch in New York? No Moosehead for me; I don't go north of Fifty-seventh Street. Say day after tomorrow?"

10

That's sufficient. I don't have to prove this. Neither could Yakkie, as it turned out. Kates was that good. Nothing was true about what she claimed to be her name, family, hometown, college, law school, marriage, children, environmentalism, goferhood. Kates said it all about herself when she said, "Nobody." It's just not possible to get to her who, where, when, how. It's all gone. The foster family Monastersky clue didn't work out. Maybe Kathy DePaulo. Maybe anything. When I said that the Goods' power can buy privacy, I meant it. When Kates said about Hollywood, "They don't care. I love them. They don't care," she meant it. Whoever Kates is, she's solidly safe before the mast.

I haven't tried to reach her again. I think sometimes that she might miss me. But then I think that she's figured out that since I don't write or call, I am never to be trusted. She does *cheat*. I don't mean about *Killed the Beast*, what I suppose was her motive to close on me. Her company changed the title, the ending, the reason for its existence, and someday they might make it. But that's okay, because my idea was wrongheaded. No happy endings for KK. And even that original unhappy ending, with KK dead on Thirty-fourth Street, that's half wrong. Beauty never killed the beast. The beast is still climbing, and beauty is still screaming. If they put my wrongheadedness in production, they'll pay off Yakkie and me, probably accurately, since Kates must know you can't cheat Yakkie and get away. (Don't try it, Kates; Yakkie's a tough guy too.)

Kates cheated *me*. I was a close-up who didn't even get close, but she, the fisherperson's fisherperson, takes no chances. My darkest make-believe is that someday I'll risk visiting Yakkie again in Never

Never land. Kates will sail by. I won't be able to recognize her. She's wretched retching madness. I can guess that the only connection between one Kates and another is the quest in her. She put love's harpoon in me, and then, when I went belly up, she abandoned me because I'm just Tip Paine the traveling salesman, not that famous white whale.

Yes, here's Ahab the last time. No one knows where he came from either (no family, no friends, all business) or truly why he was so angry. Moby Dick took his leg, so he was out to take Moby Dick. But why? What was before? Something big took Kates's teeth, so she's out to take it. But why? What was before? What made her so tough? Was it what Yakkie says, "Chills"? Or was it a fire like the one that failed to consume Ahab, branded him with white lightning down his side?

"Like a hawk's beak," it does peck my brain, but I'll never solve it. Herman Melville is history. Ahab and Moby Dick are paper. And Kates, she's out there doing business, prophesying, "I grin at thee, thou grinning whale! . . . Oh, oh! oh, oh! thou grinning whale, but there'll be plenty of gulping soon!"

Pathfinder Loses the Trail

McKerr's Claim to Fame;

Uncas Falls Again

1

My imaginary best friend, McKerr, a penniless pilgrim, quit and divorced a beautiful Texas millionaire after eight years of passionate marriage. This is a claim to fame that humbles most men except sports heroes, though it's a small detail that McKerr shares a birthday with Dave Winfield. I witnessed McKerr's folly from the first cute meeting to the farewell crimes. Along the way I got to play best man, major guest, minor wheedler and at the finish a savage scalptaker who got what he wanted by using some very strong, very bad medicine.

It was the spring of 1980, and wake up in America was in the sweet breeze like Candidate Governor Reagan's homely anecdotes. McKerr and I were drifting along Broadway, discussing Schenectady. McKerr is two percent Mohawk, five hundred percent Scotch-Irish, and he coincidentally hails from a bend on the Mohawk River that the map calls Schenectady, the flacks call "Home of General Electric" and McKerr's genius has transformed into a center of the world to displace Jerusalem. McKerr himself says Schenectady is "the end of the trail," and he knows everyone in America who started there, ended there, passed through or lies about it, such as Kurt Vonnegut, Pat Riley, John Tudor, William, Henry and Alice James. Then there are the truly important locals, such as Mohawk war chief Joseph Brant and the frontier heroes Natty Bumppo the Pathfinder, Chingachgook the Big Serpent and Uncas-afore-he-fell.

McKerr is a curator in two spectacularly useless genres—Schenectady and eighteenth-century combat in New York State. He knows the Battle of Saratoga like his apartment, and he will someday defend Fort Ticonderoga to the death from the condo crowd. All these arcane episodes are critical to him not only because they created America out of the wilderness's lumber but also because they relate intimately to nothing in America's deforested morning. Bluntly, McKerr is a loony Yankee. I call him Pathfinder, after Natty Bumppo, and I follow him merrily.

It is a mystery to me how I could have stood by that first evening and watched him charm the astonishing, dark beauty we met on Broadway. I should have known she was not for him the moment she crossed our trail. "Hi," said McKerr to her with typical Yankee eloquence. "Hi," she returned. She's from Texas, and she dresses plain and down. Her name is Amanda (exactly right: "worthy to be loved"). Though she was bred River Oaks, Houston, McKerr would quickly find out that she was descended from several Reb potentates, including General George Pickett himself and most of his staff.

Their first contact did resemble the first day at Gettysburg. (Gettysburg is another McKerr obsession, though secondary.) Nothing much happened, as the major divisions were not gathered. McKerr, it emerged, had espied Amanda in passing once or twice before when he had stopped to talk to various Columbia College lowlife and Amanda had been a bystander. Now it was Billy Yankee and Johnny Reb face to face, and I was history's neutral observer, like a traffic chopper hovering above Little Roundtop.

That first McKerr-Amanda skirmish, it must have been passion I saw, though I missed it. He's tall, rangy, unflappable, persuaded by flintlocks and Fenimore Cooper, deeply Union blue. Handsome women find him desirable and his timeless pilgrimage irresistible. Amanda is tall, rangy, shaky, poorly read, apologetic about her riches, speaks Oriental languages and is devoted to her large, vigorous, very wealthy family. All shapes of gold diggers find her unbelievable. It was a match made on dingy, springy Broadway, Tip opines, and if anything explains what happened, it must have been true love.

The courtship was offstage to me and probably not air-conditioned, same as that summer. I didn't even have a PC starcruiser then, still banging away on an IBM old enough for Jack Kennedy's staff to have used when they signed off on President Diem's hit. I was a baby salesman; my first modest royalties were simple pleasure and my first independent producer was correctly chary with my option money. I sweated out the heat in my garret off upper Broadway and waited for McKerr to drop by to update me on Amanda.

"She's all right," he reported with a frontier grunt, "except she's descended from Pickett."

I should have said, What about the millions? What about Houston? Do you know how hot it is down there? That your wool pants make you a foreigner to them? That they've never heard of Schenectady and don't respect Mohawk nothing and think the Union a junta? I said none of this. Worse, I encouraged him. I blame myself now. I had recently disengaged from a man-eater named Ms. U., who had started out a Christian virgin in my barbarian paws and then, after a couple of years of heady little sacraments like SoHo rendezvous, marathon orgasms, Florentine junkets, had finally married Mr. U. the artsy-craftsy financier right in front of my backside. It was a miracle that I had been rescued from Ms. U. by her treachery, yet my longing was still too far inside her perfect *vagina dentata* to see that I was safely out of harm's way. Tip Paine was Scribe Romance that summer. He wanted every hero to marry ever heroine and live like Pompeians. Instead of being a pal to McKerr I was a redcoat parson saying marry the damsel, shuck your skins and start a little Mohawk River homestead near the fort like Henry Fonda and Claudette Colbert, raise Texinaires and pay taxes, *abandon the wilderness*.

What hooey. McKerr must have recognized it. He procrastinates routinely. His idea of tactics is to use a knife when varmits stumble by your ambush. Here he had a lush beauty so in love with him she could not stop blushing, and he was lounging around the same way we fish on the Battenkill. Cast this way or that? Move downstream or stay here? Dry flies or wet? I could see McKerr checking the water level on his waders. I snuck up and kicked him in. Don't cast, McKerr, you're the trout, swim.

"What's the rush?" McKerr asked me. "I've never been to Texas, have you? I hear it's hot and the water's no good."

Amanda's mother showed up late summer to reject McKerr. I was standing next to him at the cocktail party Amanda organized with a bevy of Houstonians-do-New-York when Mother Amanda did the deed. McKerr's a smoker, she's a smoker. He had the ashtray in his hand. She said, "So have you lived in New York since college?" and then stubbed her cigarette out so hard that she was clearly trying to burn a hole through his hand. McKerr, sweaty in his buckskins, ignored the move. Pathfinder does not mind Tory/Reb matrons. Usually they don't come close because of the bear grease in his hair.

Still Mother Amanda wanted him buried at Gettysburg with a stone marker: "Unknown, July 4, 1863." If her love-struck idiot daughter couldn't see what he was, a damn Yankee sniper, then she was going to back him off with field guns. She didn't say, "What are your people?" or "Why don't you go back to Africa and get lost on Kilimanjaro?" (Africa is another McKerr obsession; he walked it Cape Town to Cairo when he was twenty-one.) No, no, Mother Amanda is no procrastinator. She salvoed, "And what do you do?"

This made McKerr mumble and me grin. McKerr does McKerr; that's an old joke about very few good men, and it's an enviable career. But how to explain it to Mrs. River Oaks? Do you try humor, asking, "What does a two percent Mohawk do?" Do you try romance, saying, "He's a pathfinding, hawkeyed, deerslaying, *la longue carabine*–toting citizen, ready to fit the Frenchers if they ever try for Albany again"? Or do you do as McKerr did, mumble, wait, mumble, roll another cigarette?

Mother Amanda pressed her attack as her great-grandfather Pickett would have done. "Amanda tells me you didn't go to college?"

Since McKerr wouldn't defend himself, I corrected the record that he went to Africa, then to college.

"Oh, you did, college too?" said Mother Amanda. "Just later than usual? That's nice. Do you have any professional plans now?"

McKerr accepted the apartheid card from Mother Amanda. She left town assuming that the system would work, maybe not perfectly, but enough so no African Yankee like him could ever stay the night inside the concertina wire. All Mother Amandas, I have observed, make this same blockheaded mistake. They say, "That man's an ape, and you're my beautiful child." They say, "If you marry him you'll swing from trees until you fall." They say, "No, not him, anyone but him." Why do they do this? Do they like their roles? Do they secretly despise what Father Amandas are trying to hold together with mercenaries and diamond mines?

Within days, McKerr and Amanda had blown the wire with a bangalore and set a wedding date, Halloween in Houston. I approved in goony admiration. My low-grade gold from Hollywood meant that I could throw ten-dollar bills at McKerr's reluctance and my own common sense. McKerr was reluctant, I emphasize, not resentful. This despite the fact that the Amandan family flew him down to Houston a week later and, after the family sniffed his bear grease, ushered him before lawyers, where he was quietly and firmly lectured about many documents that he was not allowed to read.

After he got back, McKerr and I discussed those documents that he was not allowed to read. "It wasn't so bad except the heat," he said about the Amandan family law office. "They served iced tea before they started talking." (Lawyers are a minor amusement to McKerr; he assumes they're descended from the guys who used to hang around the fort gates, welcoming the settlers and advertising that for a fee, they could read, write and bend the judge's ear.) Nonetheless we knew what those documents were. They were the truth of marrying money. The lawyers call it a prenuptial agreement. Penniless McKerr had been politely informed that he was ineligible to become anything other than penniless McKerr forever. You come into the compound in skins and a funny hat with a tail, they said, you leave in the same stuff, undrycleaned. This was not my idea of true love. I avoided the implication that his *leaving* was what they cared about and wanted and would throw money, law and long-distance tricks at until he skedaddled. Rather I emphasized the make-believe. McKerr was going to be happy. I was going to be happy, happy is where we all were going to live as soon as we got out of Houston's heat.

2

The nuptial weekend was mined with large clues that happy was where he'd been and McKerr was wandering off the trail. But remember, it was very early in America's morning, Governor Reagan was a week away from the presidency and Tip was ignorant that what was coming was the tramp of money, which would drive all frontiersmen deeper into the wilderness. McKerr sweated out the jumbo-jet hop by keeping his eyes inboard. Pathfinder does not believe in leaving the earth to get somewhere he can't hike to in a month. The fantasy hotel McKerr and I endured was polar, silent, smooth, and I was new enough at fantasy bivouacs to enjoy it all—piano bar, room service, salesmen in blue suits making gabby phone calls in the lobby, hoteliers grinning vacantly, beautiful women trailing Ms. U.'s scent. "Forget it," McKerr told me when I started following one blondine blindly. "You don't know how lucky you got when she got away." I asked if this was a jittery groom. "Forget it," said McKerr.

Amanda's family was rich to us, but to Houstonians they were just well off. They do live in the sacred groves called River Oaks. Then again, River Oaks is okay; even Democrats live quietly next door, and if President George Bush had owned a Texas home back then, it would have been as modestly patriotic as all the other mansions out that way. I noted neat lawns, large families, imported landscaping and a very early trend toward German cars. I asked McKerr, "Why German?" He said, "They're roomy."

The rehearsal dinner was at the Bayou Club. It did show money.

The Bayou Club is one of the compounds in the area that do not accept applications from trash like us. But there were no limo ferries or whooping preppies named Chilly or Dilly. The club was more of the quiet fantasy sort, a planter's big house that got diverted here on its way up to Memphis. Dark servants and southern cooking appeared, Texans bumped each other, saying "Howdy, howdy!" and everyone was out by 10 P.M., saying, "You come back soon, hear?"

McKerr and I intended to go straight back to our fantasy hotel for coffee and doughnuts. Somewhere along the way we were shanghaied by a couple of Galveston lawyers, whom we liked a lot when they took us to a normal-sized tract house. There was a beer-and-tequila party in progress, with other beefy lawyers and cut-off-clad divorcées who were not fussy about burping, hollering, and moaning with the accurate "I gotta piss real bad, but I'll be right back, darlin', don't you move." I liked a busty single mother named Goldie. She kept rearranging her blouse and saying, "Beer makes a girl grow; you find bellies a turnoff, do you?" I gazed upon Texas anew. They have fun down there; don't listen to their bellyaching. It's a right roomy place, where the women drink from the bottle, stash pistols with their knickers and say strange things to strangers, such as, "I like a man when he sweats."

By the time we did get back to our refrigerated room, ordering eggs and coffee because Texas doesn't comprehend the bagel, McKerr and Tip thought they had the Amandan family solved. They were okay —punctual, possessive, competitive but okay, almost like us if they hadn't been born rich and we hadn't been born Yankees. Amandan money was not earned like the proverbial Texinaire swag, all of sudden from oil. Amandan money is dull real estate. Oil barons come and go (and there's been a lot of going since back then); however, the land charges rent eternally and can be adjusted anyway you want.

Early Saturday morning McKerr said, "Let's find high ground." We took a walk in downtown Houston to assess Amandan family holdings and to reconnoiter these Texans in sunlight. McKerr sweated his skins through. "What kind of October is this?" he asked. I made a thin joke with what I'd been reading about Governor Reagan's campaign, about Bill Casey's theory of an October Surprise that might miraculously stampede the electorate for President Carter. McKerr said, "Carter couldn't surprise Bambi."

Everyone driving by knew we were foreigners, because Texans do not walk anywhere. It's the heat, of course, and Sheridan's old wit that the devil would live in Arizona and rent out Texas to suckers. It's also that Texans believe in riding around. There's no landmark in Texas to head toward, and riding the range is local entertainment. It's also easy, since the landscape is all downhill from nothing and worthless-looking. The Texinaires fret about this and have hired modern science to erect magnesium-and-glass towers in geo-synchronous orbit at one meter. McKerr and I dwell on the island of tall buildings; size and building materials don't impress us. What did about Houston was the antigravity of the towers. All America west of the Delaware can look propped up like a facade. Houston was not that. I've told you—it floats above mother earth. Houston's not a city. It's a star base for aliens sucking on dinosaur lunches until we either wise up and tax petrol like gems or tuck it up and go nuke.

McKerr and I were too persuaded by mockery that morning to think futuristically. We grumbled about how Texans say "Howdy" way too much to be sincere and otherwise dress, eat, grin and lust like Americans with too much beef in their diet. I suppose Houstonians would smell funny to an Oriental fish eater just as Tokyo smells funny to Texas. Tip Paine the poultry eater smells funny too. There wasn't anything generous about what we said that morning—cheap cracks about longhorns, short vocabularies, how it was weird that the Texas Railroad Commission ran a vast state that has less railbed than Burma. We did find the highest natural point in the city, a sod-covered artificial mound near a plaque saluting the astronauts. "High ground," said McKerr, taking his stand. He peered down an avenue dusty with recent construction. "Who'd volunteer to fight for this?" he asked. "There's no water." We declared that we'd climbed Mount Houston, ha ha; time to get dressed for the priests.

I stood at the altar watching a human sacrifice and saying nothing other than "We will" when the cant-happy Episcopalians asked us spectators if we would do everything to honor and preserve this adventure. In a lovely church on a blue-sky day McKerr and Amanda tore out and exchanged their hearts. I was the best man, so my job, I supposed, was to keep the bleeding from becoming mortal, a decent responsibility if you drop your guard just a little and get sentimental about marriage. I also had to present myself solemnly, since I was one-fifth of McKerr's scouting party in Houston. I nodded to the hordes of Amanda-lovers, who asked me so politely, "Who are his people really, have they really gone to Africa to get lost on Kilimanjaro?" McKerr's dad is dead, his sensational older brother is a shrewd no-show at ceremony. This meant his cheery, no-nonsense Scotch-Irish mom, the daughter of a New York City police chief, was the only family member supporting McKerr through the afternoon reception at the Amandan manse.

Two other McKerrites did show, both Schenectadians-in-New-York. There was a crafty lawyer nicknamed Touter, who is really a flute-playing sweetheart. And then the stunning tv star whose stage name is Beatrice, pronounced Be-a-tree-cha! with gusto.

Keep your eye on Beatrice. She speaks in husky wittiness—"Oh, look at their hair. The beehive lives!" Yet she's a dark lady. I call her Contessa B. She can do Ida Lupino meets Madonna on cue; she sings, dances, flirts, snorts, rides limos bareback and toys with boys from Hollywood as if they are Italian ices in ethnic flavors, particularly Jewish. Back then she had just assassinated her way out of the Equity stand-ins and was making a tv pilot in Hollywood while simultaneously jetting to demiporn in Spain. "Oh, I have a body double," she told me of the Spanish gig. "It's just drafty on the set." She was gowned in a leggy blue cocktail dress that fit her hips like a proposition. I backed off when Contessa B. squatted down. "I've gotta work out the jet lag cramps," she explained. "Back flips are best, but I'm not wearing the right underpants."

Beatrice's appearance at Houston was an October Surprise to McKerr and a curse to Amanda. Beatrice and McKerr grew up together, same high school, several grades apart. She introduces herself as the sister he never had. If you believe this you're as credulous as Tip.

Amanda wasn't fooled. She gathered her wedding gown hem and challenged Contessa B. "Maybe you'll want to nap; you look tired from the trip." Amanda is simple about men, money, her mother and my motives. Yet she can be a dead-shot cowgirl about outsiders like Renaissance starlets. If Amanda did anything obviously wrong about McKerr (and I don't truly think she did; I think it was her mother and the legend of Natty Bumppo that did her in), it might have been choosing not to whip back her antique beaded lace gown, draw her derringer from her garter belt and plug Beatrice in the heart. Use a silver bullet, darling, just in case.

I made a pachyderm of myself at the reception, the post-reception fiesta and especially at my post-fiesta rendezvous with an Amanda pal named Mayro, a strawberry beehive with honey lips. I also wore a ten-gallon straw hat, bragged about how Bob Duvall wanted to do my first screenplay, pretended to be a hands-off Puritan who wouldn't think to unbutton a honeybee in glowing chemise. Mayro believed me. "You're a writer?" No. "Well, whatever you call it, you're not a poor boy, are you?" Poor salesman, yes. "You won't be for long, I can tell, you just hold on, I know the economy's gonna bust out like wildflowers." She drained her margarita. "You ever seen the range just bust out?" Mayro was driving us fast by then. I was holding her bouquet while she did racing changes on the loops that lasso Houston. "Tickets for speeding?" She laughed. "You worry about that? This is Texas, darlin', Texas."

Eventually Mayro swung her suburban roadster by her tidy ranchero to mix me lemonade and explain her divorce by way of her daddy's suicide, her momma's gin, her own banking career. "We're just shoveling it out to anyone who raises his voice," she bragged about Texinaire banking practices. "South of the border, they're dumping the mangos right out of the baskets to haul it away." I note here that America's morning started before Reagan's dawn. Mayro's vice-presidency was trading money for bad checks. I must have sounded negative that night, a poor salesman yet unaccustomed to the banking idea that our debt is my wealth. Mayro challenged my doubts. "Get in line and get yours, Tip; you're free, white and Republican, hear? You think they earn their money?" World economics settled, the remainder of the evening was routine pachyderm games. Mayro played the blind girl: Is Tip a wall? a snake? or winged?

The next morning Mayro rocketed me to the ramshackle train station to say farewell to McKerr and Amanda. They were off to a honeymoon in New Orleans and then a riverboat trip up the Mississippi. McKerr had rejected a return by air. He assumed if he got to Pittsburgh he could walk in. McKerr was subdued, Amanda was aglow, I was grumpy, Mayro was scheming. My parting line to McKerr sounded like a warning hoot owl. It had come to me vaguely that we had trekked here to scout, only to be bagged by the local talent. He mumbled, "Forget it; it's the heat." Right, I thought, big comfort. McKerr lit up and grinned. Amanda kissed me. "I'll take care of him now," she declared.

Mayro rocketed me to the local polo club to display me to one of her ex-darlin's. His name was Mr. Judd, and he looked splendid in jodhpurs. He told me we should have lunch when he was up to New York for the bank. I heard this as modern Texinaire for "Get out of town pronto." Mayro was electric—the horses, the mallets, two shootists exchanging pleasantries, her nipples pushing out her blouse like lean-to poles. "You don't ride?" she asked me. "Well, you come on back 'n' we'll set you up just fine."

Mr. Judd galloped his pony up and down the field, the tailgaters shared Tabasco sauce, Tip fumbled with his pipe and chatted with an ancient about the rules. Polo's not a bad game. It's lost a lot, though, since they substituted a bamboo ball for the severed head of an enemy prince. I tried to imagine how the Mongols would have done against these bankers. The notion of "right of way" would have flummoxed them until they figured the referees can't watch the ball and back-stabbing all at once.

Later I took Mr. Judd's pronto advice. Mayro wanted to rocket down to Aransas and explore the gulf on a yacht built for two. "You don't sail either?" she asked. "What do you do?" I directed her roadster to the airport, though not before we stopped off at the fantasy hotel to collect my bag and permit me to explore Mayro's lean-to one more time. I don't like trophies, yet Mr. Judd's height in the saddle urged me to tell Mayro I was taking her scarf with me—hang it on my Sharps gun rack, ha ha, muse about lady bankers. I didn't like how much she liked this malarkey. "My scarf?" she bluffed. "That's not what you really want, is it?" Tip blushed and hoped Mr. Judd would use that mallet on her lovely head before she rocketed up to the city to take me to lunch too.

3

That was the courting and wedding. I have less to say of the marriage, because I wasn't invited. Once Amanda had her man, she figured she didn't need me around to keep him. For six years I had to force my way to the McKerr table to preach my opinion of matrimony. Everyone had one of those; we were all guilty of having an opinion of matrimony. Mine was distinct for growing hostile. At the table I watched and wheedled, snipped and sniped, eating Amanda's cooking and speaking against her whenever McKerr permitted.

For example: "Yeah, but I like her," McKerr would explain to me when my derogations cut. "She can cook."

"You can cook," I would slash back, "and she's going way past the kitchen. Look at this place, it's *swept*."

McKerr would usually allow, "She does clean up a lot, but that's women," and then he would usually break contact.

Why did I speak ill of worthy-to-love Amanda? Jealousy? Maybe. Pride of place? Maybe. Savagery? Maybe. I told myself I was a big boy who didn't want nothing but the good old days when boys were boys and girls kept apart at half musket shot.

For further example: "Girls are all right," McKerr would often inform me. "You're not patient."

"That's likely," I would always admit.

"They don't want much," McKerr would instruct me. "They build up the campfire too high, but what else do they want beside the kid? You've gotta trust 'em a little."

"Not likely," I would always admit.

There was one creature who was not guilty (not at first), and that was Little McKerr, born two years into the marriage, named Nicholas by Amanda for her long dead grandfather and called by McKerr and me Uncas-afore-he-fell.

If you don't know Fenimore Cooper you're robbing yourself, but I'll treat you by cribbing the greatest of the Leatherstocking Tales, *The Last of the Mohicans.*

Back in eighteenth-century New York, when the forest was absolute wonder, Natty Bumppo, the hawkeyed, deerslaying Pathfinder, and his faithful red friend, Chingachgook, whom Pathfinder called "Big Serpent," roamed the wilderness with Chingachgook's only son, Uncas. Uncas was the last of the celebrated Mohicans, a clan related to Mohawks and Delawares but royaler somehow, first-rate Americans. A plot intervened, and naive Uncas, trying to save two white girls who had no business in the forest, was slain by a bad Mingo named Magua, a good-bad man with hard-minded motives.

Uncas's death broke Chingachgook's heart and weakened Natty Bumppo so that he and Chingachgook drifted deeper and deeper into the wilderness to escape the rottenness of civilization. Every intelligent boy lives the tale at first hearing and not just Americans. The shrewd Russian general staff makes it required reading for the officer corps, and this alone is why the red bear is never to be treated as a declawed berry snorter.

Patriots McKerr and Tip believed ourselves blessed by our Uncas. "Two hands, two feet," said McKerr, "that's the package." He was ratlike at first, then pink and useless women's work, but by the third year McKerr had him in his first handmade moccasins. That Halloween, the fourth wedding anniversary, we added a breechcloth, eagle feather and historical war paint, complete with ersatz turtle tattoo on his chest. "What's the turtle mean?" Amanda asked. "Chieftain? The turtle? That Magic Marker's not going to make him sick, is it? Can I wash it off now?"

McKerr was studying the Mohawk tongue in order to pass it on in casual repartee to the guileful little tape deck in a child's mind. The war cry was easy, but even simple imperatives, such as "Bring (me my) supper, squaw," were twisters, and the proverbs, such as "Kill a deer before you see it" and "Be the stream, don't follow it," were Joycean gobbledygook to my untutored ear.

Uncas learned and honed, a terror if you didn't get the stone knife away from him fast and a scarily good shot with the bow. They were only suction-tipped arrows, but the boy aimed for the throat. Uncas became in quick time our ultimate video game, the half lad who could sneer at white men in their ugly cars and speak boldly against the Frenchers. "King Louis is the enemy," McKerr instructed. "Say it: King Looey—bad medicine." Uncas also showed easy camaraderie with the wee savages who roamed his stoop. Indeed Uncas could make the local ADC (welfare) kids seem only half savage. They envied his war paint, and there was an incident over an eagle feather that warned the bullies Uncas was not to be hit upon. It wasn't worth the sweat. Redmen are said never to forget an offense; they'll be back forever.

I describe perfection for McKerr. Yet there are plenty of hints in just what I've told anecdotally as to the trouble. McKerr refused Amanda's money beyond rent support and victuals. He insisted that his family continue to camp in his make-believe wilderness, which was actually a three-room apartment in a neighborhood that is the other side of the Upper West Side's DMZ. McKerr can stroll Broadway and see the battle of Harlem Heights at 121st, where patriots fit the redcoats yet got licked, 1776. To modern eyes it's where Broadway dips toward ransacked Harlem. Down the slope are badly, badly battered human beings who didn't get wake-up calls in America's morning. McKerr and I have both been mugged casually every other year. The hooligans use guns, knives, brickbats and strangleholds and flee like the night. We both know how to communicate with the blueboys from the local precincts: "Two of 'em," McKerr has testified several times. "They said, 'Be cool, man, be cool.'" We also know what to think when the ADA tells you the judge accepted their guilty plea and, since McKerr and I were not too killed to testify, let them walk on probation if they'll go back to school. This is routine danger in a city where many bad guys are drugged, terrified of themselves, armed like assassins, yet at the same time demirich guys (like

Tip) insist upon our liberty to live on the next block in renovated co-ops.

McKerr and I understand this like winter (and by the way, cowboys out there, we're not allowed to carry guns or fight back much). No surprise that Amanda did not understand or that Mother Amanda was speechless when the Amandans first taxied to a dinner at McKerr's camp from their fantasy hotel midtown. I do not mock the Amandans for their shock. Who would believe? Harder, they come from a state where they are allowed to carry guns and Fourth Amendment rights for perpetrators is a fortune cookie. Amanda was never roughed up by the hooligans, not so that it was passed on to Houston, but it's obvious to anyone, even non-Texinaires, that living in Dodge City, you have to dodge fast.

Uncas's fate was not joked about. There was the background jeopardy. "He's just a child, a little boy," Amanda protested when we joked about his scrapes. "They kicked him down for a feather." Also there were the nonschools ahead of him. "Have you ever visited that place?" Amanda asked us of the neighborhood grammar school. "They have chains on the door, bars in the kindergarten." There was the winter the boiler broke and icicles formed in the bath, and there was the holiday McKerr, Amanda and Uncas were in Mexico with the Amandans and a few weary drug addicts worked over their apartment with precision and left a needle. All this was not dealt with directly, as suited McKerr's temperament. Meanwhile Amanda was much on the phone to Mother, assuring her no one strange was in the next room. "It's the radiator," she explained. "It's working."

Uncas himself presented more philosophical trouble. "His name is *Nicholas*," Amanda started insisting now and again when the warpath wore her down. "You try to discipline a child whose father tells him he's a chieftain." McKerr reluctantly accepted the alteration in his make-believe. The boy was Uncas to him but the firstborn grandson of inherited wealth to others and also the namesake of the family's icon. Worse, Uncas-Nicholas's great-grandmother was alive and fiery at ninety-something, and it emerged over the years that what was on Mother Amanda's mind often had first been designed by her mother, Mrs. Nicholas the First.

Remember, our full alias for the half lad was Uncas-afore-he-fell. The felling began again every time the Amandans jetted this threatened little family off to their holiday retreats. Texinaires, lacking other weather than hot, celebrate the major holidays by a lake or seashore, preferably out of Texas. Uncas would go off in his traveling skins and return in PGA mufti. He would switch from a parley about how to make a fire out of sticks and shavings to wanting to have that Texas Ranger story read aloud for the fortieth time so he could get excited about the pony his uncle Amandans had taught him to ride at the ranch. I thought the worst trail sign was when Uncas was called to the phone to say "howdy" to his great-grandmother the wicked empress and then came back to miss the bull's-eye badly.

McKerr's folly was not caused by Uncas's falling, however; that was a flank maneuver by the Amandans, and Pathfinder can rabbit run. I am not sure I know what the truth is, though I saw enough of it happening, and I encouraged McKerr's disaffection with mischievous certainty. The Amandans were wrong, I declaimed, McKerr was right. They were wealthy without working. McKerr was poor because doing McKerr doesn't pay the king's script. And Amanda, I said, she's a sweet, smart, kind person, but she's no squaw and does Chingachgook halfheartedly, about what you'd expect from a cowgirl. I left out the part that I was Chingachgook and wasn't leaving.

Amanda understood all my troublemaking without spying on our powwows, even if McKerr and I had them more and more at my garret or (when I did get in the bank line and get mine) my co-op. This might explain why she persuaded McKerr, in the sixth year, into retreating from his imaginary forest up to the real one in the Catskills. She leased them a clapboard colonial on a spectacularly sleepy branch of the Schoharie and started preaching settlement. "We'll have a garden," she said, "and you can fish every day, and there's a real school for Nicholas, where they don't treat them like little convicts."

That following year I missed McKerr extremely and Uncas more than I can admit. I was much away myself then, being demifamous and cashing demilarge checks, yet my pomposity, while fun, was hollow compensation. I blamed Amanda and her family for my cold campfires. They were wrong, I prophesied, and they would fail.

When McKerr began turning up in the city now and again, mumbling and grinning that he needed a vacation from casting in icy brooks and gamboling in haunted hills where the deer are thicker than settlers, I, faithful Chingachgook, took my stone knife in hand and used it. Recall that Pathfinder's nickname for his faithful red friend, Chingachgook, was "Big Serpent." I was that, whispering in his ear, the proper snake accusing him of woman's ways and civilized nakedness and offering the fruit of my knowledge. You're only two percent Mohawk, I argued, you're mostly a Scotch-Irish exhibit, grandson of a New York City police chief, curator of yourself and musty legends. What use are you up in a clapboard gaol in a tidy village where the hunting season is enforced and what's left of make-believe are the cannon holes in various stone walls? You can't do McKerr in a genuine bought and Orientalized compound, I argued, you need the wilderness in your potato brain, and all that's left of wild things is here in New York City. I turned and turned this serpentine nonsense so that I got to believing it much more than McKerr.

He listened. Pathfinder must listen to Chingachgook; it's the leatherstocking rules. "They're all right," he said of the Amandans. "They call too much." And, "They keep asking me what I'm going to do," he said of his mother-in-law and father-in-law. "What do I say? How do I tell them I'm doing it?"

I returned sneaky sympathy. Pathfinder was way ahead of me, however, so far off the trail that what I thought was him helloing was actually him farewelling.

McKerr loved his white keeper Amanda, worshiped the falling Uncas, but the wilderness was calling him, and an evil spirit had appeared to soothe his melancholy and partake of his game. I reintroduce Beatrice (Be-a-tree-cha!), the actress Schenectadian, who by then had assassinated her way out of starlethood, had abused and abandoned several agents, producers and a coked-up star or two, and was campaigning for the villainess role in a major miniseries while holding down several gigs in Eurotrash movies in Spain. She was hot, and McKerr was a hawkeye she wanted to bag. I didn't see for some

time—I was much preoccupied with my own aggrandizement—
but when I did note McKerr's oft mention of statements by Contessa B., it was too late. I had played mischievously to get McKerr
back and had then lost him to a snake who dwarfs me, a serpen-
tess who suns on golden rocks and swallows game many times
her size.

McKerr's visits to the city increased and lengthened, not just a
post-Thanksgiving retreat but a post-Christmas encampment. He
now openly bad-mouthed the Amandans: "What do they want from
me, law school? Where's that? For them, money's law school. It's
sick." This after the Amandans had kidnapped him to a resort for a
family wedding, where they'd thumped his absence of ambition, his
rude dress, his penniless prospects.

Meanwhile Contessa B. was at her heartless work. The woman is a
dark vision. Not just superbly photogenic but limber, lyrical, greedy,
ruthless, well-traveled and fork-tongued. "Is he there?" she asked on
a call to my apartment one night, looking for McKerr. "What do you
think, Tip, how long does he have to put up with her bullshit? She
threw out his old wool pants!"

Also I think Contessa B.'s much too good in the bedroll. If I
sound envious of McKerr, it's true, I was, and the part of me that
celebrates nature's way to toss up these femmes fatales admits that
when the devil cuts the right deal we are none of us safe from
things that go hump in the night. Oh yes, her self-pity was good
camouflage. She'd call me past midnight from some fantasy hotel
in L.A. or Spain and groan like a wallflower about how hurt she
was, how she couldn't sleep but had a wake-up for makeup in five
hours, how she only wanted the best for McKerr because she loved
him, and why couldn't he see that Amanda was a bleeder who was
feeding on him? Her best lines, ones that I fell for every time,
were delivered once a month: "I've told him I'm not talking to
him anymore until he wises up and chooses. Do you understand,
Tip—we're finished until he decides."

Yes, yes, I would reply, yes, yes, a triangle can't make it in a
two-dimensional world like tv. I didn't actually make the crack about
tv. I should have, in order to protect McKerr. But I was spellbound by

Contessa B. too. She's an alarmingly beautiful woman. And she doesn't ever not act, so that when she's playing the part as your friend or lover, you're convinced. Who can talk back to Ida Lupino on a riff? And also, truth, I was glad to have her slither and hiss while I returned, guilty as a bloodstain, to the safe role as wise, faithful Chingachgook. More truth, I had a new plan that was an old plan, dreamed up by Fenimore Cooper, and I've cribbed it already. Naive Uncas falls while trying to save white women from their out-of-placedness. Pathfinder and Tip, heartbroken long-striders, slip back to the wilderness to escape the rot.

4

The finish is the start. McKerr procrastinated in a circle back to Pathfinder in the wilderness. Amanda took up with weeping, mother's lawyers, painting lessons at Woodstock and then much more weeping. Contessa B., foiled by McKerr's guileless virtue, moulted one more skin and slipped off with another producer. She promised never to wend our way again, though this was an acceptably obvious lie. "I'm done with you," she told McKerr. "You're never to call again, never to write again, just stay away, I'm done with you! You're a cheap, selfish bastard, and that goes for your friend too!" (I wasn't fooled by this; McKerr's hawkeyes drift off the path too often for me to trust him alone out there.)

What about Uncas? He became Nicholas, an Amandan for the twenty-first century, a red lad growing into his worst enemy, the dude cowboy.

As for Tip, he's very happy. The wild turkey is sweet, the campfire is warm, the Frenchers are due again in the spring to try for Albany and maybe New York. Meanwhile the redcoats, our tremulous allies until the patriots get organized in Boston, just marvel at McKerr's steady stare and my scalp bag. Yes, my hip-hung and criminal scalp bag, much yellow and red hair with dried skin attached. It's time for

Big Serpent's confession. I also have two brunette lockets, clipped sneakily from Amanda and Contessa B. I used very strong, very bad medicine to get rid of the womenfolk. I've admitted my skulduggery to Pathfinder. He's said he doesn't care.

"They just wore me down," explained McKerr. "It's a lot of responsibility, as they kept telling me."

"*They?*" I prodded. "You mean them back in Fort Houston?"

"Forget it, they're all right," said McKerr of the Amandans again. "It's just different in Texas, too hot."

I've left out much sootiness about the eight years. Such as Banker Mayro the vice-president's scandalous drunk that night in Greenwich Village, followed by her botched suicide back in Houston in glowing chemise. More bloodcurdling events I've skipped: Contessa B.'s off-camera abortion; McKerr's mother trying to hold Amanda up at the wine cooler after Amanda's miscarriage; Uncas's scarlet fever after a Texinaire fiesta. There was also unholy tomfoolery down in Houston that took casualties like Santa Anna—Mrs. Nicholas the First cashing chips and waltzing off with Old Nick in spurs! Mother and Father Amanda's divorce! Father Amanda's instantaneous remarriage to a troll!

What would it serve to work all this routine rot in? Pathfinder and Tip know civilization isn't our way. We do have the wilderness to ourselves. We're in winter camp right now. The sky is gunsmoke, my knife is sharp and his musket, Killdeer, is gunsmith cleaned. Soon, when the great horned owls *hoo* and the half moon parts the cloud veil, we'll turn from the fire and watch for Uncas's ghost. He'll come toward us without a sound—no snapping twigs clutter his path—and he'll be smiling in that Mohican manner, lord of birch and brook trout and ten-point buck, so beautifully the last of his tribe, McKerr's true claim to fame.

It comes to me now to make another claim, a large, nasty one, suited to the sort of cutthroats that McKerr and I must never be again. We did the deed, you must understand, we solved Fenimore Cooper's leatherstocking tale stranger than he did. We fought them all to protect dear Uncas. But their civilizing ways got him away from us. So we sneaked into that fortress called matrimony where they'd trapped him, jailed him, condemned him to death by wealth. And finally, to keep him forever ours in make-believe, we set him free. Two musket shots. I aimed.

4

In the Tunnel of Love

Black Monday, Tuesday,

Wednesday, Thursday, Friday;

Holmes Paine on the Case;

Tip the Croquet Player

1

T he Third Reich is a low hobby of mine, well behind Wells's Time Machine and cowboys like Gordon Liddy. So I was in lazy humor when I booked a posh cabin on a ferry out of Helsinki and sailed for my first visit to Germany. Truth, I was headed deep into Deutschland to visit my colossal baby brother, the centurion, on guard with our elite armored cavalry at the right flank of the infamous Fulda Gap.

Our branch of Paines are citizen soldiers the same as Ms. Liberty herself. The first Paine in America quit England the same year Lord Protector Cromwell quit his earthly travail for a colony in hell. Subsequently the Paines fit the forest and swamps of the Carolinas for a century of dirt farming, child-making and potshotting at the Occaneechis and Susquehannocks. Moving on, there were several Paines who fit the Frenchers behind Braddock and Washington, more who fit the redcoats behind Washington and one who fit the redcoats again in the retreat from the burning Capitol Building in 1812. (Yes, remember the redcoated devils burnt our Capitol and the President's House too, so what is this unbalanced anglophilia?) The Blackhawk Indian War had a Buckeye farmboy, the Mexican War had a vagabond who died of cholera en route and the Civil War was so crammed with Paine boys on both sides (half of whom called it the War of Secession) it's impossible to figure. After that I lose count until the one great-uncle who vanished in the Belleau Wood and of course my own dad landing on Omaha Beach *before* H-hour and my mom too, the dark-eyed WAC at Fort Benning who dazzled the armor candidates. We Paines didn't rise in the ranks. We served as junior fodder and went home. None of us current boys did Vietnam, an odd credit to us and a Paine judgment of that war. We didn't have to, we didn't want to, we didn't.

Now in armed service is the mightiest Paine our branch ever produced, a six-foot-seven Paul Bunyan who is called Bunyan. He's got legs like booster rockets and a bronze-plated chest, an igneous jaw and aquamarine eyes, a soft-spoken tongue and a brain suited to a countinghouse. Bunyan's also my baby brother—I named him Bunyan, an eldest brother's privilege—thirteen years behind me, with three other big Paines in between. In truth, my parents have never known how often they must pray to thank God almighty for visiting them with such luck, four healthy sons and then Bunyan too. He's loving, kind, studious, honorable, naive like spring and hardy like fall.

The army didn't seem to know what to do with such a throw-weight specimen. If there were fire they'd issue him a platoon and a sergeant named Blackwatch and point. When they brought him back down the mountain in a bag, they'd pin a ribbon on the gore and speechify about why we fight. Yet there's only a Cold War out there for our legions, so instead they spied him right out of Fort Benning's OCS as an honorable bricklayer. After searching around in their ratings, they put him where it counts for boys and girls so far from home—the adjutant general's cadre. He became a postman.

It was the genius of the morning's buildup to build down to keep the peace. The mail must get through, right, it's why we fight too, right, and what better station for a blue-eyed behemoth who can read, write, pray, count and shoot than a postal detachment at the frontest of the front lines, toe to toe with the Russkis on the German frontier. When that dreaded black weekday arrives (Saturday or Sunday aren't black, they're holy or bloody; blackness is prole work) and the Warsaw Pact divisions rev their T-80 engines and punch out NATO like the champ laid low, how philosophical it will be to have ink-stained, stamp-happy Bunyan in the MIA lists.

Marcus Aurelius would understand and approve of Bunyan as postman. You remember him; he was the last Roman emperor worth remembering, some eighteen centuries back. He served his time in hell, called back then the German quagmire. Maybe you don't remember. Rome was the capital of the world, and its empire stretched Britain to Palestine, Abyssinia to the Danube. North of the swampy Danube was end-of-the-world trouble—the German quagmire. The German tribes were bloody-minded savages, scary like nightmares and tireless like floods. Marcus Aurelius camped on the Danube and held back the Germans like a log dam. He wasn't all warrior-king, however; he'd been educated to philosophize, and he called himself a Stoic. Simply put, Stoics were princely social climbers who philosophized. Accordingly Marcus Aurelius never wasted his best centurions on the idiot recruits, slogging over sylvan kill zones and sipping cholera. He kept his handsome captains close at hand, perhaps as postmen, to remind him with their fierce obedience that all poor souls are burdened with corpses—no need to abuse the specially beautiful corpses while they're alive.

Marcus Aurelius was much on my bookish mind as my ferryboat eased out of Helsinki harbor. We were bound hard for Mecklenburg Bay at Travemünde, a Baltic port serving Hamburg. It was a Finnish ship, muscular, clean, very fast, on jet engines that parted the Baltic overnight, and it was stocked with muscular, clean, very fast Nordic beauties who do publicly sauna in small towels or not and do confide in excellent, grinning English, "There's nothing dirty about it to us, you understand."

I ogled the Scandinavians, whom I like most all the time; they're fun even when they're melancholic, they sensibly favor trim houses, sunny weather and lake water. However, like Marcus Aurelius I kept closest watch on the Germans on board. Too many war stories, too much bloody-handed history, from Rome through the twentieth century, all warned me that there must be something mysteriously scary behind the pleasant German mask of Nordic propriety.

At smorgasbord dinner that night at sea I chanced to be sitting at a long table suddenly occupied by polite German voyagers. I say polite because they used utensils, smoked quietly, discussed music and back-packing with passion and now and again remarked on the excellence of Finnish cuisine, especially the reindeer meat.

I eavesdropped sneakily. When one tense lad caught me cocking my ear at a political quip and asked me *auf Deutsch* if I was American, I pretended noncomprehension. I speak German well enough. (Nearly as good as my Russian and equal to the six other European tongues I've picked up; there was a reason the army coddled me and the NSA hired me: Tip Paine has a sad-sack tabula rasa brain.) However, I didn't want these Germans to think I understood or sympathized with a pickle in Deutschland.

As supper finished, the serving tables were removed and dancing began on the center deck space. Old and young patted their stomachs and tramped to the beat. I delayed my exit to ogle more blond hips. Sometime between a polka and a waltz, while I was lighting my pipe, one of the Germans appeared at my side. She'd caught me listening in to her chitchat earlier and now asked me in broken English if I was American. I nodded this time. She pointed to the swirling polka. *"Der Tanz. Wollen Sie tanzen?"* She paused and guessed, in English, "Dance me?"

It was a simple request. Europeans believe in exercise after dining, and being shipboard, this means pandemonium to music. It's not romantic to them, more like folkish calisthenics. I convinced myself that I could further reconnoiter the Germans by dancing with one— but not a polka; we waited for a waltz.

It wasn't entirely research. She was attractive, and I was vain after several weeks in Russia being a know-it-all. Her name was Frau Jodl (Yodel), no relation whatsoever to the ex–field marshal. She said she was a registered nurse returning from three years with the Finns in Africa for the Swedish Red Cross. Her story was amazing, and I heard just pieces of it because her English was hilarious. "Africa, *der schwarze Kontinent*... black continent? Where is the Africans, not the same all there."

For my own black, secretive reasons I continued to play dumb about German. Frau Jodl's husband was not mentioned. She was in love with Africa and a Dr. Swede too, who had broken her heart. She was returning home to visit her family before going out to Zimbabwe again to inoculate the fly-covered doomed. The Euros are wild for Africa; they think it's outer space and they're cosmonauts.

I knew this, so rather than fritter away our time about the famine, I guided her confidences back to Germany and her family. Her hometown was Nuremberg, deep in Bavaria. "You like Bavaria?" she asked. *"Den Wein und die Berge?"* I wanted more than wine and mountains. I wouldn't go so far as to polka, and I figured she could drink me into the Baltic, so I used romance, the stupid obvious insincere ploy that works eventually anywhere and fast shipboard.

Buxom, strudel-crisp and fair Frau Jodl was a nurse who was used to clumsy passes. She was also a Bavarian, accustomed to pretty words and rendezvous. What persuaded her to me was a mystery. She had not heard of my books or movies, was unimpressed by money, had outtraveled me by an astronomical unit, regarded America a greedy *Kind* in and out of tantrums. More, I dance badly and dress like a croquet player. Say it was the Baltic moon, a swift passage and her whim.

The three Finnish backpackers who picked us up at the bar might have helped. "Are you Yank?" asked the big redhead in Brit slang. "You're big like Yank blokes." Frau Jodl was amused when I took pity and let the girls use the shower in my stateroom. Frau Jodl and I sat by, sharing schnapps and watching the picture window of a porthole. The ship kicked up white water while the pink beauties shed their punker black and emerged from the hot water like buttercups. Finnish schoolgirls are gorgeous and eager for everything. While they gagaed me (Lord Tip in his mature cabin), Frau Jodl got to play my acquaintance at first, then my sister and finally the role she liked, my mother. "They are young," she declared. *"Du bist es nicht."*

Meanwhile I loosed her broken tongue about the Fatherland. It wasn't easy, having to pretend to learn the words to ask just as she was using them. Papa saw five years' service in the Panzer Grenadiers. After he was wounded the third(!) time, he was a fireman. Her uncles traveled all over Hitler's map, one lost at sea in a U-boat off Ireland, two privates lost in the Ukraine, none at Leningrad or Stalingrad. Many other uncles and cousins survived in bad shape. One was now a prosperous apparel manufacturer and another sold for Audi. No one, to her knowledge, had served in any of the major murder gangs such as the storm troopers and their infamous panzer divisions: Das Reich, Der Führer, Hermann Goering, Totenkopf. Her papa, the ex-Grenadier, was about to retire after forty years in a winery.

"You know dis *Wein?*" she asked. *"Er ist leicht und..."* She used the German word, the gerund for *kühlen,* and I almost gave myself away when I translated the obvious for *liebfraumilch,* "quenching."

Maybe I did reveal my deception. She talked more and more *auf Deutsch* after that, not about the dead and buried Third Reich but about her dreams and the romantic Baltic. Hers was love talk, which resembles itself in most languages. "I'm an adventuress," she said slowly in German, testing me. "It's a job where I come from. You Americans think everyone either stays at home with children or goes to an office."

My trickery undid me in the end. The Finns kept up slangy patter while angling for my spare beds for the night. Finally they perceived that Frau Jodl was not leaving, and they left. We elders then alternated in the shower and were sacked out as cozily as knots when conquering Yankee Tip tricked himself and nonperformed. She, Bavarian nymph, charitable way past my experience, seemed to like my detumescence more than my bombast. "There is a proverb," she told me, "that you can't walk crooked on a straight path." Worse, she actually sang me a lullaby.

There were no shenanigans early the next morning. Frau Jodl pounded off to consult with her traveling companion, Nurse Heidi. I was pleased to meet them both for a properly dressed smorgasbord luncheon. "You're a writer?" Heidi asked. No. Frau Jodl helped her friend. "He makes a lot of noise, but he's not so tough. Believe me, he's no fascist." (Fascist is a very old word, from the Latin for a bundle of rods and an ax, a talisman of state authority; it's also fair to say that it's slang for prick.) The nurses laughed.

I had rationalized my fascist failure at fascism by then and was comforted. Daughter of a Panzer Grenadier, I argued to me, mother of one in time. Tip Paine wasn't going to risk creating another grim-eyed *Soldat* for the Fatherland. By the time we docked at Travemünde I was returned to Marcus Aureliusizing. The good Stoic wrote in his sensible book *Meditations* that a man should love nothing that is not woven in the pattern of his destiny. Relax, Tip, I translated to myself. Germans are just not your style.

2

I had deeper prejudices waiting offstage but checked them while transferring from ship to German shore. It was a typically gray June afternoon on the rolling north German plain. My travel agent had arranged for a huge blue car to meet me on the quay (I don't go where I can't be driven), and it was an expected first lesson in Germanness that, unlike everywhere else I've been on this earth, the driver and car were punctual and obliging.

I felt eager for exploring, when Frau Jodl's voice surprised me. "Herr Paine, aren't you going to say goodbye?" I was surprised how quickly the nurses had passed through customs, given that they were nationals returning from Africa. As for me, the officials had treated my bald eagle like a *carte blanche*, which both pleased and worried me. "Herr Paine, Tip, you didn't kiss us goodbye," continued Frau Jodl. Heidi manhandled her giant bag to the ground and asked me of the Mercedes, "Is this yours?"

I was nabbed, another getaway in the trash. My choice now was selfish American or showy gentleman. I didn't hesitate and introduced the car, a pet at their pretty feet. "Oh, Herr Paine," said Frau

Jodl, *"wunderbar,* how kind!" She didn't bother with my ruse anymore, telling me in exacting German that they were in a hurry to catch their train at Hamburg (south), but hadn't I said I was going on to Berlin (east) before I wandered my way to Bavaria?

I surrendered again. I was their pet too, yet my escort duty was short-lived, no suppertime negotiations. Nurse Heidi's mother would be at the train station at Frankfurt exactly on time, and if Nurse Heidi, a plump fret cadet, wasn't on the train, *ach Himmel,* what would happen? I had no answer and watched the ladies hop from the car at the Hamburg Bahnhof and flee toward their schedule. I was relieved and figured I didn't actually have to call Frau Jodl next weekend, though she had kissed me farewell nonmaternally and said, "You're a funny fellow. You should call me; I'll show you Bavaria. And I promise, no more polkas."

My driver swirled me through downtown Hamburg so I could glimpse the new architecture. I also wanted to imagine what sci-fi/ spy guys Auden, Isherwood and Spender might have seen sixty years before, when they'd arrived to burn up their golden youth. Auden's puppy land is gone as if it was make-believe. The real fire storms arrived with wings in 1943. Hamburg was (and is) home port of IG Farben, once the gunsmith of the Third Reich. The Allied bombers put it to the torch. You might argue this as the way of war, and you'd be right. Then again, our bombing incinerated German children where they hid, regardless of creed. I am not so tough, it's true, and I stared at the canals and park streams we drove by. I was playing make-believe, trying to hear the huddled ghosts still screaming for mama.

I heard only car horns and speed. Yet another truth of the famous phoenix when it does rise is that it aims to flap away specters too. Hamburg is Marshall Plan original. And then we were on the autobahn and bound for nightfall in Berlin, moving at one hundred and fifty kilometers an hour and getting passed. Until we took off, I had admired the tidy shops, streets, people and clock towers, all correct and up to the moment. My harder thoughts were these: Landscaping by phosphorus bombs. Bird seed by President Truman. Prosperity by hard work, thrift, luck.

These were the good Germans, the guidebook said so, so why did I bear them such hardhearted prejudices? Because I often brood like a Roman Stoic and they don't? Because they build cars as good as tanks? Because they believe in schedules like invasions and executions? Because they smile and smile at large Yankee nabobs? Everyone's forgiven them, I've heard it said, except a few million long-remembering Jews and one or two Russian peasants.

So why was Tip (who's read the casualty lists where it asserts that the Third Reich surrendered as unconditionally as carbon) so suspicious? Marcus Aurelius wrote, "Look beneath the surface for the intrinsic value." I was looking. The Federal Republic of Germany is extrinsic like ingots. I did not want the dull gleam to fool me. What was deep down inside this polite rushing clock?

3

This "deep down inside" cliché is my flimflam, what writers call pointing, because I know where I'm headed and you don't. I wrote it when I was tired and much crankier about Germany than I've yet admitted, so, excuses made, I'll get on to the Tunnel of Love.

For three days my car zigzagged the northern plain like a plush scout craft. From Berlin we drove back across to Cologne and then south on the Rhine so I could see Remagen. You don't remember if you're under fifty or not related to a Second World War vet, but Remagen was very famous for ten days in March '45. Our army was stalled along the Rhine River, unable to cross because all the bridges were blown and the Wehrmacht was dug in apocalyptically on the opposite shore. That is, all the bridges except one railroad span at Remagen, where their dynamite had failed. Our First Army's III Corps' Ninth Armored Division blasted its way to river's edge and captured both ends of the bridge on March 7. Victory in Europe followed, the American army pouring into the breach like a tidal wave. It just so happened that my dad's combat engineer company was attached to III Corps. On the tenth day, Dad's company was assigned to climb onto the Remagen bridge and glue it back together after all the barrages and tank crossings. Platoon leader Dad tossed a coin with another platoon leader. The winner platoon got the dry-footed bridge work, the loser had to go down into the Rhine River mud to tidy up our pontoon bridges, then being impolitely shelled, rocketed, bombed and strafed by the desperate Germans. Dad lost the coin toss, and he was standing on the banks of the Rhine when the Remagen bridge above him failed and shuddered and collapsed of a sudden with the winner platoon of engineers on board.

I tell all this because I'm here telling it because of a toin coss. I lunched in brand-new Remagen and watched the Rhine, where I might have ended before I began. My thoughts were crankhood: What're the Germans, nuts? Did they think the American army crossed the Atlantic for a bluff? All those men and machines rolled up to the Rhine were gonna turn around because the Germans were tough? Ike was gonna say, "Oh, my mistake, I guess we're not *sincere* like you Germans." I also thought, Forty years isn't long enough; I can still hear the toin coss and the shelling, rocketing, bombing and strafing directed at Dad.

My big blue car descended into rural, undulating and fairy-tale Bavaria at Schweinfurt am Main. I said farewell to driver Jurge (who was eighteen, unctuous and a furtive doper) and waited at the train station for brother Bunyan.

Bunyan was late arriving. Our army works its junior officers scrupulously. I entertained myself by counting our M-1 Abrams blockbuster tanks on the railcars until Bunyan appeared suddenly on foot. "You're here!" he announced happily. "I wasn't sure you'd make it. I mean, you're here!" He laughed like my baby brother, but he looked quietly ferocious in officer fatigues, that superb commando-style sweater bearing his first lieutenant gold stripes. He was bigger still, and it had only been a year and a half since I'd last seen him, at Mother's Christmas.

"How do you like it—not much, huh?" he asked. I said the M-1 tanks were amazing. "No, the town, Pig's Crossing—that's what we call it." It was a wet day, and Schweinfurt's depot is a commuter pit stop scarred by graffiti. I returned that I was fascinated by all of it and went on to comment about Berlin and Cologne. I also used some German on him, to trade language skills. He frowned at this. "It's okay; you don't have to," said Bunyan. "We don't, you know, need it much."

"How's that?" I asked. "Bavarians speak English?"

"Negative," said Bunyan. "We just speak American."

I soon learned that our army does not encourage its troops to parley *auf Deutsch*, and though Bunyan could do it fairly well, he'd become all army. This was a clue for my investigation, and I turned it over while we hopped into his low-slung Japanese speedster and reconnoitered the environs.

It's called the Tunnel of Love—*der Liebestunnel*—and Bunyan told me about it as soon as we passed over it. "It's right beneath the road, about a kilometer long; you can see it best in winter," he said. "The snow melts first over it."

We were north of the clean, quaint town, midway between the two bivouacs of our armored cav. East of the road I saw the larger barracks set back behind a treeline. Behind a stone wall nearby, there was a concrete column topped by a familiar surly eagle with an enchained swastika for a perch.

"It's the only real swastika I've seen," said Bunyan. "They just leave it there." He explained that once upon a time, those stone barracks had headquartered a panzer regiment. Down a ways, west of the road, Bunyan indicated our armored cav brigade headquarters in a flat glen. That was also where a Luftwaffe field used to be, he said, and our guys had moved into the same shabby wooden barracks and converted the old airfield to a tank and helicopter parking lot.

What was instantly important and confounding to me was that tunnel running a kilometer odd between the two bivouacs. The Hitlerites built it for an air raid shelter and armory.

"They flooded it when they retreated," Bunyan explained, "and we've just left it that way, too dangerous to go into because of the unexploded ordnance. Not doable."

Bunyan didn't know why it's called the Tunnel of Love; it just is.

der Liebestunnel. There were more clues in what Bunyan said as we spun back through the town to his private digs (officers live "on the economy"). I got very suspicious.

"You use the same barracks?" I asked.

"Sure," said Bunyan. "It's cheaper than building, and what the heck, they're built pretty good."

"The swastika eagle is left in place?" I asked.

"Yeah, I've wondered about that," said Bunyan. "They must have figured it didn't matter."

"What do you mean, cleaning out the Tunnel of Love is not doable?" I asked.

"Hey, I just got here," he said, "but it'd be a mess down there. Who's gonna pay for it?"

"What sort of front-line bunker is this?" I asked.

"The frontest," said Bunyan. "We're the Blackhorse, Tip. The hostiles are just forty clicks north. Nothing between us and the Gap but speed."

He meant the Fulda Gap. "The Gap" is mythological warrior-talk for a future killing field around the farm town of Fulda, to the immediate northwest of Schweinfurt and the Tunnel of Love. The Gap is where our shrewdest war planners have been expecting the reds ("the hostiles") to invade civilization since the Potsdam Conference, summer 1945. Bunyan was telling me that East Germany was an easy drive north, especially in an Abrams M-1 jet-engined tank at 70 kph. He was also telling me that his armored cavalry regiment, the elite Blackhorse, attached to our Eighth Infantry Division, was at the right flank of the first day of the end of the world.

Shall I repeat this? What sort of frontline bunker was Schweinfurt am Main? The sort at the end of the world on black Monday, Tuesday, Wednesday, Thursday or Friday.

Soon enough we were lounging in Bunyan's flat back in town. I came out of the shower to ask dumb questions about that black weekday to come.

Bunyan answered bluntly, "We go into the woods and keep going." I asked which way. Bunyan pointed out his window, over a row house and a park, west toward Philadelphia. "Thataway," he said.

I peered outside. I asked if he meant regroup? fighting withdrawal? last-ditch deployment?

Bunyan shrugged. "Geez, Tip, I don't know and don't want to. I do what I'm told and—don't think about it."

Good sci-fi/spy form, I thought. I'm your brother, but you might know what you don't know you know, so say zip. I pushed him anyway. I said that we've got just half of an armored cav *regiment* at Fulda, the other half here at Schweinfurt on the right flank. I asked how many *divisions* the reds were pushing through the Gap.

"Hey." Bunyan laughed. "You ever seen what *one* armor division looks like when it's coming at you?"

What we were discussing with slight order-of-battle facts but with much common sense was that when WWIII's Defcon Five sounded a klaxon blast, meaning invasion by hordes momentarily, our guys were to pile onto anything with treads, wheels or blades and bug out. Schweinfurt is a crater waiting to happen, doom incarnate. I had flattered myself when I'd spotted the nuke plant bubble east of town, and I'd thought, Well, if it's really bad, they can put an arrow into the container building and no one will want the Main River valley for a hundred years. But our army isn't thinking about slow death. Bunyan's armored cav is to get on their black horses and advance backward to Switzerland, because this part of Bavaria is scheduled to be kaput instantly and forever.

Look at the map, where East Germany sticks a knee into West Germany's belly. Belly button Fulda, to the northwest of Schweinfurt, is a sleepy town on the sleepy Fulda River, anchoring a gap in the hills between the Fulda and Main rivers, which quickly becomes an armor autobahn. The Main River valley takes your normal red T-80 driver zigzagging straight to the Rhine, where some red guys turn south for Spain and other red guys turn northwest for London.

I understood right then that what's said to be between the Cold War and Comrade Sheriff of Nottingham is this exquisite rolling tank country of north Bavaria, where the farmers outproduce nature and the wine is quenching. NATO's muscle, SHAPE (back at Brussels), isn't going to wait for a fighting withdrawal back to the Rhine while the good guys mobilize Frenchers and Brits and resupply from America by container ship. Forget that WWIII sci-fi/spy charade in the books—how we'll have eight days of warning time while the reds concentrate their divisions; how we'll have ten days to slow them down before we have to go nuke. On the first day, *in the first hour*, the brass is going to sigh, maybe tell Washington, if the satellites still work, sigh again and then make Bavaria and Hesse a moonscape with some gigantic weapons, which for no reason don't scare voters because they are called conventional. The tiny, tiny nuclear ones aren't going to be used at first, not because of fainthearted taboo but because, like gas and germs, they tend to drift the poison back on you willy-nilly.

By the end of that first black weekday, however, the tiny, tiny nukes are gonna seem a mercy killing compared to the conventional cloudbursts. On that first black day, Bunyan will be going backward, not from their range finders and smart-bomb lock-ons but from ours. Tom Clancy and Larry Bond, my admired mentors, listen up: No counterattacks, nifty Stealth takeouts, Custer II last stands. Here's the actual battle scenario: Black weekday. Bug out. The end.

I overenjoyed this bleak vision that night at dinner with Bunyan. I was picturing myself moving from one prearranged fire-coordinate to the next as we spun through the farm fields to a potato soup restaurant and then back to his digs. I am usually excited whenever at futuristic ground zeros—Empire State Building, Capitol Dome, Eiffel Tower, Pantheon, Kremlin—but to be inside a future former river valley is my kind of appalling fascination.

(I'll make a note here for the strategic treason discovered since my visit to Bavaria four years ago. It's alleged that one of our sergeants, a guy my age, sold out the Eighth Division's escape plans to the reds. Units, routes, coordinates, life expectancies. Sold them out not for politics but for cash and hormones. If true, then my dear Bunyan was one of those boys you sold out, Sarge, and I have a private vengeance and long memory. If true, freeze in hell, Sarge.)

That evening none of my fancy patter bothered Bunyan. He knew his big brother was always making believe. He told me about his post office work load, his shirking mailmen, his superlative efficiency reports. Bunyan was a postman, not a tank driver, and getting the mail through required as much precision and speed as any armored beast.

Then he changed tones and told me that he didn't really comprehend the Germans. They were pleasant but not friendly, happy to take his marks but unhappy about his uniform, his professionalism, his fact. He had the best time when, on days off, he dressed civvy and drove down into Bavaria, away from our bivouacs.

"They don't like us," he summated flatly. "We spend a lot of money, and they don't like us. No fraternization."

I asked if the whores were excepted.

"They're mostly Americans too," he answered correctly, "and *I* don't like *them*."

"Ahem," I tried. "Certainly the German army [*Die Landswehr*] must appreciate what we're doing here."

"Nope," he said. "They're crummy soldiers; just look at 'em. Good cadres, bad recruits; it's involuntary for them, and they hate it. Drugs and stuff."

I listened and speculated. I think I even dreamed about the Tunnel of Love that first night. Then again, being buried alive is called a nightmare. I was trying to put *der Liebestunnel* together with what I'd seen of arisen Germany and fancied about our bug-out war plans. The tunnel didn't fit. And neither did the lone swastika eagle and the local antipathy to our boys.

Weren't we here defending Germany from the reds? Perhaps gratitude was overmuch, but tolerance required more than taking your money and grinning. So? Why hadn't we taken down the swastika eagle and cleaned out the Tunnel of Love? Why were we here until we were needed and then bug out? And what to make of this astounding opinion from straight-arrow Bunyan that the *Landswehr* was crummy? Germans bad soldiers?

Mostly, though, my curiosity was fantastic, since it was my intuition that the mystery about the new Germany could only be solved irrationally. This palaver isn't trickery; I truly didn't know then.

"Look beneath the surface," whispered Marcus Aurelius, "for the intrinsic value." Okay, Emperor, I responded. What was in the Tunnel of Love?

4

Bunyan had to leave me the next morning for an officers call at Eighth Division HQ back at Frankfurt. He was apologetic about my having to spend the weekend alone, but this was monthly duty.

"Well, the brass likes it," he explained. "We sit at long tables, and then there's dancing. I think they're trying to be like the British—you know, *esprit,* those regimental messes, pass the brandy with expensive cigars. We don't do it very well; we like beer and rock, and hardly anybody smokes."

I packed him off and went for breakfast in town. I was content to wander around, send cards to Mom and Dad and my other brothers, maybe take in Hollywood *auf Deutsch.* Also there was Frau Jodl at Nuremberg.

That sunny easy day in clean quaint Schweinfurt led to a grim but incomplete discovery about the Tunnel of Love. Tip had forgotten, until Bunyan mumbled it on our driving tour, that Schweinfurt ("Pig's Crossing") was where the Third Reich's ball-bearing factories had been. That the Allied air forces had pounded it flat once upon a time. I thought nothing more of ball bearings until I wandered into a beautiful bookstore after lunch. I spotted several glossy volumes with B-17 pinups on their dust jackets. Schweinfurt, I read quickly, had suffered a black weekday once already. It's still called Black Tuesday hereabouts, summer 1943, when our Flying Fortresses came in a V of V's and did murder.

You might recall that black weekday if you've ever seen Clark Gable, Walter Pidgeon, Van Johnson, Brian Donlevy and Edward Arnold in a B&W flick called *Command Decision* (1949). It's a claustrophobic movie, all reaction shots of the strain of command, but it bites harder when you accept that it's based upon a genuine event. The plot was sci-fi/spy. Our Eighth Air Force convinced itself that it could shorten the war by sacrificing hundreds of our flying children in order to destroy the Third Reich's ball-bearing factories at Schweinfurt am Main.

1 1 6

I recall now that the first four times I saw *Command Decision* as a kid it made sense to me. Shorten the war, maximum effort, pound the Nazis, bite your mustache, Clark, attack—and when the first day's recon photos show the target was surrounded, not buried, go back, go back again, rubble the rubble. When I was an older kid, the 1972 Christmas bombing of Hanoi/Haiphong harbor (our B-52s pounding peasants hiding in concrete baskets) alerted me that strategic bombing isn't sage tactics. The next four times I saw Clark Gable wincing as yet another B-17 crash-landed in England, or Walter Pidgeon calculating losses by not trying to count aloud with his fingers times ten, it occurred to me slowly that, well, WWII was different (this is the peacenik line), sacrifice meant something then, terror-bombing was proper for devils who worshiped genocide.

That bright Friday in Schweinfurt, sashaying along the serene Bavarian cobblestone square, admiring the exquisite barometers in the windows and sipping sumptuous beer, it finally came to me that I had missed the dark joke of that movie all these years. More, since it was loosely based upon fact—the double strike air raids against Regensburg and Schweinfurt on Tuesday, August 17, 1943—I had also missed the weird proposition in the Eighth Air Force's daring. Fly six hundred bombers naked beyond fighter cover to bomb fairy-tale Bavaria? For ball bearings? To shorten the war? What?

I detoured back down to the train depot to inspect where the factories had been. I found there was still a plant there; it made machine tools now and it looked solidly built on stone foundations, efficiently sited across from the rail lines. I stepped back and considered how unusually flat the railyard and factory compound were. Bavaria rolled. This was potato pancake. I stared at the stone foundations and fancied I could see where the old stone met the new. The pictures in the glossy books were no help figuring what happened; they were mostly snapshots of craters filled with craters and many numb civilians trying to remember they were breathing.

Command Decision is the Hollywood version of the story from our side. I was now standing on their side. I studied the high sky and tried to hear the B-17 engines in geometric combat boxes at twenty-four, twenty-five and twenty-six thousand feet, see the dustballs of flak, imagine what I would look like through a bombsight.

Ball bearings? Who's kidding? It was summer 1943. The Russians had thrown the Nazis back at Stalingrad, the British had thrown the Nazis back at El Alamein, our guys were driving across North Africa. Yes, the war was millions of casualties short of finished, but ball bearings? That's esoteric sci-fi/spy, same as targeting the nailmakers to get at the king amount his charger. All our brave children dead or missing for metal marbles? Huh? I couldn't figure it. General Curtis LeMay led that first Black Tuesday raid, a strange dark hero who would go on to fight the Cold War with SAC and consternate common sense by running on George Wallace's ticket in 1968. I wondered, in my Bavarian consternation, if there was explanation with tough, brave, self-sacrificing, ruthless and finally wrongheaded LeMay. Did we do it because we wanted to show we could be wrongheaded? Not for ball bearings but because we wanted to show that even when we were wrongheaded there was nowhere to hide, that America, right or wrong, could and would heave machinery and men like spittle until we won?

At the same time, the Tunnel of Love did make better sense to me now. I had thought it an extravagant, extraneous air raid shelter, built with slave labor and fitted out with linoleum, Bauhaus chairs, chandeliers(?), among the ordnance pyramids and stripped-down Messerschmitts. I had pictured an aphrodisiacal gallery, hanky-panky splayed on 88 barrels.

Now I understood it had been the local Führerbunker, the only safe place during those black weekdays when the earth moved upward. For that first Black Tuesday had been followed that fall of 1943 and several times in 1944 with many more black weekdays of combat boxes of B-17s, B-24s, B-26s, Lancasters. Our side didn't just goose Pig's Crossing one summer's day; we came back and back to stamp out its goose steps.

I wondered who got privileges in the Tunnel of Love. The panzer regiment would have been in Russia. Could there have been enough Luftwaffe families to fill a kilometer? No. The civilians must have had lifeboat access, VIPs first and last, many children. Okay, I thought, out there in modern Bavaria were many fortyish farmers who had vivid memories of horrible days in a strange chamber while the bombs fell and the rear guard made whoopee with grass widows.

Der Liebestunnel had been a nightmare, I reasoned, now mostly gone.

My dark thoughts returned to me. On our side: Why had America launched bombers at Schweinfurt?

On their side: Why was *der Liebestunnel* still intact? The mystery of it. If our army didn't care for the grimy labor, why hadn't the now prosperous chamber of commerce cleaned it up? West Germany had remanufactured itself, dug up each unexploded bomb no matter the danger, melted down every 88, rebuilt cities in place with a curator's meticulousness when possible. Schweinfurt's town hall bragged about its age. Nothing was to have been left of the Third Reich. *Der* "not doable" *Liebestunnel* was either an inexplicable freak or a bone-rattling clue.

5

Yes, this is a mystery yarn about Germany. Don't take notes; all the clues are coming back, and in Sensurround. I've shelled, rocketed, bombed and strafed you with details because I'm fighting back, and my adversary is what's in that Tunnel of Love. It was important to me to find out, and if it's not to you, maybe I haven't told enough jokes so far, maybe also I'm carried away by Marcus Aurelius's recommendation to dig, dig, dig for the intrinsic values, to solve the case with overheated words rather than the fire that has never worked permanently.

I rang Frau Jodl that evening, after watching Eddie Murphy razzing Beverly Hills in German made me feel homesick for silliness. We chatted entirely in colloquial German about my serendipitous week, and she actually said "*Jawohl*, Herr Paine" when I hinted at her driving up from Nuremberg and showing me the Bavarian hinterland.

She arrived Saturday at exactly 9 A.M., in a maroon Audi that clashed with her coloring. "My uncle's car," she announced. "He's trying to bribe me with one if I don't go back to Africa. My mother's put him up to it. What a deal!"

Frau Jodl was a brisk flaxenhead, with big shoulders, many curves and pale blue skin that must have harried her in Africa. That day she wore climbing tweeds, and I soon discovered why. We darted up the splendid cupcake hills to the foot of a famous brewery/monastery, Kreuzberg Rhon. The tourist buses up from Munich certified that this was what Bavarians considered weekend glee. We climbed up to the holy Gothic masonry. I balked at the crowd. There was an outdoor bazaar hawking lederhosen, mugs and trinkets, and inside the hall the long tables were packed by tipsy folk scarfing down black beer and singing wanderlusting favorites.

"Ach, Tip, you must try it," she said. "It's good luck, and this beer is famous. A love potion. On such a day, we don't have to sing, and no polkas; we can just drink a little and climb up to the crucifix."

The love potion line worked, of course; calling anything such does. Call even abominable herbal tea a love potion, and any idiot will swoon. The climb worked on me too. We went straight up a staircase to heaven, and by the top I was breathless to lean on her. The prize at the peak was a life-size crucifix. Couples carrying discreet blankets were scattering into the woodline. That was not for me, never is; as a salesman, I obey all rules. I sat primly beside Frau Jodl and admired the vast view of other woodlines shot through with lust. The far villages were orange-roofed matchboxes, darkening and brightening as cheery clouds passed over them.

Agrarian Bavaria, if you haven't ever wanted to go there, makes "picturesque" an insult. I glanced into the nearby woods. It was too cool for them to undress. I thought, It must be comical, but whose style isn't?

Frau Jodl was acting impatiently intimate: "Just put your arm around me, then."

Right. I distracted her with patter, then thought to ask what was most on my mind. Had she ever heard of Schweinfurt am Main's Tunnel of Love?

She shrugged and shivered. "It's cold up here," she tried.

I started to tell her why I cared about the Tunnel of Love.

She wouldn't have it. "You know, Tip, no one cares about that time anymore. My papa doesn't care either. It was a long time ago. No one here today was born then."

I asked if this meant it was a new Germany.

She surprised me. "I don't care if it is or not. I was born here; I don't live here. Politics is shit. You Americans, you already own everything; why are you unhappy? You, my darling Tip, why are you unhappy? So free and rich. You remind me of someone I knew once. A terrorist. It's not funny. He's in jail now, forever, with his unhappiness. I don't think about Germany or any other country. In Africa, people are happy to eat once, just once! For me, you work hard and make things happier wherever you are."

Good speech, I thought. A kinder man would've shut up. Tip asked who the terrorist was.

"He was a fascist!" she snapped. "He tried to blow up a bank! He kidnapped two girls and killed one! What does it matter now? He was the people's hero one day, so he claimed, and the next he was telling the police crazy stories about everyone he knew. That's your fascist. Heartless, brainless gangsters. Crazy, sick, crazy, crazy, crazy."

I waited to see if there was more. Then I asked if the gangster had sold her out too; was that why she was in Africa?

She leaned close. "You do make movies, don't you? I forgot a moment. You're not a terrorist, you're Hollywood."

I said I was certainly guilty of Hollywood.

She laughed. "No, no one sold me, Tip. Is that what you think? He sold only gangsters like himself. And now they're gone." She punched me and giggled. "Maybe they're in your tunnel, how's that?"

We climbed down from Kreuzberg Rhon better friends, that's certain, and while we raced off to the local resort of Bad Kissingen for more sights, I decided I was in love with her for today. She wasn't my style, true, but a good weave nonetheless, and she wore Bad Kissingen so well.

It's a village like a Disneyland for world-weary adults. Bad Kissingen was once famous for its mineral baths, the old-fashioned version of a health club. Haydn, Bach and Mozart are still playing the local bandshell. Beethoven must have stumbled upon it in his forays and fled its charms instantly for the woods, tripping over fellow curmudgeon Goethe. Everything you can dream up that is bucolic and civilized about Bavaria is replicated there, and there's a casino too. Convinced? The gardens are splendid, the swans are ethereal, the shops are baubles, the hoteliers are midwives, the churches are rococo apologia.

As we strolled this paradise, my soul started to waver. I was thinking anti-Tip, treacherous notions such as John Calvin was a French jackass; what was wrong with popism was the Italians; America was lost over the edge of the flat earth; mine eyes have seen the glory, and it's Bavarian. We supped on veal, and the meat weakened me the more, along with the *liebfraumilch* and Frau Jodl's maidenly affections. I hallucinated that I should quit common sense, propose happiness to this African angel, jettison four hundred years of Puritanism and seek the banns in a Catholic church.

I even yanked wary Marcus Aurelius into this make-believe. He wrote, "Once dismiss the view you take, and you are out of danger . . . you have rounded the foreland and all is calm, a tranquil sea, a tideless haven."

So then, Tip, I thought, renounce your German-bashing, your Bavarian-entrail-stirring. Sure, Hitler found a tideless haven in Bavaria and didn't exactly have to press-gang his barbarous crew from the local farmboys. Sure, Bavaria was a home to Nazism like Leningrad to Bolshevism, Hollywood to cokism. But that's gone! No one young enough to copulate standing up was alive back then.

I held on to my convenient counterreformation as I held Frau Jodl's waist. "Do you gamble too?" she asked, pointing the way to the casino. I made a joke about losing a coin toss in my protopast. "I think you're a lucky man. Let's see." We tried my luck in the casino, the champagne tried my synapses, and then we tried flesh again in a baroque chapel of a hotel suite overlooking a small green.

Trite consequences. Frau Jodl was another lullaby but nonmaternal for a moment. She was too much of a woman for me, yet I can fake it with the rest if I've convinced myself I'm being wickedly matter-of-fact. I did non-nonperform and was then ruined forever on German nurses when she casually sponged both of us clean. It feels good; it's also a strange love rite, not my style.

"You must sleep on your side, *Liebchen*," she instructed me as we settled down in goose feathers. "It's better for your heart and breathing." I thrashed around. There was more instruction. "Don't sleep nude; ring the porter for a nightshirt. It's chilly in the morning."

I grumbled and made a crack. "Think I need a nightcap?"

She was brusque. "You can sleep any way you want to; I'm just thinking of your health. You don't wear enough clothes for the mountain air, and your muscles are knots from the way you hold yourself. At least relax in your sleep."

She was off on another medley of lullabies. I listened like a postop patient; no nightshirt for me, but I did try to sleep on my side. This torture lasted until she slept—I'm too big to rest unless flat on my backside like a corpse burdened with a soul—and then the soft bed attacked my spine.

I confess I get even moodier after sex. Also I'd been dreaming badly since landfall in Germany, and Thursday night's Bavarian nightmare about *der Liebestunnel* still harried me. By first light, I was fitfully visionary. I slipped out sideways and she, a light sleeper like Clara Barton, instructed, "Drink some water, don't smoke your pipe, cover your shoulders, sit by the window and you'll soon come back to bed. I'm here if you want me."

Many fine fellows I know would regard this sort of woman as a queen. She directed her energy right at my body, and she wasn't a shirker about the soul either. For me she was a threat alert. I escaped like Beethoven from blissful Bonaparte into the sitting room. I most enjoyed myself standing smoking, uncovered, at the window. It was going to be another *wunderbar* day. The long first rays had reached the green below. There were no sounds but the hungry birds and a brook nearby, no color but the white painted stones and that hunter's green perfection grass enjoys minutes before dawn. I was cranky enough to stare and stare as I puffed and puffed.

My anti-Tip mood was gone. I stood a naked Puritan and scowled. I was chasing the Tunnel of Love. What was it? I couldn't solve it. I needed help. So I called on a make-believe friend of mine, a completely vain alter ego whom I call Holmes Paine.

More grandiosely, I fancied that the spirit of Sherlock Holmes was close by me. He had fallen into Reichenbach Falls, and I made believe his spirit had bubbled here to me at Bad Kissingen. So then I was Puritan Holmes Paine on the trail of something that I'd heard, seen, touched or imagined this last week that must be, must be, the answer to my investigation.

The crime was notorious. You know it by Dr. Watson's title, "The Case of the Third Reich." Forty years later the crime was well exposed, the victims greatly mourned, the criminals condemned. Holmes Paine was tracking a cold trail for something Scotland Yard had missed, as if Lestrade had leaped to the obvious at the Nuremberg Trials, nabbed all the correct devils, but in his righteous haste botched the trail. Netting the right gang, Lestrade had missed the mastermind. My intuition was that Moriarty, the anthropomorphized source of all evil, had slipped away again. I wanted to get him, it, whatever it was.

"When you have eliminated the impossible," the incomparable S. Holmes once preached to Dr. Watson, "whatever remains, however improbable, must be the truth."

All right, Holmes Paine summarized obediently, the eliminated impossibles were: That Marcus Aurelius didn't waste his time on the Danube trying to pacify the German barbarians. That those same barbarians didn't eventually pacify Rome forever. That, skipping fifteen hundred years of skulls and bones and what horror the Reformation and its counter caused, Germany didn't rise up out of imperial dunderheadedness to try to pacify every country on both sides of it in the First World War. That Hitler didn't happen. And (I was being meticulous) that our Eighth Air Force didn't pound Schweinfurt flat for nothing but ball bearings. Most of all, that the Tunnel of Love doesn't mean something. Those were all impossibles.

I, Holmes Paine, tried to locate the improbable and lost the scent again.

I called on Marcus Aurelius, more of his stress management. The one I like best is boilerplate for him and all us Stoics: "How's my soul's helmsman doing? This is everything. All else, within and beyond my control, is bones and vapors."

There were some very fetching bones and vapors in the nearby bedroom, but to prove to you I am a low-slung bloodhound, I report that instead of quitting my nuttiness I stayed with it. I stared down at the green. Perfectly civilized Bad Kissingen. Perfectly pastoral Bavaria. Perfectly charitable Frau Jodl. And then I saw what was right in front of me on the green below my window.

The green was used for croquet, probably for the touring English —who else plays that silly game? Someone had missed out collecting all the croquet wickets. I spied the forgotten wickets because the light was better and they were white.

That's it. The improbable solution: croquet wickets. All at once I'd solved two millennia of Germany, our bombing runs on all those black weekdays in the past and our armored cavalry deployment here waiting for all those black weekdays in the future. Most especially I'd solved the Tunnel of Love.

I know this sounds crazy, that sleepy, moody Tip could spot simple white croquet wickets on a trim Bavarian lawn and know that he'd solved the case. I'm reporting it as it happened and skipping how I'd done it. It was an improbable and farfetched solution, yet it was the truth. And it all came down to the Tunnel of Love. I knew what *der Liebestunnel* was and why they hadn't cleaned it out and what was in it.

6

You want to know, and I'm going to tell you, but my way. This isn't fast food; I do that stuff in my screenplays. This is Tip the wandering misanthrope, and I don't give a hoot if you leave off. (You're a badly read citizen if you do, and I wouldn't spend four minutes trapped in a first-class compartment with your excellent shoes, hired aroma, healthy aversions.) It's sharp-eyed readers I want along with me now, because this is a fussy, bookish case before the bar of history.

I gave you a sneaky hint earlier when I said I dress like a croquet player—whites on whites, pastel tie. This was a falsehood. I actually dress the baggy Yankee jurist at the florist's, chitchat in blue wool over the anemones. I only wear white when someone's wed or the opera is unavoidably ridiculous.

Tip the jurist now refers you to the common-law grandfather of us sci-fi/spy boys, H. G. Wells, who outraged every Victorian but Mark Twain and Bernard Shaw.

You know Wells as a shopworn scrivener, Boom-Boom H.G. with his Martians, air wars, atomic bomb, knee-jerk Darwinism and that nonpareiled Time Machine. However, Wells, after the first war had softened his mind and then the 1920s had hardened it again, bashing Fordized America, the Anglican Church, Whitehall the Insufferable and Winston the Inedible, after all that Wells got prophetic again in the 1930s, the age of the despots and their flacks right and left. Wells only flacked for Wells, and in 1936, in his insatiably bitter seventies, he published a novella that is the scariest little book I've ever read after Job. It's entitled *The Croquet Player*.

The unnamed narrator is vacationing on the French coast with his noble aunt the suffragette peacenik. He is a professional croquet player, the one thing he cares to do well in a silly world: hit a round ball with a flat mallet head through wickets on trim grass and only when it's clement. The Croquet Player thinks his dear aunt sweat-minded with her causes for disarmament, one-worldism, peace at last. At luncheon one day the Croquet Player chances to converse with an intense Englishman, who, though on holiday too, seems strangely candid. All English feign eccentricity. This one, the Croquet Player thinks, promotes his centeredness, and he has a story to tell.

The Englishman says that he has come from a wet rural reach of Britain, where the local parsonage was the best supper table in walking distance. The parson was gentlemanly, none of that Methodist love or dissenter scolding. The parson's wife was loving and a reasonable cook. The parson's one love was mankind, and his hobbies were walks with God almighty and local lore. Slowly, however, the Englishman heard tell at the table over many weeks that the best people in the village were becoming homicidal. Wives were stabbed, children vanished, clerks turned shotguns on other clerks. The parson was baffled by this mayhem. No one had ever come to service, yet he had always known they were too busy being good Christians out there. Their new deviltry was a puzzle. The parson wrote the bishop for instruction.

One other fact emerged to the Englishman at the parson's table. There was a local famous bog, bottomless and grim as it should be, and recently some local boys had dared close enough to discover bones had bubbled up from its maw. These bones had come to the parson's attention, and he was pleased when he ascertained by correspondence that the British Museum was interested. They were Neanderthal bones, evidence that this sublimely wretched neighborhood had always been a thriving settlement.

The Englishman finished his tale to the Croquet Player morbidly. The parson's wife became adulterous with the bishop. The parson murdered her in a passionate rage. The Englishman, deprived of his table, planned to move on. But first he swung by the bog at dusk. What he saw terrified him. He watched as vapors rose up from the bubbling bones and formed the image of a gigantic skull, mouth open — the rising of a death's-head.

The unflappable Croquet Player was flapped by the Englishman's tale. He arrived at luncheon the next day hoping to learn more of this bog. The Englishman didn't appear. Inquiries were made — indisposed? departed? The answer arrived from a local doctor at another table. The Englishman was his patient at the sanitarium, and, to the doctor's certainty, the Englishman had been here many years, was very mad but not dangerous, and hadn't been out of the care of doctors since he was a lad. The Croquet Player faced the truth. Everything he had heard was make-believe, wasn't it?

Wells wrote *The Croquet Player* just as the Hitlerites were rising up out of the bogs of Bavaria. It wasn't some idle romance to him. He knew that what was happening in bucolic Germany was coming fair England's way. Wells was scared, and he meant to frighten his countrymen and women to action. The message was "It Can Happen

Here." You will remember that his message failed. Wells wrote a good book that told the truth in make-believe, and very few listened. Mass murder followed.

Fast forward to Tip. That Bavarian morning, watching the sun light up the croquet wickets on the green, I was scared too. Soon enough I mean to frighten you about the Tunnel of Love.

Frau Jodl did get me back to bed that morning, there were more happy commands and wet obligations, we breakfasted easily, attended mass for my curiosity, drove back down to Schweinfurt most satisfied, and I kept shut throughout about my discovery.

Bunyan was returned in all his American glory. I was proud to introduce him and noted Frau Jodl's smile at his size and earnest politeness. I had bragged to her that there were tens of thousands more like him back in "greedy" America. Bunyan's such a treat to spring upon European prejudice.

"You're the little brother?" she said.

I corrected: "Baby brother."

She laughed. "How? What do they feed you?"

Bunyan shook her hand. "Nice to meet you, ma'am," he said, then in German, "It's a pleasure, Frau Jodl."

We invited her to luncheon at the officers club. Frau Jodl declined, saying she was best back to Nuremberg. I kissed her farewell at the car and she kissed back. "When you get to Africa, find me through the Red Cross," she said. "It'll be fun there too, and I can show you, Tip, what happiness is, true happiness." The German is *die Freude,* or joy, and it was part of her wardrobe. She was a splendid adventuress. I missed her immediately and then put her in my pantheon, while Bunyan and I drove to the club.

Bunyan told tales en route and sweetly blushed re Frau Jodl. "She's nice, huh?" he remarked. "A nurse too?"

I told tales and did not blush. After luncheon we strolled out into the brigade HQ grounds to provide me a close look at the war machines. And also at this end of the Tunnel of Love.

The well-armed sentries saluted Bunyan correctly. I liked how keen they were, faced by my baby brother, who is a princely centurion and takes the army, his duty and our country very seriously. I was the frail child here, he was the grownup.

Nearby there was one M-1 Abrams blockbuster tank out of its cage, being brushed and pampered by its crew. When you first stand next to a main battle tank you will know that war is crazy work. What else but craziness could make human beings build, man and attack with such a monster? could make other human beings try to get in its way? It's a ground-eater; they keep rubber mufflers on the tank treads when using the paved roads. Bunyan explained that when they wound up its jet engine it screamed.

"They get speeding tickets," Bunyan joked. "When they open it up on rubber treads it can clock ninety clicks, and the MPs don't like that. Scares the heck out of the cows."

"Brave cows," I said. "Would do worse than that to me."

Imagine this one microchip-brained creature coming at you at speed, then consider that it knows where you are and can swat you like a pest without stopping. Then imagine a company of them, a division's worth, covered above by our Blackhawk helicopters, which are simply octane dragons. I could see from one tank why the war planners fancy themselves medievalists. The ages are dark. Chivalry is losing to witchcraft. Every field is a joust, every contender sports treads, everybody dies.

The other armored knights were parked behind a meaningless cyclone fence. Bunyan explained that when they sound a practice scramble, the tank crews bat out of hell from their mortality to get to their creatures before they move, because they don't wait. The tank platoons fan outward *through* the fence and into the woods.

"Five minutes," Bunyan explained, "this place is empty. They give the rest of us ten minutes to find our transport. After that, you're a casualty. I didn't make it once, and never again; it's bad news."

I asked Bunyan if he'd been up to the No Man's Land on the border.

"Sure," he said, "but just for a look-see. And it's not called No Man's Land. It's the Frontier of Freedom."

"Correction acknowledged," I obeyed.

"They camp them three weeks out of four up there," said Bunyan. "It's tough on them, tougher on their wives and kids; they're mostly nineteen-year-olds, first time away from home. Brutal—the divorce rate is brutal. Up on the border they play chicken in the rain with the hostiles, and they're loading live rounds when they do."

It was time to try out my solution of the case. First I asked Bunyan if that chicken game on the border was entertainment: You guys are bugging out when it comes, right?

"Affirmative," he said. "The guys caught up on the border are KIA. We've got assembly areas to get to, then we do what we're told."

I asked my last question before I, doing the Croquet Player's work, was absolutely Holmes Paine certain. "Where's the entrance to the Tunnel of Love?'"

Bunyan wasn't sure. He waved out to the former airfield where our tanks now awaited Armageddon. "They sealed it up," he said. "It must be there somewhere, because it runs that way." He pointed east toward the old panzer regiment barracks and that swastika eagle. He sensed I was up to something foolish; he asked, "Why?"

I told Bunyan, and now I tell you. *Der Liebestunnel* is a bog of Bavaria. There must be others. I know where this one is and will mark it on your map the way it is targeted on our fire-coordinate grid design. Bunyan's armored cavalry isn't at Schweinfurt to fight the Russians, nor is our Blackhorse there as defenders of Germany. They are occupiers; we and the Russians are allied occupiers. The forty-year-old Cold War had blinded me to the original challenge when the Allies moved in. Our children are part of the army of occupation, and the Brits, Belgians, Italians are too (the French crapped out, and good Gallic riddance), and so are the Russians over the border, squatting with all their T-80 weight on Prussia. WWIII is coming on German soil, that's correct, but we and the reds aren't going to be fighting to protect Germany. *We're going to be fighting what's inside Germany itself.* That's where the bogs of blackness are. Marcus Aurelius knew it, we and the Russians know it. Germany is Europe's blackness.

Don't fuss at me. You want to forgive and forget, you're a saint. I'm not. Don't give me that Germany-the-nation-of-enlightened-geniuses argument, citing Mozart, Beethoven, Mahler, Goethe, Heine, Rilke and Mann. You know you get the very highs with the very lows. And don't try that banality-of-evil palaver on me. Evil is a monster, and it's cunning, immortal and long-brooding. Lastly I'm not listening to the most-of-them-weren't-born-then brief, because a shrewd ancient source assures me that wickedness is visited upon the sons until the third and fourth generation, and forty years is merely one ejaculation. Every land must have its bogs of blackness, I agree, but Germany has what law enforcement calls a long list of priors. What's down inside the Tunnel of Love is Black Monday, Tuesday, Wednesday, Thursday and Friday, and what's keeping the blackness penned up is our armored cavalry on guard over the exits.

This is why they never could clean it up—you can't extinguish evil; that's theological absurdity. It's what our Eighth Air Force was really after in those desperate raids at Schweinfurt back forty years of black days—Curtis LeMay and our bombing children were not wrongheaded after all; they were on target and brave beyond the rational. It's also why that single swastika eagle remains on a pillar at Schweinfurt—it's a marker buoy for our bomb- and gunsights. It's also why the Germans don't like our army's boys and girls and why the German boys are such crummy soldiers these days. We keep them crummy. We're a combat boot on their shoddy intrinsic values, and as long as the money and luck hold, we're not letting them get up again.

The Tunnel of Love is fleshless, vaporous Third Reich. It's loving itself and breeding down there. If you're not scared by this, then I guess you're one of those who say, "It Can't Happen Here Again." I offer comfort to those who know it can. Bunyan and his compatriots have got it trapped shut from both ends for now.

However, I am Stoic enough to know that good and bad come in cycles. Nothing is lost, especially not blackness. When it comes up out of the tunnel again, the blackness will have another novel jingoistic name, but it will be familiar to Marcus Aurelius. When it comes up again, our armored cavalry is bugging out and our brass is calling down all the ordnance in our locker. God help us all if it's not enough.

"How's my soul's helmsman doing?" Marcus Aurelius asked once upon a hellish time in the German quagmire. "This is everything. All else, within and beyond my control, is bones and vapors."

I answer, Our soul's helmsman is doing just fine, sir, patrolling the blackness, the black, black bones and vapors.

Before I found the Tunnel of Love I worried that the good guys might be overlooking some rotten threat. At least now I know, as the good guys do, where some worst of those bones are waiting and that vapor is wafting. Brave Bunyan faced that gigantic death's-head (*der Totenkopf*) every dusk. We croquet players out here in the land of the free have our job too. We are folly itself—hit a round ball with a flat mallet head on a trim lawn and only when it's clement. It's a silly world, and let's keep it that way as long as possible. I'm a well-paid fool.

What did Bunyan make of my solution? He giggled, and I loved him for that giggle. We looked for a movie, but he'd seen Eddie Murphy already, and the rest of the local offerings looked anti-American to me. So we rented his favorite VCR tape that summer, *The Terminator*, featuring a southern Bavarian ape as the evil that won't quit until it's crushed by American machines.

Bunyan's laughter at the movie made me relax, and I trust it relaxes Marcus Aurelius's soul too. Our best children are still on station, Roman wise man, and our Pax Americana has a few more good years until our glory goes fleeting too.

5

Writers Are Curs

1

I t's time to admit that I don't like writers. It's not their artsy lip and pet parrot called Eternal Verities, their fussbudgety prejudices and lazy labor, their cunning libidos, boastful cowardice, typeset self-pity. No, Tip, be commonsensical right away. *Yes it is.* And that they know what these allegations mean without having to touch a dictionary, yet they wouldn't know the truth about themselves if it tried to give them the wrong change for twenty dollars.

You might know some of them and have decided they are admirable folk, sweet like sacramental grape juice, long-suffering in their gentle poverty, somehow wise with their easy chatter and wide knowledge of brave subjects. I'm telling you don't believe any of it. They spend most of their three-day week with their shabby students or shabbier appliances, admit to trendy music no honest teenager has cared about since Elvis (and there's a new group who think Elvis was

133

a writer), cash paychecks like flood victims, eat the kind of tedious food that health columnists approve, claim to be persecuted by relatives and exempt from taxes, identify with every prisoner they never met and especially with the guilty ones, and regard their homebody lives as some crystal ball that can do melodramatic special effects the twentieth century left behind when its first stupid war strangled reason.

Worst of all to me, they are also bad citizens, routinely ignorant of virtue, equality and independence. They *seldom* vote, they give two-figured money to pretty vertebrates or professional scab-pickers, they mock every president of our Republic except Lincoln, and they trendily remember the Gadget, Hiss, Checkers, U-2, Bay of Pigs, grassy knoll, Christmas Bombing, Deep Throat, Desert One, contras and Dan Quayle as equivalent conspiracies (and treat none of this shopping list with the irony they tirelessly apply to divorce stories). As for their labor, which they call work—now and again, if their grades are in or their pretty second spouses keep the brats absent or their boozy New York editors call to flatter them, they fuss with underpowered computers to finish the same old sentiment in a week or five thousand words, whatever happens first. The rest of their feeble lives are dependent upon right thinking—the right videos, right tooth care, right aphorisms, right attitude about menses.

It's as predictably safe a course as the *Consumer's Guide,* with an agenda like UNICEF and winter holidays at Mom's house or not. Then there are those summertime weeks at state-funded campuses— these junkets are called writers workshops without smirking—in order to blab about writing to mall shoppers, mothers in white eye shadow and the occasional true trade unionist whose collection of sci-fi/spy books makes him the ideal taxpayer yet whom the admirable, sweet, impoverished, wise, glib, bold, snot-nosed writers shun like the GOP.

That's how I met the writer Bohdan Galster, at one of those workshop scams. He is a *literary person,* of course; that is what is meant when someone is called a *writer* these anxious days. I won't define "literary" for you, it can't be done, but if surrounding a suspect is all that's left of frontier justice's hanging the rascal, then I'll say that "literary" can also be read as sincere, enlightened, spiritual, college-prep—something like the high school homework we nonlits didn't do, can't recall, still hate anyway. Significantly Bohdan Galster is a famous famous writer writer literary literary person person—name droppable and reputation undeletable—who dazzles all the usual suspects. He is also, Tip's opinion, a braggart, a lecher, a coward, an offense to every family value urged by our media and their Kremlin, and a fellow who it was my poor luck to suffer, curse to gravesite and ghoulishly try to kick in. I do feel guilty about that last bit, and I'm fairly certain it's why I'm recording my stupidity. If there's a lesson in this folly for me, it's that when you take revenge upon someone you despise, stab in the back in the dark with a power tool and make sure death is done before you get out of town.

(Also, the devil dwells in this yarn's details as elsewhere, so keep alert, Tip construction the next half mile, pass at your usual risk.)

It was tropical Ohio in June, and it was my third trip to the Midwest since I could pay for these things. I had been hired on by the same con artists who were paying Bohdan Galster. Both of us were to teach a fiction workshop to nice Americans who should have spent their money on baseball, chocolate or air-cooled diversions. It was stupid of me to go, to take Buckeye tax money, to play a role that the mind doctors call inauthentic and mother-pandering. It was Ohio that persuaded me, since my dad's family is Buckeye back to the Revolution. I am purposefully named Tommy "Tip" Paine not for that 1776 big-mouthed firebrand republican (who's no relation and neither a hero in America in these anxious days nor a hero in the GOP but whom I openly admire) but rather for an 1864 hotheaded Buckeye bugler (who is a relation, my great-grandfather, and who helped put the torch to the South with Sherman's XX Corps, burning out another branch of my dad's family at Milledgeville, but then that was a sincerely stupid war).

Still I shouldn't have gone along. I'm no writer, no teacher, no colleague. I've already told you what I am. I'm a traveling salesman just like my dad, only unlike him I don't sell anything useful; my samples are make-believe and foolish, giving the folk what they want while stalled in air travel, roasting on beaches, sleepless against pillows. Yet I let my rude sci-fi/spy books prop me up, and there I was meeting the famous famous Bohdan Galster (BG) at the faculty orientation.

"You're the spook?" a fierce bearded fellow started. It was himself, BG, but I didn't know for a few moments. I was concentrating on the spook crack. Spook is slang for spy, hireling of the CIA, secret policeman, fascist swine. That he thought me a spook, I assumed, was because of the independent movie producer who broadcasted the falsehood that I was a veteran of the American intelligence community and who subsequently turned my first book into a modest summertime "giggle," as my Hollywood agent says.

I introduced myself anyway.

That's when BG gave me his surname and asserted, "I'm BG." I'd heard his name before—on tv—and since it was easy to assume he liked being treated as profound, I obliged while stating the obvious yes, pleased-to-meet-you, connect-a-dot patter.

"That's right; we're going to be working together," returned BG. "You take the boys, and I'll take the girls." He thought this funny and picked at his white chest hairs. He wouldn't look at me. At the time I was simple enough to believe he was distracted by the women in the room.

I know now that it was the size difference between us and that he played chess seriously. He was a Latvian giant whom God almighty made a beer keg. I am not tall, not heavy, not very clumsy, but God made me a giant mongrel anyway and then made sure I can't drink, dance, eat curry or rightly appreciate females of any species, or play decent chess (I do smoke a pipe, most wrong fashion, thank goodness).

"I haven't read your books," said BG. "Have you read mine?"

I lied, and he let it go.

"My wife saw one of your movies," he said. "She said it was gory and dull."

As ever, I apologized for making money on trash.

"Are you religious?" asked BG.

I said I wasn't even Irish.

"I am," responded BG. "Most spooks are pious, yeah? But they don't understand sacraments like marriage. I'm..."

I didn't hear the rest because a redheaded graduate student—who was named (I kid you not) Fredericka but who called herself (I kid you not) Riki—moved close enough for BG to grab and nuzzle in a way I would only permit my late dog, who was canine but no cur.

Later that evening, Riki the redhead got free of BG and approached me again for a chat. She was in charge of the workshop and the dozens of suckers who had signed up for it. She was also willing to brief me on BG after he had departed for dinner with several female students he had already tagged as if good timber.

"He's like that all the time," Riki said. "I've seen him do his act before, at a workshop down in Austin one summer when I was researching my dissertation."

She wanted to tell me about Sonya Tolstoya, her chosen academic specialty. However, I wanted to hear more gossip about BG. I kept telling her I didn't want to be here in Ohio, that I should give the money back and run away. This kept her easy midwestern soul coming back to BG, in order to assure me I would enjoy my week with him.

"He's had three wives so far," she continued, adding that he joked of having more bastards than dependents, had a new wife, who was much younger and pregnant, and made a workshop director's life hellish, demanding two girls be brought to his room, sushi, better vodka. "Anything that sounds like a Baltic Hemingway," she quipped disapprovingly.

Riki was not only an academic but also a baby writer; so I knew she was trying to impress me with right thinking. I believed everything she said about her estranged husband, her academic dreams, her troubles with late registrants. But not about BG—the Hemingway rep re stocky, bearded, boastful, serial-marrying writers is right fashion. Riki thought him a skirt-chaser in a midlife grumble who was undeniably charismatic. There was also something vague about his scarred wartime childhood. I looked up Latvia that night and discovered a tiny Baltic state about the size of Vermont; capital city Riga; pastures and timber; chiefly Lutheran; eaten by the Russians and Germans after 1918.

I weighed all this common sense the next afternoon while I shared
a round-table classroom with BG in the university's student center/
motel. He showed himself vain, crude, habitual, domineering, gos-
sipy, slippery—in sum, a famous famous writer. We were supposed to
be sharing the teaching too; however, I sat by like a chalkboard while
BG harassed each student in turn.

"Read what you have," BG ordered a fair muscleman who said he
was on disability leave from a county fire department.

The fireman began his story of a two-alarm barn fire during a
downpour. I thought it fascinating detail, and you would too; the
fellow could not write, but what he knew opened a door.

BG stopped the story as the firemen were shooting a burning goat.
"What about the peasant who set the fire?" BG demanded. "He just
watches while they do this?" (I forgot to mention that BG has Slav-
American diction he turns on and off like bottled gas.) "You're a
fireman or a goat-killer?" challenged BG. "And where's the beautiful
farm daughter? You left out murder."

The fireman showed shame. I waited while an iron-made Oregon
woman protested that there was no peasant in the story; what beautiful farmgirl?

BG was a queen's bishop on attack. "I won't listen to hormones,
grandmother," he taunted. "There's a peasant. You don't like peasants? You're a peasant!"

The iron-made Oregon woman, a potentially gorgeous grandmother at maybe thirty, tried, "But lightning started the fire."

"Hormones!" hollered BG. "Take your pills before you come to my
class! You're a peasant, don't forget! Lightning is dumb accident!
Murder makes fire!"

She, exposed pawn, held her meaningless position. The women in
the class gazed upon BG as if he were Dustin Hoffman or, worse, a
famous famous writer.

BG directed his no-neck bishop turret at me. "Tell them about fire,
Colonel Chekist."

I blinked and translated. BG had promoted me from spook for our
side to spook for their side. "Chekist" is Russian slang for spy, hireling

of the KGB, secret policeman, fascist swine. BG was either hallucinating or thought me not worth taking out. Again, my sci-fi/spy reputation was tough to shuck in a blink. That independent movie producer lied about me by telling a half truth. I've mentioned to you before that the truth is after two years as a clerk in the army, I did spend two years as a clerk at the National Security Agency. What I haven't mentioned is that the NSA is the only truly ironic credit of my life because it meant that I had, upon entrance, passed two polygraph tests to prove that I didn't know anything secretive and then, upon exit, signed that lifetime contract called the Secrecy Oath, "never to divulge, publish or reveal by writing, conduct or otherwise" secrets I don't know. My first publisher, an impotent scoundrel, ignored this fact, and I didn't object. But then that independent movie producer got slick while advertising my first movie. Since then, my NSA clerkship had been branded on all my paperback reprints along with the New York flacks calling me a junior-varsity Nathan Hale/ William Buckley.

Easy lies work in America in these anxious days, so it was useless to object to BG that I was no spook or even to explain that if I had been such the correct terminology was much more clever—agent or ops officer or black ops or my favorite, "alleged CIA contractor." I looked at BG and mumbled some high-minded palaver that fire was a major character, that if you show it you'd better explain it or admit you can't.

"See, grandmother," snapped BG, "Colonel Paine knows about fire."

I felt spared and grinned.

BG didn't care about my explanation; he just wanted to perform, and his threats at the students and me were his way of clearing the field of competition. He rumbled into a maliciously cruel story about a barn fire in Latvia. It was a stock BG peasant yarn, but I didn't know that yet. BG was the story's hero, because he had set the barn fire when he was eight years old. The peasant neighbors beat him for it. Heroic lad BG had not cared. He had done it to impress a pubescent girl who had coquettishly bathed naked in front of him.

"I was the best lover she ever had," declared BG. "Her name was Masha, and years later she married the fire because I was unfaithful."

The class sighed, the Oregonian too.

I laughed accidentally, then covered up my face. I assumed that BG had not noticed my response. I thought him a first-rate crank, trying to solve history as if it were a fairy tale. His story was clearly make-believe, but so what? He had a strange genius, and now that I think about it, my laugh was spontaneous applause. Anybody can tell tragedy and make tears, but it takes ineffable talent to tell the tragedy of the Second World War as a fable and get laughs.

The first day's class ended after BG had salvoed into the security zones of the rest of the students. That evening I judged him while dining alone in the student center's Victorian mess hall. BG fought like a grand master, I concluded, hit the center of the board with coordinated firepower, then ground them in their disorganized panic. No flanks or pawn hoards, just major pieces and a blitz. It didn't concern him that his opponents were children, vacationing divorcées and spinsters, that the field was a land-grant university in a heat wave. Bohdan Galster was a winner. No wonder he was famous famous, sold books like high heels (I sell like cheap sneakers), had a job at a famous famous college and front-page notices, petted his handsome pectorals and never buttoned his shirt above his sternum. I wanted to like him for being such a roaring guru, but then I ran into Riki the redhead, following the post-supper poetry reading, and she ruined my make-believe camaraderie.

"I have to talk to you," Riki announced, the enjoinder I know always means trouble. Afterward, at the evening wine bibbling, amid nervous cheery students, she confided about BG. "He told me that he won't teach another day with you in the class."

I pretended to understand, a bad habit I have from mother-pandering.

Riki explained very compassionately that BG said I was a pompous prig and a threat to his soul. He had used the words "threat" and "soul." Note this, *I was a threat to his soul*. Having me around, BG had pronounced, was worse than exchanging apartments with President Nixon. There was wilder stuff, about how BG knew I had murdered peasants in El Salvador and Lebanon and that he could smell corpses when I talked.

I was so hurt that I tried to recover with poor wit, mumbling that some of what BG had said was true but none of the interesting parts. I asked Riki if this slander was because I had laughed at BG's barn-burning story. I asked if he'd mentioned about my youthful foray on the Congo River, where I'd held coats while my pals assassinated Dag Hammarskjöld.

"It's not you, Tip," Riki said (I wasn't on Tip terms with her but let it go). "I've heard he's done this before. In Austin he accused Seamus Heaney of being an informer for the SSA."

Who Seamus Heaney the name droppable was she didn't say, so I figured he was a writer too and bothered to correct her. "It's SAS," I said, "Special Action Section, the British killer elite." (The details matter very much to me; they're where I begin to make it all up.)

Riki then asked if I would accept an apology from the workshop and perhaps go along with a compromise.

I got grumpy, saying that I would return the money and leave tomorrow, maybe tonight if I could find a ride to the airport.

Riki became bureaucratic suddenly, a turn that still surprises me whenever I see it in baggage handlers, diner waitresses and other authoritarians. "You can't leave," she declared. "Let me handle it."

"How's that?" I asked.

"I'll divide the class into two sections," she said, "one for him and one for you."

I lit my pipe in her face and thought, Okay, Ms. Solomon.

2

The rest of the week was public Tip-flogging. I met each afternoon with three BG defectors—the fireman, a statuesque Dakota farmboy now teaching at a Calvinist college and one of those inspired trade unionists who can weep while reading the letters of Norman Mattoon Thomas. We traded science fiction stories, agreed that Ian Fleming left his best stories in the bottle and that J. G. Ballard and Steve King were dark angels. We also read aloud from Graham Greene's early gem, *The Confidential Agent.*

I would not have talked to them about myself, except that it was clear from gossip we four overheard at mess that BG was teaching by preaching against me hourly while goosing the women in his class for stories about their abortions. So I offered my boys the presumed-innocent and shockingly dull facts of my time clerking at the NSA (America's omnipresent surveillance machine), coincidentally during the administration of a most unbreakably coded president, Richard M. Nixon. The boys were hooked, of course, even by my dull facts, since every American male I have met on airplanes and long ferry rides eventually confesses to wanting to be an agent, a case officer, an operative or, when I explain it to them, an "alleged CIA contractor" —all this for them in another life. Many of the ladies too.

The most famous alleged contractor in America is Gordon Liddy. You know this or should. Remember the Watergate Caper? The fantasy-hotel break-in that broke down President Nixon's twenty-six years of upward mobilization? Gordon Liddy means a lot to me. Gordon Liddy is my sensational muse. Mother Earth stood still the day he lectured Attorney General John Mitchell re how to destroy the Democratic Party as if it were randy, prissy Bolsheviks. Gordon Liddy was once a major player in the great game called the Cold War, my chosen area of make-believe. Spying on and playing dirty tricks on the reds is hilariously manly work. You get to wear leather, use secure lines, buy drinks at the pool for aging berets, gossip about Acheson, Hiss, Edgar Hoover, the Dulles and Kennedy brothers and eventually RMN. Writing about it is fun and funny, always looking for a way to explain MacArthur, exhume Stalin, unravel Ike's golf game, detonate Castro's cigars, certify that Khrushchev pounded an Italian shoe and that LBJ was constipated like Lincoln, et cetera great puzzles right up until you try to get the Watergate Caper back onto Gordon Liddy's original plot outline and away from that cheating end of public floggings.

That June in Ohio I hadn't taken on the Watergate Caper yet. I was still working the preliminary bouts 1948–68. Nevertheless Gordon Liddy is always there for me, wherever I snoop. He's on my shoulder right now (Tip Paine's pet parrot), and he wants me to get on with murdering this famous famous Bohdan Galster.

3

The rest of the week I talked and talked at class, mess, the evening bibbles, but my defense failed like the Cold War's dearest scapegoats, the Red Sox. I was in the stocks. BG was a strange strange genius genius too.

I knew I was named a baby-killer when it came time for the annual workshop softball game. BG showed up to cheer on his peasant girls. Riki had told me that each day BG chose two of them to keep up all night with vodka and stories. In the morning he did push-ups at the coffee machine, the only place I had seen him without his groupies. I believed no BG tales now, because I was ashamed of what I was in BG's version of the world. I was sure he had been born in Scarsdale, was married twenty-five years to a Wordsworth scholar, had twin daughters at Brown, and his accountant had him borrow to pay his taxes.

My shame weakened me at the plate so that I flied out to medium center and booted a chopper at third. Late in the game, I and my boys, playing for the bad guys since we were the bad guys—BG traitors—caught up when infield errors unloaded the bases. I came to the plate like William Casey (then still mighty at the bat) and swung righteously at the first pitch. It was a long ball, which made my circling of the bases into a gamut.

The peasant girls scowled, and that is not easy to take, good-looking women angry at you. Is even alleged contractor Tommy Magnum ironic enough for that? BG departed before we lost by winning the game. Afterward I appealed to the trade unionist. He spoke bluntly: "Forget it, the guy's a jerk." The Dakota farmboy spoke anecdotally:

"My dad won't hire guys like that; they always want an advance."

I planned to skip the final faculty dinner at week's end, but Riki insisted at the student ice cream farewell that I was her date, giving me the address of the town's only French restaurant. I called for a taxi on time and was getting in when BG charged up with peasant beauties in tow.

"Want to share, Colonel?" he asked.

I blinked, and the tallest groupie, who was the iron-made Oregon woman, watched me accept another defeat. Her name was (I kid you not) Alexandra, but she called herself (I kid you not) Sandi. I mentioned her to you before—the one BG called "grandmother" that first day in class—because I knew she was coming back into this yarn, and I did like her fair, leggy looks, and also she plays the necessary role of unnamed, unwitting co-conspirator co-victim in this homicide. Truth, I'd had a crush on Sandi since the softball game, when she had belted me for tagging her long legs out at third base.

BG ordered the taxi to a Mexican fast-food dive at the edge of town. I didn't protest, since my reward was having Sandi sit next to me. I tried hard not to listen to BG's monologue while I told her the play at third had been too close to call. She ignored me for BG, who was telling his Yucatán peasant cycle. At the Mexican restaurant BG ordered two margaritas for everyone. He ducked his head together with the other two women, both very thin and cool in expensive summer dresses, so I sat primly with the Oregonian.

She soon showed the BG talent for flogging me. She said she was an unmarried mother of two girls, nine and seven, lived on ADC welfare among pinewoods on the Columbia River, had left college for her first abortion, had solicited money door to door in her town to pay for this workshop trip. Her father was in federal prison, and borrowed heavily from her. I listened like de Sade's jailer. She belted me again when I asked the waitress to exchange my tequila for a weak vodka tonic.

"You know what a pain that is for her?" Sandi scolded. "I've worked plenty of these places, and you're the kind who always shows up. Seersucker and big tips but what a horse's ass."

We were late for the faculty dinner, so I called for another taxi. I could not stand listening to BG talk about tropical diseases of the foreskin, so I went outside to wait.

Sandi followed me; she challenged, "BG wants to know if you're buying another round."

I was enjoying this by now, Daddy Spookbucks and his accusers, so I tipped the waitress again when I paid with plastic.

Meanwhile Ms. ADC Oregon had tricked me into pushing her on a swing outback the tortilla oven. Oregonians are well-built and hard-charging. Sandi told me I was greedy, insincere, judgmental, that all I had ever done was get married in a church and divorced by mail. BG's name didn't come up, but I knew she meant I should be more like him. By the time the taxi arrived, our roles had stabilized: she was my castigator and I was her sunless slave. I tipped the waitress again for bringing out my Panama. "You didn't fool her," Sandi judged. "You're still a horse's ass."

My week-long shame undid me, and I tried to get out of the stocks. With BG in earshot, I said he was nothing but a short Svengali who threw like a girl and wore cologne. I also raved a non sequitur about how Latvians collaborated with anyone wearing a helmet.

BG made room for me in the taxi by having the skinny New York woman sit on his lap. "You know about my country?" he started, sly black eyes blinking and white chest hair flapping. "I was apprenticed to a saddlemaker in Riga. I bathed the stallions after they'd . . . you know." The beauties guffawed, and he was off on another peasant fairy tale.

At the French restaurant, a former outlet in a failed mall, Riki the redhead was furious, and I was the perpetrator. She pulled me away from the long table, now covered in after-dinner espressos, and lectured, "Most of the faculty lives here; they could have been with their families tonight. This was for you out-of-towners, and you don't even have the courtesy to show up on time. Everyone's ready to leave; we've been waiting for you. And what do I do about the check?"

I apologized abjectly. I blamed myself. I said I would pay for my dinner and BG's and the peasant girls'. Riki might have forgiven me, except that Sandi had saved a seat for me and was immediately intimate about her plans to go back to college and find real work.

Riki moved over to flirt with BG, glancing back once at me as if measuring my fangs.

I had lost my only ally. I wished I had that infamous pill sewn in collar tips, then I didn't. I comforted myself. This was silly. It was tropical Ohio. They were all routinely unhappy. I would survive, and it would only cost me some hundred-plus dollars more. Tomorrow, United Air would be my private carrier back to the real world. I didn't need President Ford. I would pardon myself out of the stocks.

BG interrupted my consolation. "What did you do to her, Colonel?" he asked me after Riki and the Buckeye lecturers had left. He was drunk on my wine and was eating from his beauties' plates. "She's disappointed in you," BG continued. "Didn't you make love to her? The proverb says, 'The pail doesn't kick the cow.'"

The peasant girls thought this profound and giggled. Right then I didn't know the truth to tell it. It was checkmate-in-one any time he felt like it. I think I tried weakness, saying that Riki was married.

Generous BG let iron-made Sandi finish me off. "You don't know anything about women or anything," she said. "How can you call yourself a writer?"

4

None of this bothered me or my muse a paid-off hoot by the next morning when I ambled down to my ride to the airport. I knew I wasn't a writer. Writers were clever curs who favored their cages as long as poetic bellhops delivered booze, bimbos, fat notices and slender royalties; the end. I felt terrific when I thought to telephone flowers via FTA to Riki the redhead. Virginal white roses; let her eat carrot cake.

My driver, an earnest grad student, hustled my bag into his trunk and made me feel even better when he said he loved my books and movies and was it true that I was a retired spook, er, agent?

How I liked the real world, where real men are make-believe assets (an asset is an underpaid alleged contractor) and every conference call means we're winning the Cold War. Then I discovered why it was such a pretty morning. It was God almighty's joke, because BG was the extra passenger in my car. He had missed his ride an hour earlier and was immediately whining that he might now miss his plane. This was not my cocky leering BG. This was a sweating unshaven older man, his shirt wine-stained, himself and his bag unzipped.

I decided not to call attention to his slovenliness by asking how he had slept. I presumed he had sat up one too many nights playing Mr. Cinderella to the peasant girls and now, pumpkin smashed and high heels broken, he was suffering the scullery maid syndrome—once a pot, always a pot. I did say that I hoped last night's taxi service had served him better than it had me. (After I had decided to abandon BG, Sandi and the peasant girls at the French restaurant—they were going cruising to a local biker bar with one of the waiters they had picked up—it had taken me a half-hour wait to get a taxi back to campus.)

BG coughed and sputtered, "I don't know."

I thought, Know what? But I didn't ask, since it was fine by me that gregarious BG didn't talk much during the trip except to whimper now and again about his plane's departure time.

The grad student handled his suburban roadster brilliantly (it's called a Trans Am), fast-laning us on the interstate like Bond on uppers. I knew he was well into the spy escape fantasy that is best used in the penultimate chapter, so I ignored the speedometer and asked happily about the passing cornfields, the local pols, the nearest air force bases. He asked me what Bob Duval was like as a screenplay collaborator and had I really written all those lines for Olivier?

Whirling into the airport maze, the grad student ran two lights and cut off the taxi line, to arrive at the Departures door eight minutes before BG's flight.

BG was a panicky ingrate, jamming his foot getting out of the car, dropping his ticket, begging the baggage clerk to get him to the gate on time.

I waved goodbye and turned back to flatter the grad student. He was so excited by his driving—he'd already calculated he'd averaged 66 mph door to door—that I went along with his plea to sign a book for him. We found two copies of *MacArthur's Ashes* at the magazine counter, and I signed one for his dad too.

After checking my bag, I was pleasantly alone, flipping through *Playboy*, wondering where that tall woman in alligator cowboy boots at the United counter was bound, when I heard my name like a whimper. It was BG, the low cur, bloated and tail-tucked.

He dragged his bag over and whined, "I missed my plane. They wouldn't let me on. It was right there! What kind of place is this? My wife's meeting me at National. I can't get her on the phone. She's pregnant and has our little girl [gasping pause]—she'll be waiting there forever! They told me there isn't a flight until eight."

I nodded at his predicament but said nothing.

"Please, you know about these things," whined BG the more. "Can you help me, please? I'll do anything you say, just help me—I have to get home."

Tip is not a charitable man. I didn't know then that I might be what can be called an alleged contractor (a well-paid asset) for the devil. Nor did I know that what was about to happen was that gripping scene where the poor weary cur cuts a deal with Old Nick. What I'm saying is that I think BG sold his soul that day. And I think I bought it for my boss the devil. Should I repeat this? *I bought BG's soul for the devil.* Further, the devil is very, very fussy about contract law. Whatever deal you make with him, he keeps to it precisely—in exchange for your soul. All BG wanted was to get home. He got nothing more.

Pay close attention; here's how it happened. I kept nodding at BG's pleading and thinking to myself, I hate you, low cur, I wouldn't help you go anywhere but to hell. I confess that's exactly what I thought. (I didn't remember until much later that BG had said that I was a threat to his soul.)

BG shuffled, trying, "Can't you think of a way? I know you can, you're a world traveler, there must be a way. Tell me, please!"

What I should have done is grunted and laughed. Instead I lost my temper at his soulless (almost), squirmy manipulation and decided to treat BG like the cur he is. I told him he could have his wife paged at National Airport.

Hysterical BG, hung over and sleepless, said, "How do I do that?"

I tried reason. I said it would cost more, but he could fly to La Guardia on my plane and catch the shuttle to D.C.

He mumbled, "Yes, whatever you say, please, don't leave me, please."

Soon enough I was leading him without a chain (curs feed on the hand that feeds them, then follow along unasked, looking for more) down the cool, empty corridor and onto my flight. What thanks did I get? As soon as we were airborne, BG discarded his beggarly role and transformed back into famous famous in time for the round of drinks. He was two rows behind me, and I listened to him start his stories to the honest taxpayers around him—loud, musical yarns that made the women laugh. He must have used his name, because while our plane taxied to the gate BG was signing tickets for his fans. The famous famous Bohdan Galster. I wanted to run. It was not our fate.

La Guardia at noon Saturday is not for a child, coward or BG. He dragged behind me like himself. Now that we were out of earshot of the adoring public, he was helpless again. He had never flown the shuttle! He had no cash! He was sure he'd get lost! Please help me!

Here again there was the deal-with-the-devil scenario, like a re-prise to guide the audience to the sinister point. BG wanted my help. I wanted him to vanish into hell. For reasons of choice hambone theater, the devil deal requires some exchange of property between the contractor (me) and the soul-seller (BG), and when really spec-tacular, a signing of an unbreakable contract in baby blood. What I had to exchange was cash American. I peeled off Andrew Jackson's grouchy faces and bought his wish to get home. BG took the money like the damned. I wish now that, since I can't change fate, at least I could have known what I was doing. It would make it less spooky to live with.

At the last gate, Eastern waiting outside to abuse its clients, BG made a heart-filled speech about what a good friend I was, that he'd send me a check if I gave him my address, that he liked my business card, that he looked forward to seeing me again at another workshop, that I'd saved his ass.

I grinned like Daddy Spookbucks should, ignorant of my true nature. I told myself that BG was a mess and there was nothing to learn from this except that after forty, writers should not be allowed more than a phone call from the tit.

BG was not blind, so he rallied at the finish. "You know, that's a wonderful woman." He meant either the redhead or the Oregonian. "Are you going to see her again? She invited me out to smell the pinewoods." He meant Sandi. "She's wonderful," he crooned. "If I was your age, I'd think about it. Start again, with two kids to raise, and she's got style."

His last line was elemental writer—cunning, well-modulated, probably a lie, leave-them-guessing; he called over his shoulder, "Did you know she spent eight months in jail for grand theft auto?"

5

I forgot about all this quickly. I went off loafing and fly fishing at my camp in Maine and then six weeks later on to cozy foolishness in San Francisco with my sweet pal Donna Marietta, a former *Playboy* objet d'art who flies the polar route to the Middle East for a crazy Japanese-owned charter (and she's a pilot, not a stewardess). Including my stop-off in North Carolina to go out on a supercarrier with my brother Sam, the industrialist, it was Labor Day before I returned to New York and faced my stack of mail. I tried to open everything in chronological order to repair my time lag. I found an envelope from BG. It was two months old. There was no letter, just a check made out for the amount I'd lent him. If you're taking notes, understand that the doomed soul cannot return the devil's payoff and that this check was the same as a signed unbreakable contract. The baby blood is coming. There was scribbling on the check: "My deep thanks."

There was also a letter from Sandi, dated two weeks before. In a careful script she went on about her kids, her dad, how surprised she had been by the postcard I had sent her from San Francisco and why hadn't I flown up to Portland, she was only an hour west? It was a peachy come-on until the last paragraph, where she wrote, "I'm still upset by BG's terrible accident. What a tragedy. I know you would say *He'll get over it*, but I don't think like that. I feel so bad for his wife and child too—what do you think?"

What accident? I reread the letter. She didn't say.

I found out when I opened (out of order) the month-old letter from Riki the redhead on official land-grant university stationery. Enclosed with my expense reimbursement of $28.17 for a week of Jell-O at the motel mess was a letter about BG and his accident.

Four days after I had sent BG off, I learned, he had tried to put out a kitchen fire in his house before the rescue services arrived. "He was very badly hurt, I understand," Riki wrote.

She did not provide details. (This was the woman who had called the Brit killer elite the SSA, but that's no excuse.) I should have figured that she was leaving out the vitals. She did add that BG was looking at a long convalescence, but "He's fighting back . . . hanging tough . . . he's not a quitter . . ." and other propaganda for what you are after you try to put out a kitchen fire by yourself. Riki closed that she was going to see BG when she got to D.C. to join her estranged husband. "We're going to make a new start at Georgetown. Wish me luck."

Luck, I thought. Then I reread the letter, editing out all the sympathy. The fact was this: BG had found another fire.

I must be accurate. I felt no sympathy for him. I laughed, and the laugh reminded me that I despised writers, literary persons, writers workshops, teachers, colleagues and before all that him, BG, the famous famous now laid low Bohdan Galster. I checked BG's check against a calendar. It was dated four days after I'd sent him off. Exactly. I assumed, to make myself feel puritanically revenged, that he had mailed it moments before he walked into that kitchen fire.

It did not come to me just then that the reason I wanted the scene so tightly shot (check, mailbox, kitchen, boom) was that it corresponded to how the devil is said to do things. Remember, the devil is a fussbudget about the terms of his contracts. The devil had held up his end of the deal—BG got home. There was a four-day delay while the devil waited for the return of the signed contract. Then it was time to collect the first installment.

However, at the time I was still unaware of my alleged contracting work. My first and only notions were shaped by irony and contempt —that BG's barn-burning peasant story had come back at him like an apocryphal SAS sniperscope shot that misses Ulster and goes around the world into a Whitehall window.

Lightning is dumb accident, he'd said. Murder makes fire, he'd said. I pictured it this way: Peasant-hero BG had charged into that kitchen fire all the while thinking he was running away to a naked farmer's daughter by a sylvan stream in Latvia.

Then I got very fancy, very suspicious. I reread Sandi's letter. How had she learned of BG's accident? Sandi wrote me of her feelings about it, not of the facts of it, which meant that she was living with the news some time now and had assumed, the way insiders do, that I shared her BG view, an odd opinion at the least. Perhaps the peasant girls had called her? But that was not a straight line. I suspected BG. He had written her while convalescing. Of course! The deviousness of these writers—quick to turn their idiocy into a long-range seduction.

I reviewed Ohio and solved the shenanigans of that last night at the Mexican restaurant. *BG and Sandi had been having a fling.* I had been the beard, those other two girls in summer dresses the hand-maidens. At La Guardia, BG had complimented me for my business card, but that last "grand theft auto" remark was his calling card, like a brand on Sandi. What a camouflage he'd arranged for his affair— demanding two girls be brought to his room for stories, suggesting serial ménage à trois when there'd only been hanky-panky with one leggy welfare mother.

How had I missed it? Did you miss it too? Review the details yourself. You don't understand women, Sandi had said to me. Smell the pinewoods, BG had said to me. If I was your age, BG had said to me. Start over with her, BG had said to me. Add these clues up as I did, and you'll understand how I figured that BG had not merely charged into that fire. He had *set the fire*, because he wanted to run away not to a Latvian peasant girl but to an Oregonian one.

BG, you low cur, I thought, you flogged me all week; and then you duped me into buying you, your bimbos and your mistress dinner; and then you made me help you get home to your *third* wife.

My reaction was characteristic devilment, though I didn't even think it was first-rate mischief at the time. I pulled out a glossy card of David's cinematic *The Death of Marat*. (You remember it: Marat the invalid writer is slumped in his bath, pen and paper in hand— one dead troublemaker, stage center.) I wrote BG a get-well-soon note. I added bluntly that he should tell fewer cruel stories. I signed it "Colonel Paine."

Then I decided this was all too BG-like. I was putting in murder and leaving out my disgust. Yet the card was small and I didn't want to waste my time explaining to him why he'd gone into the kitchen fire. My P.S. noted Chekhov's excellent advice that one should drink less vodka. My P.P.S. was vengeance: "Stop setting fires you can't handle."

It was summer's end before I thought about any of this again. Riki the redhead wrote me that she was getting divorced, moving to Austin to conserve Madame Tolstoya until she finished her dissertation and could get a real job, and by the way, she'd be passing through New York, did I mind if she called?

She wrote nothing about BG, but why should she? The guy was a winner. I figured he'd concoct some fairy tale about his accident that made him into a hero, and after he published it he'd be championed in *Time* for writing a parable of America's incompetence in the third world. Then BG would likely seduce another peasant girl and start his wicked research again.

A week later Riki called me. "I'm in Brooklyn, staying with a friend," she said. "I'll be here a couple of days. I know you don't plan ahead—how about a drink tonight?"

Negative. I lied and said I was waiting for my brother the industrialist. After some banter about her divorce Riki finally gave me the crucial details about BG (the devil dwells in details).

He was still in hospital after three months. That kitchen fire had hurt him badly, all right. *He had been blown up.* The doctors had amputated one hand and part of the other. His ears were stubs. The burns were worst on his torso, where the skin grafting was iffy. His wife was nine months pregnant, and they were destitute, without insurance in a rented house. The other famous famous writers of Washington were organizing a series of benefit readings to pay the most larcenous medical bills. BG had lost seventy pounds and was on so many painkillers that he could not sit up.

I listened to Riki's tale and waited for her condemnation. Yet she said nothing about my Marat get-well-soon card. I felt so prickly-skinned about it that I imagined the famous famous of Washington would nail my card to BG's hospital room door for everyone who visited him to curse. I got off the phone and cursed all of them like a preemptive strike. I figured that no one had noticed my crime yet, too busy weeping over what was left of BG.

My crime just got worse and came calling again. Soon after, BG's wife sent me a note saying she was sorry it had taken so long to reply to my "thoughtful" card. I read each of her kind words like an accusation.

"Times are hard," wrote Mrs. BG, "but we have a wonderful new daughter to be thankful for." She was reading BG one of my books, she wrote. "He likes the range of knowledge. . . . He calls it encyclopedic and wants you to write more about women." She hoped to meet me one day when times were better.

What did I do in penance? Not much. I did send in a check to BG's charity and did read about the benefits in the papers. I also walked myself through the caper like a criminal in pursuit of himself. That's how I worked up the similes—that's literary talk for what something you've done is like. Like homicide. Like whipping a cur. Like an alleged contractor. The truth might be that I actually am an alleged contractor for hell itself, but for the moment let's pretend that my fancy talk above is just flimflam. Whatever your opinion of these matters, there's no escaping that I am guilty of devilish misbehavior. I know it, and eventually BG, if they put him back together, will know it.

He'll know more than that too, and now I'm going to tell you the cruelest detail, one straight up from hell, one that I didn't discover until after New Year's, when I rendezvoused again with my pal Donna Marietta in San Francisco and thought to call Sandi, among the pinewoods on the Columbia River. It was a most upsetting phone call. She was very sick in bed and croaked more than talked. "Oh, Tip Paine." Sandi sighed. "Yes, of course I remember you. . . . No, I'm awake. Thank you for calling."

I'm going to tell you what I learned from that phone call but trickily, cowardly, pitilessly, glibly, *like a writer.* However, since I despise them and their nasty games, I'm giving you this chance to figure it out yourself. Recall BG's insistence that he was religious, someone who understood about sacraments like marriage. Reconsider BG's first remarks to Sandi in class, "I won't listen to hormones, grandmother" and "take your pills before you come to my class!" Ask yourself why he was in such bad shape that morning after on the way to the airport. Take seriously my clue that the devil's contract must be written with baby blood.

Time's up; just listen. A writer would tell it this way:

If Old Nick weren't so far behind in his dirty work, I would have heard from him by now—a telephone call, long distance, after midnight.

"You do neat work, Tip," the devil will say. "You're a threat to souls; we can smell corpses when you speak." (The devil speaks in the royal we, just like all world leaders.) "By the way, Tip," he'll say, "what do you know about this Oregon welfare mother who's had another abortion?"

"You mean, sir," I'll respond, "the one that hemorrhaged her like a scapegoat, made her curse God and barter her soul for drugs, left her bedridden and whiter than a rose?"

"Good detail, Tip," the devil will say. "What we want to know: is that your handiwork, Tip?"

"No, sir," I'll counter humbly, "though it's my best guess it was some writer—a famous famous one and going your way."

Sellers, Guns & Money

Peace Is Our Profession;

There Is an Irony Gap;

My Nemesis

_____
_1_

I t b e g a n o n a train. If banqueteers can't get big draws like Ludlum, Buckley or Clancy, they sometimes turn to the second rank of us sci-fi/spy guys. That's why I was southbound on Amtrak's Silver Star into autumnal Dixie, heading to the tail end of the tracks at Miami for a banquet of munitions lords along Biscayne Bay. I'd chosen an overnight Pullman rather than the two-hour jet hop because I had the time and had never rolled through the Old South like FDR headed for Warm Springs and romance.

(I'm going to play another romantic game here. It's called Find My Nemesis. That's Greek for "enemy." Here's a hint. In my world-shaking romances I introduce the bad guy right away in the first chapter —doing something corrupt like destroying his wife's thoroughbred at Saratoga rather than giving it over for sale after it's stupidly won a three-year-old claiming race, and then prophesying re the CIA, "Langley'll never know what hit them either. First they win . . . then they lose." But that's fast-buck scrivening, and this yarn is my way. Find My Nemesis.)

The Silver Star sleeper was Soviet shabby, the food approximate, the clackety-clack like a tape of my first childhood long train ride with my grandfather the Pennsylvania Railroader round the horse-shoe bend at Altoona. I had armed myself with four pulp pounds of a Peter the Great biography, and when we lost light past Richmond I made acquaintance with the ancient attendant in the empty dining car. Clearly he had worked the Silver Star long enough to remember New York steaks and draft beer in the missing bar car. I did wonder about his mourner's black armband but circled around the subject by asking where would we be at first light? where did he live in Florida? He didn't give his name, I didn't return mine, but his name tag read Wilson. It took me a while to hear the turns in his basso profundo cadences, and then what emerged was a dateless, anecdotal history of his thirty-five years in the porters union, raising a family and then raising his children's families when fate hurt his sons somehow.

It's not my experience that railroaders chat with civilians. My grandfather said it was company policy, but I think it's their version of mysticism—riding the rails produces a library of sounds, and one must listen. So it must have been grief that loosed his tongue. I never found out whom he had recently buried. I wanted to know everything about him; he was suddenly my hero into a cool Carolina night. Yet I am wary of direct questions. If folk want to tell you, they do; if not, not. I did ask if his father had worked on the railroad.

"Oh, yessir, yessir," he replied. "He got to digging in the Dismal Swamp for them. Many years back now. That's when I went up to Washington and joined the army."

This was a new clue. "You were in the service?" I asked. "The Second World War?"

Wilson wasn't as old as I'd thought. Korea, he said, which I happened to have studied, so I was stuffed with arcane facts, especially about the "colored" army units that generals Johnny Walker and Ned

Almond abused and wasted before the army invented integration due to high casualty rates in the nonblack divisions. I tried details and dates, and he nodded as if I were the veteran.

"Yessir," he finally said, "the Triple Nickels, that was my outfit."

The 555th Field Artillery Battalion was famous for valor. It fought from the Pusan Perimeter slaughterhouse, where the North Korean army trapped our boys, up north to the Yalu River slaughterhouse, where the Red Chinese army trapped our boys, back south to the last-ditch Line D, where the reds destroyed themselves on our molten barrels, up north to the thirty-eighth parallel, where time wasted reason—Korea the bloody yo-yo.

I continued free-associating. Wilson continued nodding. "Yessir, it was bad, bad. I never been so cold. . . ."

He didn't finish. I knew he didn't want to tell me. It's the bona fide mark of all combat veterans that they don't talk about it. I watch their faces but cannot read them. Nonetheless this was a Korean vet, a rare find to this day, as if the hundreds of thousands who survived the bloody yo-yo have vanished like the train service. I wanted more and tried barter.

I told him my dad's tale, tricked out of him that summer of the fortieth anniversary of D-day, about how the "colored" work battalion that came ashore late on the first day at Omaha Beach had panicked and screamed there was a gas attack. My dad's company of combat engineers was dug in on the dune ridge above the beach, and when they heard the gas attack sirens they scrambled for their masks like the doomed. Dad wasn't wearing his pants, and rather than run half naked across the beach to fetch his mask, he, a twenty-three-year-old embarrassed lieutenant, just pulled his tarp over his head and tried breathing shallowly. The hard joke was that the gas was actually a breeze of cordite from the naval guns. The "colored" soldiers had never smelled cordite, since our 1944 segregated army had not thought them combat worthy enough to provide decent training. There they were on Omaha Beach on the longest day, without weapons, cover or help, being laughed at by the naked and undead.

This was a long way around getting Wilson to tell me what it was like, seven years after Omaha, to be a member of a famous field artillery battalion, breathing cordite like opium, dropping tons of HE on those fabled communist hordes.

"Cordite," he said, "you don't forget that. Yessir, cigars's best."

I asked, "What cigars?"

He gave me the best explanation I could get that night. "I promised myself," said Wilson, laughing gently, "if I ever got back I'd smoke a good cigar every day."

His laugh made me wince when I thought about it back in my compartment. I'd met a man with a motive, and it made me feel purposeless. I like to talk about it, you see, talk and talk, and I'm unsure my motive is ever more than bookish curiosity, which is actually just *snooping*.

Wilson was cheery next morning at late breakfast, and by the time we bumped slowly to the Amtrak redoubt at Miami he was packed up and ready to depart with the passengers. I followed him from a distance. He was chatting with junior porters outside the Arrivals doors when my car arrived. An antique tall van had pulled up and flung its rear doors open to serve barbecued ribs to the club. Wilson was far away in pleasure the last I saw him, and I wished I'd thought to ask him what time of day he smokes his good cigar.

I also wish now that I'd asked Wilson, the railroader who was actually a member of the Triple Nickels, the easy soul who was actually a mourner, the guy in the kitchen who knew a lot about God almighty's mansion of many rooms—I wish I'd asked him a question that fooled me a lot that weekend (and all the time). How come nobody and nothing is what he, she or it seems?

2

My driver appeared a tight-lipped Latin. He roared through a trashy neighborhood and then onto a broad skyway that shot into central Miami. He made me for a New Yorker and suddenly asked, "You come here to lose on the Jets?"

This was chummy NFL talk; the coincidence was that the Miami

Dolphins were hosting the New York Jets on Sunday. I feigned high-stakes knowledge and surveyed the landscape. If you haven't been there recently, brand-new Miami is a Broadway musical set—tinted glass and pastel metal, sky of fake blue, palm tree tunes, the humidity even in autumn making action either a chore or sweet. That glamorous cops-and-robbers show gets it too right and then, because a camera's eye can't focus fast like our real one, misses that everywhere in Miami is as flat as the water table. Clouds are flat, streets are flat, cars are flat, hundred-dollar bills are flat off the presses. Florida from what I saw from the train is a vast links. A fair-sized god could try a sand wedge from Jacksonville to the flagpole at Miami. I was not disappointed. I decided it was wonderful that America had decided to overbuild a city in a wilderness due snakebirds and alligators. I'd heard the tales of the laundered drug money holding together the economy and about the race riots, Latino millionaires, condo scams. I believed all of it and knew at first sight that none of that mattered. Miami works because it's a dumb idea that works. That sea-green smell is cash. Wall Street does not smell of cash; the money is blips on a screen, and the harbor is dead. Miami reeks wealthy pale putting green.

There was more green in the wardrobe of those lined up in the lobby of my fantasy hotel on Biscayne Bay. They were not the calm customers I'd expected. Warbucking is a monastic fraternity, and this was supposed to be a banquet for brothers who use the Department of Defense for a credit line: the B-1 bomber that does not much work, the B-2 bomber that does not much exist, Star Wars!

My host found me. He was my age, knotty, dark and compelling—his name tag read "Associate Banquet Director Mr. Wiecek." (It's pronounced like Wheat Chex, and he's called after another breakfast cereal, Wheatie.) "You like the train, huh, Mr. Paine?" said Wiecek. "Our people mostly fly in, y'know."

Wiecek was presently joined by a hostess, a robust and dark young woman whose name tag said "Banquet Director Ms. Wiecek." They were twinned in green blazers, white shirts, dark slacks. I didn't ask but assumed that only husband and wife can look so matched. Ms.

Wiecek offered, "I'm glad there weren't problems at the station; we never had to send a car there before."

Before I could defend my antique travel plans, two stocky young men appeared from the rattan chairs. Wiecek introduced them as his "bros" Candles and Huffley. They were in pullovers, not banquet garb. Candles charmed me by saying, "Great to meet you." "Yeah," added Huffley. "We've read all your books."

I was my orthodoxally humble self, changing the subject to conceal my vanity. I asked if the restless in the lobby were banqueteers.

"Nah," said Wiecek, "not our people."

Huffley explained, "Most of 'em've come down for the Florida game this afternoon."

I tried to sound informed, asking after the Dolphins and Jets.

The boys laughed. "Not till tomorrow," Wiecek explained. "Miami's a college ball town."

Candles asked, "You a Jets guy?"

I smiled ignorantly.

Ms. Wiecek, whose name was Sally, did not miss my turn. As the boys bumped each other with predictions about ball games, she remarked, "Miami doesn't have much culture like New York, Mr. Paine; it hasn't gotten here yet. It's coming, I hope."

Wiecek harrumphed at her observation and took my bag. "Our big people come tonight," he declared. Wiecek was an organization man; it was a telling aspect of his character. He liked to belong, and he spoke in jargon that divided reality into either "our people" and the unmentioned or "bros" and "them." Like many a fine fellow, he didn't bother with the worrisome idea that all organizations subdivide in a way that leaves guys like him and me unmentioned too. "Our big people don't stay here," he said. "Company jets, stretch limos, and the old jet jocks drive themselves straight from the marinas in incredible cars."

I loved this and took a guess, asking if there'd be an astronaut.

"Yeah," said Wiecek. "Glenn's on the guest list."

"Neil Armstrong too?" I hoped.

"Nah," said Wiecek.

I kept up the small talk while they walked me up to my BOQ, the routine frigid barn suite with a water view behind heavy drapes. Huffley had excused himself at the elevator bank, saying that his wife was waiting for him in the car. Candles wanted to stay, but Wiecek gave him a sign to scoot. "See ya later, Mr. Paine," Candles closed, "Jets 'n' all."

By then I was so swell-headed I was gabbing my just-invented theory that Neil Armstrong should be in the Senate, and because he wasn't, then perhaps NASA had made the wrong choice for first patriot on the moon. I'd heard Armstrong keynote my baby brother's graduation; he was humble, strong-minded and altogether an engineer who cared about children—not my idea of a Roman conqueror. I blithered aloud to the Wieceks that Armstrong should have levered himself into the Senate to hold the Midwest fast for modest Republicans and serve as the perennial vice-presidential choice as Glenn is for the Democrats. Instead Armstrong remained a frontiersman making small, honest steps.

"Yeah," said Wiecek, "that was some walk he made." He laughed wickedly. "I'd vote for him."

Sally Wiecek said, "You never vote, Wheatie."

Wiecek harrumphed again.

Sensibly I instantly rejected my above idiotic opinion about Neil Armstrong. I also rejected the fruit basket on the table. Instead I opened the white envelope with my name on it. There were ten flat one-hundred-dollar bills inside letterheaded stationery addressing me as the Honorable Mr. Paine and stating, "Compliments of the Select Committee for American Peace." This was the banquet's black umbrella. There was a shibboleth beneath SCAP's eagle-headed logo: "Peace Is Our Profession."

Here's where half of my weekend grief began, in a casual moment of make-believe—a traveling salesman's constant jeopardy. It was the letterhead. I had let my New York speaker's agency confirm my date and had never seen the official invitation. Now in motion inside Miami's stage set, I saw the strange joke I had missed out on, or had I?

This shibboleth "Peace Is Our Profession" was strangely close to another shibboleth "Peace Is Our Profession." You might remember the old B&W movie *Doctor Strangelove*, created by the strange crew of director Stanley Kubrick and actor Peter Sellers, who plays every strange role, including the very candid weaponeer Dr. Strangelove. There's a detail in it that you don't spot the first ten viewings. General Jack D. Ripper (Peter Sellers playing Sterling Hayden) goes nuts and orders his SAC B-52 bomber wing to attack Russia. One bomber gets through, and its strange pilot (Peter Sellers playing Slim Pickens) rides the bomb down. End of movie world. Reverse the tape a bit. General Jack D. Ripper's SAC command has an emblematic shield on the wall behind his desk. The shield's shibboleth is "Peace Is Our Profession." I had assumed that Stanley Kubrick had asked Peter Sellers to play a typical SAC shield and he had just transformed himself into the real thing, since everything about SAC is funny if you find nuclear holocaust funny when played by Peter Sellers's best mushroom cloud.

The Select Committee for American Peace's letterhead was cause to reconsider. Peter Sellers was dead, yes? These munitions lords were not being nostalgic, yes? Well, maybe. At the time, Tip told himself not to carry on foolishly. In Tip terms this means "common your sense." It was Miami, I was sleeper car sleepy, Neil Armstrong was a very noble man, I had the usual stage fright about my performance that night. I waved the cash at Wiecek.

He shrugged. "Expense money—y'know, walking around."

Sally, who had been rearranging the fruit, opening the drapes, fluttering around the suite like a good mom, contributed, "It's their idea, to give it in cash. I think it's rude, like dope money or something, but y'know, it's Miami." She shrugged winningly, a female version of Wiecek's muscles, and I liked her even more—a kind person, "good people," as America used to say before hyperbole took over and good and bad seemed weak reviews.

I dropped the letterhead for the cash. To cover my glee I returned to my earlier NASA theme, asking where they'd been when Neil Armstrong had walked on the moon.

Wiecek shrugged again. "Saigon, I guess."

"Oh," sighed Sally, "Wheatie—"

"Forget it, Sal," Wiecek ordered Sally, "just forget it."

Sally looked to me for sympathy, and I held back for the riddle. Everybody knows where he or she was that day, July 20, 1969; even the then unborn have it calculated from either their delivery or their conception. Wiecek said he was guessing Saigon. I figured him for a heavy-duty Nam vet, down to the steady stare he used like a window in time when 1969 came up.

I flapped the hundred-dollar bills and said that I wanted to spend some of the swag on them later at poolside, shoot the humid breeze about Armstrong's day or any other. I used the word "Saigon" as a talisman.

Wiecek said, "Yeah, yeah, if I can get free; it won't be till late, after our people have wrapped it up."

I asked Sally if she could come along too.

"I don't know, Mr. Paine, there's a lot to do." She glanced at Wiecek, and I missed what he did; she added, "I don't think so, really, but thanks and"—Sally was heading out the door—"if there's anything you need and Wheatie's busy, just call the desk; they'll find me."

Wiecek was eager, however. "It'd be great, Mr. Paine; just what I need after this shit. It's been nonstop for six days, cuz we gotta cover the convention too." Wiecek gestured to the window and what I presumed was Miami's convention hall, where the munitions lords had been dealing all week. "Mind if I bring my bros? Haven't much seen 'em all week; they're fans of yours too."

I said certainly, it would be fun, I needed something to look forward to. I asked if he could convince his wife to come along, gesturing to where Sally had stood.

"Nah; she's not my wife anymore," said Wiecek. "We just work together sometimes. It's a little town, y'know. I'm really a stage carpenter. This gig's extra, Sal's mostly."

I was flummoxed. Not married anymore?

Wiecek provided more of the riddle. "We're gettin' divorced soon, y'know." He brightened. "But my *girl* can come along, I'm pretty sure. Her dad's one of our big people. She'll be here later. Her name's Lorelei. It's okay if she comes, yeah?"

Wiecek had to rush off. I wanted to learn about his marriage troubles, since I liked Sally a deal and Wiecek a little through her, and I didn't like the swishy sound of Lorelei. But again, if people want to say, they say; if not, not. So instead I guessed about what was only half as intriguing. Given his granite polish and Saigon amnesia, I asked him if he'd been a beret.

He nodded as if he were wearing one. "Yeah, but not green," he said. "It's a long story."

I joked that it could be a thousand dollars long, for all I cared. Mine was a stupid joke. But just then I thought I was clever and took the wave of his fist as tough-guy camaraderie.

3

I aimed to decontaminate, nap, roam around, buy a silly shirt, call my imaginary best friend, McKerr, in New York to tell him this was even better than we'd made believe. But McKerr was probably at work for the latest pirate he'd found, and I thought better of letting myself be seen in native drug lord rags. It was yet another mistake not to have napped. I wasted the afternoon in the shade at poolside, watching brown beauties in bright silk go in and out of blue water.

Too much great flesh makes me do that shy trick of imagining them with their clothes on. I was dressing up yet another Incan goddess when Wiecek turned up to say my rented whites were in my room and they expected me at the prepodium cocktail party at 6 P.M. pronto.

"Affirmative," I said.

Wiecek was taut, a man inside a major operation. He had already changed into his white coat, and I complimented his gardenia corsage. "My girl's idea," he said. Wiecek got that wicked laugh back. "Mr. Paine," he tried, "about what you said, about later—?"

I interrupted. "Call me Tip." I proposed that later we could escape this high-security zone, find out what *salsa* means. I said that we were the same age, appealing to his sense of camaraderie to impress him. I added, "We're both working; tonight's a hot kitchen we can get out of after the tables are bused."

"All right!" he said. "Blow off the kitchen, yeah! But—about my beret, we can do that before, just us, okay? My bros were grunts too, but I was closer to lifer, y'know? Huff, he flew a slick, Candy was arty 'n' like that. My girl, I don't talk about it in front of her, y'know; she's not like that. Okay, just us?"

I translated. Wiecek had been not only a beret of some sort but also a professional, several tours of duty. His friends had also toured Vietnam, flying helicopters, serving in artillery or infantry, but they were not lifers, that is, devoted organization men like Wiecek. Also he didn't want to talk about himself in front of them for reasons of warrior humility or in front of his new girl, Lorelei (the munition lord's daughter), for reasons of . . . pride? new leaf?

I said, "Sure, Wheatie, I understand. Just us."

"*You're okay,*" he said. He didn't say, You weren't in Vietnam, huh? Nam vets don't bother with this, it's not useful to them. The ones who talk at all speak with that badge-of-courage tone of dried blood. That I wasn't a Nam vet was implied, however—and also that since I'd asked about Saigon, then I was a snoop but that I *might be* all right.

I wished him good luck with the banquet. "Oh, yeah," said Wiecek, "that guy Glenn is no-show. A farm aid got him. But our people've got other big people, y'know."

SCAP's banquet did have those big guns, also lions and tigers and all manner of Russian bear-hunters. I've been waiting to impress you with the fact that the keynote speaker was Mr. Donald Trump himself. You've heard about him, at least you've heard him promoted all about. Trump is my age and sort—traveling salesman of make-believe. He's rich and famous, of course, while I am demi of both and therefore not his sort at all. I can guess that the munitions lords had asked him as the banquet keynoter for approximately the same reason they had asked me to do color commentary—Kissinger and Ludlum were previously engaged elsewhere. SCAP was trying a youth movement for its evening's entertainment, sort of Catch a Rising Star Wars comedian.

I was on time. My introducer at the prepodium cocktail party, Ms. Milly, said she loved my movies. I liked her diamonds. She stepped off a moment to dazzle someone else, and I was left alone in a crowd of back-pounders.

Sally Wiecek was suddenly at the kitchen door. I moved over to snoop the more, starting by apologizing for any trouble I'd caused her before.

"Oh, that, no, it's okay," she said. "You know we're separated? It's okay. He likes to be with his friends anyway; I never went out with them. But thanks."

She was too busy to linger, and I should have let her go, but I was feeling fretful, as if I wouldn't get to see the whole movie. I asked her if she could meet me later, separately, down in the bar. We could talk about Miami's future culture.

"Yeah, well, maybe. Thanks, Mr. Paine. I know you're trying to be nice, but—but I don't want to get in Wheatie's way."

Ms. Milly returned. Sally smiled more winningly than any rock and rushed off.

Ms. Milly spoke cutely about how hard young women work these days and then guided me back to her job. She must have known Mr. Trump well, because he kissed her on both blushed cheeks before turning eight degrees southeast to shake my hand cleanly. I reminded him we had met before, at a GOP fund-raiser in California. He responded cleverly: "I've enjoyed your books. The ones with me in them are the best."

I liked him for this, since I haven't written him in yet. Then again, I have liked him every time I've seen him. Being near him is like being near sci-fi/spy bliss. No reason to solve him: he's just fresh —a young Milky Wayan who *knows* what the galactic center feels like, a billion black holes snorting stardust for kicks.

I did have one other prepared remark. I asked him if he recalled where he was when Neil Armstrong walked on the moon.

"At work," he said, deadpanning himself. "I've been at work since 1947."

I faded. Guys like that should have the last line. He's genuine make-believe future history incarnate.

That's a typical Tip Paine sci-fi/spy irony, part petting and part whacking, and since it's a new subject and because I know it's coming up shortly, I shall define "irony." Like "nemesis," it comes from the Greeks. They had this word for fib that we have inherited as irony. The Greeks also had this smart-ass named Socrates, a shrewd wino who hung out in the marketplace gutter and who you could never be sure meant what he said. Often the word and the man are put together, so that you get "Socratic irony," that is, smart-assed fib. The Greeks didn't make much of this double-talk either and made Socrates drink poison. Today, Greek replaced by American at the center of the galaxy, it might help to think of irony as a tiny joke that very few folk get. Altogether this makes irony mean a smart-assed fibbing tiny joke that at least one person laughs at and others find poisonous, while select authorities find cause to feed that poison to the guy doing the ironizing, called the ironist. There's a simple aphorism to remember this dictionary gab by: Nothing's what it seems.

The banquet was not poisonous; sherbet to open the palate, two kinds of wine before another kind, nouvelle cuisine fish something and good water. I was seated on the dais between Boeing Aerospace and Ford Aerospace, whose names were Spiker and Gorra and who competed by claiming they loved my books.

Gorra of Ford flacked Stealth technology: "It's a beaut, yessiree, and it can zoom!" Spiker of Boeing was an aerospace guy too, but he was working underwater counterdetection and didn't care to duel about high-altitude cloaks. He did quip, "There's software coming that'll make Tom Clancy out of date like a spyglass."

I liked them. They were genuine sci-fi/spy. It's commonplace for us make-believers to be buttonholed by Department of Defense guys and told about gizmos we should put in our books. I have a signature response. I say I'm low-tech Cold War: Machines break, mistakes work, gunplay is useless. I'm also used to it that the DoD guys don't smile. For Spiker and Gorra I added the detail that I think invisible planes and submarines are cheating and goofy, like a bomb that kills without a bang. This is a quick example of irony.

I eat only vegetables when I have to speak, and regard wine as treacherous. The silvery bear-hunter who introduced Mr. Trump went on properly long about dear old fighting-tough morning-wake-up blood-and-titanium America resplendent, ever prepared to fight two and a half wars simultaneously while never striking first and building up to build down, peacemaker peacekeeper pièce de résistance—the party line continues like this and always sounds Grand Old Party. (I confess here that I'm a registered Republican. It's a family trait, like the *tock* in the cerebral artery that will kill me post—seventy-five.)

Donald Trump dominated the evening like a comet. Perhaps you've come to think of him as a luxury huckster (marble bidets, honest roulette, superhero sportsmen), but he's got the same realpolitik that guys like Kissinger do ("What works, *I* did"), and he's not grumpy about losing yet. Also he must be thinking of bypassing Capitol Hill and going for Foggy Bottom. He let his long hair fall over Central America first, then the tragedy in Lebanon, the insanity in the Persian Gulf, and Gorbachev the Maybe/Maybe Not Terrible. He must have given the speech before in various order of threat axes. It was reassuring in a Cold War way. I listened while fussing with my champagne flute, dropping in bread crumbs and trying to read a make-believe message from Langley. I used this bit once and had a message appear that turned the plot sideways to a rescue in London.

That night I got mush and walked right past the warning sign that said that I was thinking too much, a poor move if you have to perform. In Tip terms, I was uncommoning my sense. Losing sense soon follows.

Mr. Trump was done and cheered. After the silvery bear-hunter emcee made some good jokes about Miami, I was on the platter. They applauded generously. I aimed to tell my best Cold War Hollywood story. General Walter Bedell Smith was an early director of the CIA, and in late 1950 with paltry funds he had to build an Oriental network from scratch to try to figure what the Red Chinese were going to do in Korea about our Eighth Army. You'll remember that by then our boys had recovered from the Pusan Perimeter and were rolling up to the Yalu River, to piss in it and at the Red Chinese across the border in Manchuria. So, as the yarn goes, clean-living Bedell Smith went to Bangkok to meet with a possible secret source at the most secure place in town, a Shangri-la whorehouse, and who did he find was Mr. Big Talk but the actor Ralph Bellamy, on a binge. The Thais worshiped Ralph Bellamy for his second-banana job in the famous B&W screwball-comedy film *The Awful Truth*. By 1950 they either had got him confused with the movie's lead, Cary Grant, or didn't care, since that was one of those films that played Bangkok for fifteen years because of the Second World War blockade. More, the word in Asia was that Madame Mao of Red China fame, a movie star herself, was in love with Cary Grant and maybe Ralph Bellamy, so it was logical to the Thais that Bellamy/Grant would know what 600,000 sneaky Red Chinese soldiers were up to in Manchuria.

If none of this is logical to you, then the Cold War is not your kind of code game. It's a fun and ghastly tale, even if I do tell it too much, and I knew this was the right audience since unlike Donald Trump's and my cohorts, the boomer crowd, these silvery folk could remember that what was about to happen east of Bangkok and south of the Yalu was MacArthur's apocalypse. I was rambling along describing Bellamy/Grant's costume, how he didn't know who Bedell Smith was and assumed he wanted an autograph, which he signed, "Cheers, Cary," when I lost sense. An image of the Korean vet Wilson floated up beside me.

Instantly I was way off the silly point and speculating out loud what time of day Wilson smokes his cigar to block out cordite. I'm sure now that what triggered the Wilson story was that half the men in the room were smoking cigars. I was watching the red tips twirl through the stage lights, and I was breathing the tobacco. Sight and smell are the handmaidens of hallucination. At the time, however, it just seemed a natural segue from "Cheers, Cary" in Bangkok to Wilson's "It was bad, bad. I never been so cold," about Korea. Gradually I realized that there were likely more than a few Korean vets in the audience, and while it was okay to joke about CIA shenanigans in Bangkok, it was not okay to joke about the horror of Korea. I knew I had to bug out. I mumbled how Wilson was fine when I last saw him, feasting on ribs and heading home.

Then the first part of my weekend's grief—"awful truth" says it lamely—closed in on me. I was sweating, hoarse, terrified, cigar-smoke queasy, but I couldn't get off the podium. Worse, I had Cold War Hollywood on my weak mind. Watch now, this is how nightmares work: suggestion becomes terror. I glanced at Donald Trump grinning at me. *And he was being played by Peter Sellers.*

It's an old peacenik joke that Dr. Strangelove's foreign accent and freeze-dried wig made him resemble not the radical weaponeer Edward Teller (who was the intended target of satire) but in fact Henry Kissinger, who in 1964 was nowhere near the galactic center. I will not labor the joke. It's too spooky. See the movie, laugh or not. But what was happening to me on the dais was nightmare standing-in: Edward Teller played by Henry Kissinger played by Donald Trump played by Peter Sellers—all of whom were grinning at me.

Vain body-snatcher Peter Sellers took the next challenge. He also played Tip. If you've ever been stuck at an open microphone, you know the out-of-body feeling. But Tip was suddenly sharing the mike with a genius of irony, one of the smartest-assed fibbing tiny jokesters since Socrates.

"'Peace Is Our Profession,'" Sellers-as-Tip blurted to the audience, "the promise on your stationery, ladies and gentlemen. I want to close tonight by asking if any of you have ever thought how very close that is to another 'Peace Is Our Profession,' from the movie *Dr. Strangelove.* You remember, the genius Peter Sellers's finest ninety-four minutes on earth."

Peter Sellers said this. He explained nothing, a non sequitur from Mars. Yet general officers and munitions lords listened as if he'd just said, "So you're the leaders I've been taken to."

There was anxious laughter like firecrackers. Sellers-as-Tip continued, "The late General Jack D. Ripper isn't the brightest symbol of modern American strength. Unless we've realized that, since Jack is gone, we ourselves must now close the irony gap with the other side. The irony gap—"

The firecrackers were at my side. Sellers-as-Trump was chuckling and urging Sellers-as-Tip to go too far. I had to regain myself long enough to get off the podium, but how? Meanwhile Sellers-as-Tip locked on his target—the banquet.

"But that's another problem we sci-fi/spy boys are working on," said

Sellers-as-Tip, "late-night blazing, closing the irony gap on a bunch of Moscow ironists. Sure, we say SDI is Star Wars, but so do they! Sure, we have bombers so peaceful they don't fly too good, but so do they! Yet—and here's the gap that worries me—they are way ahead of us where it counts. *On tv.* They get to say Lenin meant well and Stalin made mistakes. They get to say invading Berlin, Hungary, Poland, Czechoslovakia and Afghanistan is maintaining order. They get to say all those skulls in Siberia are reindeer. . . ."

I swallowed. Not Sellers; I swallowed. I could hear what was coming. This cold warrior boilerplate delivered, Sellers-as-Tip was about to finish with major smart-assedness. He was about to deliver a version of Peters Sellers's last line in *Dr. Strangelove:* "And the reds get to go on tv and boast, 'Mein Führer! I can walk!'"

The sketchy applause saved me before Sellers ranted the *mein Führer* line, which would have killed me. No matter the context, guys who make billions on guns & ammo just don't find the idea of *Führers* on tv funny. I don't know why.

But what was important was that the audience thought my swallow was a period. More, I argue now that the very *sketchiness* of the applause jarred vain Peter Sellers just enough that I was able to get back to my seat without him. The nightmare was over, though I didn't dare look at anyone for fear they'd be you-know-who.

I finished off my mushy champagne like good water while I studied my losses. Ralph Bellamy and Cary Grant abandoned. An innocent Korean War hero somehow mocked for his common sense. And the coup de grace so nutty I couldn't summarize it.

The banquet broke up for after-dinner lobbying. I was alone at the dais, and then I was in the hallway being buffed by more of the Ms. Millys. I returned their flattery and waited for authority to tell me my bag was packed, get out of town. It didn't happen. The munitions lords withdrew hastily in cadres to determine everything back at the marinas. By nine-thirty (lords favor early public events, late private confabs) I was down at the fantasy hotel's frozen bar, sipping a madcap soda.

I'm aware now that the reason they weren't annoyed with me was that no one had listened closely enough to decipher my ranting. It's commonplace with comedians that if you look all right and are making fun, then the audience feels all right and thinks it's fun. Significantly, none of the banqueteers had mentioned Peter Sellers to me. No one. As if he was gone, had never been there.

I accepted this, however, because it's hard even for me to watch *Dr. Strangelove* for the twelfth or twentieth time and want to talk about it. Peter Sellers goes too far. He makes me sympathize with the Athenians who nixed Socrates. That movie is too ironic; it created an irony gap in Hollywood that can't be closed. "*Mein Führer!* I can walk!" is a last line that makes every last line since sound dull. That movie should be destroyed. First show it to the Russians so they understand the threat, then get the talkers at Vienna to agree to a scheduled mutual irony reduction, then make all the prints and *VCR* tapes of that movie drink poison.

Nevertheless that night Tip had created an irony gap for himself. This, more than Miami's staginess or my napless stage fright or my snoopiness, set me up for part two of my weekend grief. I did it to myself. I separated from smart-ass fibbing/tiny joking in order to get off the podium, and that meant I left Sellers-as-Tip behind. I forgot that it's funny that nothing's what it seems. Tip Paine ironist confronted Miami deironized.

4

By ten o'clock I was soberly stupefied at the frozen bar. The cable tv was replaying that day's Florida State game, and I was not thinking too much. Sally Wiecek appeared like a mom who's run out on the dishes, folding a hand towel into a square as she maneuvered the empty tables toward me.

"I really can't stay long," she began. "I'm done but have to check that the caterers didn't leave with more than they brought. It would've been a lot cheaper if we'd used the regular staff."

I said the banquet had been smooth, she'd done a good job, how about a beer?

She wanted wine, then squirmed until I asked the bartender to provide her with cigarettes. "I quit, y'know," she said. "Until the separation, I'd quit. I didn't want my kids starting up like me, so I quit." I soon learned that there were two children, one Sally's and one Wiecek's and hers, girl eleven and boy five. I asked where they lived and how long she'd been a hotelier, an honorable profession I depend upon like savvy pilots. But Sally didn't want to talk about herself, and I was glad she understood I was not flirting. I wasn't even snooping hard any longer, just happy to be with a pleasant person, both of us out of the kitchen.

After a few kind words about liking as much of my talk as she'd overheard, Sally got to her open motive. "You like Wheatie, don't you?" she asked. "I mean, you don't know him, but he's a good guy. He's my sweet palooka."

I laughed for her affection. I suddenly wished I had the luck to be called "my sweet palooka" by a sweetheart like her.

"He talked about you all week," she said. "He's a big fan. I'm sorry I haven't read your books. I do read, y'know."

I tried to soothe her, asking after her favorite books.

She returned to Wiecek. "He's going through a bad time. I guess we both are. Did he tell you about us?"

I told her what he'd said, then risked upsetting her by mentioning his "girl."

Sally was lovably angry. "Her, that *person*, Miss Sugar Girl! She picked him up, y'know—that's the way he tells it—at the playhouse; picked him up like that!"

It must have been a wild story. Sally didn't tell it; she concentrated on right now. "What do you think, Mr. Paine, about Wheatie? Does he seem okay to you? I'm asking, I guess, because you're, y'know, not from here and you write about men like him."

I said I wrote about happy endings but that I understood her question, so I asked a little more. What I learned was A&E channel Vietnam, Wiecek the draftee who kept volunteering for rough duties during a ruinously stupid war and who was soon enough a brown beret doing special chores for the army in 1966 and after. I'd never head of brown berets, but I do know about special chores. Wiecek was trained to be a commando, a small-team operative, an attack dogface out of helicopters, riverboats, darkness. Warrior lingo has many slang names for them, and they all mean killer elite.

"Then he got shot." Sally winced as she said it. "In the back. They gave him a Bronze Star, and he came home. That was 1969, Mr. Paine, why he didn't want to talk about it."

I told Sally that none of them wanted to talk about it.

Sally wanted to. There was a quick survey of their romance. She'd met him after her divorce, when she'd been in tender shape, with a child to raise. Wiecek had been in crazy shape, on army disability. Sally had glued him together and taken him home. "We were okay," she kept repeating at each new achievement. Then came another Wiecek change, in the 1980s. It's called the Vietnam syndrome, and his version was that he started hanging out with other vets, went to Washington for the Vietnam Memorial wall dedication, said he was feeling much better about the army and Vietnam, and then—

"He won a piece of the state lottery," said Sally. "Not the big one but big enough. The lottery—that's what I think caused it: he won it using his serial number. And we had more money altogether than ever before, so Wheatie got into real estate with his friends—his *bros.*"

I sighed, because the lottery is too modern to make sense. The big thinkers say that Wiecek's problem was raised expectations leading to rebellion and despair.

Sally said all this much better. "He's lost again like when I met him; he's got money, but he's lost—y'know how horrible that is, to watch and feel so helpless? My ma says he'll grow out of it, but I don't know, do you?"

I puzzled: Boy / beret / back-shot / Bronze Star / disability / marriage / Vietnam syndrome / lottery / sugar vamp. I was lost like Wiecek. Without irony, remember, I didn't see that Wiecek was a one-man weather forecast due for another change any day, a sunny one. I mumbled in confusion.

Sally and I might have figured some of this out if we'd had more time. However, while she was reviewing their marriage again, mentioning that Wiecek was now taking their son out on speedboats with the other woman, "Miss Sugar Girl," we were invaded by the sweet palooka himself. Wiecek appeared like a point man, still in his whites but looser muscled and sashaying through the tables as if macho with bandoliers.

"Hiya, Sal," he said cheerily. "Mr. Paine, yeah, Tip, ya were okay, okay, we were crackin' up in the back, ya really blew 'em away, great story, Cary Grant and Madame Mao, great story."

I said no one had laughed very hard.

"They laughed on the inside," Wiecek reassured, "and that cigar stuff, great way to get in good shit, I never got that those Korean grunts knew about good shit, we figgered they did opium and Jap beer, okay!"

Wiecek and his tongue were much looser, eau de marijuana sitting on his big shoulders like a monkey. You notice, too, that neither he nor Sally mentioned Peter Sellers? At the time, I was grateful. At the same time, I noticed little else. The details I provide here are hindsight. Without irony, I was one-eyed—an invalid, no depth perception, missing at least half the action.

Sally saw everything. She might have fixed his bow tie if he'd sat next to her. Instead he pounced onto the stool to my left, so that I was separating the separated. Sally said, "We've been talking about you, Wheatie."

"Yeah, great," he said, ordering a beer with a hand flick as only genuine tough guys can do. "Ya gonna write about me, Mr. Paine— Tip? I saw some heavy shit." He laughed wickedly again. "Those movies they're doin' now, they're okay, but we weren't like that, y'know; the Nam took a long time, and the bad stuff went down *slooooow.* Shit, I don't remember the barrages, that was way back there, way way back, and I was in a buzz for years. But how they gonna do that in a movie? *Buzzzzzz,* bang, *buzzzzzz* bang bang, *buzzzzzzzzz?*"

He was funny, and I did laugh.

Sally must have heard this as desertion and went on a solo patrol. "He's not writing about you, Wheatie; he's interested in happy endings—isn't that right? Maybe he's gonna write about me."

"Yeah, you sound happy," taunted Wiecek, who was truly tough to withstand Sally's tough love. "Have a brew, Sal, and quit that." He meant the cigarette. "Come on, Sal, it's bad for ya."

Sally puffed hard and salvoed again. "Maybe he's gonna write about me—why not? I was there. It wasn't a *buzzzzzz* for me."

I had leaned back to avoid the fire, but this was news. I asked if Sally had been in Vietnam.

"Yeah," said Wiecek. "Tell him about how rough it was to feed the chickenshit brass chickenshit." He addressed me: "She was volunteer. That's how she scored her first husband, the looey—get that, little boy looey got Sal and got broke."

"Yeah, well." Sally stepped down to leave before Wiecek counter-attacked. "Your first wife didn't get broken, Wheatie; she's got her *bull*shit together." Sally patted my shoulder. "Thanks, Mr. Paine—Tip—and don't, y'know, don't play the lottery. It's for *palookas.*"

I got down to say good night, failing to make her smile. I'm never more upset than when I know a nice woman is going to cry as soon as she's out of sight.

She sighed. "I've got to get back; I'm still working."

Wiecek waved goodbye mockingly and gulped his beer before he remembered his manners and me. I tried once to awaken his dopey head, by saying that Sally was a serious woman.

"Yeah," said Wiecek. "Ya really gonna write about her?"

I was loyal enough to Sally to speak bluntly, also cranky enough to talk too much. I said that I didn't write about Vietnam; I wrote about the Cold War. That routine hot wars weren't funny to me, they were stupid all the time and usually sad too: no happy endings and a rare few almosts. I added that another reason I didn't write about Vietnam was that I hadn't been there and wasn't dishonest enough yet to hawk it as if I were running for public office.

Wiecek heard little of this; he did understand that I wasn't being funny, so he returned his version of why no Vietnam for Tip. "You guys'd write about it if we'd won," he said. "That's what's wrong with those flicks—all losers, not like yer books."

I tried another explanation. I said that I might write about Vietnam someday but that it wasn't finished yet. "It lacks a punch line," I declared. If I'd said this with irony it might have convinced him; instead I said it flatly.

He misunderstood flatly. "It's over, Mr. Paine. I don't believe what ya say. It's over. I'm here to tell ya it's over and I'm gonna get *on* with my life."

I didn't correct his distortion of my remark. I knew the Vietnam War was over. It ended April 29, 1975, White House time, when that last slick popped off our embassy roof in Saigon to leave behind ruination, coincidentally on my birthday. I get to mark two strange events every year, the other one as some women I know remember their abortions. Also I was not in a mood to debate politics with a man who was certain about everything when he said it. I changed directions, saying that the rumors of the Cold War being over were greatly exaggerated and that was why I liked it. This SCAP crowd was the brass's brass, and they were talking hard every day.

"Shit," grunted Wiecek, "I looked at their stuff at the convention hall. It couldn't stop a round, so it couldn't stop a troop. Shit, how're ya gonna fight when you can't handle mud and belly-crawl in guts and shit? Yeah, machines don't puke, but I betcha if I puked in one of 'em it's junk."

This was a crude but irrefutable opinion of the prospect of the Department of Defense's war planning. After two minutes, a battle-field is gory junk that only a naked animal could survive. I grunted back to show him I believed him, liked him, too, for being so dopily, blockheadedly accurate.

Wiecek finished his second beer. "I guess ya don't want to hear about my beret, huh—since ya don't write about the Nam, what's it to ya?" I accepted his judgment. "It's okay; I don't like to talk about it much anyway. It's not good to, they say, and"—he laughed wickedly again—"it's like I said, *buzzzzzz*."

I supposed he'd depart. I'd had enough of his folly and wanted to be alone with mine.

Wiecek was single-minded. He recovered quickly from anything, and he had a hidden motive. "My buddies, y'know, Mr. Paine—it's early yet. I wanted to make sure, y'know, that ya meant what ya said. Cut loose this laager?"

5

I should have declined. Most of the bumps in my life result from my not declining. Instead I let myself go along, and I've told you why. Without my irony, everything had flattened like Miami. I had this brilliantly snoopy idea that if I could keep passing Wiecek's tests— understanding the precise Nam vet word "laager"—then maybe I could figure how to help Sally by convincing Wiecek he was an idiot to leave her. I was the idiot to get involved in someone else's marriage; that's something you do only when you're sure you can be hilariously smart-assed and can fib your way out as fast as you got in.

Not Tip. He was one-eyed Uncle Fixit. And when Wiecek's "Miss Sugar Girl" turned up momentarily at the frozen bar, I didn't spot that she'd been waiting in the wings for a signal that I was okay, double okay.

Lorelei was orange, not only her color but also her breasts, hips, cheeks, scent. She was wearing a warm-earth ball gown shot through with tropical chartreuse and I think dull gold. She kissed Wiecek on the neck and introduced herself. Then she did the college-didn't-change-this-belle twirl to me. Lorelei the knockout handled Wiecek like a trainer. He was her love-drunk Polish property who did he-man work, looked swell in whites and got very silent in her presence.

Lorelei started, "Wheatie and I just love your movies, Mr. Paine, though he says they're not as good as the books. I haven't read them, but I will now."

I said, "Call me Tip," and smiled, waiting for her to call me "you Yankees."

She didn't disappoint. "Daddy asked me to ask you if you're kin to that other Tom Paine, the Yankee one, 1776 and all that."

I returned my flimsy calling card of a conversation piece, saying no, no, he spelled it different, ha ha. (It's true until 1776: Tom Pain.)

She cooed, but she probably would have cooed if I'd told closer to the truth, that I was kin to one of Sherman's avengers.

Wiecek pounced down when Lorelei said, "Wheatie, why don't you go ahead, honey, and see that everything's ready." He was gone on command.

I wanted to ask, What was ready? but Lorelei's orange was on home ground and in blossom. She skipped around the plantation a few more times, Daddy this and Daddy that, and I ushered her back to the late twentieth century by asking about Wiecek.

"Have you known him long?" I tried.

"Of course!" She glowed. "But he's getting divorced, you know, and that takes time."

"He's a nice fellow," I tried. "A little rough but nice."

"I've never met a lover boy like him!"

I tried harder for Sally's sake, saying that he didn't seem like anyone Lorelei had ever met.

"Oh, Wheatie's just like Wheatie," said Lorelei, "but he's sensitive too; if you knew him better you'd see that. He's had a few bad breaks —he told you about Vietnam, didn't he?—but he's gotten over that now. He's going into real estate—did he tell you that?—and that's something I know about. I'm a realtor, Tip, honey; are you interested in a condo? I've got some out on Key Biscayne that the owners want to unload fast." She leaned close to whisper, dosing me with scent. "It's a secret, but there's lots of South Americans who buy without looking and then change their minds, or the *Federales* change it for them, you know."

Yes, yes, I thought. An orange realtor with condo secrets to sell, I thought. She was charming and smart. She must have known I'd chatted with Sally, and so she was eager to flirt her way around any disapproval I might show. I didn't dislike her as I'd supposed I would. She was fine-looking and persuasively pro-Wiecek. Well, at least pro-Lorelei with Wiecek attached. But this is keen hindsight. I wasn't thinking clearly at all at the bar, otherwise I might have picked up on that "sensitive" remark—a former weapons locker is so very sensitive, a man-stealing belle is so very sensitive-minded.

"Can I ask you a question?" feinted Lorelei. "Are you really interested in Wheatie for a book, or am I making you fidgety?"

She was perfect—I wouldn't have air-brushed a sweat gland—and Wiecek was perfectly wrong for her. I wasn't so dull I couldn't see that nor that their sin and sex must be Roman, the flesh being orgiastic for strange opposites. This last Tip opinion was why I was strong enough to try once more for Sally. I figured Lorelei and I were not opposites, two salesmen of the uppity class, so that I could wade through her grove and shake her. I could have made a pious speech; I was feeling like a marriage counselor. Rather I stuck to facts, saying that Wiecek wasn't a realtor, he was a husband and father, that he'd had *a lot* of bad breaks and *his wife's mother* thought he'd grow out of them eventually.

Lorelei looked a little hurt, but she was not absent of personal wisdom. "Wheatie and I've talked about that, Tip, honey, and he's the one to make his own decisions, don't you think? We do get that for ourselves."

Right, I thought; good reply, Lorelei.

Lorelei was not through. She had a prepared trap to show me how happy Wiecek was with her. She finished her champagne cocktail like many a woman I have admired from afar and said, "Wheatie and I have a treat for you. We've had our little drink, so come on now with me, no peeking."

Here's where I could have used a smart-assed fib to get out. Yet I'd taken my snoopy shot for Sally and surrendered like Wiecek to the other woman. Lorelei abruptly maneuvered me out of the frozen bar, past the pool, down a soft-lit walkway between centipede grass to the fantasy hotel's quay.

We looked down upon my "treat," three cigarette boats bobbing in Biscayne Bay—black-and-silver Pall Malls, their engines on dragon's-breath idle—and manned by a squad of vets with bimbos in hail poses.

Lorelei laughed wickedly. I recognized where Wiecek had learned his laugh. "Aren't you surprised?" she said to me. "I just knew you'd be; it's like that scene in your movie."

(This was not untrue, though it was Helsinki in spring, there were ice floes, renegades, assassins stalking George Marshall.)

Wiecek helped Lorelei down and then hopped on the quay with me to introduce the squad. Candles and Huffley I already knew, their wives I nodded to, then there was burly Marconi, sunny Sonny something, tiny Lagruber and another beefcake, nicknamed Clydesdale, along with consorts.

Wiecek added about the cigarette boats, "It was Lore's idea, sir, it's the best way to see it after dark."

I missed the obvious ambush fashion in all this, except that "sir." I knew then that there was cash involved. Wiecek was blunt, it was three hundred dollars for each boat, my Amex card as deposit. The fey greaser standing by the lines took my money and card, no receipt. I got down beside Lorelei, and we launched into the black bay.

6

It was not pleasure, nor was it truly dangerous. Cigarette boats are huge, oceangoing Porsches, suited to drug running and well-framed tv movies. The experience is hijack high jinks. We ran out in tight convoy, then turned three abreast to come round back toward Miami's lit towers. Wiecek gave the wheel over to Huffley, the ex-slick pilot, who proved expert at making white-water waves. The three boats played ribbon-cutting games with their backwash. I sat blankly, jammed against Lorelei and Huffley's tall wife, whose name I missed in the roaring.

Presently I began to release my grip on the floating cushion, but then they got this swell idea to run the boats at speed within arm's reach of each other so they could pass out the champagne bottles liberated from SCAP's largess.

I hate speed, and speed on water is meaningless. It's the fly fisherman in me: water is for wading or floating, black water is for reflection. There must be speed limits in Biscayne Bay, at least that close in to the mansions, but then why were we being hailed by other maniacs out for an evening thrill under a gibbous moon? There are no cameras! No one cares if you go fast! Lorelei jabbered, Wiecek kept a joint lit in the wind, Huffley's wife streamed her hair. My stoniness was misunderstood as suave.

Eventually they tired of water speed and backed the boats together for other accelerations. Wiecek's marijuana was replaced by cocaine. This thrilled them, because that dry powder was too expensive to pass safely between three boats bobbing aft together like bumper cars.

I hate drugs more than speed, and don't call me a dummy for being in Miami's cocaine snowdrifts and expecting innocence. It's a dark prejudice of mine. Sci-fi/spy insists that drugs are for torture or doctoring after torture. I insist there's no place for drugs in what needs talent, like my adulthood. I refused when Lorelei offered.

"It makes it go *sooo* fast," she said. "Tip, no?"

I said *no* very unironically. No like no public official means anymore. No like Citizen Paine said to the tricky king of England, 1776. You want to hear what Tip sounds like when he's being immovably negative? "No," I said. "No."

"It's okay," sniffed Lorelei. "You don't feel like it."

"Lighten up, man," said Wiecek, seated at Lorelei's feet. "It's cool, we thought ya'd like it, but it's cool."

I got cold-minded, telling Lorelei and Wiecek another unironical Citizen Paine opinion. Citizen Paine said, *'Tis time to part.* Tip Paine said, "I want to go back now."

Lorelei tried, "Oh, honey, it's early yet and—"

I tried the truth; it works sometimes. I said, "I'm afraid of black water, Wheatie. I want to call New York and go to sleep."

Wiecek grunted. "Aren't ya... what about the party later?" I thought he was kidding. He wasn't. "At Trump's house?" he asked, pointing toward these islets that serve as part of Miami's mansion row.

Lorelei explained, "We hoped you'd invite us along—oh, please, pretty please."

Here was their motive at last. I was more than a celebrity or deep pocket; I was an access code. Rich and famous Donald Trump had yoked a large team of munitions lords and driven them back to his

Vanderbilt bungalow after the banquet. I hadn't even considered going along, because I regarded myself paid off. Now it emerged that busboy Wiecek and company wanted out of the kitchen through the front door. It was such a silly idea that I didn't say no, I laughed—wickedly like Lorelei.

She laughed back in the original and tried, "We won't embarrass you. My daddy's there; it's okay."

I told Lorelei she should take them to the party if Daddy didn't mind. She ducked that one, so I knew that Daddy did and would. Just then I could have taken the long way home and agreed to their scheme. But remember for the last time I was separated from my sense of the ridiculous, so I didn't see the joke in bringing along a squad of Vietnam-vet, lottery-winning, coked-up realtors to a lordly confab I was happy to be out of.

Here's how I sound when I'm unhappy and a hard touch fearful. "Please," I said, "take me back to the hotel."

The boys and girls started arguing among themselves. One girl said, "I *told* you." A boy said, "Let's forget it, man." Another girl said, "It won't work." Then they chattered about me as if I were ashore. "He's a shit, then, man." A jagged speech mentioned me crudely as "one of 'em."

At some point, and I missed it, preoccupied by the bad notices, a tool of the vet trade appeared in an adjacent boat. It's called a revolver; this one had a long barrel. When it was fired it sounded as trite as it is. It made the boys macho and the girls wince and giggle. Candles the gunsel ejected the spent shells and proposed, "Let's get him back and have some fun, then. We've got the boats for the night; it's cool."

I hate guns more than speed or drugs. They scare me so much I make them funny in my books, and that's why my protagonists have my phobia—it's funny to me—agents, renegades, colonels, all afraid of guns. I realize now that Wiecek and company were enjoying themselves again; having abandoned the fantasy of crashing Trump's party, they were trying to climb into the fantasy of speedboating. They were vets. Speed and drugs and sinister "tphuts" are as nostalgic to them as rock music.

Bobbing in Biscayne Bay close off mansion row, it was my turn to misunderstand. I needed Peter Sellers. I only had terrified of speed/ drugs/guns Tip. I crouched up and started a pompous little lecture. I stole the salutation from Sally.

"*Palookas,*" I declared, "you're middle-aged *palookas.*" Rhetoric descended from there. I told them to put away the coke and gun and get me home and themselves home to their kids. I told Wiecek that he was a middle-aged crybaby as well as a palooka. I pointed to the mansions and said that they're the lords, we're the servants. That we're not invited. "You palookas, me, Wilson—not invited!" I cited Wilson again, saying he did his war and then did thirty-five years saying "Yessir" on a ghost train. "Don't talk about your war," I said, "but don't talk about it without me around to listen anymore. Get me back."

In the balmy breeze I was cruelly unfair, but then that's part of the wit about that idea. Fair is sports talk, where you drive or hit the ball, not an ideal. And by the way, if you were expecting this scene to transform into genuine violence—heavy drugs and guns, kinky romance—then you're unfair too. These were middle-aged citizens, not gangsters. I'm a salesman, not Tommy Magnum. It was flat-minded Miami, not tv. Also, heavy carats, big guns and kinkiness were back at the banquet.

These middle-aged citizens did try to respond to my big mouth. They made accurate remarks like "What?" and "Who's a palooka?" and "You're way out of line there, mister."

Lorelei said, "We'll take you in, Tip, honey; no harm done."

Wiecek was more accurate as he took command of the boat and cruised evenly back toward my fantasy hotel; he whispered, "Shit, man, shit, a guy can't have no fun no more."

7

Tip got himself landfallen that night, safe as a cabin boy, and he got his irony back after a bad night's sleep. I was not so amused by my conduct that I wanted to see the kitchen help again, so I canceled my Amex rather than reclaim it from Wiecek. My bug-out plan included sneaking out of town on my Visa inside an Eastern jet headed north just before NFL kickoff at the Orange Bowl. I exit fast a lot like this; it's a theme in my notes. By the time I got back to New York I had stopped blaming myself for snooping around in someone else's triangle while at the same time mixing it up with the ghosts that vets carry around like backpacks. Peace is *not* a ghost's profession.

My final detail here is that challenge I made to you to find my nemesis. You've figured it out. Tip's commonsensical enemy is Tip, who likes to talk and talk about it. And he's not quitting; he's got to close that irony gap. Someday I'm going to go on tv and shout, "*Mein Führer!* I can walk!" and laugh really hard, because, dear Wheatie, a guy can have fun if he keeps in mind that nothing's what it seems. Not Sellers, not guns, not money—none of them are what they seem, thank heaven. And if I get to heaven I'll ask Peter Sellers how he did that mushroom cloud nicknamed *Das Ende*, ha ha.

(No, that's not my end. I got a card from Donald Trump, saying what a pleasure it was to meet me; it was superbly done and untouched by human hands. I got a valentine card from Sally *and* Wiecek that winter, and it was very human, Wiecek adding a note: "Let me know when you're ready to write about it," and Sally adding, "You're my palooka too."

(I'm glad the cards come from most different addresses. I can set them side by side and see that they're just fine separate. In the kitchen, Wilson, Wiecek and Sally are lucky cooks to guard against that infamous mushroom soup bubbling over. And in the banquet room, Trump guys in white and Lorelei gals in orange are the funniest kind of Strategic Defense Initiative all by themselves and my proof why that random nuclear apocalypse ain't gonna happen except in the movies. If it did—Tip smart-asses in the tiny library—then God almighty's mansion of many rooms would lose its staircases and the star-sucking crowd would be busted down with the rest of us. And that's *too* ironical for this galaxy's entertainment, I guarantee. Cheers, Tip.)

Murder by Paine

Fly Fishing, Horse Racing,

House Hunting, Art Collecting;

Holmes Paine on the Case

1

My imaginary best friend, McKerr, and I were up at my camp on Moosehead Lake last August, failing to deceive brown trout with our gray ghost flies. Bored by bad luck, Tip suffered a notion to go house hunting. I studied the local newspapers to chart a course along the Down East coast of Maine, from Cape saltbox to Federal blockhouse to Victorian pastry. I wanted a fourth address to hide in when my two in New York turned New York and my camp turned Arctic. I also wanted house pride. I just plainly wanted, a forty-year-old who'd never mowed his own lawn.

McKerr rejected bluntly. "It's the hole, the *hole*. What lives in houses? Dames." If you recall McKerr's personality, he's a loony Yankee, a hawkeyed deerslaying *la longue carabine*–toting crank who roams in the make-believe of the eighteenth century's New World wilderness and whom I call Pathfinder after Fenimore Cooper's timeless, guileless genius, Natty Bumppo. Accordingly McKerr regards settlement as an enemy of reason and any bivouac close enough to the fort to smell cooking to be deathly. He was right as usual, but I didn't listen and thereby hangs a tale of greed and murder that it was my grim task to solve before it hanged us like the sad folk who did actually die and the ones who have gotten away so far.

On the third day of my campaign to go house hunting, we were on the lake at sunrise, floating serenely and losing grumpily. Brownies can laugh, and we were their idea of comedy. McKerr took a break to divert himself with yesterday's *Racing Form* about the Saratoga meet. I was at the bow, solving a knot I'd invented by casting left-handed.

"Say," started McKerr, "what's the hill here?" We'd drifted into the pine shadows that brownies call home. "It's Blind Mountain, isn't it?" asked McKerr, who thinks topography is as profound as fishing. Moosehead Lake is surrounded by rolling bumps that McKerr pretends are Abenaki maidens in repose. Blind Mountain resembles a tired rump. McKerr dropped the *Racing Form* and cast. "If it works," he prophesied, "it works." The mystery was solved when in an illegally short time a laughing brownie guffawed his streamer.

"Blind Mountain!" rejoiced McKerr. "A nine-to-one long shot in the Whitney tomorrow!"

Several hours later we were at McKerr's Land Rover, striking a bargain. Yes, I'd go along with his genius to connect a stupid trout with a horse race (the next day's Whitney Handicap at Saratoga) if yes, also we built into the ten-hour drive to Saratoga a detour by way of real estate. It was logical at the time. McKerr had been weakening toward my house make-believe ever since I'd discovered that he had never collected the forts Down East. And there was a beauty called Fort George at the port village of Castine, where there was conveniently a realtor I'd phoned.

The feature race at Saratoga was McKerr's smoke. Castine turned out to be mine. It's on an idyllic peninsula that points into Penobscot Bay like an arrowhead, commanding the river up to Bangor and the sea lane due west to Lisbon. On the map it looks perfectly well seated where the pines meet the granite. Up close it's a widow's fairy tale, dozens of pristine clapboard manses that were built by seafaring

plunder and that now berth horticulturalists and decelerating ancients. It's dominated by the Maine Maritime Academy and in the
summer favored by those yachtspersons who amuse fish everywhere.

"The big house," McKerr mocked as we drove into Castine. "No
crash-outs in a century."

I should explain that recently McKerr had acquired the jargon of
1930s gangster movies. It was my fault. I was working on a screenplay
about the crash-out of cocaine cowboys from the federal pens where
they are now kept like goats, and to help my make-believe I'd cast
McKerr in the feature role—Pathfinder as public enemy. After a
week of nonstop VCR tapes, he was a buckskin mobster, I was his
oily mouthpiece. That's also why the long shot at Saratoga. It was
method acting, a play-along notion to shade his character.

We parked on Water Street in a foggy, salty rain, one of those
squalls that flirt with the shoreline. McKerr was ready to collect Fort
George and get out of town. I invoked our bargain and ducked into
the real estate agency, a fancy niche in a beautiful brick triple building dating from the Revolution. U.S. Customs was upstairs, and the
stone steps in the hallway were worn by two centuries of quarrelsome
Tories.

I hoped for an easy parley. Instead I was confronted by what
sounded like rent war. A chubby middle-aged Yankee, Boston by his
accent, was carrying on impolitely with the realtor's secretary. "Yeah,
well," protested the chubby Yankee, "tell her that when her checks
clear, mine will!"

The secretary smiled weakly at me while writing down the Yankee's
bluster. "Can I help you?" she asked me. I mentioned my appointment.

Meanwhile the chubby Yankee was appealing to McKerr. "Tell
your friend she writes her checks underwater."

I heard McKerr play mobster: "Swells, they're all the same," but
then I was distracted by the secretary's sales pitch.

"Mrs. Ives apologizes, Mr. Paine," said the secretary, speaking of
her boss. "She's late getting back from a ride with her daughters; can
you wait until three? She has some real bargains to show you."

"Bargains, haw!" mocked the chubby Yankee. He was one of those overweight men who appear clownish when upset—jerky motions, roving eyes. "Fireplaces propped on poles, beams cracked half through, haw! Come to my shop, gentlemen; I'm an *honest* junk dealer."

He pounded out the door but not out of the building. In the hallway he popped a hatch to descend a stair ladder to what was once the building's carriage house.

The secretary flushed. "I'm sorry, he's upset; he's a nice man really."

Outside McKerr mumbled, "Bargains, bargains."

I was now so annoyed at his sarcasm that I insisted upon lunch at the first café we chanced upon, walking uphill toward the fort. McKerr hates lunch other than caffeine and nicotine. The plump café owner, Mrs. Roche, served us immediately, a generosity I claimed was impossible in the real world. I told McKerr it was a fine town, why hold the white paint and rosebushes against it? I argued that it was seafaring once, the ghosts of the salts were omnipresent. I told him to focus on that, not the yacht marina or the lilac shops.

"Yer goin' soft," lipped McKerr. "Not a dunker in the place, java's thin as an alibi."

Eavesdropping Mrs. Roche, a round ruddy grandmother, asked if we were off a yacht.

"Fishermen," said McKerr happily as if proposing a cover story for two gunsels on the lam. "Him, he wants a house."

Mrs. Roche brightened. "There're some real bargains this season."

McKerr crushed his cigarette. I knew that if I didn't intervene quickly McKerr was going to get us tossed out, so I told Mrs. Roche we were looking for diversions while we waited upon a realtor. I asked if there was anything out of the weather.

Mrs. Roche shrugged. However, a slender wan fellow next to us at the counter spoke up. "Excuse me, but do you know the Wilson Museum?" We bantered pleasantly over lobster salad while he explained. "Some friends of mine are giving a flint-knapping lecture this morning; are you interested?"

My informant was Father Phillip from the fishing island of Deer Isle, at the southeast rim of Penobscot Bay. He also asked after my house hunting. It just so happened that his congregation was tightening its belt and selling off the parsonage in order to build him an efficiency apartment in the church basement. Perhaps I might be interested in a twelve-room Federal? A "real bargain," he said, with a sea view and four wooded acres. He spoke as if burying a lover. "We've done a deal of restoration, the teak panels, broad-plank floors. It needs children, though, with five bedrooms. Are you . . . ?"

"No, Father," I admitted. "Divorced."

"Pity," Father Phillip said, "but there's time, Mr. Paine, plenty of time, and a house up here tends to make babies."

"Not a selling point," I said.

"You can be Uncle Scrooge, then," Father Phillip said. "Does that suit you?"

Exactly. I liked him, a gentle smart fellow. I've often met parish priests like him and wondered why the Roman Church insists upon its Cardinal Humbug image when it has such good men in the ranks. I thanked him and took his card.

As we were leaving, Father Phillip said, "I know a lot of the best houses around here, if you need an impartial opinion. Watch out for the fireplaces and beams."

McKerr kept mumbling, "Bargains, bargains," as we set out in the rain for the Wilson Museum, up Perkins Street past cut-gem Capes and Federals. Halfway there we chanced upon a find that astounded McKerr. An open field at the waterline is all that remains of the first French trading post in North America, established 1613. Champlain himself landed here in 1604 and named the peninsula Pentagoet. For the next two centuries it passed back and forth between the Frenchers, their Indian allies and the British. We stood beside the sealed-up well of Fort Pentagoet and enjoyed a time voyage. Forget Jamestown, a sickly backwater the tremulous English never believed in. Here at Castine was the nursery for the northern empire that England and France fought over until it became the U.S.A.—a grassy field, a rocky shore, a seascape of choppy water and pine islands to the south.

McKerr's Pathfinder blood was up. "Clever Frenchers," he said. "Good anchorage, fresh water, gun platform, pirates' den."

McKerr's new mood marked his quick conversion from sorehead to romantic in the rain. As soon as we walked into the children's hour at the Wilson Museum, he fixed upon the dark ponytail of a beauty in jeans, whose fate it was to connect us like a sinking fishline to the murder that awaited us like a tourist trap.

She was Assistant Professor Iphigenia Incavagglia, a Coast Guard Academy grad teaching at one of her alma mater's rivals. She had a Roman nose, a briny temper and a figure that would have blessed the bow of a clipper. Called Effie (she hates Genie), she was wowing nine kids in the museum's main room with the Indian lore called flint-knapping.

McKerr knows these things, how to choose and strike a stone with a stone or antler billet to fashion an arrowhead or a speartip, and he stood by nodding as Professor Incavagglia and her assistant, an MMA cadet, demonstrated. Then it was the kids' turn, and McKerr surprised me by crowding forward with the grammarians to take up a sample and flint-knapp away.

"You've done this before," said the Maine Maritime Academy cadet assistant a might snippily. His name tag read "Moon."

McKerr tossed down his rock and declared, "Cleavage's wrong."

Cadet Moon sniffed.

McKerr squinted.

Cadet Moon, brunet and clear-featured, was as trim and attractive in his uniform as McKerr was baggy and woodsy in wool. Cadet Moon examined the rock, then reached into his kit bag for a beautifully made leather case that resembled an old-fashioned ship surgeon's pouch. Inside he had stone and antler billets arranged like instruments, along with neat little finished arrowheads. Cadet Moon took his lore seriously and took up McKerr's discarded rock to make a series of weird whacks with a square-headed billet.

McKerr scoffed at the fussiness. I thought this knapp duel ridiculous, except that I was certain McKerr himself was fussing to get Professor Incavagglia's attention.

Eventually Effie did come over to profess. I'll skip the flirtation. McKerr had reverted to taciturn Yankee know-it-all, which can be insufferable. Effie on the other hand was as casual as her ponytail and a most patient listener. Soon enough introductions were made, fussbudget Cadet Moon had returned to the kids, and McKerr's blarney had moved from the stone age to modern romance.

Effie reported that she taught history at MMA and was certain we'd enjoy the local lore. "Castine's an open-air museum," she said. "All the way back to prehistory, ruins upon ruins, every rock's been pissed on ten thousand times the way you pissers do." She laughed. "Most of you anyway."

"I told you this was a great place," said fork-tongued, love-struck McKerr to me.

Effie asked me, "And you want to live here? That'll jolt the town. You're under sixty and—no wives?"

We harrumphed in unison. The rain had stopped, and there were blue patches to show the squall was moving on. We were now a trio walking up Battle Avenue above MMA's stately grounds to the second-oldest fort in town, the British-built Fort George. It's just earthworks today, its compound used for a baseball field, but once Fort George commanded the bay west and the narrow neck of the peninsula east. We climbed up to walk off the earthen ramparts of the fort. McKerr and Effie were trading eighteenth-century anecdotes, which accelerated into boy-girl competition. They used me as the ignorant child.

"The kitchens were there," said Effie, "all the best coins too—those that the scavengers've left."

"The arsenal was there," said McKerr. "They made a tomb of it."

"Paul Revere was almost here," said Effie, topping McKerr's blarney. "He was a colonel—the quartermaster for the invasion the patriot cause sent up from Boston in '79 under a Saltonstall, to drive out the redcoats. It was a disaster, and they had to scuttle the flotilla. Revere got court-martialed. Only his friends saved him later."

"Redcoated devils," said McKerr, who was truly impressed and gazed upon Effie like a Mohawk princess at his campfire.

Effie was further interpreting Fort George through the ages, when we were interrupted by a bizarre invasion of our own. A blue Bell helicopter fluttered in from seaward, swung over the Maine Maritime

Academy and then settled gradually down behind second base at Fort George's center. Four fashionable folk in foul-weather gear climbed out and strolled in a circle.

"Bozos!" cried Effie, charging down the rampart straight on to the chopper. It was eighty yards, and McKerr and I caught up only in time to hear snippets of her fury at the pilot. ". . . National landmark! . . . You know better. . . . Get out of here!"

The fashionable gang of four drifted back toward us, two sleek dames with boozy pallor and trim flanks, who were escorted by a pair of genuine Tory usurers.

"Can I assist here?" asked the tall gray one—Rheinmann, he said, off the big boat out there in the bay, *Platinum.* "We meant no harm. My friends and I . . ."

Rheinmann's was such pleasant malarkey that it must have been his Oxbridge accent that put McKerr on the warpath. There was also Effie, who had thrown herself into defending Fort George without considering that yachtspersons come and go without rules.

The combat was brief. McKerr slipped back to the helicopter's tail, popped a panel and held his fishing knife appropriately close to the fuel line. Pathfinder's mayhem was afoot.

The pilot ducked out, shouting, "Get away!"

"No; you get," said Effie, "before you can't."

There was more to the contest, but Effie and Rheinmann did the talking while McKerr played silent torpedo. Such subtlety always works—why argue if you've already won?—and we three had a rude laugh afterward as we wandered back through the campus toward Water Street. We were so pleased with ourselves for having repelled a helicopter that McKerr tried blatant seduction. He proposed a weekend foray to his home hunting grounds.

"Saratoga?" said Effie. "Tonight? Oh, I wish I could—oh, let me think!"

McKerr was zigzagging most uncharacteristically. It was good for him, this love at first flint-knapp, and I felt grand as Uncle Tip the chaperon.

"You can get away, Eff," I argued. "We'll sack out at McKerr's mom's house in Schenectady and make the first race easy."

Effie was giddy. "You've got to let a girl think." We halted at the parking lot outside her office. "You two are more excitement than I've had . . . well, can you give me some time to think?"

This was disenchanting. There was mention of her small child, her mom, other divorced details, but still she'd started out a frontier woman, only to retreat toward American domestic. My realtor appointment was a convenient break in the action, so we arranged a rendezvous with her in an hour and continued to the agency.

The town center was livelier now with the fair weather blowing. The yachtspersons were floating around doing their laundry. The biggest tourist spot in town is the Maine Maritime Academy's training freighter, USS *Maine*, tied up beside the new-built engineering hall. We avoided the day-tripping tourists and stopped to buy tobacco in a market and to ogle some of the sailing beauties. Women off yachts look ratty, too much gin and sun and not enough shampoo; they cover it up with funny colors and randy eyes.

McKerr ignored the women. He only had eyes for the enemy and pointed to the huge ship offshore, Rheinmann's two-hundred-foot diesel yacht *Platinum*, under Canadian sail and now mounting its Bell helicopter again. "Cheesy redcoats," said McKerr the mobster. "As if they still have rights—oughtta make 'em swim with the fishes."

Realtor Mrs. Ives was still not returned, though it was half four. The secretary was very apologetic and asked if I was anchoring the night in the marina.

McKerr said, "We're volunteers, Mollie, not *them*."

Joining in his patriot temper, I asked if there was a twelve-pounder for sale we could bring to bear for some fireworks.

"If you mean antiques," she said, "there are several nice shops."

I took her little map and we walked down to the marina to eat ice cream and speculate how we could scuttle *Platinum*. We even drew up a plan on the map and befriended the adolescent waitress to ask if there were any freebooters in town looking to go buccaneering for Old Glory.

She giggled. "Are you serious? This town? It's dead."

Meanwhile we were eavesdropped upon by two yachtswomen at the next umbrella. I favored the fair one, flat tummy, broad abeam, tiny burnt nose and pageboy two weeks past the last blond rinse.

McKerr caught her staring at us and boldly proposed, "You Mollies in-ner-rested? A Castine tea party—plank for the peerage and ransom the swells."

They weren't Mollies. The fair one was Jilly, the brunette was Connie, both off a fifty-nine-foot charter in port, a Hinckley Southwester, *Arctic Loon*. It was a loony day because not only were they our age and therefore too old for us, not only were they usurer-married, but also their husbands weren't flying in until Sunday and they were "in-ner-rested" in our loony chatter.

I dummied up after introductions, since McKerr was in command. "We run your cutter alongside after dark," he proposed, "grapplers away, and then slit every throat that don't choke."

Vodka tonic Jilly asked, "What are you two talking about?"

"Make-believe, Jill," I explained. "It's what we do."

Bloody Mary Connie said, "We aren't that bored, if you're serious."

I tried to amuse them with a version of McKerr's tangle at Fort George.

"You cut the fuel lines?" asked Jenny. The truth no longer mattered; they were a lot tipsy and a little intimidated, which probably explains how, when we made to walk away, they said they'd follow along if we were really going antiquing. "A cannon—is that what you want?" asked Jilly.

"Muskets, repeaters, anything with pop," said McKerr, flicking at the fishing blade on his hip, pointing out to *Platinum*. "Make her for crew of sixteen; cabin boys won't fight."

"Eurotrash," I added excessively. "They'll strike their colors as soon as we show ours."

Connie blinked. "My husband's Canadian."

We rejected the first antique shop, and I got McKerr aside from the dames to say we'd best lose them before *they* got serious. McKerr understood. In all the world there is nothing so game as a vacationing mother temporarily landfallen without kids or husband. (Also McKerr and Tip regard adultery unworthy, the sport of settlers.) It would have worked—Jilly and Connie were coming to their senses since it was time to meet their yachting buddies for fresh booze—but we then chanced upon one more antique shop.

This one was set into the lower-level side of the triple brick building housing my real estate agency. The fashionable gang of four off *Platinum* was idling at the door. Lord Rheinmann had his back to us and was talking into the shop. McKerr strode up the warpath silently.

The first shot was fired by the shop owner, however, who happened to be the check-bouncing chubby Boston Yankee we'd met upstairs. "That's what you say!" he barked at Rheinmann as he used his bulk to push him farther out the door. "And I say Christie's is in New York if you can't take risks!"

Tip applauded. The Yankee was roly-poly pink-faced out of control, but he knew the Third Amendment, about not having to suffer foreign troops. He looked at me anxiously, then bowed. "Thank you, gentlemen."

Rheinmann turned, to find McKerr in his face. "You again!" Rheinmann exclaimed. "What is—? Never mind."

McKerr knew his lines: "Fit the Frenchers with the redcoats, then Gentleman Johnny at Saratoga with the Frenchers, then watched Cornwallis sail away, world turned upside down."

"Are you bastards *on* something?" asked Rheinmann in retreat. "Because if you are, I'm sure there's law in this town for riffraff."

McKerr grunted. It was Tip's turn. I hummed them "The World Turned Upside Down," a rowdy just-say-no-to-drugs tune in 6/8 time played that day at Yorktown the patriot cause just said no to Cornwallis and he departed like a pimp, also played one day soon after when Castine just said no to King George and the English empire quit their last stronghold in New England.

There were more stuffy words but not from us, and the *Platinum* gang departed like swells.

The Yankee introduced himself. "Bob Littlefield," he said. "Welcome to my shop. . . ."

We returned our monickers and ambitions.

"You want what?" asked Littlefield. "Twelve-pounders?" He roared. "Come in, come in; plenty of trinkets for your ladies." Jilly and Connie raced up to assure Littlefield they were not our ladies. He roared again and started talking.

Littlefield was a Yankee in every way but the most obvious—he rambled. Otherwise his character fit his shop, a jammed-full junk heap under the broad beams, paraphernalia from fiddles to swords to prints and oils purposelessly without order and dusty dank through the years. "My rent's low as the beams, so I sell cheap," he said. "Look at those beams, cut from a frigate, one solid piece of cedar, please touch, it's the fun."

Littlefield plopped down on the only corner of his desk clear of stacked paperbacks. I realized that there was a scraggly fellow in jeans and gray T-shirt sitting behind the desk reading *I Rode in a Flying Saucer*. Littlefield ignored him even when he bumped a stack of paperbacks that tumbled onto the UFO fan's lap.

I'm not sure how Littlefield got started on politics, but soon he was discoursing on the Democratic Party in its glorious Depression days in Back Bay Boston. "A man needed work, it was dignity then, not like this crowd today. My dad did roofs one week, sewers the next, anything at all. It wasn't the money, it was the work."

Jilly and Connie were fascinated by the trays of Victorian semiprecious stones. Littlefield whipped out bags more, then produced a gem box of lapis lazuli. "From Pakistan, you know; got it at a flea market in Portland, ladies," then he was on to a story of how he first came to Maine.

"I've a house up at Bagaduce," he said, "old farm town up the road. Paid twelve hundred cash for it in 1964. Old lobster who sold it took my money and said, 'Would've taken less.' I took the deed and said, 'Would've paid more.' He's still up there, hates me for what he could get for it now, a hundred thousand, more."

McKerr was scouting in the corner, so I got to be the available ear for Littlefield's monologues. Littlefield was discussing the federal deficit when Jilly interrupted, "I like these; how much?"

At this point McKerr beckoned me; he was holding a box of coins stamped with King George, but what he cared about was the oil portrait hanging beyond the rubbishy stuff. "You recognize that face?" McKerr asked me. "And look closely at the bark in the background."

I obeyed, and here is where fate again played a trick on us. The oil painting was a clean lovely Federal-era portrait of a very old bewigged man. Strangely the old man was wearing a U.S. Navy midshipman's uniform, circa 1800. The nose, the mouth, the eyes were eerily unmistakable. But what provided the best clue was the name of the little ship (bark) painted in the background, *Captain Death.*

You don't know this, but Citizen Paine began his adventures as an English commoner named Tom Pain, who ran away to sea at sixteen and signed on a privateer he called *Captain Death.* It wasn't until he was thirty-seven, a disgruntled father and civil servant, that he ran away again, to America, to flack for Benjamin Franklin and soon after author anonymously the pamphlet that turned the world upside down, *Common Sense,* 1776. The American and French revolutions followed, with the man now calling himself Tom Paine a noisy player. Yet after all this, a lifetime of fire and thunder, his boyish escapade on *Captain Death* was the one autobiographical detail he liked to brag upon. Citizen Paine ended his life in poverty and infamy on a farm in Westchester, New York, dead of pneumonia at seventy-two in 1809, forgotten by the nation he birthed, without family or friends when he was interred behind the farmhouse. There are no known portraits of him in his dotage. Even his bones were lost when a creepy English lord disinterred them for a memorial back in London and misplaced them en route.

So what was this—a portrait of ancient Citizen Paine playing the boy sailor? I started to ask McKerr.

McKerr shushed me and addressed Littlefield. "That's mighty nice, mighty nice."

"You've found my beauty," said Littlefield. "Best thing in the shop except for that American impressionist there." Littlefield ordered his scraggly little assistant to clear a path in the trashy prints between us and his "beauty." UFO boy was a timid factotum, who retreated instantly when Littlefield began his sales pitch.

Littlefield did not mention the critical name, but then again he didn't know the portraitist either. Just got it last month from an estate sale in St. John's, he said, don't have time for the research, he said, that's why it's cheap. Down in New York it could be worth a fortune, he said, but he wasn't paying those rents so didn't charge those prices.

McKerr spoke at the right moment. "How much?"

"Eighty-five hundred." Littlefield didn't grin. "You won't believe this, but I lowered the price this morning, same for the impressionist there. You like it? Twelve-five."

I was hovering at this other supposed treasure, a fuzzy landscape of a whaling port that I wouldn't have bought as a stamp, but then I know nothing of the art history game except that the swells play it nastily.

"I'll tell you," said Littlefield, "it's been a slow season ever since that crash last year, slow." Littlefield was on to national politics again. "It's going to come down, all of it, and then what's land worth, what's anything worth?"

"Bye-bye now," called Connie. Jilly and Connie were excusing themselves lamely. "Maybe we'll see you later," cooed Jilly. Her gaze needed a tonic recharge, and I felt bad for her. (No I didn't.)

Shrewd Littlefield leaped to offer Jilly a parting gift of garnet, presuming this would deepen our interest in his precious paintings.

I mumbled as much to McKerr. He said, "If it's what we think, it's better than a house. Shut up."

McKerr entered into some Yankee bargaining of his own. I thought them fair matched, two Yankees conversing without eye contact. "Portrait like that..." from Littlefield. "Frame's beat up..." from McKerr.

Some time later we were outside the shop door, having knocked fifteen hundred dollars off the price and trying to get away from Littlefield's greedy gamesmanship.

"I've had other interest, gentlemen," he said, "the Maine Maritime Academy for one, fine piece for their collection, so I can't keep it aside, you understand."

I missed how it happened, but suddenly Effie was nearby, makeup applied, hair combed out and a good denim skirt to show jogger's legs. She hailed us and then addressed Littlefield cheerily. "Don't rook them, Bob, they're friends of mine." Effie pounced down from the street level onto the walkway and bumped McKerr like a lover. "His coins are bogus," she said. "Arrowheads are good. He keeps his best stuff up at his house."

"Friends of yours?" said Littlefield, adding oddly, "They're kind of gentlemanly for you, eh, Eff?"

Effie ignored the crack and asked what we were buying.

Greedy schemers Tip and McKerr grabbed her before her archival mind exposed our tactic.

"Sunday morning, we'll be back here," said McKerr to Littlefield. "Seven thousand cash."

Two Yankee traders shook hands on the deal with the same sort of solemnity their forefathers used to acquire New England from its native residents.

2

Effie backed out of our invitation to Saratoga. Her mother was visiting for August and wasn't persuaded that a thirty-five-year-old divorced mother of a preschooler was mature enough to run off with unknown men for a weekend at a New York racetrack. Put this way, Tip's and McKerr's moms would have voted with Effie's. We three dined at the Victorian-built Pentagoet Inn, and then we lingered so long at the table and in the picturesque common room that I had to kick Effie out so we could get on the road.

"See you at church," she said.

"After church," said McKerr, who thinks preachers agents of the crown.

"Well, don't spend it all on horses," she closed. "I like generous meals with generous men."

Ten hours later we arrived in Schenectady in woozy exhaustion and sacked out at McKerr's mom's house. We'd spent the drive talking out our scheme along with the other attractions of Castine, chiefly Professor Incavagglia, whom McKerr so favored it worried him. "Just a dame," he said. "Nice gams, nice neck, but a dame."

Neck? I let that go and won't call much attention to our afternoon at the track either. Our plan was brilliantly stupid and didn't have a chance. It was supposed to go this way: Tip lends McKerr a thousand dollars. McKerr puts it on Blind Mountain, a pretty pony listed that morning as nine to one in the Whitney Handicap. McKerr wins, repays me my grubstake, we drive back to Castine and he buys Citizen Paine's portrait of madness, which is priceless.

If you've ever been to Saratoga you know it's the most beautiful track in America—casual, pastoral, homey—and also secretly the best track in America for desperate long shots on the nose. (Let's leave out the fact that our choice of the horse's nose was based upon a laughing brown trout out of Moosehead Lake.) I have no excuse as to why I went along with McKerr. I just follow Pathfinder. No one, not the *Daily Racing Form* nor OTB's touts nor the crusty guys around the picnic tables, picked Blind Mountain even to place. By race time Saratoga's computers showed doubt too, by extending the odds to eleven to one.

No suspense. Whitney Handicap, mile and a furlong for three years old and up, with a quarter-million-dollar purse. Blind Mountain, with a career earning of $90,324, carrying 122 pounds and J.D. Bailey on a fast track, goes out fast, holds through the far and near turn, then gets trapped on the rail in the stretch and miraculously places by a length, a nose *behind* the winner.

All this is sensible. Except that it didn't happen this way, and ten thousand dollars of winnings is too fat to make a single roll of hundred-dollar bills. We stared at the results on the field board. We sweated while waiting out the results of the photo finish. The crowd groaned when the announcement confirmed the ridiculous fact that Blind Mountain had won by a nose.

McKerr rolled four cigarettes. I lost my best traveling pipe. Together we learned once more why gambling is not for the easyhearted and sudden plunder is very upsetting.

I remember the drive back because we stopped at the IV Corners market in the paper mill town of Rumford, deep in the Maine woods, to tank up and debrief.

"Are we doing this?" I asked.

"Shut up," said McKerr. We bought ugly pizza and paused at the river to admire the evil profile of the paper mill's stacks, which were backlit by the green glow of aircraft warning beacons and which spewed a sulfurous stink that appeared to rise straight from Old Nick's pipe.

"Are we doing this?" I asked again.

"Shut up," said McKerr. We did take one more break, outside Rumford at the point on the Androscoggin River where Benedict Arnold first met trouble when his hodgepodge expedition to conquer Quebec City drowned in the falls that used to be there. McKerr finds spiritual muscle in this sort of wackiness. "Are we doing this?" I asked the last time. McKerr said nothing.

Castine was silent at first light. I'd arranged us a second-floor room at the Pentagoet Inn so we could sleep off our defeat. Since we'd won, we were noisy slipping into our bunks. Also McKerr found he'd rather chain-smoke than sleep, so he set off to walk the town and wait for Littlefield. I missed the next few hours happily, the last peace I would have for several days, since now it's time to show you how murder followed greed, ours and theirs.

You've heard of or met most of the suspects and material witnesses. The first victim was Yankee Bob Littlefield.

McKerr woke me with the news. "Dead, murdered, Friday night after we left. The old Roche woman told me. She says his boyfriend stabbed him, then ran back to his trailer and got a shotgun blast from *his* wife."

I made McKerr repeat the sequence (there was clearly a gender problem here), and then we got to what we really cared about. I asked, "What about Citizen Paine?"

"The shop's locked up," said McKerr. "County sheriff's tag on the door."

We bought breakfast at the Castine Café in order to chat with our source, round Mrs. Roche. Her version was what is called lurid. Friday night Bob Littlefield went home to his house up at Bagaduce and got murdered. Everybody knew he was a "funny sort," she said, which is rural Maine code for homosexual. Littlefield had a handyman named Levi Gilbert, a local bad boy who'd done a stretch in state prison for vandalizing summer cottages. Levi Gilbert used to live in a trailer off Route 199 with his wife and two kids. Now he was a "funny sort" too, said Mrs. Roche. Levi Gilbert's wife had filed abuse charges against him in the past, and he was under court order to leave her alone. Meanwhile Mrs. Gilbert had taken up with Arthur Moon, another local boy, who was a "good sort," the nephew of a Captain Lincoln Moon in the Hancock County sheriff's office.

I interrupted to ask if Levi Gilbert was a scraggly little fellow partial to UFO books.

"Flying saucers, you mean?" said Mrs. Roche, nodding her head.

I also asked how many Moons lived around here.

"What d'you mean?" said Mrs. Roche. "Moons're a big old family, here to there." She frowned at me. "I'm a Moon too, if you're asking."

She finished off with the official police version, via the local deputy sheriff, Jack Ladue: Scraggly bad boy Levi Gilbert murdered Bob Littlefield the way those "funny sorts" do, then went crazy and attacked his estranged wife's trailer while she was asleep inside with her kids and new beau Arthur Moon. Mrs. Gilbert shotgun-blasted her husband in the leg and fled with new beau Arthur Moon and kids for help. Levi Gilbert bled to death before the police got him to the hospital. Case closed.

Tip fancies himself Holmes Paine now and again, but he's no Dr. Watson, so I'll cheat a bit and tell you right now what McKerr and I did not know until after some strange goings-on. None of Mrs. Roche's nor Deputy Jack Ladue's version of the two murders was true. You do already know that S. Holmes's profound contribution to modern philosophy was his maxim: "When you have eliminated the impossible, whatever remains, however improbable, must be the truth."

On to the impossibles.

We abandoned breakfast and drifted outside, a muggy morning, the wind from the west. Castine's churches were ringing the call to worship. I said something vague about Littlefield's luck.

McKerr said something vague about our luck, then gruffed, "Littlefield's dead, and how're we gonna get our painting now? My painting!" McKerr challenged, "What are we gonna do about it?"

We should have left it there, walked to the Catholic church to flirt with Effie, gone back to our laughing brownies. But ten thousand long shots was too heavy for us, and we buckled to greed.

I asked McKerr if he'd heard Mrs. Roche mention anything that could be called a motive for little Levi Gilbert's rampage?

"Robbery?" tried McKerr. "And it's not gill-burt, it's jill-bear, Frencher name—anything's likely."

"Okay," I said. "Refight the French and Indian wars later." I tried to sound analytical. "Littlefield was bouncing checks, right? And the biggest money he'd seen all summer is in your fishing vest, right?"

"Not robbery?" asked McKerr.

"Eliminate greed," I preached, "which in this case would resemble robbery, and the other madness men kill for is family, which in this case would resemble jealousy."

"Jealous of what?" asked McKerr.

I agreed, "Yeah, what?" It didn't seem to me that a timid ex-con reading UFO books would be in a mood to commit a crime of passion within the night.

McKerr said, "They're saying they were queer."

"They said worse than that," I mumbled. "And even if they were lovers," I returned, "jealousy requires a third party."

"You got a lotta rules, mouthpiece," McKerr teased.

"It's not me," I grumbled. "It's tv." I organized my thoughts. I argued that robbery was the best motive for now, and there was only one thing Levi Gilbert could've thought worthwhile to kill for—the bundle in McKerr's vest. "But before the payoff?" I asked.

McKerr repeated his challenge. "What are we gonna do about it?"

Momentarily we were down to the triple brick building on Water Street. The building was open on Sunday because U.S. Customs upstairs never closes.

Conveniently for our larcenous plan, we found the missing Mrs. Ives working at her secretary's desk.

"Mr. Paine," she began, an attractive silver lady in riding clothes. "I'm so sorry about Friday; how good of you to . . ."

Sales patter continued, and I drew her out about her bargains. My ruse was very nervous-making, and my bowels rumbled while I stalled Mrs. Ives long enough for McKerr to slip down the carriage house ladder through the dead-bolt hatchway in the hall to Littlefield's shop and to return.

I'm not sure what I would have done had McKerr done what we'd considered—exchange seven thousand dollars like a pack rat for the Citizen Paine portrait. Fortunately or not, he didn't do it, because he couldn't. While I was chatting with Mrs. Ives over photographs of enormously expensive lawns, McKerr came in softly.

"...love to take you around, Mr. Paine," said Mrs. Ives. "This afternoon is booked but—"

McKerr interrupted. "Tomorrow."

Mrs. Ives then made a strange turn that two decades in New York have taught me how to decipher. She looked at McKerr, at me, back to McKerr, then swallowed while tucking her silver curls behind her diamond earrings. I'd said no wife. She'd said, "Oh." Now she was asking her matronly sense of proportion if we were homosexual. Tip is usually entertained by such wrongheadedness. Not this time. Mrs. Ives was suddenly a sleek hag to me, and I attacked, mentioning to her what we'd learned of Littlefield, Gilbert, murder.

Mrs. Ives spoke sympathetically at first: Terrible tragedy, town's abuzz, nice man, did I know him? Gilbert too? Sickening to think. The realtor finally reemerged. "I hope you don't think Castine's like this."

"No wife-beating?" I taunted.

"What do you think of us? The worst around here, well, speeding and poaching."

"No robbery?" I taunted.

"Oh, a little, but really no one locks their doors, but—"

"No drugs?" I taunted.

"—you know Maine," she said, stopping hard. I waited on the drugs boilerplate. She smiled. "You're from New York; I almost forgot." She sighed. "This is the willy-wacks, Mr. Paine."

Then she was bizarrely on to a non sequitur story about how last year she had invited a homeless boy who'd quit a yacht to stay in the room above her stable and care for her horses, and soon after he'd disappeared with some of her jewelry. "I got a card from him last Christmas," she said, tucking her hair again. "I know I should have prosecuted, but it wasn't very good jewelry, and I didn't want trouble for my daughters."

Mrs. Ives was another textbook Yankee who rambled, and given that she thought us two big-city gays, she was probably about to invite us to go cantering if we didn't get away.

I used the excuse that we were going to church.

"Oh," she said, "but services are just about over. Except at the Trinity Chapel."

That's right, nice hag, I thought, we're going to count Tories. I said that I'd see her tomorrow.

The sun was cooking off the muggy damp. The marina parking lot down the slope was like a stock car race, with the rentals firing up to go for victuals.

Soon as we cleared all earshot, McKerr was back to his mobster jargon about what he'd found in the antique shop. "Joint's been tossed, not that the heat's careful, and guess what's missing?"

I translated: Littlefield's shop had been searched by the police. Citizen Paine was missing. Also, McKerr added, the American impressionist painting was missing.

Conspirators Tip and McKerr stopped off in the grocery to buy tobacco and confer over the Sunday papers. The *Bangor Daily News* weekend edition had a late-breaking and abbreviated account of the two murders, replaying Mrs. Roche's version by way of deputy sheriff Jack Ladue and adding the detail that the state attorney general's office and Barracks J of the state police were investigating in cooperation with the county sheriff. The case wasn't closed, not yet.

Of significant note to me was that Captain Lincoln Moon and Deputy Jack Ladue were listed as the officers first at both crime scenes. I showed McKerr the paper and offered the guess that maybe Littlefield had taken the Citizen Paine portrait and the American impressionist back to his house for safekeeping. That still didn't make much of a robbery motive for Levi Gilbert.

"But your lovers' tiff," said McKerr. "It don't figure, shamus."

"Right," I agreed, lost in the willy-wacks, a word I liked. "What now?" I asked McKerr the Pathfinder.

McKerr said, "The dame knew the stiffs."

He meant Effie. This was a convenient direction, since we were on it already, out Perkins Street along the shoreline. Just past the open field that was Fort Pentagoet stands Castine's prim new-painted Catholic chapel. It's actually an 1830 farmhouse that was converted to a chapel after the First World War for the Irish servants of the Yankee lords. We idled among the Japanese cars parked on the lawn. The bell sounded out an earnest crowd of middle-aged ladies along with not a few nuclear families. Effie emerged with her cute kid and very tall mother, who was wearing a Pro-Life button. Tip made a remark to McKerr. McKerr ditched his cigarette and approached warily.

"You're back!" cheered Effie. "Did you win? You won!" Formalities waited upon Effie's sweet hug of McKerr and his swag-filled fishing vest. "Let me see. Mom, look, he won!"

Effie's dark-eyed mom was Mrs. Kielly (Effie wasn't born Roman after all; at least a half-Irish maiden), and Mom's glance at us was suspicion itself.

Handsome McKerr wasn't helping himself as usual, so I tried flimsy chatter—saying we were fishermen on holiday, we were happy to meet her.

Mrs. Kielly remained matronly cool, and I could guess that a hundred one-hundred-dollar bills was why. Charm as I might, we were northern sharpies to her. "You're on vacation?" asked Mom. "All alone, are you, no families?"

Effie instantly invited us to her house for lunch. We were fending this idea off as if it were the Inquisition, when our little contest was interrupted by the arrival of a fair, muscular fellow in a washed denim suit. Effie drew her kid close. Mom went from cool to ice floe.

Meet the knothead deputy sheriff, Jack Ladue. "Hey ya," he said. "These're them, Eff?"

"Yes, Jack," said Effie. "They came back, like I said."

The momentary silence was what can be called a town and gown love affair not prospering for demiadult reasons. What I'm saying is that divorced Effie and divorcing Jack were lovers, but their relationship was ending: perhaps because Jack hadn't removed his wedding ring, as Effie had; perhaps because Mom's visit was a time-out during which Effie had reconsidered her attachment to a knothead; perhaps just because.

Jack Ladue reached for my hand. "You're Tommy Paine. Hey there ya. . . ." There were more colloquialisms, followed by, "I've seen that

movie of yours; great. When Effie told me . . . I've never met someone like you." Jack had a strong callused grip, stubby fingernails, a
cop's mustache and a belly at maybe thirty. He was the kind of cop I
like when he's driving away being a cop.

Mrs. Kielly frowned at Jack because he wasn't driving away.
McKerr made a smoke. Effie kept up salutary patter.

Finally Jack caught on and said he must get his kids home. "Hey
ya," added Jack, grinning at McKerr, "d'ja win there at the track?"

McKerr was reaching for his tomahawk, so I intervened with a
statement of fact. "Yes, he did, Jack."

"How 'bout that," said Jack. "Welllll . . . Eff, Mrs. Kielly, see ya."
He nodded and left.

I waited just long enough for Jack to take the lead to his Japanese
4 × 4 (navy, newish, fog lights, two grammar school kids waiting for
him) before I pursued with a hail.

"What's that, Mr. Paine?" asked Jack.

I flattered his knothead about his notice in the paper.

"Yeah, that's right; Eff said you knew Littlefield."

"More than that, Jack," I said. "I kind of liked him; good guy for a
Democrat." Jack didn't laugh. "So tell me, Jack," I continued, "why'd
Levi Gilbert do it?"

"Well, sir," Jack offered, "it's not my first murder investigation, but
ya know, they were more'n buddies, ya know." Jack bared his stained
teeth. "Levi, I went to school with his brothers—his folks're real
upset."

I was returned to thinking about a motive for the murder. Robbery
didn't make good sense, so I tried the other possibility, jealousy—
that is, some sort of family falling out. But what family? There
seemed only one family connection in the case. I asked Jack how the
Moon family felt about their boy Arthur running around with a
woman who'd put him in harm's way?

Jack had a goofy habit of blowing up his cheeks when he was
thinking. "How's that?" he asked.

"The Moons," I said. "I hear they're a big family around here. How
do they feel about Arthur getting attacked by Levi Gilbert and then
ducking fast when the shotgun went off?" Jack still wasn't showing

comprehension in his law-enforcement eyes, so I listed a Moon collection: Mrs. Gilbert's beau, Arthur Moon. Investigating officer Captain Lincoln Moon. The café owner Mrs. Roche the Moon. Then I added for thoroughness Effie's little helper at the Wilson Museum, Cadet Moon.

"I gotta say I don't get what you're gettin' at, Mr. Paine," said Jack.

I realized that whatever I was getting at, Jack wasn't going to help me along. Most un-Holmes-like, I tried a guess. "Was Levi Gilbert a Moon too?"

"Well, not recently." Jack laughed. "The Moons're a big family, here to there."

I made one more guess, just for fun. "Are you a Moon, Jack?"

Jack Ladue said, "Not close, Mr. Paine," and laughed again. "Hey there, you Hollywood boys..." He swallowed something, and I missed it. "...don'tcha?" Jack talked some more but unhelpfully; the dimwit local cop wasn't unprofessional: case under investigation. "See ya," he finished.

3

Citizen Paine was missing, McKerr was romancing, I was sleeping too heavily at the Pentagoet Inn, until McKerr woke me again for dinner near six. I told McKerr he needed his rest too. There was some mumbling about a nap at Effie's office. I asked, nap? office? couch maybe? McKerr said nothing. Twenty-hour drives, wobbled brains and so forth, but this was obvious hanky-panky.

Later I was mischievously silent when Effie joined us for dessert at Mrs. Roche's café. She'd changed back into her jeans and looked sexily radiant sitting close to McKerr. "Are you really going to buy a house here?" she asked me, "or are you two up to no good?"

McKerr grumbled when I asked him if he'd blabbed our Zurich bank numbers too.

Effie said, "You think that painting's at Bob's house, huh?"

I bypassed her felonious guess, and we ambled down to the rowdiest bar in town, a quayside pub with moldy trimmings and futile lighting. The yachting fleet was in, as dads or moms joined their sunburned families for tomorrow's adventures. I asked for a table away from the hormonal monsters (aka teenagers) and was rewarded with my back to grouchy grammarians. McKerr nurses caffeine, I sip seltzer; Effie, however, was a professional sailor and was soon launched boozily into her life story. I hurried her ahead to the current facts about the hip crowd in old Castine.

Little surprise that Bob Littlefield, she said, was the generous host of what passed for local underground culture. He'd held large parties at his Bagaduce farmhouse and was extremely well liked by as many as despised him.

"Why're you asking all this?" tried Effie. "You don't believe Levi did it, do you?"

"Nope," I said.

"Okay, okay," said Effie, "I don't either, it's terrible—except that he did. Levi's been trouble for years."

Impolitely I asked if this was the sheriff's department or the history department talking.

She said, "Hey, give me a break. I knew them both; they were friends of mine!"

McKerr glared me down. I didn't back off, asking if Effie knew the new widow, Mrs. Gilbert.

"She's one of those poor human beings they beat and beat until she's mindless," said Effie. "Levi wasn't her first bad move and won't be the last. Up here, it's a battered woman's nightmare. You ever hit a woman, Tip?"

Nice tack, Eff. I repacked my pipe and liked her the more.

About this time we were interrupted by fate again, in the person of the grass widow blondine Jilly. "Remember me?" she started off, plopping down and handing me one of my paperbacks to sign. "This is you, isn't it; we figured it out last night—you're Tommy Paine the writer?"

Wrong, Jilly, but her autograph hunt was for starters. Effie now enjoyed herself encouraging Jilly's adulterous affections for an available best-seller (Tip). It emerged that Jilly's husband had found a reason to stay in Highland Park, and she was tipsily alienated from her pal Connie and the rest of her yachting party. Flirtation followed inanely, colored by Jilly's erotic oohs about McKerr's winnings and her erotic gasps about Littlefield's murder.

Eventually I didn't like Jilly the Chicago public relations honcho less. Eventually also Jilly made her move and invited us to act out her marital discord on the fifty-nine-foot charter *Arctic Loon.*

I'm skipping the giggly shore-to-ship transfer in the dinghy and the general suspiciousness of the midwesterners toward Tip and McKerr. Because sometime after we'd arrived we were chilly on deck playing count the constellations, when one of the husbands, who didn't know Betelgeuse from his old Guccis, asked the cook to bring out the dope.

The crucial clue came up soon. Jilly was down in the head, arguing with Connie about Tip. Effie was in McKerr's lap, competing for space with the Benjamin Franklins. The so-called grownups were buzzed out, passing the evil weed in a circle. Then one of the husbands—Jeffrey, I think—let out a holler at the sea and said, "Yeah, man, great shit—you wouldn't believe how hard it was to find around here. Worse than the sixties! F——ing economy's gone nuts! Coke's ghetto cheap, grass is like out of sight! It's like your books, there." He was now addressing me. "Commo plan, dead drop in a field and what's it called, the pad; blinking headlights. This crazy hillbilly and Mammy Yokum."

Mr. Jeffrey was trying to impress me with sci-fi/spy jargon. His mumbo jumbo adds up to a dope deal. He liked being the center of my attention, so he repeated himself with a detail. "It was like some movie—they're operating out of that junk shop below Customs, for chrissakes. And ya gotta drive to a pickup in the woods at these trailers with hillbilly goons staring at you. It was the movies!"

I let go a broadside. Where, when, how, who? My dopey source was defensive, but his answers did include that the dope purchase had been at a certain antique shop and the dope pickup had been Friday night at a trailer, well inland. I didn't bother telling the midwesterners that their expensive vacation had transformed them into probable material witnesses to murder. Instead I signaled McKerr, who caught on right away.

Effie got touchy when we took her forward to the boom. "Okay, okay, so you know now," she said. "Everybody around here knows about Bob."

"We didn't, Eff," I said.

"Why should you?" said Effie. "You're not from here."

McKerr laughed at her logic.

Jilly came forward then to butt in. "Hey, what's going on? You're scaring my friends—"

McKerr said, "You should've told us Effie."

"Okay, okay," Effie tried. "I'm sorry, but Bob's dead, and what's it matter now?"

Mobster McKerr said it best: "We thought he got it for our package. Instead he got it over a deal."

"You don't know that," protested Effie.

I urged Effie's logic into the fact that dope wasn't mentioned in the newspaper, that an ongoing attorney general's investigation was. I asked her how come her boy Jack Ladue was spreading fag murder gossip when he knew it was dope.

"Okay, okay," repeated Effie, then she sighed. "Jack's like that, you know. Sneaky."

4

Again what McKerr and Tip should have done was let it go. It so happened that my new dope-robbery theory (greed) was as wrong as Jack Ladue's dope-robbery /"funny sort"/ rampage theory (greed with a twist), but I didn't know that and, truth, didn't care. What McKerr and I wanted was our Citizen Paine picture, and now that we had a way of arguing it out of the picture, we got sneaky like Deputy Ladue. This is a roundabout way of saying that what followed was knotheaded.

I could blame it on the dames. (Nah.) Effie wanted her McKerr, and Jilly wanted her revenge on her absent husband. This led to a bedding arrangement at the Pentagoet Inn that resembled wartime

London—two couples, one and a half rooms, foolish silences, much giggling, girls in and out of the bathroom. It made me restless, and while struggling with aggressive Chicago, Holmes Paine withdrew from carnality to reconstruct the crime of murder. (Mind doctors are not wrong: sex and death are terrific for make-believe.) Jilly finally settled down, and I held on to her rump like a talisman.

I might have dreamed. I imagined Littlefield alive, then dead. I asked him, who did it? He wasn't talking. I tried Levi Gilbert. He was whimpering while he bled to silence. I asked Tip: Does a man stab his buddy, then run to his wife? Turn the world upside down: If I stabbed Jilly, would I run to McKerr?

The answer was *maybe*. But only if I wanted something beside sympathy. Like money to get out of town? Say battered Mrs. Gilbert was holding my money from the dope dealing. That made her a partner and her new beau, Arthur Moon, a partner. They blast me and run. How convenient that my death gets explained away by my alleged previous crime.

Now Tip was back to the beginning: Why did I stab Jilly? Because she's jealous? nasty? stupid? Because I'm jealous? nasty? stupid? Because she's got something I want and won't give it to me? It didn't add up, I thought, as the gumshoes might say. Not elementary, I thought, as Holmes might say.

It was 5 A.M., with first light in the window shades. I sat up and realized McKerr was already awake and smoking pensively. I summarized my confounding case in whispers.

McKerr said, "Right, mouthpiece. Shut up and get dressed."

In not much more time we were Land Roving to Bagaduce. The smart part of our plan was that we were visiting the Littlefield crime scene. The stupid part was that we needed Effie along to guide us, and that meant Jilly wouldn't leave herself out.

Bagaduce is a crossroads in the willy-wacks ten miles inland from Castine, along the bank of the tidal Bagaduce River. Once it was mean farming on small parcels in soil stolen from the forest. Nothing grows there now but trees, not much lives there now but low-income natives and well-fed wildlife. Bob Littlefield's farmhouse and attached

barn, set close to the road and catercorner across from another farmstead, needed paint and roofing. We motored around back to the
woodpile, near the pantry door. Public enemy and mouthpiece
quizzed sleepy Effie.

"Jack said they found him in the tv room," answered Effie. "He was
tied up, you know, awful, awful."

I played Clue big-city style. "So you say the handyman in the tv
room with a knife and...?"

"Yeah, naked," answered Effie. "Yeah, tied up. I don't know how
he did it, okay?"

McKerr and I didn't have to force entry, because the door was open
except for the sheriff's sticker, which we agreed we didn't see. Longtime
New Yorkers, we've been to murder scenes before. It's upsetting but also
exhilarating, voyeurism times ten thousand. The kitchen smelled
musty. There was a Littlefield mess of collectibles and unwashed dishes.
There were two quarts of blueberries rotting in the sink. McKerr noted
that the utensil drawer and the knife rack were empty.

"Crime lab boys must've taken them," said McKerr, "looking for
the weapon."

In the tv room the corduroy lounge chair was blood-soaked. There
was also a rancid smell, which was clearly the dried gore. I lit my pipe
into a volcano and McKerr made extra cigarettes to cover the worst
of it.

"Tied up," said McKerr, pointing at the chair. "That's how it's
done."

I agreed; a sick part of human sexuality is bondage. There were
blood flecks radiating from the chair onto magazines, rug, stereo, tv,
as far as the window bank.

McKerr turned on the tv, to discover it was set on the VCR.
McKerr punched the machine, and we discovered there was a color
tape of a supine boy masturbating his sizable self to classical music.
"Brahms," said McKerr.

"Video of the plague years," I mumbled.

We quickly inspected the whole junk-filled house. Again I don't
know if we'd have done it, but it didn't happen, no Citizen Paine or

impressionist to be found, so none to be acquired.

We heard Effie and Jilly knocking on the back door and ushered them in.

Jilly said, "Please Tip, can we go, please?"

Effie said, "You're being crazy."

"Not yet," I said. "It's time to reconstruct the crime."

McKerr volunteered to sit in the lounge chair as it had been left, in the reclining position. I took his knife. Effie and Jilly peeked in on us detective ghouls.

"I'm bound," said McKerr. "Am I watching tv?"

"That's not funny," said Effie.

"What's remote control for, then?" teased McKerr.

"From all the bloodstains," I argued, "Littlefield bled to death slowly." I indicated the tv. "The VCR tape was played halfway through. So it was either off or the killer turned it off, otherwise it would have finished and rewound automatically." I turned the tv and VCR on.

"You stab me from behind," said McKerr. "There's no angle from the front."

Jilly whined when she saw what appeared on the tv screen accompanied by the Brahms. "Look, look!" she said, pointing. "What is that?"

"Mood music," said McKerr. "Porno to you."

Jilly was aghast. "I don't believe this—look, look!"

"It stinks in here," Effie said. "I'm going out to the car."

"Me too," said Jilly. "Shit."

Holmes Paine ignored the dames to continue his search for a motive. How did a dope deal gone bad explain such butchery? Littlefield and Gilbert were partners, they'd sold much dope before, so why should they fall out to murder Friday night?

"It doesn't figure," I said to McKerr.

"What does?" returned McKerr.

"Wilderness existentialism later," I said. "You don't butcher your naked and tied-up partner in his lounge chair while watching porno because of greed. You do it because you're crazy, all right, but not over money. The only other possibility has got to be jealousy."

"Rules, rules," mocked McKerr. "Now you're gonna claim it takes more than two."

"I'm gonna claim it takes a family," I argued. "But what family? What kind?"

"The mouthpiece is asking me?" said McKerr.

"No, I'm asking the police," I said, "who probably aren't asking any questions at all. They probably figure they've got Littlefield's murder solved. They're probably concentrating on Levi Gilbert's murder because of the dope angle."

"Yeah, well, the cops tossed this place," said McKerr. "If you don't have a motive, you don't have the weapon or the autopsy either."

"That's tv crime lab talk," I argued, "and murder generates so much data that the courts have to solve it with subsequent events like a bartered confession from the suspect or another crime."

"You're mouthing off, mouthpiece," adjudged McKerr.

It was time to go. But before that I imitated one of my books and circled the house for random clues. Littlefield's Ford compact was trashy like his life, showing his taste for large candy bars, small colas, *Art & Antiques*. I liked the Sierra Club sticker. I rolled up the windows, to protect it for any relatives he might have. It was full light now, the first traffic appearing on the roadway, so I gave up part one of my investigation and ordered McKerr to part two—the Gilbert trailer.

Effie was against this expedition but obliged with directions—out Route 199. We clocked it as a twenty-minute drive from Littlefield's house to the wooden post of mailboxes at the turnoff onto a dirt road. There were two trailers in a glen. The red trailer wore a police sticker. Backwoods poverty is rust and woodpiles. The other trailer showed smoke and a woman's face at the curtain.

McKerr said, "This is bad medicine."

I asked Effie which way to Levi Gilbert's dope field?

Effie cursed me with a sailor's mouth, which made Jilly say, "I wish I could do that."

Just then the other trailer produced a stout bearded country fellow slinging a shotgun and easing down the steps while staring at us.

"Twenty-gauge, side by side," McKerr said, "tell me why we're not gone," and then amused himself by driving in reverse back up the slope.

"You're f——ing lunatics!" cried Jilly, who slapped at me. "He was gonna shoot us!"

As we were driving away at speed, I argued that every trail doesn't produce a lead. But my companions were disgusted with Holmes Paine's methods and told me to shut up. I was making notes on a dollar bill, when Jilly revealed she's a woman who resents criminological intellect by hopping onto my lap.

"I'm hungry," said Jilly. "Thank you for asking."

McKerr, enjoying his escape fantasy, teased, "How about lobster for breakfast? It's not bloody."

"Eureka," I announced. "Stop the Land Rover." I leaned forward and asked Effie where my new theory lived—the old lobster who sold Littlefield his house for twelve hundred in 1964.

"You mean Chester?" said Effie. "Well, why?"

"Simple, Eff," I said. "When a man gets murdered, ask his oldest enemy why."

We were soon back at Bagaduce. Eighty-nine-year-old Chester J. Stairs turned out to be the farmstead catercorner to Littlefield's. Chester's Victorian farmhouse was forty years past sound. The wraparound porch sagged less than the roof. The farm's true delight was the menagerie of small animals—puppies, kittens, goslings, chicklings, piglets, real kids, and a *real* owl in a chicken-wire cage.

"He's famous crazy," explained Effie as we walked around to the back. "No one knows where the animals go when they grow up. Bob says—said, Chester has a fountain of youth." She meant the boarded-over well in the backyard. Jilly was joyful with the puppies feeding on her shoelaces.

McKerr tried the door, asking, "So how do we get an audience?"

Effie said, "Just wait."

Chester took his awesome timelessness emerging from the goslings. He was a tiny, knobby, hairless, brownish soul with warts like freckles and a small, steady gait.

I suddenly solved his menagerie—their youth kept him alive. I started a speech, but he didn't seem to hear me.

Chester sat on his porch steps, tugged at his woollens and nodded at Effie.

"They're friends of mine!" she shouted.

After more shouting, Chester the Deaf demonstrated once again that Yankee stereotypes are rambling motormouths.

"... want to know about murder?" he began. "When Queenie Thompson killed Montgomery Frye, she folded him in the icehouse; found him in '19, when she sold off for his debts."

No, Chester.

"When Niles McAdoo chopped up the two Ruths in '28 ..."

No, Chester.

"... the Bagley boy back from the war ..."

No.

The listing continued. With his memory, Bagaduce was a twentieth-century murder capital. Eventually I brought him to the past weekend by shouting, "Bob Littlefield! Levi Gilbert! Did you see anything strange last Friday night?"

Chester peeked at the overcast sky. I was sure he was going to tell us something profound, at the least solve everything. Instead Chester plucked up a kitten and left the earth. "It's not they wouldn't take me." He held out the kitten. "Like Noah, I'm patient—sons, wives, six hundred years old. I'm ready, don't you know, work, appetite, clean living, that's my secret! They're coming back, don't you know. Can't tell you when, but look here, look. Like the book says, 'Noah has won the Lord's favor.'"

"Help us," I asked. "Who's taking you where?"

"Them! You know." He erected his hand upward. "Spacemen! Wiped out evil once and will again, and I'm theirs when they come back, red 'n' green 'n' blue, don't you know."

McKerr grinned, proud as usual of the Yankee talent to make a nation without making sense. Effie thanked Chester for his timelessness.

I did have one more silly question, the reason for which makes no sense to you, but take notes anyway. "Chester," I asked, "did the red, green and blue spacemen come recently?"

"Just look!" he said. "Like the book says. They're looking for 'a just man and perfect in his generations' and that takes work, don't you know!"

I thanked Genesis 6 and called for a retreat to a pancake breakfast, no blueberries.

5

McKerr's detention ruined Monday afternoon and evening. I'd been out with Mrs. Ives and was just back to the Pentagoet Inn from debating quarter-million-dollar real estate. I didn't blink when I found McKerr in the common room, watching the grandfather clock like a condemned man. I'd last seen him on his way with Effie to face her mom after her overnight stay, so I started a joke about Mrs. Kielly the inquisitor.

McKerr tossed his cigarette into the fireplace. "Sit down, shut up and listen."

I was rocked by McKerr's report, especially when he got to the part where Deputy Jack Ladue cruelly picked him off the street in front of Effie's house. I panicked when he described how he was treated over at the courthouse in the county seat of Ellsworth.

"State police, two of 'em," reported McKerr, "grilled me for an hour, that good cop/bad cop routine. How come I have ten grand on me, where's my ID, who vouches for me, ever been arrested, want to call a lawyer?"

By then I was spinning around the common room, checking my wallet for my lawyer's number in New York.

"They took my knife," said McKerr. "My best knife! Said they wanted to help me. Took my knife and told me not to leave town."

I asked if they also asked about our two and a half illegal entries of crime scenes?

McKerr just got angrier. "I wouldn't tell 'em nothing. Not your name, my address, nothing. I know a railroad when it's coming at me."

"That was thick," I said, "very, very."

McKerr snorted. "Nobody tells me where I can go." He pounced up. I knew he wasn't bolting. Pathfinder doesn't groan, watch movies or do anything normal when depressed. He roams. "Nobody," he said, and left me hard.

I didn't see him again until the next morning at breakfast. By then I had called my lawyer, my accountant and my brother Sam, the industrialist (this last for a family matter but also because Sam had once handled financing for a management buyout deal most favorable to the citizens of Maine and was on a first-name basis with its popular governor). I had also called U.S. Customs and the U.S. Coast Guard. In sum, I was well prepared to calm McKerr down with some legalistic savvy.

Nonetheless McKerr came into the breakfast room at the inn scowling at the fact that I was breakfasting with Jilly. She had let fifty-nine-foot Arctic Loon sail without her and was flying on to her mother's (where her kids were stashed) when she felt like it. If I wasn't telling a murder mystery I might pause here to preach about the dread of adultery. (Just say no to yourself, okay?) I was listening once more to Jilly's fury at her unsatisfying life as McKerr pounced down on a chair that can't survive buckskin backsides and started with his own fury just where he'd left off.

"Have the coppers been here?" he asked.

"Drink some coffee," I tried.

"I want my best knife back," he said.

"Make a cigarette," I tried.

"I'm gonna make that Frencher Ladue eat his own ears," he said.

"Long night with the black bears?" I tried.

McKerr grinned hostilely. "Let's burn this Tory hole out."

Jilly wasn't sure he was joking. I knew he never joked about Frenchers, Tories or massacres. I had to get him off the warpath before I provided some important details about our trouble, so I told him that Effie had come looking for him early that morning. She was very anxious, I added avuncularly; it was less than inspirational of you to wake her up last night at midnight, then pound off.

"She's in love with you, dummy," said Jilly, who was practicing extreme statements on us in preparation for her campaign back in

Chicago, "and you go off without telling her anything."

McKerr gave me the who-is-this-squaw? look.

"She was crying and crying," said Jilly. "I had to hold her. She waited all night for you. What's wrong with you men?"

Jilly's report was actually an abbreviated version of Effie's hysteria. Effie had burst in upon Tip and Jilly around six that morning and swooned on McKerr's empty bed.

Jilly continued to lecture McKerr with regard to his misbehavior. It was a generic monologue and first-rate. I could hear that Jilly's husband was in for major courtroom damage. I left the table long enough to make a crucial phone call. When I returned, Jilly was finishing McKerr off. "She thinks she's responsible, and you blame her, don't you? So typical!"

I kept shut because I had a typical Tip surprise for all concerned (you too) and was enjoying my genius. Consciousness bashing eased soon after, and we walked Jilly across Main Street to her room at the Castine Inn.

"Am I really going to see you later?" Jilly asked me.

"Dinner, Jilly," I said. "Just make sure Effie's there too."

McKerr waited a dozen strides away and then exploded. "You'd go nuts if they'd picked you up. You wouldn't stop yowling till they were wiped out. We're out of here, mouthpiece, out, out, good riddance!"

I agreed, to McKerr's astonishment, and we got in the Land Rover and motored up Route 166 in silence.

McKerr spotted Jack Ladue's trailing patrol car by the time we reached the intersection with U.S. 1. North was Moosehead Lake; east was Canada. McKerr cinched up his fishing vest and delivered a mobster line. "Let's lose the copper."

"Good, good," I said. "Go east." I was teasing him, because I knew reason wouldn't work and didn't want Pathfinder armed with a two-ton vehicular weapon.

McKerr bought my make-believe about beating it across the border, only to discover at high speed that we were in the county seat of Ellsworth in fifteen minutes.

"What're you gonna do," McKerr asked, "send me over?"

I humored him with Hollywood lip. "Not today, sweetheart," and got him to stop off at the county courthouse.

Country boy Peter Irving was waiting for us. Pete was a real mouthpiece (recommended to me by my New York lawyer), whom I'd hired the night before. Jack Ladue was parking behind us just as Pete popped into the backseat and started at McKerr: "Say, so you're the fella causing this excitement. Pleasure to meet ya." Pete's corduroy three-piece, balding blond head, clean shave and bow tie were perfect. So was the copy of one of my paperbacks; another eager autograph hound. "What fun, Tip," said Pete. "Don't worry about it; nothing else today but tax cases."

Jack's timing was knotheaded too. He strolled up to the Land Rover and peered in McKerr's window, sniffing. "Clocked you at seventy-two there; anything to say before I write the ticket?"

Pete Irving blew Jack off. "Wheels of justice, Jack. Just follow us; we've got a date with the coast guard at Southwest Harbor."

Pathfinder's a hero because he doesn't worry about law and order. He's straight and true and knows that what goes on in settlements is not. Why talk as long as he's moving? McKerr said nothing as Pete guided our drive south from Ellsworth onto the famous resort island Mount Desert, where Acadia National Park dominates cliffs and mansions. Southwest Harbor is a boomtown, with traffic jams, condos, the Hinckley shipyards and a fishing fleet that reaps crustacean treasure. It's also Down East headquarters for the coast guard.

Southwest Harbor also has the supremely famous Claremont Hotel, a luxury inn that is to Yankee croquet what Fenway is to Yankee baseball. I'd picked the Claremont for a comfortable rendezvous with the law, but we arrived to discover that the coast guard hadn't arrived yet. So Pete and Tip enjoyed a few hours bashing wood balls with wood gavels on a rolling lawn overlooking the spectacular coastal tide. McKerr sat by on the lawn, still refusing to talk.

"What's wrong with him?" asked Pete. "Doesn't he know?"

How could I explain that nothing was wrong? Pathfinder was roaming in make-believe. And no, Pete, I explained, he doesn't know and doesn't want to, not until he gets his best knife back. Also not until that knothead Ladue, parked next to our Land Rover in front of the hotel, vanished with the Frencher empire.

But you're not wearing leatherstocking, so now it's time to tell you what I'd figured out so far.

Holmes Paine had eliminated many impossibles. Levi Gilbert didn't murder Littlefield. If he had, the state police wouldn't have taken McKerr's knife, wouldn't still be looking for a weapon and therefore still looking for a killer. And Levi Gilbert wasn't killed for bloody-handily attacking his wife and Arthur Moon at the trailer out of rage. He might not have attacked them at all. Because they three were three-fourths of a dope gang, and that night they three were fighting over a payoff that I figured the state police were holding as evidence. And what triggered the ghastliness of Friday night at the Gilbert trailer wasn't an argument over the future gains from the sale of Citizen Paine or even the two-hundred-dollar buy by Jilly's yachting buddies. No, there'd been a big dope buy that night, say kilos' worth, big bucks' worth, that had been dealt not at the trailer but at Littlefield's farmhouse. And what had needed that big a shipment was a big ship, and what had bought it was in the red, green and blue landing lights of the Bell helicopter off *Platinum.*

(Recall: Littlefield had shouted at Rheinmann, "Christie's is in New York if you can't take risks!" Recall: Chester's non sequitur about UFOs, "They're coming back, don't you know.")

What Holmes Paine had left was part of an improbable truth. Friday night the Bell chopper had landed at Littlefield's. Large cash had changed hands. Levi Gilbert had then gone off to his trailer to make the split with his wife and Arthur Moon. Levi had arrived at the trailer just after his battered wife and Arthur Moon had dealt with the midwesterners off *Arctic Loon.* The midwesterners had vamoosed. Simmering dispute had proceeded to shotgun blast, the weapon of choice in that unhappy glen.

If you don't like this, you're right, it's got twenty-gauge holes.

The biggest hole was who killed Littlefield back at his farmhouse and why? I didn't have an answer at the Claremont Hotel because I didn't know what the state police knew. (I was Holmes without Scotland Yard.) I could assume there was something wrong with the county sheriff's original theory that it was Levi-Gilbert-in-the-tv-room-with-a-knife-out-of-robbery rampage. Pete Irving had passed on the courthouse gossip that the two times of death didn't fit—Gilbert had died first, Littlefield later, much too much later. I already had ascertained the detail that Littlefield had died naked and bound in a lounge chair, a position he must have gotten into at some leisure probably long after the big payoff from *Platinum*'s Bell helicopter.

Though I couldn't explain it all, McKerr's detention had forced my big mouth. The night before, I'd played dial-a-deal and sent everyone over: Jilly's *Arctic Loon* party as material witnesses; *Platinum*'s gang as material witnesses; and realtor Mrs. Ives as the money launderer for the dope ring. (Recall: Littlefield shouting, "she writes her checks underwater.")

This last was truly sketchy, and if Mrs. Ives could ramble her way out of the accusation, so be it. I was angry. Mess with Pathfinder, you're going to get messed. I figured that when the coast guard brought in the yachters I could eliminate more impossibles and figure not only Littlefield's killer but also what I truly cared about: Who took Citizen Paine?

Such was Holmes Paine's genius that sunny croquet afternoon. Pete and I were sipping iced tea at the shoreline lounge bar when we sighted a small coast guard launch heading in. The sweet ancients at the tables around us were excited, since we'd told them everything and they were older than Agatha Christie.

I didn't know where McKerr was and didn't wait for him as we charged out to the end of the wharf. I did let Pete do the talking. Rheinmann was not on board the cutter. A square-built ensign told us that *Arctic Loon* had been intercepted in Machias Bay and wouldn't be in until after dark. *Platinum* had crossed into Canadian territorial waters Sunday night and been boarded by the RCCP.

"It'll be a while for them," said the ensign, "but if there's contra-band"—he paused, a veteran in the drug wars—"it'll go worse for them over there, believe me, much worse; they got room in lockup over there, lotsa room."

Pete Irving earned his fee: "You won't need Mr. Paine anymore?"

"Tomorrow," said the ensign. "Check in tomorrow."

That was the vague end of my great solution. No yachtspersons, no confessions, no Citizen Paine.

Pete was sympathetic, "Well, there, Tip, maybe you overplotted. What you say, it's all possible, just in no hurry to work out. My experience, justice grinds slow and small."

McKerr was watching us from the rocks at low tide. I waved all was well, which wasn't accurate, but it made me feel better that he signaled back Pathfinder style, hawkeyed and grim.

6

What this mystery lacks is the sort of haphazard violence Hollywood favors. The gunshot at Tip in the night, the blackjack at McKerr around a corner or that foolish favorite the car chase, where McKerr and Tip are run off Route 166 into the gentle but dangerous shoreline. If that's what you want, change the channel, because it's my opinion that murder is not a crime spree, it's a phenomenon.

Hollywood always cheats when it solves a murder by adding on more violence to lead the way to the bad guy. The truth is that a murderer is so frightened by what's happened that if he or she doesn't get nabbed in the first twenty-four hours, then afterward he or she will become the most lawful of citizens. And since most murderers are as ordinary as pumpkins, what you have before and after the madness is you or me or any jack-o'-lantern. Accordingly homicide investigation would be impossible without two strange facts. One: Most murderers know their victims intimately. Two: Most murderers eventually confess, even if they deny their own confession forever— something just clicks in the brain, and out slips the truth.

Then there is a third strange fact, which Tip can't prove, and which is an indifference to the police. After the crime, a murderer becomes a textbook victim. He or she acts wronged, vulnerable, weak-willed—a pumpkin thrown out of the patch and left to rot alone, unloved, waiting to be squashed.

At dinner that night (Tip, Jilly, McKerr, Effie) back at the Pentagoet Inn, I blithered all this big think out, along with my failed grand solution.

McKerr showed interest (though it might have been the beef), asking, "There were four crimes, right? Two dope deals, two murders, none of them linked?"

"Correct," I said. "Not one, two, three, four; rather one, one, one, one."

"Wait a minute," protested Jilly, sipping her wine. (Jilly wasn't as shocked as I'd supposed at the pursuit and arrest of her former yachting pals. Truth, I think she kinkily liked me for it.) "And you say that poor man," she continued, "in that awful chair, that he was murdered after Levi Gilbert was murdered?"

"Correct: afterward, much afterward," I boasted, "by person or persons unknown. For reason or reasons unknown. That's the crucial unanswered question here: *Why was Bob Littlefield murdered?* If you can say why, you can probably say who. Yet whatever the motive, whoever did it is now the wimpiest of victims."

Effie was our conscience. "Bob's dead!" she scolded. "A lot of people are going to jail! And you're joking about it! I live here!"

McKerr tried what is great sympathy for him: he touched her hand.

"Okay, okay," said Effie. "Jack's a pig for hauling you into it, but still it's a lot of pain for a little town, and you're laughing at us."

Jilly provided big-city truth. "Drugs are everywhere, Effie; you can't say you're safe here. I read where it's the biggest cottage industry in Maine. You did know about it, everybody knew, and it came to this. They"—she meant me and McKerr—"just kicked back. They're crude about it, but why not? That poor man was butchered, and someone's getting away with it."

It had taken appetizer, entrée and much palaver to get to this impasse of argument. McKerr called for a walk before sweets. We strolled as two couples in the moonlight down Perkins Street to our favorite grassy field in town, Fort Pentagoet. Tip and Jilly stood romantically at the waterline. I was enjoying the affection of someone who knew I hadn't sent her over with her former pals.

Uncharacteristically McKerr went along with Effie into the Catholic chapel. There had been a memorial service that afternoon for

Littlefield and Gilbert, and the lights were still on inside, folk coming and going in clumps.

"The town feels guilty," Jilly observed. "I do too. If I were home I'd go to my pastor. If you weren't such a crank, you'd feel guilty too."

"Sure, Jill," I preached. "Guilt is routine, but nearby there's a specifically guilty soul, and it's not me. Nail the bastard, hang the bastard, then gnash about the celebrated human condition."

"You're so full of it," adjudged Jilly.

Correct. But now the tricky part. McKerr wasn't feeling any more forgiving than Tip, and when he and Effie came out of the chapel he dropped back with me as the girls led the way toward the ice cream parlor.

"Your setup today, too fancy, mouthpiece," said McKerr. "You want to get a man, track him, don't wait on the flat feet."

"I'm full of it," I grumbled.

McKerr agreed. "If you weren't out here feeling proud of yourself and goosing the girl, maybe you'd've come along inside there."

"What?"

"Yeah, well," said McKerr, "guess who's on his knees back there in the pew?"

"I don't guess," I lied. "What are you talking about?"

Now McKerr told me what I had walked right past, what his hawkeyes had spotted and then tricked out of weepy, vulnerable, guilty Effie in the chapel. "The Brahms," said McKerr wickedly. "Guess who's little-boy whack-off on the videotape?"

I knew the truth as soon as he named it, and started toward Effie to confront her for holding out on us.

McKerr grabbed me back. "No more fancy stuff, mouthpiece. I say face the man."

"And say what?" I asked.

McKerr lit a cigarette as he declared, "Face him and make a deal for my painting."

I started something pious about greed.

McKerr wouldn't wait on my situational ethics. He called to the dames that we'd be along momentarily and then led the path into the chapel. A local folkie was playing chords on a guitar. There were several older women muttering at the rear and more near the confessional box to the front. I was for circling our prey in the second pew. McKerr led directly.

Maine Maritime Academy Cadet Moon looked up from his prayers. I report I was afraid, and that is exciting when you remember it later. Cadet Moon was in his pretty uniform, a tense cipher. A few times I've actually looked at a man who's in serious trouble with the law. None of them look alike save this—they are dazed, slow, brittle (my victim theory). I won't pause now to tell you why I knew Cadet Moon was the killer, or near to; I'll just say Holmes Paine was elementarily sure.

McKerr was pathfindingly sure. He stepped in front of Cadet Moon and didn't say more than was necessary. "You don't look any better with your pants on."

Cadet Moon looked away.

McKerr added, "We want the painting, *my* painting."

Cadet Moon didn't move. We didn't move.

It was my turn to talk. I laid out our deal. Still no motion. I can guess now we'd all gone too far and didn't have a next move.

Inconveniently, Effie and Jilly didn't trust us as far as a trout laughs and came rushing into the chapel. Jilly looked fretful and Effie frightful.

I told McKerr we were leaving, and we grabbed the dames before they ruined our scene with questions. It was a struggle, but the chapel intimidated their protests. Back out on Perkins Street we needed a little muscle and some false promises until we got them moving toward Main Street.

Then came hollering. "You're crazy!" cried Effie. "What were you going to do to Billy?"

I mumbled, "Didn't know his name was Billy."

"You can't go around accusing people!" she declared. "Do you think you're God!"

I mumbled, "Is this a catechetical quiz?"

"Shit," she cursed me, "you're worse than Jack!"

Jilly helped some. "What did they do? They didn't do anything."

Effie repeated herself to communicate the point that what we'd done was get ourselves born some irreverent day in the past.

I listened to Effie's tirade longer than I wanted to, because McKerr was in charge.

McKerr tried silence, and then he tried warpath. "Your private copper snatches me and you say nothing! Now you're yelling because we're tracking the right man!"

At this Effie stopped gasping imprecations. I thought she was going to bolt for home, kid and mom. Instead she took Jilly's arm and, once we'd regained Main Street, ordered us to get her ice cream. "Chocolate chocolate, and be quick about it."

The dames waited outside while McKerr and I lined up behind more pastel yachtspersons and unwashed blondine. This delay gave me a chance to review with McKerr our latest plan to recover Citizen Paine. I used sci-fi/spy jargon. Stakeout, trade-off, exfiltration.

McKerr asked, "No coppers?"

I said I needed one phone call but no police.

Outside again, we four enjoyed our cones as we drifted up toward the inns. It was time to part, and I did it flatly. "Good night."

Effie and Jilly protested immovably. They had their own plan, but first they wanted to hear ours.

I refused to say more than that we wanted Citizen Paine back and didn't give a hoot what happened to Cadet Billy Moon or the whole guilty little town of fag-bashers.

"We're going along," said Jilly; she grinned at me. "Otherwise we're sending you over."

Effie addressed me. "You act so smart—well, shit on you. I'm gonna be there to defend my friends."

She thought we were headed to the courthouse in Ellsworth, so I told her the truth. "We're not turning anybody in, Eff," I said. "We're getting even and getting out."

"What are you up to?" asked Effie.

Jilly teased, "Probably grand larceny."

I told them, and now I'll tell you, since there's time while we four piled into the Land Rover to drive out to Bagaduce to wait at Chester's farmhouse across the road from Littlefield's.

Holmes Paine had eliminated many impossibles, and here's some more. Bob Littlefield wasn't murdered by his dope ring partner Levi Gilbert, nor was he murdered by a thief or silent partner. That is, greed was not the motive.

Bob Littlefield was killed by a lover. That is, jealousy (family) was the motive. An unusual sort of family, a farfetched sort of family grouping, yet a family nonetheless. I had reasoned correctly and then doubted my own reason.

More, the crime didn't happen during the dope deal with *Platinum*. It happened much later that night. And the weapon wasn't a kitchen knife or McKerr's fishing knife or steel at all. That's why the state police were stumped. Littlefield was stabbed by an antler, what flint-knappers call a billet. You saw it in Cadet Billy Moon's fancy leather case Friday morning when he knapp-dueled McKerr at the Wilson Museum.

What I'm *not* saying is that Cadet Billy Moon did the deed. I couldn't and didn't know that as we waited at Chester's farmhouse from 8 P.M. until 10 P.M.

Our stakeout wasn't uncomical. We shouted with Chester about UFOs while Effie and Jilly drank Chester's whiskey and rubbed puppy ears. McKerr insisted upon climbing up the sagging roof to monitor the passing vehicles with his field glasses. Eventually we were joined by genuine mouthpiece Pete Irving, whom my single phone call had beckoned. By then Effie had told us more than we needed to know about the underground shenanigans of Castine, Bagaduce and environs.

Homosexuality is ordinary, average, unexceptional, as commonplace as churchgoing; end cosmopolitan sermon. Out in the willywacks, however, homosexuality makes some folk outlaws. In sum, Littlefield's house was a hideaway for a lot of cramped, troubled souls who huddled together for affection and mutual support.

Something very stupid had happened that Friday night. Dope deals, hot cash, vacant promises, loose-lipped dreams joined together with dope-smoking and probably bondage and sex, and then had come a sudden threat to someone in the homosexual family group who thought he was being left out.

That was who we were waiting for. Whoever had felt left out that night had murdered Bob Littlefield with the sort of hatred that can only come from love. And I didn't or couldn't know that someone was Cadet Billy Moon.

What I did believe was that terrified Billy Moon believed that the Brahms tape left behind in the VCR at Littlefield's would destroy him. Whoever else was with him and Littlefield that night would panic too.

Yes, none of this might be true. It could all be my smoke. Except that there's this modern version of S. Holmes's maxim that declares, "If it happened then it must be possible."

As proof to myself that my solution was accurate, there was the deal that McKerr and I had offered Billy Moon in the Catholic chapel.

"We get Citizen Paine," we'd told him, "we forget the tape, we just forget."

Nervous Pete Irving lit his eighteenth cigarette. "Lights on the road," he announced. It was near ten, the eighteenth car to roll by. Pete was there to protect me and McKerr from local revenge in case our plan blew up. Pete didn't like any of it, but I was the paying client, and so while he fussed at us he did oblige my loony ambitions.

The eighteenth car turned into Littlefield's. Pete said, "Shit, bingo, shit."

McKerr hopped down from the porch roof. "Let's do it."

I asked Pete if he was satisfied. "Yes, yes," he said, "but, Tip, we're out here alone, and I'm advising we call somebody. I mean, they could be killers—shit, you say there are killers!"

I wasn't really sure of the next part, but McKerr was. When he's on the warpath he stays on the warpath. McKerr and I left behind the noisy Land Rover and ordered Pete to drive his quiet Saab across to swing onto Littlefield's drive, lights out, waiting. We walked. McKerr was too angry for me to control, so I didn't try. We smoked and waited, leaning on Pete's car's hood.

If you're wondering why I wasn't worried about violence, the kind Hollywood's hooked you to with its cheating screenplays, then I'll ruin the surprise right now and say that nowhere is it written that a priest is dangerous. That's right, Father Phillip of Deer Isle, who had sent us to see "some friends of mine" at the Wilson Museum Friday, was Billy Moon's lover too (and perhaps Bob Littlefield's lover too?). In any event, Father Phillip was the third member of a homosexual family triangle that had collapsed Friday night when Bob Littlefield bragged about his sudden wealth (dope kilos sold, paintings tagged for sale) to youthful Billy Moon. Meanwhile (sitting nearby?), Father Phillip was facing his imminent reduction from a federal gem of a parsonage to the penury of a basement efficiency.

My plan to recover Citizen Paine might have worked—our challenge, their trade-off, retreat to Moosehead—if not for the fate that had been harrying me and McKerr since he'd caught that laughing brown trout.

Father Phillip and Billy Moon rolled their car up the road and stopped as Pete flipped on his headlights.

McKerr took the lead position. Pete got out of his car to back him up.

Father Phillip and Billy Moon got out of their car and stood close together. They were the victims here. We were the highwaymen.

I called out our deal once more, this time with a self-infatuated twist. "Give us the painting," I proposed. "We'll deposit seven thousand dollars in the collection plate tonight."

I felt terrific, if you're curious, full of it, tricky and greedy too, Holmes Paine on the case. Then my genius lapsed. I'd overlooked the knotheadery that came roaring out of the woods across the road, dear jealous Jack Ladue in his 4 × 4, fog lights blazing. Our stakeout had been staked out.

Farce lacks rules. Jack tried Hollywood. "Freeze, all you bastards, freeze!"

McKerr tried disgust. "You Frencher ass!"

Pete tried reason. "Jack, put the gun down, Jack; it's Pete."

Then the Land Rover rumbled up and contributed hysteria. "Jack, what are you doing!" cried Effie. "Stop it! Stop this."

Jilly turned out to be a screamer too. "Please, Tip, please!"

The singular calm decency in all this was Father Phillip, who held a sobbing Cadet Billy Moon while he talked Jack Ladue out of his fantasies.

McKerr and I glanced once at each other. Say goodbye to Citizen Paine.

7

Who murdered Bob Littlefield? I know, mostly. You know, mostly. Tough question: So what? It's after New Year's now, six months since the mayhem. Neither Father Phillip nor Billy Moon has yet confessed, nor has either been arrested, nor has the attorney general got a case. Billy Moon did withdraw from the Maine Maritime Academy, yet that wasn't a confession of anything but that he'd been exposed a homosexual in a town that lives in splendid nature but doesn't want to acknowledge all of nature's ways. Nah, that's a sermon. He just quit, okay? And Father Phillip has gone on compassionate leave from his parish. Once again, this wasn't a confession of anything.

There's more earthly nonjustice. The Penobscot dope ring (the *Bangor Daily News* called it "the Gilbert Mob") was shut down, yet no one was indicted for Levi Gilbert's "accidental" death. The *Platinum* gang jabbered its way out of Canadian courts (Rheinmann was a Canadian, brother of an MP). The *Arctic Loon* bunch found our coast guard more troublesome, and two husbands pleaded no contest to the misdemeanor of buying a controlled substance.

It may entertain you that McKerr was detained a second time, accused of threatening a peace officer (Jack Ladue). Pete Irving laughed the charge off easily.

Also Tip was lectured by the state police for interfering in an investigation, and there was rudeness about my breaking and entering a crime scene. I accepted this as the price of telling the truth. Silly as it sounds, the truth is a great defense if you're only a little guilty.

There's some reward too. Mrs. Ives dodged the drug-laundering investigation, yet was so frightened by what I'd tried that she proved an excellent realtor after all. She found me my house here in Castine.

It's a colonial lodestone, the original part 198 years old, with twelve rooms, eight fireplaces, three baths and a Victorian gazebo—all of this pleasure on one acre of lawn (now under snow) and set up close on Perkins Street near Fort Pentagoet. I'm leasing, of course, since this demirich guy cannot afford the prices in America in these anxious days without larceny so sweaty I'm not qualified. Nonetheless the kitchen is long and warm, the owners are ancients in Florida and the water pipes are so good even I trust them.

There's also a widow's walk out of the upstairs hall, which McKerr favors for watching the bay in case the Frenchers or Tories try anything imperial against us again. I don't have any furniture to fill the house up with, so we've concentrated the antiques left by the owners in the long parlor. Effie's been working on the curtains and bathrooms, female obsessions I find dearly hilarious and McKerr knows is a threat to his liberty. Jilly stopped by here the week after Christmas with her two kids, a separation opera on its way to ski in Europe. She volunteered advice about wallpaper, floors, crockery, then she broadcasted her deep conviction that I need a microchip-brained kitchen. Effie's and Jilly's kids were most entertaining around the Christmas tree, I admit. They also beat me badly on the Mac games. I find children a threat to my liberty. Humbug.

McKerr and I are adjusting to our house pride. The main fireplace has a mantel that a tall man can lean on, and that's worth a lifetime of trouble to have. It's cedar of Lebanon, said to be carved out of the shattered foremast of a coastal brig that foundered last century. We've set a clock on it, along with hurricane lamps and my pipe racks. We've also hung it with Pathfinder's powder horn collection and surrounded it with all manner of stoking tools. It's agreed, however, that the wall above will remain blank until such time as we track down our picture.

Yes, Citizen Paine is why I chose to settle here and why McKerr roams the peninsula like a prisoner, trapped in a settlement his make-believe forebears wouldn't have bothered to burn out. We're not giving up, and I like our chances. Here's why. The town is impressed by our tenacity, its most notorious outsiders dining daily at Mrs. Roche's café. Jack Ladue drives by every night, hoping to catch us torturing rabbits. The Moon family, here to there, speaks our names like invocations of Old Nick. I wasn't entirely wrongheaded about the Moons, by the way. They were trying to protect their kinfolk from scandal, and I think Captain Lincoln Moon, whom I've never met, has me on his enemies list. Meanwhile the Moons, here to there, know we won't go away until we have what we want. Also Pete Irving is an excellent dinner guest, providing all possible police leads to the latest burglary cache that might produce. And Effie has set her students to researching every itinerant portrait painter who passed through New York 1803–1809 and might have done a favor for a mad old man forgotten by his country. I've even contacted Littlefield's relatives down in Boston, explaining as earnestly as I can that when Citizen Paine is found, we're ready to complete the deal struck in a handshake. They're not uninterested, just confused by my kind of obsession.

I don't tell them about it, or Castine, because it requires an uncommoning of sense. I did tell Pathfinder, and he said, "Shut up."

I'm eager to tell you anyway. Holmes Paine has eliminated the last impossible. What caused both murders that Friday night wasn't only the usual suspects and their kindred of Cain—jealousy, family, greed, robbery, fear, love, hatred, accident. It was also antique madness. Call it murder by Paine. And I have determined that the murder came off a tiny ship painted just for fun in the corner of Citizen Paine's portrait—a bark named *Captain Death*. There will be no justice until we recapture her and raise her most famous midshipman to his glorious place above my mantel and in American history. Improbable, yes; so's the truth.

Gordon Liddy Is My Muse

Lost Love Story of the

Watergate Caper;

School for Scandal;

Tip Names Deep Throat

1

"It started with an instruction to me from Bob Halde-man," recounted John Dean to his president one gray morn-ing in the Oval Office, "to see if we couldn't set up a *perfectly legitimate* campaign intelligence operation over at the Reelection Committee. . . ."

President Nixon listened and pondered. The tape recorder was running. The date was March 21, 1973. Richard Milhous Nixon, sixty, was at the zenith of his power. After his landslide reelection the previous fall, the Dow-Jones had breached 1000 for the first time in history. He had used B-52s to engineer a peace accord in Vietnam, opened a channel to Red China, baited the Russian bear to a stand-still and sent twelve lucky men to walk the moon. After twenty-five years in public office he was correctly regarded as the most successful citizen ever to occupy the White House.

The truth was that at this very moment all the world waited on President Nixon's dark genius. He was one of the smartest men who ever played themselves; not even his namesake Richard the Lionheart did it better. If you can read John Dean's words and not reach for a cigarette, not crave caffeine or chocolate, not feel your heart, then you are either a trendy child or a willful ignoramus. You are there, this happened on your watch, it is your life.

". . . That is when I came up with Gordon Liddy," continued John Dean. At thirty-three, fair, mild, fastidious John Dean was counsel to the President. His job for the last nine months had been to follow a plot that would not stop, that Dean still thought was once *perfectly legitimate*, that he still believed he had started once upon a time accidentally on purpose.

"They needed a lawyer," continued Dean. "Gordon had an intelligence background from his FBI service. I was aware of the fact that he had done some extremely sensitive things for the White House while he had been at the White House and he had apparently done them well. Going out into Ellsberg's doctor's office—"

"Oh, yeah," said the President.

President Nixon was well aware that what John Dean was saying was only half informed, that this ex-G-man Liddy, whom the President had never met, had once worked with a secret White House truth squad called "the Plumbers." President Nixon knew that the Plumbers, under White House orders, had committed felonies coast to coast in order to silence leaks to the press. Also the President knew the Plumbers were responsible, Labor Day weekend, 1971, for breaking into the office of the Beverly Hills psychiatrist of Daniel Ellsberg, a broken man now on trial for betraying top-secret Pentagon files.

". . . And things like this," continued John Dean. "He worked with leaks. He tracked these things down. So the report I got from Krogh was that he was a hell of a good man and, not only that, a good lawyer and could set up a proper operation. . . ."

President Nixon listened and pondered the more. The top-secret, voice-activated tape recorder in the Oval Office missed nothing—

the hesitations, a jet roar from nearby National Airport, the scrape of good shoes against the desk.

The President and John Dean conferred for one hundred minutes that morning and for another forty minutes that afternoon. They were eventually joined by two men known as "the Berlin Wall"—chief assistants to the President Bob Haldeman and John Ehrlichman. Yet all those shrewd, cautious men remained bamboozled by events, at loggerheads over what was to be done to contain the epic constitutional crisis that was once called the Watergate Caper.

President Nixon summarized repeatedly their collective frustration that day. "Well, the erosion is inevitably going to come here and all the people saying, well, the Watergate isn't a major issue. It isn't. But it will be. Something has to go out. Delaying is the great danger to the White House area. . . ."

Later, at day's end, the President fumed, "What the hell does one disclose that isn't going to blow something?"

John Dean called Watergate "a cancer within." Tip doesn't like that metaphor; I prefer "caper." "Caper" has the right wit, it projects the adventurous meandering, brainy stupidity, twists upon twists, the sense of a great game being played without rules but with players who outranked all others in America. Even with a scorecard you had to be there every day to stay in the game. Players changed sides willy-nilly. Men and women promised, lied, swore, perjured, joined, ran away, betrayed their friends, country, loved ones. One brave woman died in a plane crash, gave her life to protect her husband and her president. And everyone on every side was guilty of something; no one survived innocently. They played for keeps. There were no higher stakes. At the end it became simply and scarily a tyrannical contest.

"This is a war," President Nixon once said on tape about Watergate. "I want the most comprehensive notes on those who have tried to do us in . . . they are asking for it and they are going to get it."

Hear this. The most powerful man on earth sat on his throne and named the game. Get me or I'll get you.

Watergate also became a national mania. After all these years I still love to play the game. No one ever wrote a better sci-fi/spy story; no one ever will. For Watergate alone America is the second-grandest story on earth. The truth is that even when we blow it, America spellbinds as the magnificent fool, the self-mocking hero, the righteous bozo, liberty's darling.

Try to remember it now as John Dean tried that March day to recall it for his president nine months after the birth of the caper.

It began June 17, 1972, in the District of Columbia. The weather was gloomy, the East Coast suffering the onslaught of killer tropical storm Agnes. The time was soon after 2 A.M. The place was 2700 Virginia Avenue, the Watergate Hotel Complex, new-built where Rock Creek enters the Potomac River. Private security guard Frank Wills, twenty-four, a black man who was never employed steadily again, accidentally discovered surgical tape over the lock of a basement door. He called the D.C. police.

Soon after, upstairs on the sixth floor in the offices of the Democratic National Committee, three investigating police officers surprised five burglars. The five were exceptional in that they wore surgical gloves and carried out-of-date telephone bugs, a walkie-talkie, cameras, film, tear gas pens, and many hundred-dollar bills in serial sequence.

There were also the strange details that the men were registered under aliases in rooms 214 and 314 of the Watergate Hotel. That they had been seen eating a lobster dinner together earlier that evening at the hotel restaurant. That four of the burglars were from Miami, with notorious CIA connections back to the Bay of Pigs fiasco (Operation Mongoose). That the fifth was an ex-FBI, ex-CIA security specialist named McCord.

Where were you that night? Asleep? On a date? Watching tv? Tip was clerking for the NSA in Scotland. Specifically I was getting breakfast in my rooms outside our sub base with a recent visitor, my old pal Eleanora, who was explaining to me about her IUD, how she'd almost bled to death before she'd had it removed.

Actually I was half listening to Eleanora, because the radio was broadcasting the BBC's Saturday morning headlines: B-52s over Vietnam; George Wallace facing surgery to remove an assassin's bullet; Clifford Irving and wife, Edith, sentenced for the Howard

Hughes fraud. Simultaneously out there across the Atlantic my country was walking through a taped-open door in time like a child passing through the birth canal to cry, "Hello, history."

New heroes and new villains passed through that taped-open door too, and at the head of the pack, at the center of the birth, were two men who didn't get nabbed that night.

Alerted by a lookout, the two ringleaders of the burglars—who were in fact the White House truth squad called the Plumbers—got away.

Handsome, gaunt E. Howard Hunt, fifty-three, Brown graduate, WWII vet, ex-CIA operative, sci-fi/spy novelist, jazz enthusiast, partial to spycraft, his happy family and make-believe, got away.

And Hunt's twin in crime, handsome, chipper G. Gordon Liddy, forty-three, Fordham graduate, Korean vet, ex-FBI agent, lawyer, NRA enthusiast, partial to his happy family and make-believe, got away.

Howard Hunt rushed back to the Plumbers' lookout at the Howard Johnson hotel across the street. Hunt said, "Well, they've had it." Hunt ordered the lookout, an ex-FBI lug named Baldwin, to pack up the bugging equipment and "Get out of town." Then Hunt telephoned a young lawyer friend and told him he was coming to his house. They needed to arrange bail for the five nabbed Plumbers.

What did Gordon Liddy do? He walked through that door too and was born my muse. "Hell of a good man," said John Dean. True, but Gordon's so much more—cowboy, clown, father, paranoid, philosopher, fool for all seasons.

This is Gordon Liddy's yarn and mine too, for it's time Tip got back to his muse's beginnings. I've got something strange to tell you and to tell Gordon too, because Gordon Liddy is my muse and I can't keep shut about it anymore. It's the lost love story of the Watergate Caper. For one man so loved his country that he gave it everything —his life, his family, his fortune, his reputation, his conscience. It's also why it happened the way it did, a sci-fi/spy story on runaway. The door's opening. Born again. I'm walking through. "Hello, Gordon."

Gordon Liddy Is My Muse

My baby brother, Bunyan, met me at the Tucson airport Saturday
morning. I was on the first leg of my journey back in time to Gordon
Liddy. It was January 1989, so this took some planning.

I was en route to a week at Gordon Liddy's Firearms Security
Academy in the Sonora Desert, sometimes known as Gordon's
School for Scandal. I wasn't traveling as Tip Paine the salesman,
however, but rather incognito, because I knew the one person Gordon would never permit near him was a snoop with an agenda, and I
was that. I was after my muse. I'd never met him, never seen him in
action, and I wanted Gordon Liddy right there in front of me for
some Q&A and for one more strange desire. I wanted the truth, the
whole truth, nothing but the truth about the Watergate Caper.

Giant blue-eyed baby brother Bunyan was all genuine hero. He
was now Captain Paine, on a weekend outing from the army's Military Intelligence Officer Advanced Course at Fort Huachua, located
sixty miles to the southeast on the border. Bunyan was retraining for
military intelligence, a counterintelligence officer, headed for more
armed service with our legions around the world. I'd wanted to visit
him at Fort Huachua—the army's spy-catching institute—but as
he'd explained on the phone, "Fort Gotcha is nowhere, Tip, an old
cavalry fort from when there used to be Apaches. There's nothing
here but a K mart and McDonald's and honky-tonks. Besides, I can't
tell you about any of the interesting stuff here; I've got clearance and
you don't."

The Apache ghosts and honky-tonks sounded wonderful, the interesting stuff sounded delicious, but I'd accepted his opinion and
arranged another kind of holiday for us, one that I knew would please
his growing sense of authority in the world of genuine sci-fi/spy.

We left his car in the parking lot and picked up a rental Cadillac
which had been paid for by a Finnish friend of mine via her London
office. I could be traced through this arrangement, but it would take
time and some luck. We made a quick tour of boomtown Tucson and

drove into the hills to Old Tucson for lunch. Old Tucson is a magical place, a wild West stage set, where John Wayne and Clint Eastwood have walked before the cameras. Hollywood likes it chiefly because there aren't any telephone or power lines.

Bunyan loved the intrigue so far. He did want more facts and deserved them, since I was using him for cover too. "You're going to see Gordon Liddy, right?" he asked.

I fumbled a taco.

"And you're using the alias Wilcy Moore," he asked, "right? First off, who's Wilcy Moore?"

I showed Bunyan the only ID I'd kept in my billfold. It was a picture of Wilcy Moore, the ace reliever for the legendary 1927 Yankee team known as Murderers Row.

"Oklahoma dirt farmer Wilcy Moore," I explained. "He could throw a nerveless sinker all night, anywhere he wanted. The Yankees called him the Fireman. After the Yankees won the '27 Series in four straight, Wilcy Moore bought two mules, named one Babe and the other Ruth."

Bunyan nodded at his nutty brother. "So, posing as a relief pitcher, you're going to play terrorist for a week in the desert? Cut yourself with a Special Forces knife, learn how to break down a Kalyshnikov blindfolded and spy on girls with a sniperscope." He laughed. My centurion brother doesn't play soldier; he also knows I'm afraid of weapons. "It's been twenty years since you did basic; you've forgotten how to pull the pin. Is this a joke? You're paying seven thousand dollars plus expenses for a week on fantasy mesa? Baloney! What're you really after?"

I said I was after Gordon Liddy, ex-G-man, ex-con, tv star, owner and boss of Gemstone Enterprises, a firm that was part security consultant and the other part this mercenary academy in the desert.

Bunyan didn't buy it. We walked down hard-dirt Main Street in strong January sunshine. This was my first trip to Arizona, and I loved it already. I grew up persuaded by tv westerns such as "Gunsmoke," "Bonanza," "Wagon Train" and "Have Gun—Will Travel." Bunyan, thirteen years my junior, grew up persuaded by tv fantasy such as "M·A·S·H," "The Hulk" and "The Six Million Dollar

Man." Cowboys aren't crucial to his sense of humor, though he un-derstands Eastwood, even if Bunyan thinks he was too old in *Heart-break Hill.*

"This Liddy guy," said Bunyan, "he's a cowboy, you said. That's why we're here?" He gestured to the stage-set saloon nearby. "You're trying to tell me something? The Watergate thing made him a cow-boy. Tough guy, hard core. But I don't get it. Who cares about him anymore? I mean, Tip, no one remembers Watergate. I don't. It was all over when I was in the sixth grade."

I asked, "You think it's nostalgia?"

He said, "I think it's over."

This was rough to accept, but I did—not that it was over but that savvy Bunyan thought it was over. It was time to be big brother and sell Bunyan on my opinion and ambition. So after we sent postcards to Mom and Dad and got back to the car to start our drive to the Gila River, I told Bunyan the story of the Watergate Caper. I didn't need notes; it's printed on my left brain, all the name and dates and too many of the quotes.

Bunyan listened carefully and drove General Motors fast. "What's DeVille really mean?" he asked. "It handles like a boat."

The Sonora was spectacularly not dead that afternoon, a desert like a stage set for the first landing on Planet X, flat roads bracketed by startling naked mountains, all this landscape filled up by the jumping cholla cacti and wild asters and the spectacular plainness of the creosote, not to overlook a single bizarre saguaro cactus twisting like the entrails of a trident-topped demon. General Phil Sheridan pronounced that the devil would rent out Texas and live in Arizona. By nightfall at our motel in Gila Bend (registered as W. Moore and guest, Bronx, N.Y.) I understood Sheridan and was intimidated by the Sonora. But nothing, not even the Mexican food I avoided, stopped my blither.

Richard M. Nixon the prince of darkness 1972. Mitchell, Stans, Kleindienst, Gray and Helms his demonic lieutenants. Haldeman, Ehrlichman, Dean, Colson, Krogh, Magruder, Clawson, Mardian, LaRue, Sloan, Porter, Strachan and Chapin his corrupted underlings.

Liddy, Hunt, McCord, the Cubans, Segretti, the lawyers, the bag-men and sweet dotty Rose Mary Woods his fallen agents as well as his sacrifices. I laid it all out, the Plumbers to CREEP to the Ervin Com-mittee, Oval Office tapes, Saturday Night Massacre, impeachment, resignation, exile.

Bunyan finished my untouched burritos, and we took a stroll out-side the restaurant to admire the Milky Way, which appears to roof the Sonora as if Arizona were a giant planetarium. Gila Bend has little more than a great name, trouble with the hard-luck reserva-tions, and the routine franchises that make every immigrant Ameri-can town the same shopping center.

We were buying ice cream when Bunyan interrupted my discourse. He'd caught on, no dummy in five languages. He'd realized that his big brother was obsessed by the Watergate Caper because I thought that something about it was still unfinished, not the truth, the whole truth, nothing but the truth.

"I saw the movie on tv," said Bunyan, "the Redford and Dustin Hoffman movie. I saw it a long time ago, but it was great, they got 'em. *All the President's Men.* Sent them all to jail. What you're say-ing, it's amazing, Nixon 'the prince of darkness.' But he admitted it. So what's the big deal? Gordon Liddy, he did time, he got out, he's famous now, I see that, sort of, because he never talked. Isn't that why he's famous—he bit the bullet and never turned? But it's over."

I'd sold and sold and not advanced my bill of goods a bitten bullet. I replied stubbornly, "It ain't over yet."

"Geez," said Bunyan, "you're like the world's dustiest old man-hunter. Seventeen years later. It's history!"

I sighed and quit. I wanted to say more, but I believed I shouldn't. I was on a loony mission, and I didn't want my backup to know more than necessary about the operational details, just in case it fell apart.

This frustration didn't last long. A child I loved had stabbed me through my dusty old heart, so on the way back to the hotel we found Gila Bend's video franchise and I rented *All the President's Men* and the more famous *Deep Throat.*

Bunyan's more a prude than I am—another generational gap—

and he wouldn't watch more than five minutes of Linda Lovelace's slavishness before he switched to William Goldman's top-drawer screenplay.

I gave Bunyan a viewer warning. Hollywood played loose with the details of who said what to whom and when. Hollywood cut out many crucial characters at the *Washington Post*. Hollywood fashioned its version entirely from Woodward and Bernstein's cluttered point of view. Hollywood certainly ignored the information available on the Oval Office tapes.

"Still, follow the logic," I said, "follow the logic. Find the black, black hole."

The show finished. "Okay," said Bunyan, "I'm supposed to tell you why you're going to see Gordon Liddy. And if I'm right, will you tell me I'm right?"

I thought, What was this? Had baby brother caught the Watergate bug too—trust nothing, no one, not even what you see?

Bunyan continued, "I say it's something to do with Deep Throat, this guy who ratted on the White House."

I was packing up my kit, only new-bought doodads, underwear, a Yale tie and a pair of boots I'd broken in a month before.

"Am I right?" asked Bunyan. "Deep Throat? Deep Throat is the hole in the logic? Your black hole? Woodward and Bernstein don't get the story unless he keeps feeding them. He's like a God's-eye view, a very heavy asset. And they never say who he is. The story doesn't hold together unless you know who he is, is that right?"

"God's-eye view," I said. "Good, Bunyan, keep going."

Bunyan reversed the videotape until he came to the part where Deep Throat, played eerily by Hal Holbrook, blasts Woodward's incompetence at one of their underground parking garage meetings.

"You're missing the overall," sneers Deep Throat Holbrook. "They bugged, they fouled people, false press leaks, false letters, they canceled Democratic press conferences, they investigated Democratic private lives, they stole documents and on and on. . . ."

Bunyan froze the picture and said, "There. Deep Throat knows it all. And when he says, 'Your lives are in danger,' is he kidding?"

"That's poetic license," I opined. "DT was thinking of himself, not them, never them."

Bunyan then made a Watergate-rookie error. He reached a conclusion without working up to it piecemeal, the same sort of mistake Woodward and Bernstein kept making all that fall of '72. Bunyan said, "You think Gordon Liddy is Deep Throat?"

"Negative," I declared. "Look at the facts as they are known. Seventeen years later, Woodward and Bernstein refuse to name their phenomenal source, originally called Mr. X on the in-house reports at the *Washington Post*, nicknamed Deep Throat by managing editor Howard Simons."

I paused, not because I couldn't remember but because I was speaking too fast and I wanted Bunyan to follow my logic.

"What is known about DT is thin," I began again. "It's a he, not a woman. There was also a Miss X, whose identity was later revealed. Nor was DT a composite of several sources. He's one man."

"You're sure?" asked Bunyan.

"Affirmative," I said. "DT and Woodward conversed on the phone, though rarely and with difficulty, and in person in an exotic locale—an underground parking garage after midnight. Their meetings were set up with textbook commo plans. For example, Woodward would move a red flag to the front of his terrace or DT drew a clock face on a page in Woodward's morning delivery of the *New York Times* or they would use a one-way phone signal."

"That sounds like what you call Hollywood," said Bunyan.

"Except they did it," I said. "All this from late summer '72 at least until fall '73. DT gave Woodward and Bernstein good information, but he dripped it out like making coffee. He was also a big pain. Hinting, exhorting, accusing, whining, double-talking. Always pointing Woodward and Bernstein in odd directions. But it was scary pointing. Once he scared Woodward so badly that later that night, Woodward and Bernstein covered their conversation in Woodward's apartment by turning up a record of Rachmaninoff. They could never trust him as a definitive or quotable source. They always had to verify his tips by other means as well—FBI, prosecutors, grand jury leaks, finks at CREEP—the Committee to Re-Elect the President."

I paused again to check on my audience. Bunyan was staring. I asked, "Am I going too fast?"

"No," said Bunyan. "I was just thinking how funny 'creep' sounds when you say it. Like a famous ball club."

"CREEP, CREEP, CREEP," I repeated, listening to myself. "How else can you say it?" I asked.

Bunyan teased, "Go faster, Tip."

I obliged. I declared that importantly, Deep Throat's information was never wrong. Woodward insisted upon calling him "my friend," yet he also characterized him as sarcastic, dejected, whimsical, perverse, nervous on the phone, blunt in person, a lover of intrigue, gamesmanship, literature, mimicry. Physically DT was described as trim, not bald, tendency to lose weight from stress, not always clean-shaven, appetite for tobacco and whiskey, insomniac or near to, drunkard or near to, red-eyed, garrulous. From the beginning, DT feared he was being watched, followed or bugged. Nevertheless DT kept passing tips to Woodward, both of specific details of the Watergate break-in and of general attitudes at the White House during the cover-up.

I listed some of the known tips passed by Deep Throat.

It was Deep Throat who confirmed, in September '72, that John Mitchell was in charge of the CREEP slush fund for covert activities such as the Watergate break-in.

It was DT who confirmed, in October '72, that Mitchell had panicked after the break-in, had used Howard Hunt to track down what the Plumbers had been doing for CREEP.

It was DT who, in February '73, called Liddy and Hunt "the lowest," said that hiring them was "immoral," that Liddy had wanted to bug the *New York Times* to track down who had leaked the Pentagon Papers in 1971.

It was DT who declared, in May '73, that John Dean had pressured the burglars to take the fall in silence.

It was DT who knew that the covert activities by the Plumbers had corrupted the Justice Department, the FBI, the CIA, federal judges, the President himself.

And it was DT who told Woodward, in November '73, that the Oval Office tapes had several gaps "of a suspicious nature," probably erasures. The most notorious of them being the eighteen-and-a-half-minute gap on the June 20, 1972, taped conversation between President Nixon and Haldeman—three days after the Watergate break-in.

Bunyan was no longer staring in disbelief, he was writing fast, the way the army was training him, the shorthand of a counterintelligence officer.

He waved me to a halt. "He's one guy?" he asked. "You're sure Deep Throat is one guy? One asset knew all this? White House, FBI, Justice, CREEP, Oval Office? What kind of . . . ? And he's never been named? Never in from the cold?"

I was pleased and rewarded Bunyan. "Good sci-fi/spy talk," I said. "Listen closely."

I deepened my tone to sound authoritative. "In seventeen years there have been many suspects. Chief among them is Alexander Haig, who was Kissinger's deputy, Nixon's last chief of staff, C in C NATO forces '75–'79, Reagan's secretary of state '81–'82, presidential candidate 1988. Also suspect are the lawyers Buzhardt, Powers and Garment and aide Bull, who were Nixon's team to keep the Oval Office tapes from the Congress. Also John Sears, the Republican campaign honcho, who was President Reagan's first campaign manager, 1980. Also Charles Colson, who was counsel to the President and White House dirty trickster who *ran* the Plumbers, hired Howard Hunt, blasted the *Post*, left the White House in December '72, did seven months in jail, is now a born-again huckster in prison ministry."

I checked my audience again. I could see that Bunyan had caught the Watergate bug. His affliction was making him scribble as fast as I was blithering.

"You know, don't you?" he asked. "You know it's none of them. That Deep Throat is Gordon Liddy."

"*Negative*," I declared. "Stop guessing."

"Then stop making me," Bunyan returned sensibly.

I said, "Ask me what the principals have said over the years."

"You mean Nixon?" said Bunyan. "No, no, he wouldn't talk about it. Ehrlichman and Haldeman? Dean?"

"Correct," I said. "John Ehrlichman, who did eighteen months in jail, now sixty-three, a celebrity and bitter hack who lives in Arizona."

"Is it him?" asked Bunyan.

"Stop guessing," I ordered. "John Ehrlichman says DT never existed, that he was a composite of sources."

"How about Haldeman?"

I smiled and reported, "Bob Haldeman, who did eighteen months, now sixty, an L.A. realtor and bitter hack. He says DT is John Dean."

"Is he?"

I reported, "John Dean, who turned coat in May '73 and ratted to the Ervin Committee, did four months, now forty-nine, a Beverly Hills celebrity and bitter hack with his equally bitter wife, Mo. He says DT is Al Haig."

"All right, all right, I understand," said Bunyan. "Everybody blames everybody." Bunyan copied down the suspects and drew arrows, a Holmes Paine in the making. He asked, "What've Woodward and Bernstein said?"

"Good question, and the answer is nothing," I reported. "Carl Bernstein, now forty-five, millionaire celebrity and ABC correspondent in London, infamous for his dumping of wife Nora Ephron, famous as a billy goat, says nothing. Bob Woodward, now forty-six, millionaire assistant managing editor for investigations at the *Post*, author of five best-sellers, says nothing."

"I read Woodward's CIA book," said Bunyan, "*Veil*, the tell-all book on Bill Casey. He's a big deal. Sure knows his tradecraft, though I don't know why Casey told him so much, *if he did.*"

"Be more suspicious," I advised, "and you're right about Woodward. Bob Woodward, obsessed by the CIA, Yale grad (prep school of spookery), navy vet, multiple married, as star-struck a journalist as on earth. Still he says nothing. But, Bunyan, you didn't ask me *how* Woodward and Bernstein have said nothing."

Bunyan drained his soda pop and lobbed the can at me. "You're not gonna tell me; all this and you're just selling me a story—what you call make-believe."

"Correct," I said. "Once-upon-a-time."

"No, it's not," he said. "It's why you're going to see Gordon Liddy, isn't it? It's why we're here?"

"Correct."

"You're being weird," he opined.

"Correct," I admitted.

It was tough to shut myself up, but I did and wouldn't tell Bunyan any more than he'd already learned that night. I faced a big covert day and needed to review my act in my sleep.

At 7 A.M. I was fuzzy about my ambitions. Maybe this was a dusty old manhunt. Maybe nobody did care. No, Tip cared. The Watergate Caper was alive as long as there were missing pieces. Deep Throat's "overall" wasn't everything. As long as there was a hole there was no truth, and Deep Throat was a black, black hole incarnate.

Bunyan and I breakfasted in the hotel café while discussing how I wanted the scene handled at the Phoenix airport, where I was to be met by a limo from Liddy's School for Scandal. We got on the road for the leg in. Bunyan was *not* in uniform; I thought that would have been indiscreet and wrongheaded. We practiced our Spanish and French, a difficult switch from boyhood American. And we reviewed our commo plan—the telephone signal that I'd give every night if all was in order, the crash alert I'd give if I needed emergency exfiltration.

It was a fun rehearsal, since I didn't really think any of it would be necessary. Gordon Liddy was a nationally popular flake, not a bad guy. Robert Conrad played his life story as if U. S. Grant were still President. Gordon's "Miami Vice" episodes were first-rate hambone. Gordon was also one of Phoenix's local heroes, a favorite of talking headers, college campuses, syndicated sound bites. Yet I was prepping for him as if I were parachuting into Persia.

Of course there was the unspoken detail that I planned to cross Gordon if I could, yank his ball and chain to get what I wanted, and if he suddenly transformed himself to Gordon Liddy, paranoid avenger—the man who did forty-six months in a federal pen in a rage of silence at his enemies—then I'd need to get out of the Sonora desert as fast as I'd gotten in.

When the highway signs finally read Phoenix International Airport, Bunyan switched off the C&W radio station, patted my kit bag and said, "A week from now, Tucson, promise?"

"Affirmative. Super Bowl Sunday," I agreed. I said that I'd be done with Liddy and we'd find a cowboy bar in Tucson to watch the game and tell more stories.

"That's not it," said Bunyan. "You'll tell me who Deep Throat is, promise?"

"Deal," I said. "Meantime, do your homework. Read *The Presidential Transcripts*, *The Senate Watergate Committee Report*, and Woodward and Bernstein's two books, *APM* and *The Final Days*. Also study photocopies of the pertinent pieces in the *Post*, June '72 to August '74."

"Oh, yeah, forget the work the army has me doing all week that I can't tell you about," said Bunyan. "And where'm I gonna find all that stuff? I don't rate access to a satellite uplink."

I liked my reply. "Backseat of your car at Tucson, in the bag I stowed just in case you got *nostalgic* with me and wanted to know."

"Geez, Tip," said Bunyan, "you're really over the hill here. Turning forty does this?"

I grunted.

"Sorry," said Bunyan, "but you're playing me for a dummy, and I rate better, Specialist." Bunyan was being snooty, the officer corps talking down to us enlisted grubs.

"Tell me," he ordered, *"how've* Woodward and Bernstein said nothing about Deep Throat."

Fifteen minutes to Operation Muse, I gave Bunyan these crucial clues fast:

The only interview Woodward has permitted on Deep Throat was in *Time* magazine, May 3, 1976. Woodward said, "There is a Deep Throat, and he is not a composite.... My editors at the *Post* know he exists—though they don't know who he is.... When we wrote *All the President's Men* (February 1974) he declined to be named.... He has a career in government. He thinks that while he might be a hero to some, he would be a rat or a snitcher in some eyes. . . . Someday he'll come forth. If he were to die I would feel obliged to reveal his name. Someday he'll write a really fascinating book. Carl and I would like to work on it with him."

"Wow," said Bunyan when I finished; he changed to the slow lane, wanting to take notes. Nevertheless I knew this was printing on his left brain too. "Woodward said all that? That's a lot of nothing, isn't it?"

"Here's the punch line," I declared. "The *Time* guy asked, Why did he help you? Woodward said, '*It was an act of conscience—a result of his own disillusionment.*'"

Bunyan sneezed, the family allergy to the desert. "Deep Throat's a strange guy, huh? Hero or rat?"

We were into the airport loops. Bunyan was prepped, I was set. Spanish between us, he carries my kit bag, we don't shake hands, he keeps his sunglasses on, expect them to take a snapshot of the license plate, if there's trouble we speak only the Corsican dialect we'd both learned from reading a comic book. I gave no final instructions; my baby brother is a pro, my foil in make-believe.

"I've got to ask," said Bunyan. "Gordon Liddy. If he's not Deep Throat, why're you doing this?"

I confessed, "My muse knows, he knows it all, only he doesn't know he knows. Now he's going to tell me. And, Bunyan, another clue. *Cowardice makes heroes of us all.*"

Bunyan groaned. "What an easy clue!"

"Green light," I said, "here we go. Begin Operation Muse."

3

Phoenix is another desert boomtown that opens every morning at dawn and closes at 4 P.M. There's nothing significant to say of it other than that it's fenced in by snow-capped purple mountain majesty and it needs lots of piped-in water, so I'll get on to Gordon Liddy.

My muse preached twice to his students that Sunday, first at the get-acquainted buffet luncheon at our fantasy hotel in downtown Phoenix, second at the dress-up dinner in a private dining room. In between, the students—there were eleven of us—were stroked by Gordon's staff of instructors. Our instructors were actually mercenaries, who were eager to demonstrate to us that they had manners that suited the boardroom as well as riding shotgun or rescuing the kidnapped from savanna jungles.

Do you know about the mercenary academies? The easiest way to understand their appeal is to think of a fantasy baseball camp where you can rub elbows with old pros. It's not lunatic fringe. Merc academies attract executives, cops, retirees, the rich, the restless, both foreign and domestic vacationers.

Gordon's merc academy was colorful because of him, but it was one of dozens throughout the South and West. They're operated by vets from military and intelligence services, ours and theirs, guys on pensions who've learned how to sell their talents to the private sector. Their personnel category would be security consultant. Some merc academies advertise, others recruit by word of mouth, those I don't know about accept applicants only from friends.

Gordon's used all three methods, useful for me because when I talked to his bursar in December I had emphasized that I wanted a single room: $7,800 ($1,220/day plus incidental expenses) in a bank check for one week in the desert, anonymously.

To the instructors I was Mr. Moore of Bronx, N.Y. The big one, Choat, a cueball-bald South African émigré, asked me, "If you're active duty—I'm not asking, but if you are—Mr. Liddy has the standard request. No taping, good?"

I brilliantly swallowed my smile. "Not even photos, Mr. Choat," I agreed. I wanted to call him Sarge; he had squad leader SADF tattooed on his irises.

The fair wiry instructor Fluegeman, a Spanish accent in a tight suit, debriefed me in my hotel room. "Your application says you want Stage One training, Mr. Moore; also specialize in wire security and motorcade tactics."

For kicks I restated my requests in Spanish.

Fluegeman didn't like this. Maybe he thought I was going to ask him what Pinochet was really going to do. Fluegeman provided me with a class schedule and three wonderful books—*Manual of the Mercenary Soldier, Walls Have Ears* and *How to Motorcade*. He also gave me a videotape of motorcades in London, New York, Rome and Seoul.

"Mr. Liddy will be meeting with you, with each student, one on one, sir," said Fluegeman. "You're scheduled for tomorrow evening at Desert One."

"What's that?" I asked.

"At our base camp," said Fluegeman, "we rent a motel for the week. Near our training grounds."

My muse made my day. At the luncheon he was handsome and correct in loose jeans and waist-length brown leather jacket over a black-and-white checkered shirt. His watchband was rattlesnake, his watch was one of those rugged mechanisms called a chronograph, with more dials than the Spirit of St. Louis.

I could see that Gordon's personal clock had aged. There were only white wisps for hair; he shaved his baldness. His face and hands were cracked from the sun. Nevertheless he was a vigorous fifty-nine-year-old, no paunch, good chest, dark eyebrows over a bright gaze that squinted from too much desert, a crisp voice that was never vulgar. And there was that signature mustache, walrus proud.

Gordon circled the room, working us like a diplomat, abrupt handshake and heartfelt welcome. He didn't like to be touched, so I backed off a step before I told him he looked better than Colonel North.

He grinned under the mustache. "Who?"

"A short marine," I said. "Heart on his sleeve, eats ribbons and congressional marble."

"Mr. Moore, you're not a marine," said Gordon, "I'm not a marine, but my *son's* the corps to me; let's leave it there."

I thought, Good reply, muse; cover up with fatherhood. Gordon envied Ollie North; why else would he change the subject? Gordon never got his day on tv to tell off the Congress, and I realized it really burned him. Of all the what-ifs in his life, I thought, that must hurt hotly.

Gordon's lunchtime preachments to us were only preliminary propaganda, however—of the "This is a week you'll remember" variety.

Gordon did brandish his motto, *Fiat voluntas tua.* This is Latin for "Thy will be done." It was also the first thing he said to the press when he got out of jail in '77. It's also Signor Machiavelli—the correct worshipful reply of every lieutenant to his prince, no matter what is asked.

At dinner Gordon flew all his colors at once—red/white/blue/black. The scripture lesson was from Signor Machiavelli, Chapter 14: "A Prince, therefore, must have no other object or thought, nor acquire skill in anything, except war, its organization, and its discipline."

"Americans," continued Gordon, pillar-erect at the staff table, "don't understand this like our foreign guests."

We eleven students were seated at two round tables. I'd counted two married couples, a pair of executive secretaries, a pair of Singapore Chinese, three middle-aged white guys of indeterminate nationality, including me (not a Bob Mitchum or Rosalind Russell among us).

"But it's as true today as it was five hundred years back," said Gordon. "What we're teaching you is how to defend yourself against terrorist warfare. The terrorist is . . ."

Gordon preached the NRA line, as well he should have. This right-to-bear-arms boilerplate got him kicked out of the Treasury Department and into the White House and history twenty years back. I also heard his remarks as the economy of persecution mania, good salesmanship to the executive branches: There are lots of them, only a few of you; arm yourself or you're humpty-dumpty.

There was a shocker at the end, though. Gordon said, "I also care about the environment, the coming devastation by industrial pollution, overbuilding, reckless disregard for nature. Out there's the most beautiful desert in the world, but if something isn't done soon . . ."

What was this? Suddenly my trip was unexpected fun. I set aside my Deep Throat chase for the moment. Gordon had moved on, muse for the 1990s. But green?

I watched the motorcade videotape in my room and made notes. What could possibly interest a secret policeman about ecosystems? Could it be religion? He was raised a Latin-mass Catholic, a believer in belief, but still—Loyola, not St. Francis. Gordon was the G-man who nabbed a ten-most-wanted guy in Denver at gunpoint. Gordon was the ADA who ran for Congress in 1968 with adverts promising, "Gordon doesn't bail them out, he puts them in." John Dean had once told President Nixon re Gordon, "Strange and strong. His loyalty is—I think it is just beyond the pale." President Nixon had asked Dean, "He hates the other side too?" Dean had said, "Oh, absolutely. He is strong. He really is."

So how could Gordon have turned green? When Gordon got out of jail in 1977, he sneered to the press that John Dean could sing the title castrato role in *Der Rosenkavalier*. Gordon's autobiography, *Will*, was agitprop for dead-shot sentinels, guys whose tooth care is barbed-wire Nietzsche.

It didn't figure, but there it was, green Gordon. Tip had a lot to learn. I placed the all-clear call to Bunyan and dreamed nothing.

4

Gordon's Desert One was a quick hour north of Phoenix in a river valley where the Lower Colorado Valley borders the Arizona Upland. To a tourist it was a Yavapai County motel (ten rustic cabins behind a gas pump/novelty shop) en route to Prescott west and the Grand Canyon north. To me it was where those amazing mountain ranges take a break for a thin river and abandoned hot springs.

The Sonora is a gigantic phenomenon, and I was stupefied. I've marveled at Louisiana's Cameron County and South Carolina's Beaufort; I've worried the Colorado Rockies might fall on me and fled the American Falls and Big Muddy because I imagined I was being dragged in; I've sometimes lived where Maine's forest finds the granite. The Sonora is none of the above, rather a living heaving wasteland.

I knew it meant something that Gordon loved the Sonora so much that he'd exiled himself here from doing hard time for the highest office in America. But what did it mean to him? Hell on earth seemed too easy. Besides, the Sonora is too gorgeous to be simply demonic. You can see for miles and miles and miles, and if you're not careful that old urban bugaboo called agoraphobia will ruin your holiday. Still, when those spring showers spot the hills, the spectral flowers suck and bloom and ever-dear rainbows jump rope.

There was a winter shower that morning. By the time we had stashed our gear in our rooms and gathered for the morning debrief, the air was bathed and perfect.

Choat said day one was guns & ammo. We climbed back into the academy's Chevy bus and bounced into the hills a half hour to Gordon's Desert Two. Imagine Old Tucson built by Edgar Hoover as a miniature golf course—facades, pop-up targets, demolition cars, firing range, all this amidst a wondrous landscape where the mountain peaks were snow-coated.

I'd made small talk with both of the couples by then, Brits named Sylvester and Californians named Andersen.

Mr. Sylvester asked me, "Are you a soldier, Mr. Moore, do you know about these guns?"

He meant the traveling armory laid out for us: an assault-grip shotgun; the standard-issue assault rifles, including the Israeli Galil; also submachines guns likes a Ruger and Uzi and the prize-looking Spectre.

Mrs. Sylvester, a golden-tanned snob, said, "We just have to fire them once, Bobby, just in case." They were bankers headed for South Asian usury for Barclays and regarded Gordon's as a bizarre holiday, tax deductible.

Rat-a-tat is not the sound you hear when you squeeze a Spectre's trigger. It's a fifty-clip, shoots smooth if you can call it a polite word, and it doesn't kick up.

"Notice the stability," Choat lectured, "and the ventilation is good, no overheating. It's state of the art for terrorists now. Italians will sell any Arab. You can fire it one-handed; try it."

Mrs. Andersen, fiftyish and square-shouldered, said, "Wish me luck," and let go like a shootist. She didn't aim, but the target evaporated. Mr. Andersen considered his spouse anew (surely this was a randier holiday than Lindblad to Antarctica) and soon enough fired a whole clip.

Lordy, I hate guns. I'm not going to review my phobia. I stood by and admired the mountains while the others chopped up the range.

My refusal intrigued the two executive secretary students, Ms. Luonoso and Ms. Novak. At picnic luncheon under a canopy, Ms. Luonoso started, "Can I ask you a question: why you didn't—you know—shoot?"

Her partner, Ms. Novak, interjected, "He doesn't have to say, Jane."

They were in their forties, rings but no bands, both greasy with sunblock and dressed in matching parkas. From what they'd said without prompting, they were here to expand their skills on their employer's time. (You've heard of it, the Bechtel Corporation, worldwide construction outfit, golden parachute of State Secretary Shultz.)

"You're lucky really," said Ms. Novak to me, "to be free not to shoot. The men in my life, well, my father was navy, sixteen-inchers [smile], then missiles." Busty prim, cropped tinted brown hair, Ms. Novak pretended to cinch up her safari suit. "It's not what a woman ever gets a chance to say yes or no to," she added. "It's assumed *no*, you understand?"

I did. The Singapore Chinese were eavesdropping, Mr. Wan and Mr. Ton; they were from a region of old-fashioned piracy that has cause to worry about gunplay.

Ms. Luonoso, round, prim and blondish, addressed me again. "You know, we were trying to guess last night what everybody does. Have you got guesses, Mr. Moore?"

I said I didn't like to guess.

I saw Ms. Luonoso's suspicion lock on. Her make-believe had just transformed me into a precious-metals smuggler or weirder. She said, "I think you couldn't be a soldier, could you? Mr. Choat, he told me they think you're 'active duty.' What's that mean exactly?"

Operation Muse was working, though not as I'd planned. Gradually my compatriots came to treat me as Mr. Moore from Planet X. During the afternoon exercise—small arms for us, a shoot-off by the instructors—I fielded a few questions from the couples but otherwise was left alone. In sci-fi/spy talk, I was sanctioned—that is, licensed to be strange and strong. What I'd hoped would attract Gordon was isolating me.

The navy daughter, Ms. Novak, watched me as if I were an endangered species sunning on her lawn. Later in the day, when the air was cooler and the firepower hotter, she approached me again. "What's that funny smell?" she asked me, holding out her hands.

I told her.

"Nitrates? On my face too? How do you get it off?"

Gordon joined us in the afternoon to show off in leather and shades. He was still a dead-shot G-man, the tree-busting magnum his weapon of choice. However, he spoke admiringly of a new tool called the CZ-75.

"Finest super-nine handgun out there," said Gordon, "and it's made over there." He pointed east in disgust, way east, as behind the iron curtain. Then he did the macho magazine load favored by tv cops. Without hesitation he blasted air.

The students were now so taken by gunsmoke and sinister tphuts that they lined up to try Czechoslovakia's champion.

"For you ladies too," said Gordon. "It's got punch, you can drop what moves at twenty-five yards...shames our Beretta...double-action trigger..."

Gordon was gun crazy; that wasn't news. After supper back at Desert One, he preached weapons to us with a slide show. What passion Gordon showed was for Freudian witticisms, such as "penetration" or "cocked and locked," or how many clips you can store in a Velcro-zipped holster. I hoped he'd pontificate back around to his ecodreaming, but not tonight.

Fluegeman stopped by my desk (they'd converted one cabin into a video center) and told me Gordon needed to reschedule our powwow. "You understand, Mr. Moore, the ladies need special attention; they don't know firearms."

"Sí, señor," I teased, knowing that it takes time to track a rental Cadillac shaped like a fishhook.

Tuesday and Wednesday were up early and play hard at survival tactics, both in the hills and at Desert Two. I liked the advice about how to light-plane-crash ("Stay near the wreck, it's your friend," said Choat. "Signal with the landscape"), but much of it was campfire horror tales. Fluegeman had a great line: "Torture is conversation; talk back, keep talking, live in the land of a thousand excuses." The other students were now pals in paranoia and after supper roared off to Prescott with the gladiators for bar-hopping.

Tip stayed behind in his cabin to watch videotapes and to wait for Gordon. Wednesday evening he bit my door.

"You're antisocial," he said as he walked in, not sitting. His leather jacket squeaked. "Miami Vice" had dressed him in white, wrongly against type. Gordon was black ops down to black socks in his dyed black shitkickers. "How 'bout a drive?" he suggested.

His Bronco was leather comfort and hard shocks. He popped Verdi in his cassette system and accelerated his Bronco. "I don't know much about you, Mr. Moore; you got a clearance you can mention?"

I knew he was hooked by my ruse and I could now play the game crooked. Perversely I wanted to chat with green Gordon and mentioned the Sonora.

"I've driven it from the Mojave to La Paz," he said. "You know the Baja? Men get lost down there; the compass works, but the brain doesn't."

I said Mexico scared me, that I'd heard it called a cargo cult without a rudder.

"You've mentioned scared," said Gordon. "You've said that to Choat: scared this, scared that. The men I've known who scare like that are priests. Who aren't scared of much, when it comes to it. You're not Catholic?"

We drove through a mountain pass and crossed the Verde River, picking up a sign for Montezuma's Castle.

"You like monuments?" asked Gordon. He was loose-tongued now with his memories of the desert. His affection was genuine; he liked to camp out, ride horses, find fossils, be a cowboy in the age of antibiotics and ineradicable viruses.

I did enjoy his company. It was never intimate, but it rewarded with authoritative detail. He'd introduced godliness, and so, as we motored, I turned to thinking that he should have been a Jesuit, nothing between him and righteousness but sacraments, a wine bottle and ineffable grace. I wasn't ignoring the blaze of rage in his chest like all his shoulder chips melted down to critical mass. Jesuits could handle that, I supposed; just don a hair shirt and head for the equator to harass savages and feed leeches. If you wanted paternal and sancti-monious militance, Gordon was your daddy.

We stopped at the turnoff to Montezuma's Castle, a national mon-ument of cliff dwellings carved like antediluvian Manhattan.

"How 'bout a walk?" asked Gordon. "You smoke cigars, don't you? Real antisocial."

I'd given up my pipe for the week, a change in scent to throw off the trackers. I was getting by on a carton of cigarillos, which made me queasy after five puffs.

"I'm doing all the talking," said Gordon. "Thing is, I don't know what you want to hear. Not motorcade tactics, mmh? Wire security? You already know about wire security."

Tip heard the warble of threat alert.

"Why else would you make one phone call every night," asked Gordon, "when you say maybe ten foreign words?"

I gave him no credit for monitoring my evening all-clear calls to Bunyan on the motel line; Doris Day could manage that.

We stopped our stroll abruptly. Gordon's leather squeaked as he crossed his arms commando style.

"So what I'm saying is," he started, "you say you're flying in from New York and arrive in a rented car with a bodyguard. You won't use a weapon and don't mix or drink, and nobody ever called you Wilcy nothing. Clothes bought in Arizona, boots out of a catalogue, the Gila Bend matchbook's a plant, haircut is college boy and the beard is a week old. Just like you, a week old. You're a week old, Mr. Moore."

Gordon pointed his jaw toward Polaris and declared, "Your money's good, Mr. Moore, but you're as keen on antiterrorism as the Apache."

Magnificent muse, I love you. I told him that I'd made a mistake. (Which was true; too big a blank is a name in lights.) I felt wicked then and asked how he would have done it.

"You could've called me at the ranch," snapped Gordon. "My line's clean. Give me a date and address. You think I can't travel clean? Interview me, polygraph me, check me out—I'm clean."

Whoa, muse, you just left me in the desert. I'd disguised myself as Wilcy Moore the Fireman to avoid being spotted as a best-seller looking for a plot. I'd been prepared for him to name me a wheedling reporter or even a magazine ghoul. I'd been ready to bail out to Bunyan if he made me for any kind of snoop. But not this twist. Was I following him?

"I've been thinking it might go," Gordon mused. "I've had feelers since '80. Casey wanted me, I hear. He knew I'm putting my shoulder into Central America. That I've got contacts down there. Not a Rolodex; live bodies who owe me. Why didn't it happen? After '84, you needed me. Hasenfus! What a screw-up. You fellows ever learn, or was it like it's said? Give up the mercs and get a big show down the road?"

I was right. Gordon thought I was Langley recruiter and this was a job interview for a mercenary contract down Central America way. Operation Muse was racing out of control. Bunyan had been my worst mistake. Some men are a uniform even in jeans. And since they'd interpreted Bunyan to be my military attaché, that made me, to them, a government man, either FBI or CIA. Gordon had guessed that I was here to assess him as a CIA contractor.

More generally my mistake had been that I had overlooked Gordon's spectacular imagination. After his Watergate indictment, in his first national interview, November 1, 1972, Gordon had said, "I've got clearances so high that the name is classified. . . ."

Gordon was a missile to the stars. He thought he had clearance by God almighty, the only name I know that's classified. If you gave Gordon a launch platform, he'd do the rest. Now I was trapped in a triple-ply lie, not student, not journalist, not Langley.

I couldn't solve this beneath limestone cliffs. I kept shut and we got back to his Bronco to accelerate.

Gordon was overexcited, and because he was very smart he popped in Mozart and smoked slowly. "You tell them," said Gordon as we approached Desert One, "that I'm not done yet. It's not a job to me. I wasn't looking for a pension like that Poindexter operation. They can count on me to go where they say and finish it like they say. You know that, don't you, Mr. Moore?"

I had to ask, "Finish what, Mr. Liddy?"

"*They* know," Gordon pontificated. "*They* don't get the White House without us. Bush didn't get the White House without us. The men who take the fall. You want to see my records? Fine. When I got out I didn't have a dime, and Carter's people tried to turn me. My children were growing up without me, and they used them on me. Cruel, it was cruel. I told them I'd go back in and finish twenty-one years before I'd turn."

("Strange and strong," John Dean had said to President Nixon. "His loyalty is—I think it is just beyond the pale.")

"We'll chat again," finished Gordon as we arrived back at my cabin. "I know you've got rules, people you've got to talk to."

I nodded meaninglessly.

"You're young in the service, Mr. Moore; still you know that it's not men, it's the cause. When that's just, you take your chance hard, do what has to be done and survive what comes with what luck you've got."

(I checked his text later, Signor Machiavelli, Chapter 25: "It is better to be impetuous than circumspect; because fortune is a woman, and if she is to be submissive it is necessary to beat and coerce her.")

"I'd do it all again," said Gordon.

I stood next to his Bronco and asked with a sober smile, "'Thy will be done'?"

"No questions," said Gordon, "no regrets."

5

The strangeness of persecution mania is also its strength. It is so logical that it can be useful. George Gordon Battle Liddy was never a renegade. Like a microchip motherboard, he took orders, he needed orders.

("He's not talking," Haldeman had explained about Gordon to President Nixon in the Oval Office while they were discussing Gordon's silence before the prosecutors in 1973, "'cause he thinks he's not supposed to talk. If he is supposed to talk, he will. All he needs is a signal, if you want to turn Liddy on.")

Yes, Gordon went too far—he broke the same laws the routine secret policeman would have broken—but he got there logically, never without what he called clearance. When CREEP asked him for a master plan to disrupt the Democratic Party in the '72 election, he drew up Operation Gemstone and pitched it to John Mitchell. Bugging, kidnapping, blackmail, prostitution, character assassination—black ops warfare. When the attorney general of the United States scoffed at him, Gordon proposed again and again, until what was left got nabbed at the Watergate Hotel.

Gordon's loyalty *was* beyond the pale, because that's where too much of patriotism went in the Cold War. He'd been raised in the church, educated by Korea, the bloody yo-yo, trained by Edgar Hoover, honed in Dutchess County politics and Treasury Department shenanigans, sanctioned by the White House itself and teamed with the tireless black ops rigor of Howard Hunt.

Then fate cut Gordon loose at forty-two. My age, he was just about my age when they put him in the stocks and tortured him for being Gordon. How tortured? He was prosecuted in the courts, reviled in the press, laughed at by the pros, jailed for years to do hard time without any support from the prince he'd served. Worse, he was tortured for doing something that was said to be puerile. The White House mouthpieces had called Watergate a third-rate burglary, and this qualification just slid over to the seven Watergate break-in defendants. They were called third-raters, pranksters and, worst of all, brainless blunderers. That's torture beyond mercy. Maybe you're still laughing. You're wrong to laugh, and I'll tell you why.

Gordon Liddy was a very serious person. It is my belief that what happened to him could happen to anyone who takes orders, believes in luck and excels at the Cold War or any kind of war. He went through that taped-open door and got handed a clown mask and big feet. He thought it was his job to put them on, so he did, in silence. Yet Tip says it is wrong to mock him for his stubborn obedience to his aggrandized and unreal prince. Don't ask Gordon what he did. Ask yourself what he did. Gordon didn't take a fall for make-believe, he took it for the presidency, our elected President, and therefore for us all. Gordon still won't admit to this, for his own strange strong reasons, but it's fair-minded to say it. Gordon went into hell in 1972. We sent him there, we kept him there, we won't let him come back; too busy condemning other damned clowns.

Pay attention. What might have happened to Gordon the faithful criminal bozo?

By June 1972 President Nixon was ahead by twenty-three points in the election polls. His approval rating was staggeringly high for an election year, at sixty percent. The Democrats had axed their strongest challengers themselves. You flatter the Liddy-Hunt gang if you say their dirty tricks took even a knick out of the Democratic contenders. The jackasses did themselves in. Hubert Humphrey was rejected for being a loser, Scoop Jackson for believing in the Cold War, Ed Muskie for crying in rage when he called a slanderer named Loeb a "gutless coward," Ted Kennedy for being a plain coward at Chappaquiddick.

The strangeness of the Watergate Caper must always include its strange genesis. President Nixon had panicked in the early spring at a meaningless poll that put Ed Muskie the angel ahead. In quick time, President Nixon had reversed the poll by pulling the last American ground troops out of Vietnam and sending in the air force to bomb the peasant reds in a rage of so-called honor—result, approval rating of sixty percent by mid-June.

President Nixon's maneuvers worked brilliantly. By June he could have defeated anyone alive (there are no angels in politics) without raising his voice or a dollar. Yet months before, still worried by Muskie's meaningless popularity, he had sanctioned John Mitchell to organize the reelection campaign as if it were a war on the Bolsheviks. And by June President Nixon didn't bother to turn off the covert war he'd ordered. He let it go ahead. John Mitchell had obeyed orders. He had arranged for a CREEP counterintelligence-sabotage game, raised a war chest of sixty million dollars cash and aimed to throttle the Democrats to death. Hence Gordon Liddy's Operation Gemstone. Hence Howard Hunt recruiting a midget named Segretti to "ratf——" the Dems coast to coast. Hence the break-ins on the candidacies of Muskie, Humphrey, Jackson, McGovern, and also the wiretaps on the Democratic National Committee. Hence that amazing morning of June 17.

But without Watergate, how far could Gordon have gone? Nothing could stop his boss Nixon, so what could have stopped Gordon?

By Election Day 1972 the press had exposed the general nastiness of CREEP, including Watergate. Listen to me: the voters *knew,* and they still voted Nixon back in like an emperor. Nixon massacred McGovern, a candidate so blinded by his own goodness that he dumped his VP candidate Eagleton as if he were an abortion. Listen to me again: it's not true that the citizenry didn't care about Watergate when they voted. (Magruder estimated it cost the GOP a million votes, and Nixon joked, "Was I supposed to win by twenty million?") It's that the presidency does not go to goodness. It's a chief's job, a national ceremony, and the citizenry likes its chief part nasty, part funny, all hard-core boss. If he can't ravage his opponent, how's he gonna do against the bad guys? You want rules, stick to beatification and other nonblood sports. Politics is life, and that's very often rage and slaughter. Laugh at the President, curse him; you respect him because he takes his chance hard, does what has to be done and survives what comes with what luck he's got.

I'm describing Richard Nixon as well as Gordon Liddy. The answer to what might have happened to Gordon is more and more of the same. He was a missile, and he was well launched June 17, 1972— onto the Justice Department, federal bench, a man paid to be at the sharp end of the stick. If you scoff when I say FBI director G. Gordon Liddy, then you are a fool. Remember anonymously inept L. Patrick Gray, Nixon's FBI director, who dumped the contents of Howard Hunt's safe in a fire or a river to protect Nixon, yet then confessed to the Congress. Gordon would have eaten that evidence and chased it with belladonna, while toasting a portrait of Hoover.

You don't like what-ifs? You don't like to speculate about what might have happened to Gordon? Then you're a nearsighted fatalist, and you've learned nothing from the past. Folk base decisions as much upon what might have happened as upon what actually happened. President Nixon was always trying to interpret his cover-up of Watergate on the basis of his rise to prominence in the Alger Hiss–Whittaker Chambers case. President Nixon mused: What if Hiss had walked away? What if Chambers hadn't ratted? What if "the establishment" didn't hate him for getting Hiss? If today you ask for just the facts of what happened, then you're probably a propagandist like John Dean, who told President Nixon in March '73 about the cover-up: "You see, you could even write a novel with the facts."

What I'm telling you is that at some point after all the laughing it's important to take Gordon Liddy very seriously.

Gordon has also gone beyond a novel. I love my muse because he is beyond facts and fiction, and that means myth.

When I left Gordon that night after our drive, I realized that he was where I could never go, and I could not then and cannot now honestly say I wouldn't want to go there if fate had fallen on me instead of Gordon. This is envy, what the mind doctors say is crystalline malice. You can love so much you can hate. But I'm not standing off and claiming to be a better man. My envy has made him my muse.

Would I have done what Gordon did? I repeat that he was just about my age when he did the deed. Would I have done the same? Or would I have said no to the White House, to the President of the United States? When? Why? Am I a better citizen because I think I might have said no or because I admit I might not have? Machiavellian fortune favored young Gordon like a witch. He went from Catholic preppie to Nixon's dagger in twenty years. Fate pulled him up, pulled him down, then released him into Arizona. But what heights he reached! Only a man who went so high can take the fall as far as he tumbled.

The rest of us sci-fi/spy salesmen are fourth-raters to his third. When he said, "Thy will be done," he meant it like the pope. He gave his prince Nixon his life, liberty and sacred honor. Is that a slogan to you? It wasn't to Gordon. He'd done black-bag jobs for the mountain, and he lived in the desert. Howard Hunt once said he wanted to be the Alger Hiss of the right. What did that make Gordon? He did the deed, took the fall and never blamed his prince. Such men are rare but do exist in American history. Nathan Hale? Yes. Benedict Arnold? Maybe. Robert E. Lee? Yes. How about in the twentieth century? MacArthur? Ha! Where in literature is such a man? Lancelot? Maybe. How about Raskolnikov?

6

Thursday and Friday were more cowboys and fantasies at Desert Two. The scenario was how to survive hostage taking. This included my motorcade game. Choat showed us mannequin decoys, where to seat the bodyguard, what speeds and dispersal plans were best—that a motorcade is one car or a dozen, that you must keep to a schedule, keep moving, know the exits. We were also locked up in a room and shown how to arrange our clothes, sit, count the days, what foods were best. "Don't eat candy," said Fluegeman. "Sugar makes you pliable."

I'm skipping much of the patter among the students, since that was routine loveboatsmanship—a motley crew on a vacation cruise. I must mention the navy brat, Ms. Cleo Novak, however, because after my drive with Gordon I saw that I needed to recruit her as an inside foil. I wasn't going to get Lancelot du Gordon to open up unless Guinevere was pouring wine.

Cleo Novak and Jane Luonoso blossomed on gunpowder and intrigue. It's another story how once women get past the taboos of controlled violence they take to it better than men. For them self-defense is continually credible.

Cleo and Jane also got aggressive. They kept probing me until on Thursday night they kept me up so late drinking and teasing that sex would have been simpler.

Cleo Novak was a straight soul, and I did like her. She conversed in snippets, self-derogatory and wistful, reviewing her early marriage and divorce. She had no children, her dad was retired and her mother was a senior counsel in the California state legislature. There was also mention of a hospital president (a Mercedes M.D.) who was camping out on her door back home and begging her to marry.

"His daughter was Kappa like me," said Cleo. "We're like sisters, and I hate it."

I let Cleo and Jane speculate about my motives. Yet by Thursday night, the rumor around was that my "active duty" meant Langley. Tangled webs catch honeybees too.

Sweet Jane was husky about it. Langley made me a tv hero, and since I wouldn't answer her questions she decided I'd chosen Cleo. "Well, you two, don't be late," cooed Jane as she departed my room. "I'll wait up."

Cleo Novak topped her cup of vodka and put her feet on my bed. "I think you're probably just another jerk," she said. "Why don't you defend yourself?"

Since walls do have ears, I suggested a stroll by the local cactus, where I told her half the truth, the first step in recruitment.

"You're not a spy?" said Cleo. "You're a writer?"

"No," I defended myself, "traveling salesman."

"Whatever you call it," she said. "I don't read those kinds of books; they're really such silly boy stuff."

"Accurate," I said.

"That was your movie?" she asked after titles were mentioned. Cleo was a nonsmoker and slapped my cigarillo away. "I know what you are," she said, "you're a selfish shit. Just a new kind to me. I don't like it."

I had a sneezing fit in the mountain desert air, then tried some facts and admitted to my interest in the Watergate Caper.

"This can't be about Watergate," was her last remark when I took her back to her cabin that night.

It was almost her first remark the next evening, Friday after supper. She expanded: "Really, it's about Watergate? You're not nuts? You say that macho old fart"—Gordon—"knows who Deep Throat is? Do you care about this, or is that a lump in your throat?"

"Allergies," I tried.

"And your real name is Tip Paine?" she asked. "Shit, why can't I meet normal men?"

I had a recruit, sort of. I waited on what her will would do.

"All right, I'll help you as long as I'm having fun."

To make sure she was having fun, we went for another moonlit stroll so she could pose under starlight until I tried to kiss her. I was sneezing again, and she told me to blow my nose. Very funny. I got ready to kiss her again. She ducked me. Then, to make very sure I knew she was in this for the game, not the payoff or whatever my silliness could return, she started talking.

Cleo had a secret too. I'm going to skip more scenes, because I was after what Gordon didn't know he knew about Deep Throat and not romance with a clever, careful patent attorney whose assets top a million and who was no more an executive secretary than I was Bob Mitchum.

Bechtel, what a bland cover story. Alias Cleo Novak (real name, Salter) was cofounder of Pacific Superconductor Corporation of San Diego, California, the second private company to be licensed by our government to produce the superconducting film that might someday readjust the bottom line. What did she care about mercs in Central America or bugs in the Oval Office? She was trying to make electricity spill like John Dean. As Cleo said it right before she shut her door in my sneezy mug, "Power, Tip, I'm going to make it so cheap men like you are out of business. See you tomorrow, tyro."

Saturday was graduation. We students were briefed as if we were touring brass and driven out to Desert Two to watch several capture-the-flag games by Gordon's instructors joined by the local merc population. Yavapai is Barry Goldwater's home county, one of those last ditches that aim to make the Russkis die on the bayonets, so the boys played hard. Bang, boom, pow. Scenario 1 was kidnapping, 2 was hostage rescue, 3 was reprisal. I might have these jumbled up, but you get the idea. There was even a helicopter assault, very exciting. Choat yelled, "Choppers upset the bad guys, the noise is your friend, use it!"

I was entertained, but mostly I watched Gordon. He was still in leather and shades, and he chatted with us while he posed for group photos. When the dust settled he handed out diplomas we'd paid for (discount)—oak boxes containing an inscribed CZ-75: "*Fiat voluntas tua,* G. Gordon Liddy 1989."

Gordon made his roundabout move to me back at Desert One. He and the phony Bechtel girls were already chummy. Gordon was New York charming, a raconteur and ceaseless gentleman. I found the three of them harmonizing at the Chevy bus as the instructors loaded baggage. Everyone was lighthearted for leaving, saying their goodbyes with the usual exchange of addresses.

Gordon finished a Sinatra tune and asked me, "You don't sing, Mr. Moore?"

"He sings okay," said Cleo.

Gordon presumed intimacy and frowned at me. What sort of ops was I to fool with a civilian? He made his pitch anyway. "I can give you a ride back to Phoenix, if you're interested."

"We are," said Cleo. She was enjoying this too much, but it was too late to rethink my plan. Recruit-foil Cleo continued to misbehave when she strapped on her new automatic and paraded like a top-heavy gunsel.

I argued with her after the other students had left in the Chevy bus. She said sharply, "You're not getting anywhere unless I help you, isn't that what you said? F—— you if you're not grateful."

Here was the setup. Late afternoon in the Sonoran mountains, Gordon cruising his Bronco, Cleo bubbly between us, and my grand and expensive scheme to interrogate Gordon Liddy in bad shape.

Cleo ordered a detour by way of Montezuma's Castle. "I hear you two had quite a chat there," she said. "I want to see it."

Gordon grunted and asked her about me. "What else did he say?"

"That you want to go back on active duty," said Cleo, "leave your family and screw natives. I don't believe it. You're an old man, a monument, ha! You've earned your retirement."

"Is that what he says?" Gordon asked her about me.

"What does he know?" Cleo teased. "My dad thinks you're a hero. I told you, my dad was at Leyte Gulf. He says if you take the king's shilling you keep firing. Isn't that right, Gordon?"

The two of them were happy to make me an absent object, and their chatter continued to the limestone cliffs. Montezuma's is worth a visit if you like apocalyptic screenplays. In the daylight I could see that it was never Gotham, it's more like Cincinnati, queen of the desert, now littered with beer cans. We walked to the base and watched the shadows move up the wall.

"Places like this scare me," said Cleo. "It's not long ago enough. Like a savage high-rise; look at the handholds."

Gordon glanced at me. "What's this scare this, scare that?" he asked. "What's happened that your generation talks about scaring so much? My kids aren't scared of anything."

"Oh, yeah?" quipped Cleo. "And why should they tell you if they are?" She kicked the dust. "When your father's Captain America and has faced the guns, what can you tell him about anything?"

Gordon blanched. Cleo had found a soft spot I hadn't realized Gordon had. But when I saw it I also saw that it made sense. Punch a cowboy long enough and you find a failed parent; all that restless moving on gets you a bad reputation and very tired, melancholy too. Gordon had long claimed he had no regrets except that the Watergate bugging failed. I no longer believed him. He was cluttered with doubt—what might have been, what was lost.

I thought, He's a victim.

It wasn't until twilight, when we cleared the wilderness for the suburban tracts around Phoenix, that I asked a direct question. "What are your plans, Mr. Liddy?"

Gordon sucked desert air and started a speech. "God and the American people have been so good to me all these years," he said, "whatever comes is fine by me."

"That's bullshit," Cleo declared. "If I caught my dad talking like that I'd have him in for tests. Tell it like it is, Gordon, there's no bug here."

Gordon glanced at me again. Wasn't I going to defend him? Negative. I saw that he'd gotten lazy. He was used to the victim's gruel of pity and charity. Cleo was yanking his ball and chain far better than I could have done. I returned a blank smile.

Gordon said, "I've made my mark, and if it's not deep enough, then you tell me. I've traveled America, eighty-four thousand miles crisscross, and the young people, they understand that patriotism has risks, that—"

"More bullshit," Cleo declared. "You got caught, and none of them think they will; that's why they're children. My dad told me that you never think the gun's aimed at you, it's a surprise when you get it. And when you got it, they left you. I remember you in handcuffs on tv. I'd go crazy if that's what they'd done to my dad. Ford pardoned Nixon and left you to rot. If the navy did that to their men, they couldn't man a tug. Wake up, Gordon! If I were you I'd hate them for what they did. They *used* you. They screwed you."

Cleo bumped me. My turn.

I couldn't do it. It was too sad. Cleo had gone too far. She was stronger than either I or my muse. Her myths weren't ours, and that made her strange and strong, too, and very scary to me.

Gordon changed the subject, back to green. "You'll have to come back when the desert blooms; the colors..."

I'd solved one puzzle. Gordon had gone green the way usurers get philanthropic and statesmen take up the paint box. He wanted a safe hobby for which there was no sensible opposition.

At the end, at the hotel door in Phoenix, Gordon was magnificently courtly. "When you're back this way, you've got a friend in Arizona, and he's got plenty of friends."

Cleo blushed. "You old lizard, you."

I failed to find a significant word. I felt bad for deceiving him. I'd let a lie hang fire just the same as had President Nixon and his lieutenants. Tip had primed Gordon and then left him to dream falsely of what bang might have been.

Gordon shook my hand. "Pleasure, Mr. Moore, and keep 'em scared back there, if that's what it takes now—good 'n' scared."

7

Operation Muse was a fizzle. Worse, Cleo was disgusted with me.

"You could buy me dinner," she taunted, "you could buy me off, but you couldn't buy a judge if she were your mother. Where back East are you from? Christ, you're a wimp."

Correct. Tip lacks the assassin's blade—the "switchblade mentality" Deep Throat once told Woodward the White House had. We went to our hotel rooms to decontaminate and change. Then Jane Luonoso joined us in the dining room, where Cleo kept up the barrage. I drank wine I didn't like and can't afford. Where does Phoenix find a ninety-five-dollar bottle from California?

Jane tried to be pleasant, "You're a movie writer, really? Are you going to get a screenplay out of this?"

This just made Cleo ornerier. "Yeah, he's like Mary Worth—he *is* Mary Worth: what a well-placed scarf can do for a chin."

I'd hoped the after-dinner sweets would salve Cleo, but no, they just seemed to excite her rebukes. She dragged Tip and Jane into the piano bar and got boozy mean on Napoleon brandy. "You don't get answers 'cause you don't ask questions," Cleo accused me. "Get your nose outside. You think they're a silent majority? Get with it. You can't shut them up."

Cleo made me dance with Jane, then with her, then the two of them started harmonizing with the chanteuse at the piano bar.

I was unhappy but at ease. What could they do, make me sing? It was gambling night in Phoenix. The NFL had arrived that year, and everyone with a belly bumper was arguing tomorrow's Super Bowl at the bar. I watched the weekend cowboys and waited for a chance to defend myself.

Finally Cleo fixed bayonets. "He was right there; why didn't you say, 'Old man, who cut off your balls?' I mean, Tip, Tip! You want to

2 7 5

know who Deep Throat was, so ask! Deep Throat! They called him after a castrating slave, and you couldn't ask Gordon who—"

I rallied myself in order to grumble that Gordon didn't know that he knew.

"Bull!" said Cleo. "Every woman knows who done her wrong, and they *know* they know. Come on, Mary Worth, tell us who did in little Gor-do weir-do. If he was a woman I'd say who got into his pants, but that sounds too much like rape."

"Don't," Jane warned Cleo, "don't start."

Cleo laid her arm across my shoulders and yanked me close. "Does rape offend you, Tip? Don't be embarrassed." She was slurring her words, altogether nasty. "We've both been; you ever been? You know who did it; you don't forget."

I tried to look sympathetic. Rape scares me too. I'm never sure what to say, and I'm told I look as supportive as sand.

"He got raped, Tip," said Cleo, "and he knows it. Rape, my big Mary—what do you say to that?"

Do women actually think men talk this tough-guy way to each other? Pack super nines, brawl like punch-drunks, pop off at high noon? It's Hollywood make-believe, ladies; you've been sold trash by overpaid hucksters like me. If guys did talk like that to each other, you'd all be widows and orphans.

It turned out that Cleo Salter (alias Novak) was not Ms. Tough Guy after all, that the full metal jacket she'd been wearing was a hand-me-down from her dad, the navy commander, and it didn't fit.

I know I've done a sketchy job presenting Cleo—I've been as distracted by Deep Throat's shadow while telling this tale as I was while hanging around Gordon's School for Scandal. My excuse is that the specter of the Watergate Caper is antiromantic, that it's just so creepy an event that even seventeen years afterward it darkens anyone crossing its path.

I can add this, that later that evening, after Jane had been persuaded by a boisterous local cowboy to leave me and Cleo to our private argument, Cleo stopped bad-mouthing me. Truth, she became worrisomely gentle and intriguing.

"This really is about Watergate, isn't it, Tip?" she asked me when we were back up in my room, where I'd gotten her to ease off the booze. "You aren't just showing off, you're not on the make for me or anything?"

I told her that I appreciated her help the past week. I said that I didn't have a better explanation than to say that I was indeed here about Watergate, the caper without end. I added, "Nobody else might care, but I do; I want the whole truth of it."

"Criminey," she said, "maybe I've been fooling you and me. I thought I was clever to come out here and play cowboy. I thought guns were what made you guys weird and that if I could handle guns then I could, you know, handle myself now. Handle my business. I'm way over my head in debt. A paper millionaire, you know, which is worse than anything but invalid. Scared all the time, like you said. Or was it Gordon said you said? Anyway, you understand, scared shitless."

I sympathized. Her superconductor company was what some might call a flying leap. Everything she had could turn into the dirigible tomorrow and she'd be left holding a controlling interest in laughing-stock.

Cleo sat up, sat back, got up, circled the room, then lay down on one of the two beds and kicked off her pumps.

"I should marry him and forget all this," she said. "My doctor, I mean." She groaned in surrender. "I don't want to do that. Not tonight. Tell me about Deep Throat, tell me. God, I wish I could get lost in nuttiness like you. God, you're crazy. It must be fun to be so *craaaazy.*"

Cleo sat halfway up. "What's gonna happen if you do find Deep Throat?"

I smiled at her free-associating. An attractive paper millionaire was dizzy on one of my beds, and what she wanted from me was a bedtime story, once-upon-a-time, something to make everything come out happy. I skipped the story and got to the last line: "Nothing's gonna happen; unhappy ever after."

"That's what I thought," said Cleo, leaning back on her arm, tucking her legs up fetuslike, showing a lot of leg. "Nothing's gonna happen. All those people got destroyed, and nothing's changed. I

remember Watergate like a potboiler, one of those novels I used to
have time to read. It was exciting! But it made my dad so mad. He
couldn't believe that his commander in chief, his great President
Nixon, was a crook, and a *small-time* crook. I was in law school, and
we used to have these great fights in class about the Constitution.
Executive privilege, checks and balances, overweening judiciary, Sirica the Star Chamber and Nixon the tyrant. It was great! And those
tapes, weren't they great! Like 'You Are There'—better, because
there were gaps and you got to imagine what they were saying and
doing! Those were the days!"

Cleo flopped back and groaned again, though she was playful in
her self-pity. "And now they're gone, and guys like Gordon are all
f——ed up, and here I am a debt-ridden old maid trying to learn to
shoot guns so I don't have to become a doctor's wife like my mother
wants. Shit! Does that make sense? Maybe I'm *craaaazy* too."

I said the obvious. "You're just tired, Cleo, and a little drunk."

I did the obvious too, I admit, though I'd already rejected such an
embarrassing twist, and making love with someone you've decided
not to make love with is an odd task. I don't mean contrived, I mean
surprising, as if with one of your older sister's friends whom you have
watched go out with football stars and vanish into college but then
who suddenly turns up in your bed as a woman who knows all about
you and still thinks you're okay. I say this in supposition, since I don't
have a sister and trust all women much less than I like them, maybe
the other way around. Enough confession; even with vain bigmouths
like me something not uncrazy takes over when you take off enough
clothing and feel flesh. I was distracted, that's my final excuse, distracted, and Cleo deserved much better attention than she got from a
naked salesman inside a sales pitch that was aimed at make-believe.

Nevertheless Cleo's false intimidation did help me solve my investigation much faster than could have Cleo's genuine intimacies.

Why should this be true? Because Watergate is scary and it helps to
be scared when you think about it? Perhaps, but perhaps also that sex
with a sexy stranger who frets about death and taxes is superb for
problem solving. Did Dr. Freud say this too? Tip does. What also
helped me focus sharply on my pursuit of Deep Throat was getting

out of focus with Cleo (she made me take my glasses off too, explaining, "I don't like to see me smeared, you know, like a lab specimen").

We chatted cheerfully over breakfast early next morning. Neither of us mentioned Watergate. Instead we teased each other about our silly week together and how guns were a trite but effective aphrodisiac.

"Maybe we'll try a desert together again," said Cleo. "You never know. You ever been to the Gobi? There must be a resort there."

I said that Antarctica was the desert for me, Mary Worth in a sealskin parka with a properly displayed scarf.

"Oh, you're no good as Mary Worth, you big flirt," said Cleo. "I only said that because I was mad at you for not taking me seriously. I mean, you made a pass but you didn't try very hard, and I hate to be treated like a girl, you know, *just* a girl."

"Mary Worth," I said. "I like Mary Worth. She's the first cartoon character I've ever felt close to."

"Forget it," said Cleo. "You're too tall to wear a scarf; you forget it."

Cleo and Jane saw me off at the airport limo, and I promised not to forget them. They laughed and laughed, hugs, kisses, farewells.

All this good mood and camaraderie relaxed me. And it was while I was relaxed that I finally solved my pursuit of Deep Throat. That's the truth. I have no other explanation. I know you deserve one. How does the mind work? All those facts and guesses and experiences, how do they bump each other (if they do) and produce truth? I don't know.

I can report what I was doing when it happened. I was boarded on the hill-hopper to Tucson; I was sitting there getting revved up by the rpms of the twin rotors; I was staring at the backs of the passengers before me and straight into the flight deck, to see the compelling green glow of the control panel; I was sighing and getting used to flying one more time. That's it. And it was then, as the twin engines achieved their specifications and sent a comforting roar through the plane and me, that I experienced my vision. It was a vision that looked so clear and simple to me that I actually gasped like a ham actor at the feeling of solitude inside it.

I knew I knew Deep Throat's name. Much more, I knew I knew why he'd done it, how he'd done it and why seventeen years later he was still a secret.

I thought, See it! Gordon had told me, I just hadn't heard him. Cleo in her nasty stage had told me, I just hadn't heard her. I had flattered myself with my big talk, but now everything I had said fell apart and reassembled itself.

When you're sleuthing it's not difficult to name a name. It could be correct. It could just be a stupid wild-ass guess. And you can never be sure, even if it turned out to be correct, if you'd gotten it by luck or by reason.

What was profoundly challenging about the mystery of Deep Throat was to name that name and be able to explain how I'd gotten it and what it meant to have it. Because then I could always know, no matter what else was said, that I'd found the truth.

Nonetheless I must report to you that Deep Throat is the creepy side of scary. If scary has two hemispheres—the shocking and the creepy—this was distinctly the unknown, creepy side. You think I'm joking because the Committee to Re-Elect the President was nick-named CREEP? Maybe I am. But only because trite cracks are a good thing to make when you're creeping around in mystery and suddenly confront a black hole illuminating itself by making everything else around it appear transparent. CREEP, CREEP, CREEP. Laugh or not, I'm creeped out. It was creepy to realize all of it in a vision that day, and it's still creepy to know what I know. I'm smart about sci-fi/spy games, but I'm not creepy about them, and this Deep Throat bunkum, it makes me feel creepy.

8

Bunyan was Captain Watson at the airport gate and didn't want to wait out the Super Bowl to get to the chase for Deep Throat. His first question as we cleared the airport crowd was: "Well? Well!"

I asked for time out. Yet during the transfer from glass door to glass of beer at the Old City Jail of Tucson, a steak and barbecue bar frequented by meatheads out of Davis-Monthan AFB, I reviewed my week and assured Bunyan I could name the name.

"Who's Cleo?" was Bunyan's hesitant remark.

I frowned at his teasing.

"I guess," said Bunyan, "she was one of the other guests?"

We were seated at the bar, shoulder to shoulder with male bonding. "Stick to the caper, Captain," I said.

"Okay," said Bunyan, remembering his station as my baby brother. He pulled out his notebook, back to business. "You really know who Deep Throat is? Gordon Liddy told you, really?"

"Affirmative," I said, comfortable to stay clear of romance. Cleo was three hours behind me, and I wanted to concentrate on the issues at hand.

Bunyan nodded slowly. "And?"

I shook Bunyan off. Cleo was still too close after all, so I *demanded* a time out. I pointed to the giant tv monitor over the bar. "Let's watch the game," I tried. "We'll debrief after."

"But he told you," Bunyan protested. "I've done all this work, and he told you."

"Sort of," I said. "He told me by telling me what he is. A victim."

"Geez, yeah, that's what he's like?"

After a week of silences, foolish words erupted out of me. "An old man with a rope burn round his neck and scars down his backside," I said. "He got mauled. Only rage is holding him together. Gordon Liddy talks the cowpoke, he acts the raped."

"Whew!" Bunyan exhaled. "That's something sad, yeah?"

I said that the high-hat word was tragicomic. Bunyan was full alert and headlong. I had to slow his chase. I pulled my trophy from my kit bag, the CZ-75.

This worked exactly as a toy talisman should work. Bunyan pushed aside his notebook and field-stripped the pistol instantly. "Nice. I've heard of these. Czech, right? Walnut grip. Have you tried it?"

"Nope," I admitted.

Bunyan's macho maneuver caught the eye of the air force tech crews on the barstools.

"He gave you this?" asked Bunyan. "Yeah? I can keep it? Thanks. Are you sure? Does he carry one?"

"Sometimes," I said. More foolishness oozed. "His rage is cocked and locked."

"Hey," complained one of the air force meatheads. "You guys gonna talk, or what?"

The meathead was right; it was kickoff time, and the Super Bowl demands brusque silence, unless you're talking gambling.

I was glad for the enforced delay. I'd inadvertently upset myself by mentioning rape. It was a crucial clue, but I didn't like it. Cleo had actually been raped. I was too keen on her, too protective in reflection, to press rape as a metaphor. Then again I had to; it was the image necessary to get to Deep Throat. I needed time to brood.

I whispered to Bunyan, "Let's get to the half, then we can pow-wow."

Bunyan grunted in agreement while he reassembled the automatic and let himself get caught up in the tv picture of gladiators in tights. I knew he didn't make much of my pretentious mind-doctor talk such as rage or even my euphemism of cocked and locked. Bunyan thinks weapons are for peacekeeping and should not be asked to give peace of mind too. We are brothers. I don't disagree; I just don't agree. Bunyan's between me and the bogeymen, and that's my peace, yours too.

The Super Bowl was over by halftime. Truth, it's my notion that big games are decided on the first series from scrimmage, if you know what to watch, just like make-believe: the first remarks are the yarn. (I truly do not understand luck.)

The absence of action on the tv screen—halftime talking heads—made Bunyan restless again. It was impossible to delay him any longer; he was jumping around like a jet tank in neutral. I quit my stalling tactics, and we retired to a booth.

Bunyan started, "Do you tell me, or what?"

My mind was clear. Ninety minutes of the super x's and o's called the National Football League heaving and crashing had cheered me for my own game playing.

I said, "What. Go."

Bunyan declared, "This Deep Throat is one heavy-caliber asset. He's like you do with your books. He's got the end figured and keeps pushing the characters until they get there."

I smiled at his excellent lit crit.

"Whenever there was an obstacle," continued Bunyan, checking his notebook, "he appeared and removed it. For instance, look at the first contact with Woodward, the first one we know about: Saturday, September 16, the day after the Watergate indictments. The *Post* headline that morning was 'Nixon Ex-Aides, 5 Others, Indicted in Bugging Case.' Liddy, Hunt, McCord and the Cubans. Woodward said he telephoned Deep Throat that afternoon. Deep Throat was shaken. By what? The open line? And why? And where? Deep Throat's just sitting around where? Office? Home?"

"Good questions," I said. "Get on with it."

Bunyan said, "Woodward called Deep Throat because he wanted confirmation that the next day's story, Sunday's, made sense. Woodward read him the draft. It was the 'Spy Funds Linked to GOP Aides' story, where Maurice Stans was named as the burglars' banker and Liddy was said to be the paymaster. Deep Throat listened and told Woodward, 'Too soft; you can go much stronger.'"

I asked, "What's your point?"

Bunyan explained calmly. "What you said I should do. I'm not skipping ahead. I'm going a piece at a time. I'm beginning at the beginning. The first time we know Woodward talked to Deep Throat, right?"

I nodded approval.

"At the very beginning," continued Bunyan, "Woodward didn't use Deep Throat like a source, what reporters call 'deep background.' Woodward called him up and treated him like the *brain*. It was as if Deep Throat was already in position to point Woodward where he wanted him to go. To use him."

"Good, good," I said. "Keep going."

"It was the same all the times that we know about with those two. On the phone, at the garage meetings. Deep Throat and Woodward, the brain and the puppet. And Deep Throat was a bossy brain. His commo plan was bossy. The flag in the flowerpot, clock face in the

Times, one-way phone signals. And the way Deep Throat ordered Woodward to travel to the meets—hopscotch with cabs, underground parking garage meets. And the times for the meets, 2 A.M. sometimes running to 6 A.M. And the way he tasks Woodward to fill in the blanks. All bossy, rigid, orthodox tradecraft. Just like the books."

(You must forgive Bunyan; he's trained by Military Intelligence to speak unintelligibly. Commo plan means communication plan. To task means to bully. Tradecraft means spycraft.)

I grinned and asked, "What books?"

Bunyan continued, "It's as if Deep Throat was giving Woodward lessons out of *How to Be a Spy*. That's why the parking garage. It's how it's taught. No one pays mind to transportation depots at night —bus and railroad stations, airports, lots and garages. I suppose with time and effort we could figure out what garage they used—you know, walk the cat backwards."

"Wonderful," I said.

(How I love perfect sci-fi/spy talk: "To walk the cat backwards"— that is, to retrace the steps.)

Bunyan flipped to a new page in his notebook. "I didn't have time to follow the story day by day, what Deep Throat said, what Woodward reported in the *Post*. I fixed on Deep Throat's pattern. Woodward said later in the *Time* interview that Deep Throat was 'executive branch.' I asked myself, How come a guy who can find out what the White House is doing, how come he can work days, then carry on like a control officer?"

"Say again?"

"You know what I mean. Deep Throat was like an op," Bunyan replied. "His behavior was what I'm learning how to watch for. Except I'm supposed to walk it backwards, picking up on Woodward the puppet to get to Deep Throat the control. Deep Throat recruited Woodward. He ran Woodward. He used commo plans, route security, dead drops, pay offs of information, a safe house. He suspected he could be bugged or Woodward could be. That's an operative at work, a careful control officer."

"Outstanding ops-in-training," I said. "Outstanding."

"Yeah." Bunyan beamed. "And this puzzle. Deep Throat worked days and had time to check Woodward's balcony? Worked days and could stay up all night? No. Especially no if he suspected he was being watched for misbehavior by his superiors or by counterintelligence. If you're counterintelligence you watch for these things. If one of your troop is absentee a lot or sleepy on the job—any change of his pattern—you watch because he might be drinking or gambling or divorcing or going crazy, and if he's in a sensitive job that's one step closer to trading with the enemy. Deep Throat's pattern was night owl. He wore Woodward out. So how could Deep Throat have been 'executive branch'? What kind of daytime job would allow him so much time to roam around Washington?"

I replied cynically, "It's called the civil service."

Bunyan ignored my crack. "Can we be sure Woodward didn't make this up about the nighttime meets?"

"No," I admitted, "we can't be certain of anything Woodward said or wrote about DT. But there's this backhanded logic. Consider that a major source for clues about DT is *All the President's Men*. It went to press February '74 and was in reading galleys by summer, before Nixon resigned. Woodward and Bernstein knew DT wanted anonymity, and they built their book accordingly. They didn't know that he'd become the biggest unsolved mystery of the whole caper. We can assume Woodward meant some deception to protect DT. But he couldn't have known how it was going to turn out—Nixon resigned, all the President's men jailed, DT a seventeen-year secret rat/hero."

Bunyan mused, "What Deep Throat told Woodward. It bothers me that he wasn't ever wrong. That bothers you too, doesn't it? How could Deep Throat know so much operational detail? About the Plumbers, the Committee to Re-Elect, the FBI, the grand jury? He knew the assistants at the White House well enough to check them off like you would. You know, quick portraits for Higby, Chapin, Strachan."

Bunyan consulted his notes. "Deep Throat called Butterfield 'an ex-Air Force colonel who knows how to push paper and people.' See what I mean? It's as if he kept a character list in his head."

"Correct," I said. I wandered slightly off Bunyan's line. "But DT didn't know Butterfield was the man in charge of the Oval Office tapes, didn't know about the tapes until everybody did. And then the strangest of all, Deep Throat told Woodward about the tape gaps in November '73."

Bunyan argued us back onto his line of argument. "Deep Throat knew too much! That Segretti was small fry, that Colson received the wiretap memos, that John Dean was offering hush money to the burglars. After the election, Deep Throat said he knew that Mitchell and Colson approved the 'espionage-sabotage' operation. And in mid-April 1973 he knew Dean and Haldeman were canned from the White House before anyone else. He knew all that! And he told Woodward that it was up to the *Post* to prove it."

I interrupted before Bunyan exploded. "Make your point."

"He knew too much to be on the *outside* like a spy," Bunyan argued. "He had to be *inside* the chain of command—like a traitor. But you know what also bothers me? Deep Throat never talked about Nixon directly, as if he knew him, as if he dealt with him. How can you be insider enough to know about the break-in and cover-up and yet outside the Oval Office?"

"Brilliant, Captain."

"And it really bothers me that one time Deep Throat altered the commo plan. You remember, February '73, when he left a signal on a prearranged ledge for a second meet? Woodward took a cab to a bar, what Woodward called a saloon for truckers and construction workers—'blue-collars' was what Woodward called them. Woodward asked Deep Throat why he'd chosen a new meet."

Bunyan checked his notes and read, "'None of my friends,' Deep Throat answered, 'none of your friends would come here.'"

Bunyan fanned his hands outward and spoke his professional logic. "I don't like it when a control agent changes commo. It means panic or setup, usually both. I think that man was frightened. He was getting reckless, a burnout. He'd lost weight, he was drinking and smoking heavily. Why?"

"Why?" I asked back.

"Wait." Bunyan tapped his notebook. "And *what* he tells Woodward at the saloon meet—that Nixon was shouting that Watergate must be turned off. Shouting at whom? It had to be Dean, Haldeman and Ehrlichman, I got that from the tapes. But how did Deep Throat know Nixon was shouting in the Oval Office unless he had good access to one of those three? Unless—"

Bunyan wrote quickly. "That's my answer," he continued. "Why Deep Throat was a burnout. Someone was leaning on him. Deep Throat knew Nixon was on the rampage, that the rope was tightening on everyone, as he said. Deep Throat knew he couldn't run Woodward smoothly any longer."

I asked, "Who could lean on Deep Throat?"

"I don't know," said Bunyan, "but if Moscow Center doesn't like your act they let you know. And if you're selling out Moscow while at the same time you're working for Moscow, you know, panic city. Someone was squeezing him, or he was getting squeezed between what Woodward wanted from him and what this other side wanted from him."

I showed my excitement too. "Very good, very very. Deep Throat was like a spymaster who was double-dealing. He was dirty too, on the inside/outside, and *most* vulnerable. He didn't think he could get out, he felt trapped between two diametrical demands. He was afraid of daytime, his friends, the White House, FBI, surveillance. He used textbook tradecraft to protect himself."

"That's it," Bunyan agreed to my agreeing.

I asked, "Why wasn't he afraid of Woodward?"

"I've thought about that," said Bunyan. "Woodward was twenty-nine. He was a new reporter and very tentative. Deep Throat treated him like a student, a protégé. Woodward could have exposed him any day in the press, but Deep Throat trusted him. Like a kid brother. You trust me like that?"

I waited out his answer.

"Yeah, you do," said Bunyan correctly.

I said it aloud anyway. "Yes, I do and much, much more."

Bunyan ignored my affection. The chase was afoot, and he was onto more clues.

"There's what you call class there," he said. "They were two white men. Were they like two collegians? Like fraternity brothers? Those garage meets were like a classroom for them, the brain and the puppet, the professor and the student."

I urged, "Look where Woodward went to school."

"Yale," replied Bunyan. "He was from the Midwest." Bunyan consulted his notes. "Five years in the navy officer corps. Divorced and living alone. His salary was low, very low. Five feet ten, good-looking. A Yalie, does that mean something? Those navy fellows think they're special, never get dirty in their whites. Wouldn't wear fatigues or camouflage if you ordered them. Stuck-up."

"Army prejudice later," I said.

"Okay," he said. "I have to ask. How am I doing so far?"

He was doing superbly, though I didn't say that aloud. My baby brother is too smart a man to need flattery to continue being smart. What he had done so far was to assemble a profile of Deep Throat that fit the available facts. Bunyan hadn't bogged himself down with the give-and-take of the Watergate break-in, the burglary trial or the White House cover-up. He'd done what a detective would do when constructing a profile of a shadow criminal. It was time to move Bunyan past clues about Deep Throat to the known list of suspects.

I said, "You're doing what you're doing. You're not guessing, and that's good. Don't ask for hints either. Ready for the name game?"

"Yes," said Bunyan, pen poised. "I'm ready."

"One," I declared. "John Dean says DT is *Alexander Haig*. West Point, army general, secretary of state, presidential candidate, tv personality."

"General Haig fits partly," said Bunyan, correcting my reference to an army senior officer. "He was in the White House at the time, Kissinger's deputy with an office in the White House, right? But he doesn't fit the tradecraft. Army generals are army generals."

"Peacocks, you mean," I translated.

"I didn't say that," returned Bunyan. "If it was General Haig, it's partly understandable why he's never let on. But all that nighttime prowling? What else was he doing?"

I reported, "The Vietnam War, getting confirmed major general on Capitol Hill, jetting to and from Saigon and Paris with Kissinger while we bombed the bejesus out of Hanoi. Later he was White

House chief of staff and tried to keep President Nixon from going berserk."

"No. General Haig's not my choice," Bunyan said. "There was too much on his desk. And if he was so upset with the White House, why wouldn't he just resign his commission and call up the press openly? He was a major general! He would've been believed."

I asked, "This isn't army prejudice?"

"Negative," Bunyan determined.

I obliged Bunyan's opinion. "What you're saying is that Haig is clean and straight. What you're implying is that Deep Throat was dirty, something was wrong with him. Deep Throat was obsessed with being dirty. Someone had something on him."

"It's not General Haig," Bunyan repeated.

"Two," I continued. "*Time* magazine says the suspects include the various factotums—the White House lawyers Buzhardt, Garment and Powers, the White House aide Steve Bull and the Republican National Committee politician John Sears."

"You know about lawyers," said Bunyan. "For Deep Throat to be one of them, isn't that impossible? Do they know spying? Would Woodward have let them run him? And what could they be afraid of? They're wrong patterns, yeah?"

I said that the lawyers I knew were capable of anything but that I took his point. I added what Bunyan didn't know, that the factotum suspects didn't have the range of Deep Throat's knowledge. They had been on the scene either too early or too late. None of them had been in on everything from the Plumbers to the tape gaps. They'd had a motive to keep silent until Nixon resigned but not afterward. Bunyan was right that the factotums were clean. I added rhetorically, "If it was the lawyers, why not call a press conference? Why sneak around in parking garages or saloons?"

"We're in a saloon," Bunyan teased. "Does that make us dirty like Deep Throat?"

"Three," I said. "*Time* magazine also says another suspect is *Chuck Colson*. Special counsel to the President, ex-marine captain, now born-again fanatic."

"Marines," Bunyan scoffed, "know zilch about security. They've got cement for brains. Colson would've rammed the gates. He would've stomped Woodward. Marines don't know halfway. The corps is—"

Bunyan was preaching more army prejudice and maybe some Paine too. We're an army family.

I interrupted Bunyan to tell him that Colson did fit the range of Deep Throat's insider information. Colson supervised the Plumbers and received their wiretap memos. Colson was chummy with Howard Hunt; they were both Brown graduates and friends since '66. It was Colson who brought Hunt into the White House and through Hunt recruited McCord and the Cubans. Crucially about Colson, though he was out of government at the time, Colson learned about the tape gaps in October '73, before it came out in the press.

"A marine rat on his commander in chief?" Bunyan protested.

I reported, "They called it 'ratf——ing.' It was their cute word for what Hunt had Segretti do, for what Hunt and Liddy did by breaking into candidates' headquarters, tapping phones, planting disinformation in the press."

"I know what they called it," said Bunyan priggishly.

"It's an ugly word," I agreed.

"Just a word," said Bunyan.

"You don't like it, do you?" I asked.

Bunyan frowned. "No."

"Well, I hate the word," I said, "but it was their word, and it applies. 'Ratf——ing.'"

"Whatever you call it," said Bunyan, "you can't convince me that Colson would do it to his commander in chief. Death wouldn't protect him. The corps would dig up his bones for a court-martial. Besides, as I said, Colson isn't tradecraft. He doesn't control, he orders and blasts; body count's what marines know."

"Okay," I said, "we'll set Colson aside."

"We're not eliminating him?" asked Bunyan.

"Yes and no," I said.

"That's not an answer," Bunyan complained.

"Four," I said. "The last suspect. Bob Haldeman says Deep Throat is *John Dean.*"

"Out of the question," Bunyan declared. "John Dean! Woodward wouldn't have called Dean a friend if he were his brother. How is it possible that Dean was at the White House fourteen hours a day talking on the phone to Howard Hunt to take care of the convicted burglars and talking to Nixon to keep them all from what they called the 'hang-out,' and at night he's— No. No, no. Dean knew what Deep Throat knew, but—"

"Not the tape gaps," I interjected. "Dean didn't know about the tape gaps; he was long gone by the time they were found."

Bunyan continued his line of argument. "—but then Dean went over to the Congress and sold out Nixon on television? Why did he wait until the spring of 1973 to sell out Nixon? If he's Deep Throat, why did he wait? He was clean, they had nothing on him. Of course there is his bailout—"

"Turncoat," I interjected. "Fancy word: metamorphosis."

"Yeah, from insider to ratter," continued Bunyan. "But he'd have to be five people to handle being Deep Throat, himself, then the man who sells out on television, yeah?"

"Correct," I agreed. "Also it's been seventeen years. What's John Dean got to protect with silence now? He's already the rat of Beverly Hills. For him to be Deep Throat there'd have to be a motive for silence. Dean's a whiner; he'd turn in his dog."

"You don't like Dean, do you, Tip?"

I confessed, "Of all of them, he's the one I still can't forgive. I mean, figure. It's my problem and nobody else's. I just can't."

Bunyan teased with Hollywood blarney. "A man's got to know his limitations."

I didn't disagree. We had also reached the limits of the known suspects. I said, "That's all of them. Unless you want to debate wild guesses such as John Mitchell, Rose Mary Woods and President Nixon himself."

"Do I?" asked Bunyan.

"It'd be fun," I said, "but a waste, just like them. They wasted themselves for nothing. Nothing."

"What's that mean?" he asked. "Is that a clue?"

"Just my big mouth," I admitted. I indicated his notebook. "Read me what Woodward wrote about Deep Throat. Do you have the part where he mentions the 'love-hate dialectic'?"

Bunyan searched and found what Bob Woodward wrote once upon a time. "'Did Deep Throat want to get caught...? Was there a love-hate dialectic...? It was enough to know that Deep Throat would never deal with him falsely. Someday it would be explained.'"

I looked toward where I supposed northeast to be. "Good questions, Bob," I taunted, "even if I don't know what you mean."

Bunyan folded his hands. "Are you going to explain it? I say that none of the suspects you've listed are Deep Throat. Do I have to guess now?"

I said, "You've already told me; you just didn't hear yourself tell me."

Bunyan frowned. "That's—"

"Double-talk," I admitted.

"I don't want to guess," said Bunyan. "Tell me what I've told you."

9

The Super Bowl was done, though I can't remember who won. The meatheads were either herding out of the saloon or chomping dinner, so I ordered Bunyan barbecue and Tip avocado soup. It was time to name the MVP of the Watergate Caper.

"You've gone this far," I told Bunyan, "so walk the cat back all the way. You've described a black operation out of a sci-fi/spy novel, Cold War style. Deep Throat knew a lot, but what he knew best was the black operations. Lies, stings, press plants, media manipulation, demos, enemies list, targeted legislators and columnists, bugged offices—and then what was said to be Gordon Liddy's genius of Operation Gemstone. Muggings, kidnappings, sabotage, entrapment, vice squad fantasies. It's out of the textbooks, all right, what the CIA, KGB, SIS and so forth secret policemen practice routinely every day."

"So you say," protested Captain Bunyan Paine of the very lawful, very decent United States Military Intelligence Corps.

I bypassed political philosophy. "Who of the suspects could know about black ops?" I asked.

"None of 'em," said Bunyan, "unless they overheard how or were told or— You mean Colson?"

"Colson's very close," I said, "but he's not black ops."

Bunyan looked at me hard. "What you're saying is—the CIA; Deep Throat is the Agency?"

"Negative," I said. "No conspiracy theory, Captain. I don't believe in them, neither do you. Stay small. Deep Throat is one small, crooked and broken man."

"You're saying he's a crook?" asked Bunyan.

"Crooked. Not the same thing," I said, "but let's pursue him as you would a crook. Review for me his motive, opportunity, weapon."

"You mean like Woodward said, his motive was disillusionment?" tried Bunyan. "Conscience? Bad conscience? Guilt? Fear of getting caught? Fear of going down alone? Revenge?"

"Affirmative to all of the above," I said, "all on the hellish side of every family."

"What's that mean?" asked Bunyan.

"I don't know," I admitted. "More crackpot theory." I waved off my notion. "What about opportunity?" I asked.

"Opportunity," Bunyan obliged. "You mean like who had time to stay up all night, spy on Haldeman, Ehrlichman and Dean all day, find out about the tape gaps? Well. Some guy who's either not sleeping or is out of work. And alone, very alone."

"Affirmative," I said.

"Weapon?" said Bunyan. "Deep Throat's—" Bunyan wrote in his notebook. "The weapon was Woodward and the *Washington Post!* Deep Throat wanted page one! He got them with print!"

"Affirmative," I said. "The mightier pen. All together now."

Bunyan summated, "Black operative, out of work, guilty conscience, journalism. Smoker, drinker, depressed, mimic, showboater, executive branch, government careerist, paper chaser."

"Master of deception," I said.

Bunyan wrote more in his notebook. "That describes—Gordon Liddy?"

"Liddy's close," I said, "very, very close. The guy at the center who knew it all. But Gordon's a dumb victim. Begin at the beginning. The early morning of June 17, 1972. Who was at his side, close enough to screw him?"

"Geeezus," said Bunyan. "You're telling me Deep Throat is Howard Hunt?"

"Affirmative," I said. Creepy, I thought.

"I don't get it," Bunyan protested. "No, not Hunt. He was one of 'em. His wife died carrying hush money in that Chicago plane crash." Bunyan flipped pages. "I see how he fits the pattern. It says that he lost fourteen pounds between his wife's death in December and the opening of the trial in January. A pipe smoker, spoke Spanish, liked disguises, changed his voice on the phone, loved aliases, complained to the court that his phone was tapped in September."

Bunyan underlined his chronology and protested the more. "But he pled guilty, he silenced the Cubans, he blackmailed the White House! It was Hunt who badgered Dean for commutation. It was Hunt that Nixon knew they had to pay off. It was Hunt blabbing to the grand jury that they were really scared of—"

I didn't like the sexual metaphor, but I had to use it; it worked. "Howard Hunt screwed everybody," I said, "including Howard Hunt. He 'ratf——ed' them all."

"But, Tip," said Bunyan, "you're trying to scare me. What you're saying, it's . . ."

"Creepy," I agreed.

"Geeezus," said Bunyan.

I felt like preaching. "It's the lost love story of the Watergate Caper. Howard Hunt so loved his country that he gave himself up to rid it of a gang of scoundrels. But he didn't do it like a hero, he did it like a hooker, a prostitute, a 'ratf——er' for hire, to take everybody down with him. He was one of them. And when he got busted, he wanted to turn state's evidence. Still he couldn't be a simple witness, because he knew he wouldn't be believed. He'd just be another guy trying to lie his way out of a crime. So instead he fed Woodward the story and watched his cronies squirm."

"But why, why?" asked Bunyan. "Why'd he do it?"

"Remember what I told you, that last clue at the Phoenix airport. '*Cowardice makes heroes of us all.*' The same goes for 'ratf——ers.'"

"But what kind of hero is Hunt?" asked Bunyan.

"The cowardly kind," I said. "I don't understand what makes a hero. I know some about cowards, and being one can make you do rash, stupid things that look like heroism on sunny days."

Bunyan ignored my blither. "It's like you're describing a what?" he asked. "Like Hunt made it all up as he went along. To be all those things to all those people? To lie to everybody and then to lie about his lies?" Bunyan smiled in disbelief. "That's like what you do, Tip. Make everything up."

"Yes, it is." I smiled back in certitude. "Like a make-believer. Like a sci-fi/spy novelist. Which is what Howard Hunt is, around sixty novels now and counting."

"That was a hobby; he was career Agency," reported Bunyan.

"He wrote down what he lived, and what he wanted to believe he lived," I returned. "When you look at just what is known of Hunt's record at Langley, you're going to whistle Sousa. In the early fifties he was a minor black op in Operation Valuable, our covert war in Albania. After that he got himself transferred to the Latin American Division to use his Spanish-language skills. In '53 and '54 he was chief of psychological warfare for Operation Success, our covert war in Guatemala. In 1960 he was psy war boss again, for Operation Pluto, our first covert war against Castro's Cuba. In '61 he was a firebrand for Operation Mongoose, our second covert war against Castro, which we now think of as the Bay of Pigs."

"The Cubans at the Watergate," Bunyan remarked.

"Exactly," I said. "They owed allegiance to Hunt for more than ten years by the time he ran into harm's way and Sirica. He was Captain Black Ops. After the Bay of Pigs, President Kennedy ordered Langley punished, and Hunt and his Mongoose pals got dumped into dead-end drawers to sweat and fume for what might have been. It's not unimportant that Hunt had it in for President Kennedy, for the Kennedy family. Had it in like President Nixon did. It gave Hunt a private vengeance for taking those White House orders to ransack the Democrats aping the Kennedy legacy."

"Captain Black Ops," Bunyan repeated. "That sounds like you, not Hunt. He was the real thing, a veteran case officer."

"A spymaster," I aggrandized. "But I'm not giving Hunt too much credit. Up until the Watergate he'd only ever bossed around foreigners and mercenaries, he'd only ever played his dirty tricks and his double deals on desperadoes and hirelings. When it came to the Watergate cover-up, he was up against American citizens he couldn't buy or bully."

"You mean you think that's why he was such a shaky control officer," asked Bunyan, "why Deep Throat was so cranky?"

"Affirmative," I said. "Hunt couldn't control everything with guns and money, like his bloody old days. He had to wait on luck. He started running Woodward in September '72 and then let events guide his next move. Who broke, who ran, who lied. At the same time Hunt started harassing Dean and the White House for hush money for himself and his Cubans. He was a psy war veteran; what he'd learned at Langley he turned against Washington. He played both sides against themselves. That meant he wasn't just a double agent. He was a double double-crosser."

Bunyan's frowns frowned. "It's too much, Tip," he protested. "I can't go with you on this one. Not Hunt."

"Listen to what you told me," I argued back. "Hunt's game is what you picked up on: when you figured Deep Throat was panicky, when you said it was as if he was getting squeezed, as if he was being run too. He was between Woodward and Dean. Both sides were too much for him to control. He didn't have guns and money to hit them with. He had to charm and badger Woodward at night. Then he had to charm and badger Dean during the day. He was worse than a burn-out. Ashes. I can guess he was sleepless, drunk most of the time and tormented."

Bunyan interrupted. "You think he was ready to sell everybody out, Woodward too?"

"Yes, of course," I said with my best man-of-the-world tone. "If it had come to that. Woodward too. That's psychological warfare, isn't it? The strategy of black ops. There's nobody or nothing you won't sell out to advance the game."

"That's crazy is what that is," said Bunyan.

"I didn't make up the game," I defended myself. "A certain serpent did a long time ago. Clever fellow, likes disguises, multilingual, smokes a lot, name of the devil."

"You smoke too much," Bunyan accused.

I lit my pipe boldly and continued my case. "Hunt knew he had Woodward hooked. Woodward *trusted* Hunt. 'My friend,' Woodward called him. Friend! Hunt not only recruited Woodward; he also turned him. Woodward was way out of his depth and couldn't stop himself. Hunt was what an Ivy Leaguer like Woodward always falls for—an Ivy League burnout, a charming scoundrel, a self-deprecating confessor, a guy who's read the same confessing tracts, Augustine to Rousseau to Bernard Shaw to Norman Mailer. The I Did It School. What's more convincing than a man you might be yourself in twenty years, who says, 'I did it,' then goes on to explain here's how, here's why, here's who helped me?"

"Is that a question?" Bunyan teased.

"Woodward fell for Howard Hunt the same way I fell for my muse, Gordon Liddy. And Hunt knew that Woodward would fall for him; that's why he trusted Woodward enough to run him. You know what 'turning' really is? It's sex. Hunt courted and seduced Woodward; their affair was deep sex. What you said, the brain and the puppet. What I say, master and slave."

"You don't like Woodward either, do you?" Bunyan asked.

I ruffled. "What? I like him all right. He was a kid out there all alone, and a veteran op was coming right at him. Woodward had no one he thought he could trust to help him. No one except his control officer, who was, after all, his enemy." I slowed my explanation. "Woodward was very lucky. He got the story and it didn't get him. Lucky."

"If you're right, Tip," said Bunyan, "Woodward was stupid, too, to take that risk. That was stupid and dangerous. I'm trained that if anyone ever contacts me for anything I go directly to my CO and report everything I've done the last hundred years."

"You're a pro in uniform and trained by the best there is at coun-terintelligence," I said. "Woodward wasn't."

"I'm not graduated yet," said Bunyan correctly.

"Look what Woodward made of Hunt," I continued. "He first called him Mr. X in his notes at the *Post*. He told no one the truth of it, not even his bosses, Simons and Bradlee. It was Howie Simons who first called Mr. X Deep Throat, and Woodward went along with the idea. Deep Throat was an infamous hooker; that movie was play-ing in the Washington porn houses at the time. I think Howie Simons had picked up on the truth intuitively, without ever knowing it was Hunt."

"Geez, Tip, geez, that's farfetched."

I declared, "Hunt was an infamous hooker too, and he screwed and screwed."

Bunyan asked, "You figured this out from Gordon Liddy?"

"Affirmative," I said. *"When you're looking for a 'ratf——er,' look in a rathole.* Gordon was my last clue. Liddy and Hunt were twinned the night of the Watergate. They were hiding together like rats in the building. The panic they felt joined them forever. What I learned in Phoenix is that Gordon is still ignorant of what's happened to him. He's a victim; he likes playing the victim so much he's lazy at it."

Bunyan asked, "Gordon Liddy is a victim?"

"Yeah," I said, "a rape victim. He knows who did it to him, but he won't admit that he knows; that's why he stays the victim, that's why the rage. He was a 'ratf——er' who got 'ratf——ed' by his pal in rathood."

"Hunt's the rat?" asked Bunyan.

"Once a rat," I declared, "always a rat."

"I'm not following you," Bunyan complained.

I preached, "Gordon Liddy took the fall in public silence and pri-vate pain. Seventeen years later he's a celebrity, the unmasked vic-tim. Howard Hunt took the fall in public silence and *secret* confession. For seventeen years he's stayed underground, the masked rapist. Deep Throat got all the President's men and then President

Nixon too. Now he lives in Miami with his Mongoose pets the Cubans."

"You've checked this?" asked Bunyan, writing and doubting. "Hunt was out on bail and bond from summer '72 until he went to jail, uh, early '74, so he was available. And unemployed. Staying up all night, scheming all day, chat with Dean on the phone *and* check Woodward's balcony!"

"Double-crossers gotta put in double time," I said.

"But why Woodward?" Bunyan asked. "If you're right, why did Hunt choose Woodward? Why not Bernstein or higher up? That Bradlee fellow, the boss at the *Post*. Or any other paper?"

"Good question," I acknowledged. "I can't answer it. I can guess. Woodward was on the metropolitan desk at the *Post*, which is small-time there. A cub reporter. His assignment before the Watergate burglary was to join the team covering the Wallace shooting story in Maryland. It just so happened that one of Hunt's jobs for the Plumbers was to investigate the Wallace shooting by that nut Bremer. This was early June. Hunt actually flew up to Milwaukee to break into Bremer's apartment, looking for craziness. The Plumbers were crazy secret policemen; whatever they fancied, they pursued for strange reasons. I can guess that either Woodward talked to Hunt by accident sometime after that or Hunt called Woodward, trying to pass on black information. Maybe some other way."

"That's flimsy," said Bunyan.

"Yes, it is," I admitted.

Bunyan saw that he had exposed some of my guesswork, so he leaped to a big problem to be solved for anyone pursuing Deep Throat. "Deep Throat knew about the tape gaps," argued Bunyan, "in the fall of '73. Woodward said he called him about them. Did Hunt know about the tape gaps?"

I tried my best defense. "Hunt's buddy Colson knew. Maybe Colson told Hunt. Deep Throat did pass it on to Woodward. But that wasn't crucial. Woodward had four other sources. Deep Throat just gave him the quote that the gaps were 'of a suspicious nature.' But that was hearsay."

"So's what you're saying," Bunyan teased.

I talked faster and preachier. "Woodward got sloppy at the end. The sky looked to be falling by November '73. Nixon was out of control with persecution mania. Remember the Saturday Night Massacre? The Defcon Three alert for the Yom Kippur War? Kissinger taking a press conference to deny the President of the United States was unstable? The avalanche of calls for resignation and impeachment? Deep Throat was no longer the only one selling Nixon out."

"I don't remember any of it," said Bunyan playfully. "I was in the sixth grade."

"It is unbelievable," I admitted. "When I looked at those front pages again, I couldn't believe it, and I was there. Worse than that. I got scared reading them, and I knew how it came out. Scared. End-of-Hollywood scared."

"Like you're trying to scare me with Howard Hunt?" asked Bunyan.

I sighed repeatedly. My politics are not Bunyan's, and every time I face this fact I have to remember what a miracle America is, land of the free to think whatever foolishness you want and then think it again the next day. Write it down too. I drank my seltzer to salve my big-think voice.

Bunyan paused also, to gather his doubting forces. "There's got to be a lot of problems with Hunt," he began again, "many more than I know about. I mean, Tip, you can't document—"

"No, I can't," I interrupted. "What I'm offering is a name that fits Deep Throat's motive, opportunity and weapon. The name that is not impossible, like all the other suspects. Hunt's improbable, but unlike all the others I know about, he's not impossible."

"You always use that," said Bunyan, "you and your Holmes."

(Sigh, sigh, sigh.) "There's also this," I tried. "Howard Hunt did it the way I would have. Name all the names, hang all the bastards, Tip first and Tip last."

"You're saying this is like one of your stories?" Bunyan fussed. "But it happened!"

"And it continues," I said, "the epilogue of the caper without an end." My preaching was wearing me down. I indicated his notebook again. "Go to the post-Nixon record. What did Hunt do and say when he got out of jail?"

"March 1977," said Bunyan, flipping to the page. "You gave me the *Newsweek* clip. Here it is. He got out in Florida, before dawn to duck the press. After nearly a thousand days in jail. It says he was gaunt, broke, bitter. Hunt said, 'I've paid my price for Watergate.' He called Judge Sirica 'a vicious, merciless man.'"

Creepy, I thought, so creepy.

Bunyan continued reporting. "Hunt said the CIA 'got rid of me like they would a dead rat.' Rat! And this: he said that 'If Silbert had led me with a carrot instead of a stick, he would have had the fame Cox does today.'"

"Correct," I said. "Hunt's saying he would have ratted to the courts if there'd been a deal for him like there was for Dean."

"And this," added Bunyan. "Hunt said, 'As a CIA officer I was never charged to deal with morality.' He was hard-core, hard-core."

I prompted, "What did Hunt do that day?"

Bunyan checked. "He flew to Boston for a tv show. He changed planes three times. Hopscotch north! Still tradecraft. It says he's going on the speaking circuit. Did he?"

"Negative," I said. "Listen, Bunyan, Woodward said that someday Deep Throat's gonna write a great book, and he wants to work on it with him. Only two principals never wrote books about themselves: Howard Hunt and John Mitchell."

Bunyan startled. "Mitchell? You said that he was a waste."

"Yeah," I said, "but he's also another suspect nobody's ever seriously named out loud. I rule him out for the reason I couldn't stop laughing at the scene of Mitchell in an underground garage. Still, when Mitchell died two months back, the *Post* reporters rushed to ask Woodward for a comment. Nothing."

"You think there's a manuscript?" Bunyan asked. "A book by Hunt?"

"Yes, I do. Deep Throat's memoir, *I Did It*. To be published upon his death, one more pile of black ops vengeance. He's still a control officer out of control. Look at the saddest detail of Watergate, Dor-

othy Hunt's death in that United plane that stalled and crashed outside Midway Airport on Friday, December 8. Dorothy was the love of
his life. And when they recovered her body they found ten thousand
dollars in cash, in hundred-dollar bills, in her purse. She died a black
ops bagwoman. Leaving a condemned husband and four children,
aged nine to twenty-one. It's not hard to suppose that Hunt blames
himself for her death. What did Hunt say of her when he got out of
jail?"

Bunyan read Hunt's words, "'I wish I could have been up there
with her.'"

Creepy, I thought, creepy creepy. It was getting to me again, but I
had to pronounce the quote. "'Thy will be done.'"

"What's that?" asked Bunyan.

"My big mouth," I admitted. "Also a stupid, stupid eulogy for all
the President's men. Woodward and Bernstein too. They broke the
biggest newspaper story of modern times, they were phenoms before
they were thirty. And they never could have figured that story unless
they'd been turned and run by Deep Throat Howard Hunt."

Bunyan closed his notebook. He'd had enough. "Tip, I have to say
this. What you say, it's too much for me. It's been seventeen years.
Someone would have guessed Hunt by now. It can't be Hunt."

I cut Bunyan off to finish my sermon. "Woodward and Bernstein
are still protecting their control agent. That's textbook tradecraft too;
long after the deed the network still can't give up their boss, as if
they owe him for enslaving them. *Woodward says he'll name DT when
he dies.* Meantime Woodward's become obsessed by the CIA. The
black operatives are still using him the way Hunt did, to rat on
themselves and their bosses, to blame, confess, moan and take the
fall. 'Thy will be done.'"

"What's that mean, Tip?"

Bunyan hadn't eaten half of his barbecue. My soup was dull. I was
done too. I said we should get out into the desert air. I suggested a
drive south to Fort Gotcha, put me up in a motel near the honky-
tonks. I said that tomorrow I could snoop out all the stuff Bunyan
couldn't talk about.

"Okay to the motel and definitively negative to the rest," said

Bunyan. "You don't get inside our perimeter. No Wilcy Moore, not even a Babe Ruth homer, gets inside our perimeter."

I enjoyed being thought of as the kind of fool who had to be told to stay ignorant. "Understood," I acknowledged.

Bunyan took two more bites and asked, "But what's 'Thy will be done' really mean?"

"Malarkey," I said, "from an Italian guy who made it all up four hundred years back. Name of Signor Machiavelli. He retired to a stone bunker in the hills with a view of this big church called the Duomo, and every night he stared at where he knew he could never get to, and so he made it all up."

"I've heard of him," Bunyan teased. "Even in the sixth grade we heard of him."

"What 'Thy will be done' means is that we're all guilty. We took our hard chances, did the deed and survived with what luck we've got. Now it's time to plead. 'Thy will be done.'"

I was blithering. We were outside the Old City of Tucson Jail.

"Hey, Tip," Bunyan called, "are you really serious? My duty's to get at the truth. You know, get the facts down on paper and let others judge. But this? Mom's always telling me to watch out for you. And what you do, selling make-believe."

"Yeah," I said. "Mom's got that right."

Bunyan was in a fun mood. "You gonna tell me how this mysterious Cleo fits into this now?"

"Nope."

We got rolling out of Tucson. The night sky was overwhelming. Too many stars, too much mystery. I asked if we could go by way of Tombstone. I wanted to see it under moonlight. Maybe the ghosts had a secret to tell about the Clantons and the Earps. I thought, Doc Holliday was Deep Throat.

Bunyan had the best last lines. "What a crock, Tip, you know that? What else would you do but make Deep Throat into yourself? Geez, you almost had me there, until I remembered that you've been telling me stories since I was alive."

ABOUT THE AUTHOR

John Calvin Batchelor was born in Bryn Mawr, Pennsylvania, in 1948. He attended Princeton University, Edinburgh University, and Union Theological Seminary. He lives in New York City. This is his fourth novel.